A KINGDOM SO CRIMSON

EMMORY JARMAN

THE LIGHTBRINGER SERIES

A KINGDOM SO CRIMSON

EMMORY JARMAN

A KINGDOM SO CRIMSON

ISBN: HB: 979-8-9915352-0-5; PB: 979-8-9915352-1-2; e-book: 979-8-9915352-2-9

Library of Congress Control Number:

2024921839

To Jules—
who was the light that made my darkness more bearable.

& For those who fight unseen battles in the depths of their darkness,
searching for a light that feels impossible to reach—
hold on just a little bit longer, you'll find purpose in the pain.

"Happiness can be found even in the darkest of times, if one only remembers to turn on the light."

— Albus Dumbledore

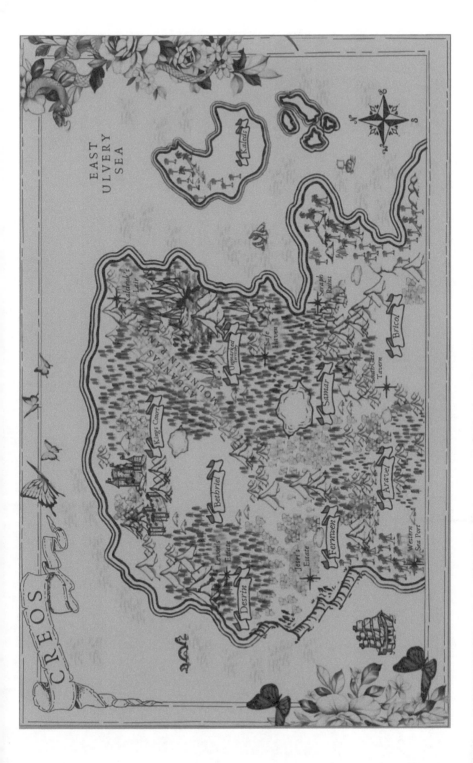

PART ONE

1

My legs started to burn from squatting on the thick branch as I stayed hidden within the tree's leaves. The wind whistled past, and I used the rustling of the leaves to blend my movements into the sound. My heartbeat pounded in my ears as I waited for any signs of Darius and his men to appear.

I played this game too often, and the routine of dull arrows and repeated games had grown tiresome. At least the arrows still stung on impact, and I could slash deeper with the dagger, leaving a more significant mark.

But this time, it was a test, and I had to follow the rules exactly: strike down, draw blood with the dagger, stay silent, and, most importantly, don't get caught.

I heard a snap, pulling my focus back to the game. I quickly aimed my bow toward the sound, blending into the tree trunk. Another snap, followed by the crunch of gravel to my left, signaled that they were trying to provoke me into making a move. Out of the corner of my eye, I spotted a sliver of green fabric that didn't quite blend into the brush beneath me. I steadied myself on the thick branch, waiting for more movement.

Another minute passed, and my arms began to ache from holding my position, still locked and ready to strike, when the man shifted, revealing a clearer target. I instantly released my arrow, striking the man down with an anguished cry.

A smile tugged at my lips as I repositioned myself, searching for more movement among the men who began to scramble nearby to avoid being hit, knowing my precision. My arrows found two more targets, swiftly bringing them down with angry cries. Yet, there were still three men left, plus Darius, that I had to take down to pass.

I quietly slid down the tree trunk, landing softly on the plush forest floor, and paused to listen. Birds sang in the distance, insects buzzed around me, and the gentle sound of water splashing from the stream behind added to the eerily quiet atmosphere.

Setting my bow and quiver aside, I reached for my dagger. Suddenly, a rush of black came barreling toward me when a swift punch landed squarely on my jaw, sending stars dancing across my vision as I held back a groan. Before I could recover, an arm wrapped tightly around my neck, yanking me backward and pinning me to his chest. I gasped for air, trying to find my footing. Gritting my teeth, I reached for my dagger, but before I could grab it, a sharp jab to my side sent pain shooting through me, leaving me limp. That was definitely going to leave a mark.

I dug my fingers into the man's arm as he tried to drag me away, squeezing the air from my lungs and leaving my body numb. Without thought, I whipped my head back, hearing a sickening crunch as pain exploded in my skull. He grunted before loosening his grip just enough for me to yank free and kick him away.

We sprang to our feet, daggers flashing as we circled each other in a deadly quiet dance. Blood trickled down his nose, and I couldn't help but smirk. All I needed to do was draw blood with the dagger or make him scream—I preferred the former.

Out of the corner of my eye, I caught sight of a blur of motion—a second man charging at me. Reacting instinctively, I launched myself at him, sliding on my knees and slicing his leg with my dagger. Blood oozed from the wound as he stumbled and fell to the ground.

Out.

He yelped instantly, throwing a lewd gesture my way, which only made me grin.

Double out.

The first man came charging at me from behind, nearly knocking me to the ground. I dodged just in time, watching him stumble to a halt. I scanned the area but couldn't sense Darius or the last man.

Pivoting quickly, I lunged at the man, now rushing to reposition himself. My fist connected solidly with his jaw, the impact sending a jolt of pain up my arm. Shaking off the sting, I flipped the dagger back toward my forearm as the man groaned—too quietly to be considered out.

He touched his swollen lip, spitting out blood, and his eyes turned feral. I grinned, shrugging mockingly to provoke his next move.

He lunged at me, his dagger slicing wildly through the air. I instinctively ducked, weaving away from his erratic strikes. Suddenly, his leg jutted out. I stumbled and collided with his fist, which hammered into my ribs, knocking the wind out of me. I held back an aching cough, clutching my stomach. Gritting my teeth, I quickly kicked his hand, sending his dagger flying. He snarled as I surged forward, blocking his next punch with my arm, and without hesitation, I slashed my dagger across his cheek, drawing a fresh line of blood.

He cursed loudly and shoved me away, a devilish grin spreading across my lips. Without missing a beat, I sprinted toward a thicket of bushes. But before I could reach them, another man emerged from hiding and tackled me to the ground. My head slammed against the dirt, stars dancing in my vision as sharp rocks cut into my cheek.

I struggled to break free, blinking through the disorientation. Then, I saw those unmistakable golden eyes grinning down at me. Calum. My breath caught in my throat as the confusion twisted into fierce, burning anger. He straddled me, his expression infuriatingly smug, and the sight of him sparked a fire in my veins.

He winked at me with a smirk, his eyes gleaming with a playfulness that sent fury surging through me. With a silent snarl, I twisted my hips, yanking him down, and shoving him off with a kick to his chest.

We scrambled to our feet, and he swung a punch at my side that I barely dodged, the force of it grazing my side. I retaliated with a swift kick to his legs, sending him crashing to the ground with a thud.

He laughed, marking him out, *if he was ever in*, and lounged on the ground with his hands behind his head, giving me another infuriating wink.

Rage boiled through me, and I readied to kick Calum in the side when Darius suddenly leaped out, slicing my sleeve and staining my green top with blood. A searing pain shot through my arm, and a crushing sense of defeat settled in my chest. I clutched my arm, cradling the wound.

Calum chuckled as he got to his feet, giving me a condescending pat on the back. "Good work, El," he said, quickly sauntering over to the men watching from a distance.

"*You cheated*," I spat at Darius, heading for the tree where I had left my bow. Darius followed, his footsteps echoing behind me.

"You asked for something different, so I thought Calum would do the trick," he said with a smug grin. "Prepare for the unexpected, Eliah. Next time, you'll get it."

I shot him a fierce glare as I snatched up my quiver and bow, anger burning in my eyes. I stormed back to the courtyard, hearing Darius's light laughter as he patted the other men on the back. Calum was gone, which was for the best; if he'd been around, I'd have lost control and beaten him alive until he learned to stay the hell out of my evaluations.

+ ✦ +

After I ran several laps around the courtyard to burn off some steam from my surprise encounter with Calum, lunch awaited me. Darius knew how much I loathed sparring with Calum and used it to throw me off balance. Sweat dripped down my back and lined my braided coronet.

"Well, you look appalling," Jesri mocked as I sat across from him. He dug into his smoked lamb and buttered yams, stuffing his mouth with a smirk. I offered him a tight, annoyed smile before biting into my dry, cold meat and stale biscuit. At least he had the decency to get me some food.

"You smell like a pig, Eliah. Wash up and make yourself presentable for tonight. Sir Alder is coming, and I don't want an *animal* at my table," Jesri spat out, quickly dabbing his face with a napkin. He stood up and strode away, clearly acting as though it was unbearable to be in my presence.

I shook my head in annoyance and reached over to finish his juicy lamb. Jesri always had the servants give me anything that was going to waste, so savoring the last bit of his meal was a rare treat.

"I saw that," Calum said, leaping onto the pergola and flopping into Jesri's chair. His ruffled, dirty blond hair clung to his forehead, and sweat soaked through his shirt. I struggled to keep my face neutral as he took a bite of an apple, leaning back and propping his feet up on the wire table. His muscles tensed beneath his damp shirt, stirring a deep, unsettling anger in me. I forced myself to look away, trying not to stare at his sculpted chest.

"Come on, El, you have to admit that was pretty entertaining," he taunted.

I continued eating my cold meat and stale biscuit, refusing to give him the satisfaction. I closed my eyes, still chewing the tough meat, and breathed in the fresh spring air, letting the wind cool my flushed face.

"Hey, don't blame me; it was Darius's idea," Calum said, his smile infuriatingly casual.

I clenched my jaw. "You accepted it and clearly enjoyed watching me fail. You know how crucial this is for me."

He pursed his lips, his dimples showing as he grinned. "At least you'll be stuck here with me a little longer," he said, sounding almost pleased.

I rolled my eyes, barely containing my fury. "As if you enjoy my company, Cal. Don't pretend. You're itching to be rid of me so you can galavant with all the ladies without a forced companion."

He furrowed his brows, about to argue.

"Tonight, we're meeting my supposed mentor. Don't screw it up, or I swear, I will slice your skin off while you sleep," I spat out, my anger barely contained. I was done with this conversation, and honestly, I did smell like an animal. This unusually warm spring was making me desperate for a bath.

"Don't tempt me," he smirked, his expression maddeningly unbothered, knowing I would never do such a thing to him.

I rolled my eyes, struggling to keep myself from smacking his infuriatingly handsome face. I started to walk away, but Calum grabbed my arm, making me hiss in pain.

"*Tyran, Cal!*" I cursed, glaring at him as I clutched the makeshift bandage that had already soaked through from the wound Darius gave me.

Calum stepped back, his hands raised defensively. "I forgot, I swear."

I grunted in frustration, throwing him a rude gesture before storming off.

"Oh, come on, El! Can't you just have some fun like we used to?" he called after me.

I stopped dead in my tracks. "*Fun?*" I spun around to face him, my voice dripping with anger. "When have I ever been allowed to have *fun*, Cal?"

He chuckled with a wicked glint in his eye. "Don't let Jesri get to you like that. You can do whatever you want."

I laughed out loud. Evidently, Calum needed to learn his uncle better. Since Jesri found me at his *perfect* party as an infant, he never stopped grueling me about who I was: an orphan with no fortune or family who cared, and the only remnants of a dowry was a torn parchment with my name on it. Still, I question why Jesri kept me, except to use me as a pawn to gain access into the King's Court by status.

Jesri was a snake and never allowed me the freedom that Calum enjoyed. Even as a child, I was constantly under his control. I used to sneak off with Calum, engaging in childish mischief and enjoying myself briefly. But those moments were fleeting and were quickly overshadowed by the crushing realization that my arrogant parents would never return. Year after year, no one came, and Jesri was always there to remind me of that harsh reality.

I lost hope and let my anger fuel within me, falling deep into the training Jesri demanded I take. He made Darius teach me how to yield a sword and a bow and to know how to strike someone with enough force to kill, all before I even turned ten.

I stopped complaining or questioning Jesri after he locked me in my room for two days without food and said it was to help me obtain *survival* skills, knowing all too well it was because I refused the offer to help get him a lady into his bed chambers—I was only twelve.

I clenched my hands in rage and disgust, the memories surging back like a tidal wave, each sharper and more venomous than the last. Calum, with all his charm and good looks—something I'd never admit out loud—was a hollow reflection of his uncle, Jesri. Arrogant, selfish, and driven by nothing but his own desires. We might have grown up under the same roof, but he was never a brother to me, and now that I'm older, I'm not sure he was ever a true friend. He had become a stranger in familiar skin, a poised parasite who thrived on the attention and admiration of others while still somehow worming his charm through me yet keeping me in the shadows.

However, I cared for him, not because he deserved it, but because he was the only one who let me be myself, who let me be free. But as we got older, he changed and warped that fragile bond between us into something I couldn't recognize. Turning more into the very snake he calls family and wanting what Jesri wants—money, women, and status—while I longed for something he could never understand: freedom.

But Cal was willing to sell it all, even the pieces of himself, for the sake of ambition. And that, more than anything, made my blood boil.

I stomped away, not caring to argue with him any longer. He scowled, throwing his hands up, and turned away, walking back towards Darius and his men patrolling the estate.

Heading for the door inside, I sucked in a deep breath calming myself and my energy for tonight. My stomach churned, knowing I was allowing them to control me like a puppet, yet I had a knife but wasn't willing to cut the strings.

2

I sat in the wash basin until the water cooled completely, chilling my body temperature to send goosebumps up and down my body. A slight knock hit the door, ushering me out of my daze. I stepped out, dripping water on the wood floors, and quickly put on my robe. My feet stung against the cool floor as I walked to the door and unlatched the lock to see Aoife smiling brightly, holding a beautiful icy blue gown.

At least Aoife could soften my dampened heart.

"Good afternoon, dear," she said, sliding past me and setting the dress down on my hard bed, which had covers so thin that they barely kept in warmth. "I don't have much time before I need to help prepare for dinner, but I wanted to see how your evaluation went today?"

I sighed and smiled at her, not wanting the anger to pick up again. "The usual."

Her eyes widened in alarm. "You're bleeding, my lady," Aoife said, pointing to my arm that had turned my robe red. "Darius is going too hard on you," she huffed with as much anger as her kind heart could take. She patted the seat next to my decaying vanity Jesri found for me from an abandoned warehouse and pulled my sleeve up, exposing several other slashes too stubborn to leave, lingering as scars and memories of failure. "Let me patch you up really quick."

She gathered the bandages and ointment, worn with use, and pushed my skin tight, pressing the salve into the cut. Pain zinged up my arm, waking me out of my murky depression. She wrapped the bandage tightly, hiding the rest of my scars and emotions with it. I thanked her as she gathered her things, quickly placing a kiss on my cheek.

"I'll be back soon to help prepare you for dinner tonight," she said, with excitement in her eyes before quickly leaving and clicking the door shut.

As I approached the bed, my fingertips brushed the soft, delicate fabric of the icy blue dress she had meticulously laid out for me. The serenity of the moment was abruptly shattered by a sharp, impatient knock on the door. It swung open before I could react, revealing Calum standing there with a mischievous grin, a glint of mischief dancing in his golden eyes. He was clearly up to something.

A surge of anger coursed through me, and I felt my eyes narrow instinctively at the sight of him. "Get out," I hissed, my voice low and laced with irritation. I pointed firmly at the door, battling to keep my frustration in check—I had no desire to deal with him right now.

But Calum ignored my command, closing the door behind him and leaning casually against its frame. He raised his hands in a mock gesture of surrender, his smile never wavering. "I've been thinking about what you said, and you're right," he began, his voice smooth, as if he hadn't noticed my anger. "You haven't had any fun in a long time. And tomorrow, you turn eighteen," he paused, his smile widening, deepening the dimples in his cheeks. "So, before you retort, let's go have some fun," he stated, his tone dripping with mischievous confidence.

I furrowed my brows, my arms instinctively crossing over my chest as I suddenly became acutely aware of my vulnerability, still dressed only in my robe. "Like Jesri would *ever* allow that—*especially* tonight."

Calum's grin didn't falter for a second. "He won't know," he said smoothly, his voice full of reckless assurance. "Jesri's too busy welcoming his highly favored guest, and dinner isn't for another two hours. I promise we'll be back long before anyone even notices we're gone."

I glared at him, hating how tempting his offer sounded. My gaze drifted to the window, where the sky was beginning to take on the rich, deep hues of sunset.

With a resigned sigh, I felt myself caving in before I could find the will to resist. "Fine," I muttered, trying to keep my voice steady. "Wait outside—I need to change."

His grin widened triumphantly, and without another word, he slipped out the door.

"Tyran," I muttered under my breath, incredulous that I was going along with this.

———— ✦ ————

The grimy and filthy town was far more repulsive than I had imagined. The air was heavy and saturated with the stench of lingering bodies and the sickly scent of alcohol. Cal had made it clear that this was not the *usual* part of town but a place where we could go unnoticed, away from prying eyes that might report back to Jesri.

As the sky darkened, the lingering chill of winter's end still hung in the air, making me grateful for my choice of long sleeves and pants. Cal seemed in high spirits, greeting several drunkards in the dim alleyways who eyed me with inappropriate pleasure. Laughing, he pushed them off before taking my arm and hurrying us into a run-down tavern. The place reeked of sweat and sea salt as if filled with men who had just washed up on shore from long voyages.

Scattered tables cluttered the entrance, leading to a long, wooden bar stained with what looked like blood. I tried to hold my head high amidst the crowd's raucous laughter and mindless drinking.

"What about this is fun, Cal?" I seethed, staying close to his side as more men turned to look at me like a prize.

Cal slung his arm around my shoulders, pulling me in close. "It's fun because you're rebelling," he whispered into my ear, steering me towards the bar where a large, husky man with a thick black beard stood.

I swallowed nervously, glancing down the long table where several women leaned uncomfortably close to sweaty men, holding them tightly. Instinctively, I wrapped my arms around myself.

What kind of crowd had Calum dragged me into?

"Two dullers," Calum ordered from the bartender behind the table as we sat down on the rickety chairs. The bartender nodded and turned to fill two small stone cups with a golden liquid.

"Dullers?" I asked, feeling repulsed as I eyed the dirty cup placed in front of me.

"Just drink it, El. Live a little," Calum encouraged, raising his cup in a toast. "To rebellion."

Reluctantly, I picked up the sticky stone cup and lifted it. Calum quickly downed his drink in one gulp, shutting his eyes and hissing before breaking into a grin, waiting for me to follow suit.

I eyed the cup warily, contemplating whether to take a sip. Just as I raised it to my lips, someone knocked my arm, sending the golden liquid splashing all over me.

I yelped in surprise as Calum hissed and cursed at the man responsible.

"Apologies," the man said beside me, his tone making it clear he wasn't.

I placed the cup back on the table, watching his back as he stalked away. Unlike the other large men in the tavern, he was tall and sculpted, with leathers strapped across his back and chest. His dark brown hair barely brushed his shoulders, and he moved with a purposeful stride. Noting he had a peculiar ruby pommel dagger at his side that glimmered in the light.

"Tyran," Calum swore under his breath.

I raised a hand, frustrated that Calum had brought me here. This was not my idea of fun. "Maybe that's our sign to head back," I stated, standing up.

"Come on, El, just one more—"

"Who do we have here?" interrupted a raspy voice. Calum's eyes widened as he quickly stood up beside me.

The voice belonged to a tall, fat man who looked like he had never bathed. Behind him stood three other men, their sun-blotched faces twisted into grimy, yellow smiles.

"No one," Calum replied quickly. "We were just leaving."

"Leaving, hm?" the man cooed, eyeing me with a disturbing delight. "Perhaps *I* can leave too. What's your name, sweetheart?" he asked, tilting my chin to meet his gaze.

I stepped back, fire raging in my eyes. "Don't. Touch me." I seethed, assessing my options for escape.

"Touch you? No," he said, clicking his tongue. "*I* won't touch you," the man mused with a sickening grin. "But they will," he gestured to the men behind him.

I slammed my fist into his nose before realizing what I was doing. The sickening crunch of bone echoed in the tavern, and a sharp pain shot through my knuckles. The room fell silent as every pair of eyes snapped to us. The man I struck snarled, his face contorted in rage as blood poured from his nose, dripping onto the muddy floor. His eyes blazed with a venomous fury.

Before I could react, the three filthy men from behind him lunged at me, their grimy hands grabbing me all at once. Calum's shout pierced the air as he threw himself at them, fists flying and striking at their arms and backs in a desperate attempt to free me. But there were too many, and they dragged me outside into the darkening night.

I thrashed and kicked wildly, my foot connecting with one man's face, sending him sprawling to the ground. Another seized my injured arm, and pain shot through me as the wound reopened. My screams mixed with Calum's frantic yells as the tavern door slammed open behind us, revealing the silhouette of the man who had bumped into me earlier.

He was on the four grimy men in seconds, knocking them out with lethal intensity. His movements were swift and precise, and a blur of force left each man crumpled on the ground. He fought with a practiced efficiency, and each strike was calculated to incapacitate them.

Once the last man fell, he turned to me, his features unrecognizable in the darkness. "Are you alright?" he asked, his voice steady despite the chaos that had just transpired, and reached his hand to me.

I nodded, still trying to catch my breath, and reached for his hand. He pulled me up with ease, his grip lingering a moment longer than necessary. "You've got a solid arm," he remarked, his thumb brushing over my bruised knuckles before he abruptly let go. I gave him a curt nod, unsure of what to say, and took a step back.

Heat flushed my cheeks as Calum rushed to my side, causing the man to step back slightly.

"El, I'm so sorry," Calum said, his voice filled with relief, though his expression quickly shifted to concern as he glanced at the man.

"You're bleeding," my rescuer noted, gesturing to my arm. I looked down and saw that my cream shirt's sleeve was soaked with blood. "Take care of yourself."

"We should go," Calum cut in, his voice tense as he glanced nervously around. He gently tugged me away, urging us to leave. The man turned and walked into the dark alleyway, vanishing into the shadows and leaving us to find our way back before Jesri found out.

— ✦ —

We returned just as the servants were setting the dining room table.

"This never happened," Calum whispered urgently as we reached the hallway leading to our rooms. I nodded in agreement, eager to forget the entire ordeal, and quietly slipped into our separate rooms.

Inside, I found Aoife waiting for me. Her eyes widened in alarm as she noticed my bloodied arm and her nose wrinkled at the grimy, alcohol-laden scent clinging to me. Without a word, she swiftly helped me out of my top before efficiently patching up my arm again, for which I was silently grateful.

"Thank you," I murmured as she finished, but she was already at my armoire, pulling out my white Spring Harvest dress and laying it beside the icy blue gown she had brought in earlier.

I raised my brows and walked over, gently touching the white dress. "I thought I was supposed to wear this for the Spring Harvest tomorrow?"

Aoife shrugged, her expression softening. "Jesri wanted you in your usual Harvest dress for dinner tonight instead. But this one," she said, holding up the new beautiful icy blue gown. "You'll be wearing for the party tomorrow."

It *was* a gorgeous gown, but everything came with a price for Jesri.

"May I ask why Jesri insists I wear this one tonight and even went so far as to *buy* me a new gown?" I asked, eyeing the blue dress with suspicion.

Aoife gave me a knowing look, fully aware that Jesri was trying to impress my so-called mentor with my appearance. The thought made bile rise in my throat, and I immediately wanted to refuse the blue gown. I'd rather be seen in a sack than cater to any man who lets his manhood dictate his actions.

I pursed my lips, fighting the urge to roll my eyes, disgusted by the memory of those grimy hands and leering eyes on me earlier in the tavern. But amid the repulsion, I couldn't help but feel a flicker of gratitude for whoever my rescuer had been.

"I presume that means this man will also be staying for the party?" I asked, glancing down at the glittering gown.

She nodded.

I clenched my teeth, exhaling sharply through my nose as I struggled to keep my anger in check. Jesri would always be the predator, ready to pounce on and exploit any opportunity that promised him wealth or fame.

Just a week after I turned twelve, Jesri put me on display before a crowd of potential elite suitors and handlers, each one evaluating whether I was *worthy* of being their pupil. He forced me to showcase my abilities in swordplay, marksmanship, combat, and etiquette. The experience was deeply humiliating, driving me into the woods in tears until I had no more to shed.

Yet, to Jesri's furious disappointment, every handler rejected me, citing my youth and naivety as reasons I was not fit for their plans.

This rejection ignited a fury in Jesri until he became terrifying and relentless. He threw himself wholly into my training with a newfound intensity, his demands for perfection growing harsher each day.

His promise to present me to another suitor when the time was right did little to ease the torment I endured. And any mistake or failure in my performance was met with brutal punishment, which carved a painful map of scars across my body—each one a reminder of his unyielding control. But the pain wasn't just physical; it was an assault on my soul, on who I needed to be. He pulled the strings and forced me into absolute obedience, enforcing his will and extinguishing any trace of my anger or selfish desires with the dreams he took that faded away with my short childhood.

And year after grueling year, I grew numb to the things I once enjoyed and became even more naive than I was during my initial evaluation. Jesri's harshness never wavered; he pushed me to the brink of collapse or unconsciousness from lack of food and strength, claiming it was *good* for my soul, and banned me from any outings outside the estate, insisting that I would sully Cal's reputation.

Jesri always had an excuse to make my life a torment. His endless evaluations were designed not just to test my limits but purely for his pleasure to see me struggle and obey. He continued this relentless regimen until he got what he wanted. Now, six years later, his promise still looms over me, and I have a sickening sense that tonight, he might finally achieve his goal.

The thought of demonstrating my skills before the man we are to dine with tonight made my stomach churn. This man was another pawn in Jesri's scheme, someone Jesri intended to use to fulfill his own desires. I flared my nostrils, shoving the unsettling thoughts aside as I tried to ground myself in the present.

Aoife helped me into my buttery white dress, which hugged me in all the right places. The skirt was inked with bright rose, lilac, and gold threads, woven to appear like tiny flowers at the hem. The sleeves puffed out ever so slightly with a tight bodice and a lower-than-normal neckline, tempting any suitor's eyes to linger longer than usual—one of Jesri's demands.

She sat me down in front of the vanity, spraying a clean-smelling perfume that drowned out the grime, and started weaving my long, dark, auburn hair into a low bun. She placed white flower buds throughout that brightened my gray-blue eyes. She powdered my lips with a hint of pink, helping my tan skin settle evenly around my freckled nose and keeping the dark hunger circles at bay. I glanced at her through the faded mirror, tilting my chin to the side to see her handiwork, hiding my scars with her touch.

"I'll never know how you make me appear beautiful," I said, pushing away some stranded pieces of hair too stubborn to stay in place.

She squeezed my shoulders, "Your beauty has always been there, darling."

——— ✦ ———

My stomach rumbled with anticipation as the rich aroma of roasted meat drifted up the staircase, making my mouth water.

I will eat well tonight!

As I turned the corner and descended towards the source of the mouthwatering scent, I found Calum slumped in an armchair, absorbed in a book. He was dressed in his formal attire, but his white shirt was left unbuttoned, revealing a glimpse of his sculpted chest and tempting me to touch him. I quickly dismissed the thought, recognizing it as his ploy to distract me. His warm eyes shifted from his book to meet mine, and he smiled with a bewitching charm.

With a click of his tongue in appraisal, he closed his book and walked over to me, his gaze lingering on my neckline. He acted as if nothing had happened earlier, fully aware that we both needed to maintain this façade if we wanted to avoid severe punishment.

"You're meant to be my escort, not gawk at me like I'm your next meal," I remarked, rolling my eyes, upset that he had taken me there for *fun*.

"But you get to look at *me* like dinner?" he purred, flirtatiously. "I saw you gawking," he said, pulling me to his side. I clenched my jaw, willing myself not to linger on his touch. We walked down the hall to the dining room, our heels clicking against the marble floor as anxiety blared into my soul.

It had been six years since I last talked to a suitor. Six. Why now? Why wait *so* long?

Calum reached out, ready to open the door. "Best behave tonight, El," he said with a scowl, flaring his hand across my eyes, acting like a Magic and looking at me knowingly. "Or else *all* this training will have been for nothing."

I dramatically rolled my eyes and forced my face into a graceful smile, fluttering my lashes at him. "Perhaps this is where I actually get *real* fun," I mocked.

He shook his head, narrowing his eyes. "That *was* fun before you messed it all up," he grumbled before bringing my hand to his soft lips. "Now show this mentor what you're made of," he whispered, giving me a wink before pushing the doors open.

Warm golden light flooded our view of the polished dining room. The long mahogany table stretched out with delicate white and purple flowers on each end. The freshly cleaned and shimmering crystal chandelier made the candlelight dance along the walls. The glassware that was set out was our finest china, with flecks of gold speckled throughout and used only to impress.

Jesri's dark eyes met mine. *Behave,* he said.

Praying he didn't know we had just snuck out before the most important dinner of his life.

Jesri rose from his seat, accompanied by a strikingly handsome man who, surprisingly, was much younger than I expected. His eyes were a vibrant seafoam green, and they locked onto mine with an intensity that made my cheeks flush. I swallowed my anxiety and lifted my chin, trying to maintain composure.

Jesri was dressed in his dark, regal suit with navy accents, and his dark hair slicked back meticulously. Jesri and Calum exuded a captivating elegance that made heads turn, drawing admiration from both men and women alike. Their commanding presence and ambition for status were evident in the way people were drawn to their influence, mostly because of the pride they got from it.

"Sir Calum Archenon, my nephew," Jesri said, breaking the silence and gesturing toward us as Calum guided me to our assigned seats. Calum inclined his head respectfully toward the man.

"And the lovely Lady Eliah Sabene," Jesri continued, his tone deliberately dramatic, ensuring the man's gaze traveled over me just as Calum's had earlier. "My orphaned ward."

I halted abruptly, my heels squeaking against the tile.

What?! The shock and anger surged through me, igniting a fierce rage in my veins.

Jesri shot me a sharp glare, signaling me to keep my composure. I curled my lip in defiance, noting that the handsome man's jaw tightened as he looked at Jesri.

"But I assure you," Jesri said, turning his gaze back to the man. "She is as much a daughter to me as Calum is like a son."

Like *he* has ever sought the title of *father.*

We sat at the table, and I struggled to control my anger. Calum gently squeezed my hand in rhythmic pulses, trying to divert my frustration.

"It's a pleasure to make your acquaintance," the man said, his demeanor returning to calm as he lifted his wine glass. His skin was a warm hazelnut, and he had short ebony hair, looking to be around Calum's age. His suit clung tightly to his sculpted arms and legs as if any sudden movement might burst the buttons. I noticed the rough, scarred texture of his hands, hinting at a rough history.

But it was his eyes that were truly captivating: a deep emerald blue that seemed to pull me in like the ocean current and beckoned me to keep staring until I drowned in them. He smiled, his gaze briefly drifting lower to my neckline before he quickly averted his eyes.

I narrowed my gaze and forced a faint smile. He returned my look with a smirk and took another sip of his wine. I turned away, subtly guiding the direction of our silent exchange.

Calum noticed the interaction and placed his hand on my knee underneath the table, gently squeezing.

"Introducing Sir Levon Alder," Jesri said with a smirk, knowing he had won his approval with my presence. "A previous regime within the King's Court."

Calum and I nodded in welcome as the footman quickly came out with dinner, swirling the air with flavor. My stomach grumbled as a plate was placed before me with roasted pork smothered in a heavenly gravy, accented with buttered asparagus, and fluffy potatoes that melted in the mouth. My taste buds danced with each bite, relishing the savor of such rich food. It took all my efforts not to dance in my chair, almost devouring the entirety of the food, until Calum squeezed my knee again, reminding me to *act* like a lady. I gave him a quick glare before slowing my pace.

I glanced up at Jesri, whose raging eyes made my food leaden. Sir Alder noticed the growing anger and helped change the density of the room, clearing his throat.

"My lady, I've heard you're quite skilled in battle," the man said with a curious smile.

I swallowed hard. "I've never been in battle," I replied, glancing towards Jesri. "But I do know how to handle myself."

"Oh, she can do more than handle herself," Calum interjected, taking a sip of his wine. "She's taken down plenty of men. And as much as I hate to admit it—" he paused, giving me a pointed look before taking another sip, "—she's managed to make me bleed and bruise more times than I'd care to count." His words drew a chuckle from Sir Alder, making my cheeks flush with embarrassment.

"It's true," Jesri added, nodding in agreement. "Just this morning, I saw her take Calum down with a swift swipe to his legs." He conveniently left out any mention of my failures, focusing instead on the more flattering details.

Calum poked my thigh under the table, and I quickly swatted his hand away. I was reminded of the only time I let him in on an evaluation, only for him to pounce and tickle me so relentlessly that I ended up wetting myself. Jesri had punished me severely for ruining *his* clothes. Calum was a master at finding my weak spots, using them to make me rebel as he did tonight, and he never missed an opportunity to remind me of those moments, often blackmailing me into sneaking out to our tree.

He poked me again, prompting me to retaliate with a sharp kick to his shin. He choked on his food, causing Jesri to glare at us with a growing irritation. I turned my attention back to my meal, focusing on savoring each flavorful bite while trying to ignore the escalating tension.

Sir Alder suppressed a grin. "You seem well-prepared for battle, at least enough to protect yourself."

"She's skilled with a bow, daggers, and in combat," Calum added with a grin. "She's also improving with the sword, though she still manages to cut herself quite often." I gave his leg a sharp tap under the table; I know he was just pushing my buttons. Sir Alder noticed and shifted his brilliant gaze to mine, ensuring he had my full attention.

"It seems there's a wolf hidden behind this lady's enchanting exterior," Sir Alder remarked, glancing at Jesri. "She will do well, indeed." My eyes narrowed at Jesri, and I started to speak, but Sir Alder interrupted. "Of course, I'll need to see her skills in action before making any final decisions."

Jesri nodded in agreement.

I cleared my throat. "Sir Alder, would you do me an honor and enlighten me on *what* I would do well in?" I grinned, hoping he might shed some light on Jesri's motives beyond mere wealth or fame.

Jesri shot me a disapproving look. "You heard him, Eliah. Before anything is decided, he needs to see you in action," Jesri said, cutting me off. "You already know enough." He waved his hand dismissively, effectively halting Sir Alder's response. I tightened my grip on my fork, struggling to keep my frustration in check.

"Please, call me Levon," he said, taking a sip of his wine while keeping his gaze fixed on me. "And I can assure you, my lady, that it will be something thrilling."

He caught on to Jesri's quiet implication, and I, begrudgingly, let it go. They couldn't keep me in the dark for long, and if it excited Jesri just by talking about it, it had to be something great—or horrifying.

We continued with our meal, engaging in light conversation and learning more about Levon's background and childhood. Jesri took the opportunity to mention that Levon was also an orphan and how well he had turned out, clearly aiming to comfort me with this comparison. It did nothing to *comfort* the pain I continued to carry, knowing deep down that those hopes and dreams of my parents return were fictitious and that they were no better than Jesri himself.

At last, dessert came out, and I pushed past the feeling of fullness and floated into ecstasy with each bite of the blackberry cream tart. Calum also savored each bite, knowing that these desserts were few and far between.

"Tell me, *Levon*. How did you and Jesri come to be acquainted?" I asked as I finished off my last piece, my stomach beyond bloated.

"We happened to meet at a tavern a few years ago," Levon began. "I was just a lad working for some...gentlemen who frequented that place. I was to be their guiding light when they needed the help home."

"A tavern?" Calum echoed, clearly surprised, and shot me a warning look. I returned his glance before focusing on my plate. "I didn't realize you ever went out drinking, especially not to a tavern."

Jesri had always considered himself above such lowly establishments and was known for his aversion to mingling with those of lower status.

Jesri smiled and patted Levon on the back. "There was a time I needed a guiding light myself," he said, glancing at Levon. "And it seems I found one." The two men shared a knowing laugh, exchanging an unspoken understanding that made my stomach churn.

"What exactly was this guiding light you were looking for?" I asked abruptly, knowing it would provoke Jesri.

It did, and he gave me a look of irritation but continued. "For you, Eliah."

His sudden comment sank unusually deep, and I wasn't sure how to answer. I wished I hadn't devoured my dessert as I aimlessly forked at the crumbs. I nodded as a sudden strike of frustration leaped from me, begging me to leave and escape the eyes of these men and the plans they refused to tell me—plans about *my* life. I suppressed a grunt of frustration. Calum noticed my state and stood, clearing his throat.

"It was a pleasure to meet you, Sir Alder. I'm sure you'll have plenty of opportunities to experience Lady Eliah's charm in the coming days." He reached for my hand, and I eagerly accepted.

"I look forward to seeing you in training, my lady," Levon said, standing quickly after I stood myself. Jesri sat still, not caring to notice my leave.

I nodded and let Calum take me away, holding my head high as I pressed the demanding anger down. We reached the staircase, but Calum led me outside into the gardens instead, knowing I needed air—knowing exactly what I needed and when I needed it. It only infuriated me more.

The sky had deepened into a velvety purple, with flecks of light blue and orange still lingering on the far horizon. We walked in silence until a sudden chill swept through the garden, catching us both by surprise. Calum pulled me closer, and I allowed myself to lean into his warmth, the familiar scent of musk and citrus surrounding me, with a hint of alcohol masked beneath.

"Cal, what does Jesri have planned for me?" I asked quietly, not letting my mind wander into such fantasies.

He shrugged. "I know as much as you do, El," he sighed, pulling me a little closer. I let him, realizing I might be leaving in a few days and wondering if I would miss him.

When Cal first attended court, he attracted many suitable ladies, leaving some with ruined reputations. He stopped acknowledging me altogether, abandoning me to his vicious uncle and Darius's men as he snuck in one woman after another. Rumors spread, tarnishing his and Jesri's reputation, and turning life into a dangerous game of walking on broken glass.

Only then did Cal remember my existence after Jesri punished him less severely than my easier punishments. And with that, Cal reeled me back in like a fish that had never seen the ocean, begging and flirting as we once did as children—creating a facade that was never real.

My skin shivered at his warm embrace, and I abruptly pulled away, knowing what this facade was. I gritted my teeth as anger and frustration ignited like a swarm of bees. The familiar metallic taste bit at the back of my tongue, sending an irritating itch down my spine.

"Tyran, El! Calm down," Calum hissed, cutting through the silence. "You'll be great at whatever you do because you *are* great at whatever you do. Just...control yourself and this *anger*. It will be your downfall if you don't learn to regulate it."

I laughed heartily.

If I could control this random anger, I would have. It was the one thing I still hadn't mastered, and it was much more complex than yielding a bow or throwing a knife. It sprouted itself when I least wanted it, pulling at every tether of my heart and mind like an unforgiving force. It was a never-ceasing presence becoming an annoying friend who never left.

"I *will* miss you, Eliah," Calum said softer, grasping my hand. I instinctively shook his hand off. His face contorted into confusion. "*I will, El.* No matter what you think of me, I will miss the company of you. And I..." his voice trailed off.

My heart stumbled, wanting to know what he *truly* thought.

"No," I spat out quickly, looking into his golden eyes. "I don't believe you will."

I pivoted and walked away, leaving him in whatever confusion he was feeling. I was furious at him for pushing me to rebel and dragging me to that disgusting tavern, and even more so for how easily I fell back under his charm. But I wouldn't let myself fall into his traps again. I wouldn't open my heart to him, only to have it be broken like my parents did.

I had promised myself long ago that I wouldn't let anyone in, especially him. He would forget me soon enough, and life would go on as it always did—with me wherever Jesri saw fit.

3

I awoke early the following morning with tear-stained cheeks and a gnawing headache that deepened my resentment. I grunted, shuffling out from under the thin covers, and rubbed my eyes to adjust to the grogginess of waking. After returning from dinner, I dismissed Aoife and fell into a puddle of tears on my moth-eaten bed. Jesri has belittled and demeaned so much of me for *his* selfish and arrogant pleasures all my life that I've become accustomed to my numb reality of failure, pain, hopelessness, and anger. And now that I might be leaving this place, it feels...wrong. As if my excitement and hopes of freedom are only glimpses of dreams I fear will never come true. Like the wishes I had for my parents to return and save me from this life—That they still love me.

I clenched my jaw—*they were just as arrogant as Jesri.*

Taking a deep breath, I forced all my thoughts to quiet.

I stood up, the cold floor biting into my toes and jolting me fully awake. As I walked to the window, I pulled open the curtains to reveal the inky dawn, with dark shades of purple streaking the sky. The sight stirred a mix of emotions and uncertainties in my heart. I took a deep breath and looked up at the twinkling stars, hoping they saw me and understood the words I couldn't bring myself to say. Hoping they wouldn't leave me for long.

I quickly scooped up my dress from the ground, knowing Aoife would be upset about having to press out wrinkles, and hung it back into my armoire. I found my tan trousers and a tight, long-sleeved knit top, slipping them on before quickly pinning my hair up. I laced up my boots and snuck out into the quiet hallway, tiptoeing into the training arena under the estate.

I began to stretch my arms, neck, legs, back, and hips before I moved on to my warmup. I lunged and side-punched the air, practicing my breathing with each swing of my arm. I continued to jog around the room before settling in front of the large flour bag Darius set out for me.

I started with a simple 1-2-1-2 combo, allowing my heart to race harder with each punch, feeling the sting of each hit enliven my murky mind and quicken my pulse. Quickly, I moved onto a jab-cross-hook-cross, tightening my core with each forceful swing. I continued 1-2-3-2, back to a quick 1-1-2. Sweat formed on my brow as my heart pumped faster and deeper with every combo. Each forceful swing sent my arms throbbing, but I relished in the contact, the burn, and the sting from yesterday's slice. I willed myself to forget and forgo those feelings that overcame me last night, replenishing them with a newfound fury for vengeance to take back my life. And take back everything that was taken from me.

Jab-jab-cross-hook-right uppercut-left hook.

I closed my eyes, pushing back memories of Calum, Jesri, and my sorrowful past, letting the anger roam free with a rageful scream that echoed off the stone walls, propelling me to punch fiercely. My knuckles stung with each forceful thrust, hitting harder and faster, letting my anger ignite deeper until I swung freely, barely catching myself before I fell to the ground, knocking the air out of me.

I opened my eyes to see flour splattered across the floor, coating my clothes and the wall behind it. I looked up to see the top of the bag barely hanging by a thread.

Slow clapping emerged from within the room. I quickly got up and whipped around to see Levon leaning against the door with a smirk. I curled my lip, hoping he would take the hint to leave.

"They told me you would be down here by morning. But I wasn't expecting to see a show, too," Levon said with a low chuckle, fueling my anger even more.

"Get out," I snapped back, noticing that the tip of my nose and cheeks were covered in flour. I wiped my face and patted the rest of my body, which left a white residue.

He walked towards me, assessing me before pushing his sleeves up. "Show me what you can do, Eliah," he taunted, squatting into a fighting stance. He flicked his fingers for me to join him.

"No," I sneered with venom in my voice.

He only gave me a smirk before lashing out, throwing a punch into my sliced arm that created a stinging pain reaching up into my neck. I grasped my arm, quickly stepping back.

"Always go for the weak point," he smirked, not caring that he split the wound, now dampening my cream top. I snarled at him, only making him laugh. "What happened? I noticed you had it patched last night at dinner. Someone playing a little too rough?"

He stepped closer, quickly throwing another punch, which I promptly dodged, smacking his hand down like a cat playing with its food. He gave me a wicked grin before he threw several more, all of which I blocked, throwing several at him. We danced like that until I landed a solid punch to his jaw, splitting his lip. He stepped back, touching his mouth, his fingers stained with blood.

"Well done," he cooed, walking over towards the weapons. "Now, let's see how well you do in swordplay."

He tossed me a wooden sword, and I got ready. I ran through Darius's drills in my head—shielding, charging, blocking, striking. But before I could move, Levon struck hard, jolting my arm with the force. I held steady, gripping the wood tight and blocking his attacks as best I could. His speed was impressive; I had to give him that.

He landed another blow, but I deflected it with speed. Its crash reverberated off the walls with an echo as I grunted, shoving his weight off. We persisted, moving in a dance of combat, our steps a rhythmic exchange of defense and striking.

Seeing an opening, I struck, only for him to defend easily and intensify my frustration. Before realizing it, he stuck his foot out, intruding on our dance, and tripped me. I hit the floor hard, my head connecting with the unforgiving tile, momentarily blinding me with stars. Gritting my teeth, I let out a low growl of annoyance.

"Here's the thing, Eliah," he panted with a smirk. "I never lose." He playfully jabbed the tip of his wooden sword at my shoulder. I swatted it away, curling my lip at him. He stepped back, offering me his hand.

"You're a cheat," I spat, shoving his hand away and getting to my feet. I dusted off more flour that clung to my clothes, looking down to see my sleeve wet with blood.

"Hm, we'll need to address that temper of yours as well," he remarked with a hint of amusement. I shot him a glare, resisting the urge to slap his handsome face. My fists clenched as I headed for the door. "Giving up already?" His voice dripped with sarcasm.

"I've had enough of playing games," I retorted.

His eyebrows lifted, a wicked grin playing on his lips. "We'll see about that."

— ✦ —

"What happened to you?" Aoife inquired, noting the flour covering my body and the blood-stained sleeve. I remained silent as I entered the bathing area, untying my boots. "It was that awful?" she prodded, identifying the anger within me and prying to get information from last night's dinner. I pouted at her, silently pleading for her to cease.

She huffed, walked to my armoire, and grabbed more ointment and a bandage. She patted my bed, and I begrudgingly sat next to her. I slipped off my dirtied tunic, noticing that the blood stained my brassiere. She cleaned and patched me silently, which was more of a gift than anything else. She turned me towards her and embraced me with gentleness.

"Happy Founding Day, my dear. And please, be careful with yourself tonight," she said, pointing to my arm. "I don't want you to bloody your new dress...nor would Jesri," she said under her breath.

I eyed the dress hanging on the partition before stretching out on my bed. "Don't worry, Aoife. I won't ruin that beautiful gown. However, perhaps some other lady would be more suited for it," I lamented, tracing the splotched ceiling within my mind.

"No one deserves that gown more than you, my dear," Aoife reassured, rising from her seat and making the bed shift. "Let's get you cleaned up. Jesri wants you to accompany Sir Alder today."

I rolled my eyes and groaned, feeling a wave of disgust wash over me at the mention of him. Just the thought of becoming his pupil made me scream for escape.

I sat up and headed to the wash basin, shedding the rest of my clothes before easing into the warm bath Aoife had already prepared. As I lathered up with soap, the scent of oranges filled the room, calming my troubled thoughts.

Was this really who I was meant to be? An orphaned nobody, burdened with unrelenting anger and manipulated as a tool by the hands of wealthy men? I gritted my teeth, feeling the anger swell within me.

I splashed water on my face and leaned forward, resting my chin on my knees, lost in thought until Aoife's soft knock broke the silence.

"Come in, I'm almost finished," I shouted, rubbing my eyes. The door opened and clicked shut, followed by the sound of heavier footsteps on the hardwood floor.

I whipped my head around to find Calum holding wildflowers, struck dumb at the naked sight of me.

"*Get out!*" I yelled. He promptly retreated from sight as I hastily covered myself with my arms. "Tyran, Cal! So help me if you're in here to tell me more about *fun*; I don't want it."

I stepped out, soaking the floor with water as I wrapped myself in my robe, my wet hair slick against my back.

"I—" he stumbled as I came around the corner, crossing my arms in front of me. "I came to wish you a Happy Founding Day and to apologize for last night."

"You know I don't like celebrating it," I snapped, not believing he was actually sorry for last night.

He only nodded and held out the flowers, "For you."

I brushed wet strands of hair away from my face and took the flowers; our fingers grazed as I forced an uncomfortable smile.

Since they didn't know my actual day of birth, Jesri decided it would be celebrated on Spring Harvest, the day I was found. Only I knew it was an excuse, for he had no intention of acknowledging me with gifts or pleasantries, as was customary on birthdays. Frankly, I could care less and detested the idea, anyway. It only served as a reminder of a day I was left unwanted.

Calum's golden eyes met mine, plunging the world into silence as he stood in a silent yearning. He stepped closer, bridging the gap between us, and my mind grew hazy with confusion. My wet feet became heavy stones, and I couldn't step away as he drew closer, further ensnaring my thoughts.

"Cal," I stated, breaking the silence and the pounding in my ears as I leaned back.

His breath hitched as he leaned in slowly. We shared the same air as a fiery sensation surged through me, catching me off guard and stirring something deep within and melting away every irrational thought.

The world around me faded as he tenderly cupped my chin and drew me closer. Dizziness enveloped my head as our lips grazed, igniting a warmth within me and rendering me liquid when a metallic twang radiated throughout the room, tickling my nose.

My heart thundered in my ears as he swiftly pulled back, letting go of my chin with a confusing look in his eye. He stiffened when a soft knock echoed on the door and quickly flung open. We immediately stepped away from each other like the two mischievous children we were, always getting into trouble. Instant regret and anger flooded through me like a sudden downpour.

"Oh, pardon me. I—" Aoife squeaked, her cheeks turning red. "I didn't know you were in here."

She moved to leave when I stopped her, "No," I paused. "Calum was just dropping off some flowers and was about to leave."

He glanced at me, nodding in agreement; his entire composure was off. "Happy Harvest Day," he said before slipping out. My heart thundered with an unwanted anticipation that left me desolate and guilty.

I managed a smile. "Help me get ready, will you?" I turned away, sensing embarrassment tightening in my chest. Setting the flowers on my bed, I moved behind the partition, slipping on my undergarments. Heat rushed to my cheeks and neck, which quickly faded because of my vexation, puncturing my heart with tiny holes and leaving me filled with self-loathing.

With an audible grunt of disgust, I headed to my vanity, using my robe to dry my hair.

"Forgive me, Eliah," Aoife said, her cheeks mimicking the redness of my own.

"No—" I stopped short; it *was* a good thing she came in. I couldn't bear the thought of succumbing to his manipulative games *again*. "Thank you for intervening." I wouldn't be evasive, "I'm grateful you stopped it. I didn't have the strength to suppress those feelings."

Her smile returned, warming her face to its usual hue. "I can always come to your rescue," she remarked, her tone gentle. "But those feelings are a good thing and worth exploring now that you're older." She paused, quickly adding, "And if I may be bold, Calum is a suitable bachelor—"

"*That is bold,*" I interjected firmly, cutting her off. She nodded with a smirk and began styling my damp hair, weaving it into its customary braided coronet.

"I hear your big evaluation is tomorrow, and Sir Alder seems quite eager about it," she remarked.

I nodded slowly. Of course, he would take pleasure in it, and Jesri would undoubtedly ensure he found the entirety of his stay to be worth telling.

"Wonderful," I sneered sarcastically, causing a pinch to my shoulder.

After she finished with my hair, she wrapped my arm in another cloth and lectured me about keeping my arm movements minimal. I agreed with sarcasm as she left me to dress in my usual training attire: brown pants, a dark green, long-sleeved tunic, and my tattered boots.

I hurried out the door, hoping to find relief from the thoughts and emotions that stirred deep within me as my stomach grumbled—hoping, too, that Jesri might be cheerful enough to offer me a decent meal.

4

"There you are!" Jesri greeted, his smile twitching as I approached the pergola. Levon sat across from him, leisurely enjoying a blueberry-drizzled biscuit. I scanned the bustling courtyard, where servants were making final preparations for tonight's festivities, hoping to catch sight of Calum for some answers.

"Come, eat while it's still fresh," Jesri invited, patting the chair beside him. I raised my eyebrows in irritated disbelief, barely suppressing a scoff. Jesri's eyes hardened, silently demanding that I play along. I clenched my jaw in disgust but reluctantly took my seat.

"And a happy day of founding to you, Eliah," Jesri toasted, raising his glass, with Levon following suit.

"Happy Birthday, my lady," Levon added with a smile.

It was no surprise that Jesri had divulged all the details of my life to Sir Alder, making Levon's casual mention of my birthday all the more infuriating. Jesri never acknowledged this day, especially since it marked the moment his life took a turn for the worse.

Jesri's foot kicked mine under his immaculate white-metal wired table he paid a handsome sum for.

"Thank you, Sir Alder," I said quickly. Indulging in a warm lemon croissant oozing with a creamy raspberry filling, I resisted the urge to let out a delighted moan.

Jesri kicked my foot again, prompting me to sit straight and shut my mouth.

"Please, it's only Levon," he said, noting Jesri's fake smile and my indulgence in more food. I nodded, sipping the peach lemonade that danced like fireworks on my tastebuds.

"Eliah, dear," Jesri began, clearing his throat. "Tomorrow, you'll be participating in a new evaluation for Sir Alder. He has some exciting things planned that I believe you'll enjoy, especially since you've expressed a desire for real weapons in the past." A faint smile tugged at the corners of his mouth. "You'll have an hour to complete it, and this will be your only test," his dark eyes bore into mine, silently conveying the consequence of failure. "So make it count."

He cleared his throat again, stuffing a piece of lemon croissant into his mouth. "Afterward, I'll need you to assist in dismantling the evaluation setup."

"Dismantle it?" I asked, almost choking on my drink.

"Yes, we've fenced off a designated area for it," he replied, his smile widening, exposing his white teeth, which shined like sharp daggers.

"But—"

"No questions, Eliah," he snapped, cutting me off.

I rolled my eyes and took another bite, my attention drifting to the distance where the remaining servants busied themselves with party preparations. They lined the tables with empty plates soon to be filled with pastries and mouth-watering dishes, arranged flower pots brimming with sweet fragrances, and meticulously trimmed the garden to perfection.

I sighed, looking down at my plate, only to find Levon's emerald-blue eyes fixed on me, an unsettling mix of intensity and sadness in his gaze. I swallowed the last of my food, shifting uncomfortably in my seat under his lingering stare.

I cleared my throat. "If I am to be accepted," I said, with a hint of vinegar. "What comes next?"

Jesri looked ready to dismiss my question, but Levon interjected. "You will come to my estate for further training," he stated, pausing to collect his thoughts and maintain the air of secrecy. "And achieve noble deeds."

"Noble? And how is any of *this* considered noble?" I shot back, my voice edged with frustration. Jesri's eyes flashed with anger.

"They are noble because only a select few have the courage to face such challenges," Levon replied, a trace of satisfaction in his tone as though my defiance intrigued him.

"I didn't know that *enforcement* counts as courage," I retorted sharply, fully aware of the fury building in Jesri as his jaw tightened. Ignoring the tension, I took another bite of food, savoring its rich flavor.

Levon's smile faltered at my response. He opened his mouth to speak, but for once, no words came out.

"So what challenges will require such *courage*?" I asked, sarcasm dripping from my voice as I took another bite. "If I had to guess, it must involve the King's Court; otherwise, Jesri would have gotten rid of—"

"*How dare you!*" Jesri's sudden roar silenced everything in the courtyard as he loomed over me. His face twisted with rage, his eyes drilling into mine with a fury that made my heart skip, almost certain he'd strike me right there. "*Do not defy me, girl,*" he seethed, his voice low and venomous. He sat back down, slowly reclaiming his composure, though the anger still simmered beneath the surface.

"Apologies, Sir Alder," he said smoothly, turning to Levon with a calm demeanor that felt like a mask. "I've tried to teach her proper manners, but it seems the wildness within her insists on tarnishing my reputation."

I dropped my fork, my hands balling into fists as anger surged through me, electrifying every nerve. The air grew heavy, thick with a metallic tension. For a moment, I saw a flicker of sadness in Levon's eyes, but it quickly faded into a dark, unsettling smile.

"Most should aspire to serve alongside King Thealor and be a part of his land, my lady. Jesri is simply doing his duty." Levon's words fanned the flames of Jesri's arrogance, and I saw him smirk with satisfaction.

My anger boiled over, and I shot up from my chair, sending it crashing to the ground. Levon quickly stood as well, his eyes filled with a silent plea that almost stopped me in my tracks.

"If you'll excuse me," I said, my voice quivering with barely contained rage. I turned on my heel, refusing to look at Levon, and stormed away. Jesri's amused chuckles echoed behind me, each one twisting the knife of frustration deeper.

Suddenly, the screech of a chair dragged across the stone floor cut through the air, and a firm hand seized my arm, jerking me back. Levon stood inches from me, his breath grazing my ear as he whispered, "The King's Match is where courage truly shines, my lady. And you possess more than enough of it."

Levon's gaze burned into mine for one last lingering moment before he let go and strode away. As he passed Jesri, I could feel the tension between them, Jesri's eyes blazing with suspicion. The anger that had surged through me just moments ago drained away, leaving behind a cold, suffocating panic. My body felt frozen, my thoughts spiraling as I tried to grasp the truth that now seemed so obvious.

A tournament.

Jesri's plans for me had been laid out all along, hidden beneath layers of training, tests, and cruelty. And this King's Match was the finale, making me nothing more than a pawn in his twisted scheme.

My throat tightened, choking off any words, any cries. The realization was crushing, a wave of dread so deep it left me hollow. I was trapped, just as I had been as a child, knowing that no one would come to save me.

—— + ✦ + ——

Unable to bear the weight of my thoughts after breakfast, I felt a desperate need to escape, to push my body until the pain drowned out everything else. I ran as hard as I could, forcing my legs and lungs to burn, chasing the edge of exhaustion.

When I finally collapsed to the ground, I retched up my breakfast, grateful that I had retreated into the colorful woods rather than defiling Jesri's pristine pasture before the party. I sat there for a while, trying to catch my breath and sift through any clues about the King's Match, but came up short.

It was well past lunchtime when I finally forced myself to stand, the need for answers driving me forward. I sought out Darius and found him at the back gates, surrounded by his men as they prepared for the upcoming party.

"Did you decide to bathe in filth on purpose?" Darius remarked, his nose crinkling at the unpleasant smell.

I scoffed in annoyance, "I need answers, Darius. What am I being set up for?" His stance became rigid, a telltale sign that he knew more than he was letting on. "What do you know?" I demanded, the taste of bile still lingering on my tongue. The few remaining men dispersed quickly, sensing the tension in the air and knowing better than to provoke me further.

"Eliah, all I know is what I've told you—"

"No!" I interrupted, my nails digging deep with my anger's metallic edge. "Sir Alder mentioned a Match. What kind of Match, Darius? And why? What is this for?" My voice trembled, a desperate plea for clarity amid the suffocating fear that I might be condemned to an unforgiving fate.

I approached him, snarling low and trying to assert myself despite his towering stature. He could easily overpower me with his years of training, large muscles, and weight. He smelled of coal and sweat, never skipping a day to grow stronger. Over time, he had become something of a father figure to me, supporting and challenging me to be resilient against the harsh words of others. He had continued to comfort me after finding me, once, in tears with scraped knees in the forest. I was so young then, unable to recall the exact words that had wounded me, but feeling their impact nonetheless.

"Eliah," he hesitated, sensing his contemplation. "Let me talk with Jesri first."

"Why?" I breathed, refusing to suppress my anger. "Why all this secrecy? Why must I always be kept in the dark, Darius? This is *my* life." My voice quivered. "It's my life," I hesitated, uncertainty creeping in. "Isn't it?"

His eyes brimmed with sorrow, silently confirming my fears. A profound hopelessness washed over me as Darius firmly gripped my arms; the weight of his silent words crashed down upon me.

"Eliah," his gaze burned with conviction. "It's an immense honor to be chosen by King Thealor. Believe that you are worthy of such recognition and that you are *more* than your training. Trust me."

He pulled me into an embrace, offering a warmth that seemed to mend the parts of me that felt lost. Speechless, I eventually pulled away and walked off, the sense of betrayal heavy on my shoulders. Each step away from him deepened my anger, cutting through me like a blade and severing the last ties to this bleak existence and the dreams I still clung to.

I refused to let this define me. I was more than this miserable life. If they chose to withhold the truth from me, I would uncover it on my own.

5

I went to the musty library, eager to search for any records or accounts regarding the King's Match. Yet, with each passing hour of fruitless searching, my disappointment grew into frustration. It became clear that Jesri had intentionally kept this information from me, just as he had with so many other things. He always kept me in the dark, controlling what I knew, feeding me only the scraps of knowledge he deemed necessary. It was his way of ensuring that I would always have to come to him, rely on him, and be chained to him.

Jesri's influence permeated every aspect of my life like a shadow I could never escape. He manipulated the world around me, crafting a cage of ignorance and dependence. The King's Match was just one more secret he held over me, another way to tighten the chains that bound me to him. As I sifted through dusty and brittle pages, the bitter realization sank in: I knew nothing about the King's Match or anything else of real importance because Jesri had made sure of it. He wanted me powerless, reliant on his every word, and ensuring that I remained under his control. For too long, I had been ensnared in his web, blind to the world beyond the confines he set for me.

Instead of the answers I sought, I did, however, find tales of ancient heroic Magics and the dark shadows that lurked within the kingdom's history, one of which was the archaic Magics called Spellcasters. I huffed out, slamming the book shut at the dark fables Jesri kept, thinking such thing as odd, and realized that the sun had dipped lower, prompting me to hurry back to my room to get ready for the party.

Through the large crystal windows, I saw the breathtaking courtyard with flowers adorning tables laden with an array of pastries, meats, fruits, vegetables, and wine. The musicians had arrived, meticulously arranging their instruments beneath the flowered banner. In the distance, the servants bustled about in the greenhouse, gently cradling butterflies designed to be released at the commencement of the celebration—a moment I cherished above all because it was the one night Jesri let me be free. As I ascended, inhaling the warm, earthy air, my anticipation heightened, knowing that Aoife waited with that stunning dress.

✦ ✦ ✦

Aoife helped me into the vibrant light blue dress; each layer of chiffon fabric flowed effortlessly and shimmered with a mesmerizing sparkle. The bodice sparkled with intricate crystals that glimmered like miniature constellations, casting radiant light beams in the golden sun. The long sheer sleeves billowed softly, trimmed with a delicate white lace hem that mirrored the neckline.

She dusted my lips with matte pink powder and lined my lashes with charcoal, illuminating my gray-blue eyes to echo the vibrant blue of the gown. She wove a delicate white flower crown and rested it atop my dark auburn hair, which was kept in a long curtain of loose curls.

I couldn't deny feeling more attractive than ever, and I was determined to counteract the rumors and lies that portrayed me as a naive, boyish orphan taken in by Jesri out of charity. Despite his claims of goodwill, Jesri never missed an opportunity to remind me of every derogatory rumor he heard about his so-called *pitiful ward*.

I hurried down the back stairs that led out behind the estate and stepped through the doors into the courtyard. The space buzzed with activity as guests arrived in wide-brimmed hats adorned with feathers, sleek trousers, fitted tunics, and gowns in every pastel shade. Musicians played melodic symphonies while servants moved through the crowd, offering platters filled with wines, teas, lemonades, and various foods.

Hiding in the shelter of the estate's west corner, I pressed against the weathered brown plaster wall, scanning the crowd for Calum's distinctive golden hair among the guests. Unable to spot him and suppressing my disappointment, I took a deep breath and ventured into the lively gathering.

I lifted my head higher, walking tall into the bustling crowd as my focus shifted to Sir Alder, seated by the gardens in a deep conversation with Lord Winslow while several ladies nearby tried to catch his eye. I couldn't suppress my laugh at the view. And despite the split lip I had given him earlier, he still looked dashing in his cream-colored suit, which contrasted beautifully against his hazelnut skin.

Perhaps it was Sir Alder who would be my oracle of information for this tournament, considering he so willingly gave me the most significant secret Jesri kept hidden for years.

"Sir Alder," I said, interjecting his conversation with the rakish Lord Winslow, who eyed me up and down with pleasure as he did with any young girl who gave him any notice beyond his wealth. I held back my discomfort, looking solely at Sir Alder's emerald-blue eyes.

"Would you do me the honor and accompany me for the opening?" I asked, smoothly laying on the flattery. I was determined to coax any information from him.

Sir Alder uncrossed his legs and flashed me a grin, revealing his pearly smile.

"Of course, my lady," he replied, rising from his seat. "It was a pleasure conversing with you, my Lord," he added to Lord Winslow, who gave me a disgusting sensual smile.

Sir Alder extended his arm, and I took it, noticing the sour expressions on the faces of the ladies nearby. Suppressing my grin, I leaned into his side, barely containing my satisfaction.

"Are you enjoying yourself, Sir Alder?" I felt his arm muscles tense beneath my hand.

"Please, only Levon," he said, adjusting his suit with a slight smile. "And yes, Jesri's estate is quite something. The people here are certainly lively."

We both glanced around at the numerous ladies, each trying to capture attention with practiced grace. I couldn't help but let out an airy laugh.

"You're the new face here, Levon. Consider yourself fortunate I stepped in when I did. Otherwise, you'd be swamped with questions and unwelcome touches, making it impossible to enjoy the excellent food Jesri is known for."

Levon's lips curled into a teasing smirk. "And it seems my swollen lip only adds to the entertainment, doesn't it?"

"You deserved it," I added, looking down my nose. "But I suppose you've redeemed yourself with that information this morning."

His brows raised, barely glancing at me. A slight smirk played at the corner of his lips as we made our way toward the front podium, crafted from fine cedar wood and painted a pristine white. Surrounding the podium were rows upon rows of flowers, mirroring the vibrant blooms that flourished in the courtyard. Pastel ribbons and delicate laces were strung at each end, softly billowing in the gentle breeze, adding a whimsical touch to the already enchanting scene.

Jesri walked up the podium with several servants following closely behind with their cartons full of butterflies. The sun dipped lower towards the horizon, casting a warm glow and painting the sky in hues of orange and pink. It was warmer than usual, and I relished the thought of summer's hot air, grateful for the warmth to train in rather than the biting cold. Jesri waited for the other party guests to fill the space around us, smiling brightly.

"Welcome, my dear friends!" Jesri boomed, lifting his hands into the air. Cheers and clapping followed. I glanced around, hoping to catch sight of Calum, realizing that this would be among the first without our customary dance at the release. A twinge of sadness settled in my chest, hoping our odd encounter earlier wasn't the cause of his disappearance.

Levon noticed the shift in my sunken shoulders and smiled gently.

"Today heralds the dawn of another chapter, a chance for fresh beginnings," Jesri proclaimed, his voice carrying across the crowd. "It is a day to honor the Creator and seek the blessings for another year abundant with growth. Growth as lush as the blooming flowers and resilient as the towering trees, bearing fruit as plentiful as the ripest berries. It's a day we cherish for new friendships," he paused for dramatics. "And for new lovers." People in the crowd whistled and hollered.

Levon looked down at me with raised brows and then out to the ladies, snickering and pointing. I couldn't stop a dramatic eye roll and felt good, for once, to be seen with a handsome bachelor among all these shallow people who had detested me for being unconventional. And now, with the new bachelor in town, I felt...different with him at my side. Somehow, I found myself grateful for all those grueling days of training, pushing my body to its limits and growing stronger. Despite the circumstances not being what I had hoped for, it was a welcome change to feel something other than self-pity.

"Today is a day for us all to embrace a clean slate and harvest our past selves by taking this new year to flourish into something greater!" Jesri continued.

He cast a glance at the servants, signaling to them. "Let the festivities commence!" With a sweep of his raised hands, thousands of golden butterflies spilled from the large cartons, filling the orange sky with specks of glittering gold and sparkling stars. A chorus of cheers and laughter erupted as the musicians struck up their festive tunes.

Levon released my arm and extended his hand toward the sky, captivated by the mesmerizing dance of the butterfly wings. A delighted sigh escaped my lips as I reached up to touch the fluttering creatures and twirl amidst the golden magic of their shimmer. His hand clasped mine, and together, we spun in joyful ease, our laughter blending with the cheers of the crowd, enchanted with delight, and I hoped this mask was enough to coax information out of him.

We cheered on, immersed in the shimmering spectacle, until most of the butterflies drifted off toward the horizon, leaving only a few lingering to keep us company. I felt utterly alive and connected to who I was meant to be and allowed myself to let go of the weight of the inevitable for the moment.

"That was the most thrilling thing I have yet to experience," Levon said, excitement evident in his voice. I snapped back to pretending and chuckled, giving him a tight smile before taking his arm once again.

"Just wait until you taste the pastries."

———— + ✦ + ————

I don't believe my stomach ever hurt from laughing as hard as I did after a little too much wine that tasted like peaches and seeing Levon's face after each bite of confections, thinking perhaps he wasn't as bad as I thought.

These pastries were undoubtedly the finest yet: tarts drizzled with a rogue spice that pricked the tongue, exotic berry-filled bonbons with the creamiest chocolate that melted like butter, candied fruit with a syrupy sweetness, and orange mille-feuille that moved our bodies into an alluring trance.

I settled into the wired chair, savoring the moment. It had been a while since I felt this happy and unburdened, finally liberated from Jesri's threatening gaze for the night. Reflecting on my life, I wasn't sure why I had allowed myself to be manipulated by him for so long.

What was I so afraid of?

Encouraged by the graceful dance of the butterflies and Jesri's speech, a newfound resolve began to swell within me. I vowed not to let my past continue to dominate me. It was time to reclaim control of my life, starting with this upcoming match.

"You're thinking about something?" Levon prodded, his words slightly slurred as he collapsed into the chair beside me, his breath heavy with the scent of peach wine.

"Perhaps you should stick to lemonade for now; you wouldn't want to miss the dancing and the grand finale."

He chuckled softly, his enticing gaze locking with mine. "Would it surprise you that I've only had two drinks? I'm not usually one to indulge, but when I do, it tends to strike me harder than most."

"Truly?" I said, surprised. "I didn't consider you to be so sober."

"Being on guard," he paused, leaning in closer and speaking in a hushed tone. "For certain things is necessary."

I narrowed my eyes. There was clearly more to him than he or Jesri were revealing. "Like what *things*?" I pressed, pretending to sip more of my wine.

"Like those who demand to know more than they should," he sat up straighter, straightening his overcoat. "I'm no fool to this flirtatious plan of yours, my lady. You won't get the information you want from me."

I clenched my jaw, struggling to restrain the vulgar retort, itching to escape. "I think the wine is getting to your head," I retorted, turning to view the crowd mingling in the golden sun.

"Care to escort me for a dance?" he said, standing and extending a hand.

"No," I said, folding my arms across my chest. "Not unless you tell me some-*thing* first."

He winked with amusement. "Your golden-eyed courtier won't take issue with me holding you close if I *do* share something?"

I stood up, surprised by his forwardness.

"I can surely tell you he is *not* courting me," I snapped. Yet, Calum's absence made my stomach twist with unease. He adored parties, especially this one, and his absence filled me with worry despite my guilt of longing for him.

He grinned. "Well, I can surely tell you, *he* might think otherwise. And *that* is the thing I will tell you."

I scowled at him as he took my arm and guided us across the stone floor, where several couples swayed to the music. The warm breeze tousled my hair, carrying fragrant floral scents from the vibrant forest beyond.

Levon gracefully took my hand and placed his other on my waist. As the other ladies watched us, I noticed a few resentful looks as he pulled me in closer, prompting me to tilt my head away, only for him to flash a smile.

"We'll be getting much closer when training starts," he mused, only loud enough for me to hear.

"You've accepted me that quickly?" I tested, irritable as his directness and ownership.

The corners of his mouth tugged up. "I'm eager to see you in action, beyond just dancing in flour," he winked. His bright eyes sparkled with anticipation, likely for whatever he had planned for tomorrow.

I glared at him and took my skirts in my free hand as we swayed to the rhythm of the music. It was like swordplay but with much less finesse and came more gracefully. I held my head high and gently stepped into each turn and swirl, acting much more ladylike than I did on most days. I let the music take us away, dancing easier than we had earlier this morning. Maybe I *would* enjoy his company.

"Tell me more about how you and Jesri became acquainted," I asked as we briefly parted before joining hands once more, following the other couples dancing.

"We met a few years past at a tavern in Bricol," he began, his expression growing weary. I waited for him to continue, but he fell silent. Why would Jesri be in Bricol? His business travels typically took him to the seaports, not inland.

"I thought you said you didn't drink? Then again, you were there as a," I paused for dramatics. "Guiding light, was it?"

He laughed. "I was recently transferred and...in pain," he paused, trying to think of words. "I thought a drink or two would be enough to dull my senses. Yet Jesri was more of a guiding light for me, helping me home after I got into a lousy brawl with a wretched man who—" he stopped, realizing he was saying too much. "It doesn't matter now. Jesri and I stayed in connection every so often and prepared for things."

"Things like me?" I said with annoyance. He only nodded, not giving me more foolish information. "What *was* Jesri doing in Bricol?"

"You ask too many questions, my lady."

"Maybe I ask questions because I *hate* feeling weak," I confessed, sensing my words resonated with him. He straightened slightly, gracefully guiding me through the dance, and pulled me close, stealing my breath. He leaned in, his breath tickling my ear. "If you prove yourself in tomorrow's training, I'll share what information I can. I understand what it's like to feel vulnerable. Things may not always appear as they seem, but it's for your own safety and success," he whispered, pulling back and twirling me again.

I shook my head, confused. "You're speaking in riddles," I said with annoyance.

"Your first riddle, Eliah, is to learn what it takes to survive."

The song ended, and he bowed low, gently kissing my fingers. He strode away towards the group of ladies swooning for him, leaving me at its center in complete bewilderment.

Survive? That's what my training *has* been all my life: to survive. What more could a match be than to survive? I grumbled in frustration, angry that I failed to coax anything out of him.

Gathering my skirts, I walked towards a maid with a platter of drinks. I took some lemonade and tapped on the maid's sleeve. "Have you seen Calum anywhere?"

The maid's plump cheeks went red at the mention of Cal. I forced down a roll of my eyes. She shook her head, "Sorry, my lady, I have not."

I gulped down the drink and placed it back on the plate, smiling at her before finding a place to hide until the finale.

————— + ✦ + —————

"With heartfelt gratitude, I thank you for celebrating our new beginnings and growth. As friends and family, let us rejoice!" Jesri's voice boomed, accompanied by the explosion of cannons, showering the sky with colorful powder that settled on the pathways below, symbolizing the planting of our new seeds, much like the butterflies, heralding new life. Cheers echoed through the air as the crowd began to disperse, strolling through the powder and allowing the vibrant hues to cling to their shoes in hopes of new promises. Amidst the crowd, I spotted Levon surrounded by ladies, giggling and swooning over his now colorful suit.

The buzz of laughter and chatter slowly dimmed into the rattle of carriages and hooves.

I moved to help clean up some misplaced glasses on a few tables when a maid intercepted me, insisting I stop, especially on my founding day. I scowled at her, dismissing birthdays as trivial and holding no significance for me beyond being a day I was left forgotten.

Yet, she persisted, and I departed with a nod, seeking solace within the estate after the party's uproar. Upon entering my room, I saw a crumpled bag on my bed. I exhaled audibly, hoping it wasn't Aoife's attempt at gifting me something—she knew I hated celebrating. I cautiously untied it and peered inside, revealing a lush lavender shawl adorned with intricate threads, creating a swirling pattern like the sea's tides. Resting atop the shawl was a small note:

The tree. Midnight.
Cal

I crumpled the note and lifted the shawl, its fabric carrying his lingering scent. It was thick and warm, with small threads hanging from each trim.

Today marks my eighteenth year, thus making it three years since Jesri forbade us from visiting our tree together, where we used to go after every Spring Harvest or whenever we needed solace, and wish upon the stars for our friendship and a brighter future beyond our dreary lives. Yet, year after year, those stars never granted my wishes, especially not for comfort regarding my lost parents. So, I stopped believing in and visiting the tree altogether, making Jesri's demand all too easy to accept. Yet, I still kept staring at the stars from my window, obtaining comfort from them despite how far away they were.

At least I never had the chance to meet my parents, making it easier to move on, unlike Calum, who never ceased to yearn for his parents' return. They sent him away to a boarding school while they ventured off to explore the world, leaving only a note for Jesri, Calum's only remaining family, stating they had embarked on a sailing journey to the East Ulvery Sea and wouldn't return until the following Winter.

Two years later, Jesri received a letter stating that Calum's parents were not returning, and knowing the burden of boarding school, he took Calum in. I still recall the day Calum received the news, seeing the weight of his world vanish within a few words. He stayed in his room for two weeks, becoming sickly and hollow. It was then that Jesri insisted he train with me, and it was during those sessions that our friendship formed. I was thirteen at the time; Cal was almost fifteen.

He was blessed with attractiveness, capable of captivating anyone who crossed his path, making his golden eyes, blond ruffled hair, and tall, strong features effortlessly claim my young, lonely heart. I beckoned to his every call, challenging myself harder as he praised me for successes, knowing how to sneak his way in and weave intricately like the shawl's threads into my young heart.

As I matured, I grew weary of Calum's games and ceased trying to impress him, recognizing his true nature as Jesri's kin. However, rather than deterring him, my indifference only seemed to fuel his determination to captivate me, leaving my heart in turmoil.

Complying with his last request before our lives separated, I made my way to the armoire, shedding my dress, stockings, and shoes, quickly dressing in black pants and a long knit tunic. I draped the shawl over my shoulders and slipped into my boots before entering the hallway, hearing the faint sound of shuffling feet echoing on the ceramic floors. Unnoticed, I slipped out the door into the dark ebony sky. A handful of servants remained, ensuring all guests had departed, and began to secure the gates.

The night air carried a chill, mingled with the scent of dust from the powder that still clung to the damp grass and walkways. I pulled the shawl tighter around me as a gust of wind rippled through my hair. The moon illuminated the path before me, guiding my steps with its radiant glow. A playful smirk danced on my lips as I swiftly made my way onto the soft, plush grounds of the familiar woods; the trees blossomed with color under the moon's luminous gaze and welcomed me back home.

6

In the moonlight, the woods radiated with vibrant colors against the twinkling stars. Each tree swayed gracefully in the breeze, seemingly in perpetual bloom, their leaves whispering enchanting melodies. I was lulled into a sense of tranquility, a gentle warmth spreading from my fingertips to the small of my back. Pollen drifted through the air like shimmering stars while insects chirped and settled in for the night. As I breathed in the earthy scent mixed with the sweetness of honey, I relished the feeling of belonging, as if this place were my true home, exuding life and vibrancy.

I followed the curve of a cluster of trees onto the makeshift path that Cal and I had created as children. The once-flat stones melted into the moss-covered ground, the greenery hugging them like spindly fingers.

I leaped onto one and instinctively knew where each stone lay within the shadowy pathway. Jumping from the last rock, I leapt, landing quietly on the gravel that led to the bubbling stream next to our tree.

The deeper I went, the more my eyes easily adjusted to the darkness. Giving my one thanks to Jesri, who had insisted on pushing my body beyond its physical limits. Whether it was sparring with Darius in the dark or confronting my fear of venomous spiders, each challenge left me bruised and swollen for days. I pushed my body relentlessly, embracing the burn of exhaustion, consistently surpassing my own expectations, and marveling at how well my body adapted to the elements around me.

"What took you so long?" Calum asked, his voice piercing the quiet and startling me. I steadied myself and approached his shadowy figure, standing next to our wish tree, a twisted mass of gnarled branches sticking out in every direction. The tree appeared lifeless and abandoned, with its thick, contorted limbs contrasting sharply against the vibrant foliage around it. Despite its barren appearance, it held a special place in my heart and was the perfect spot to gaze up and admire the shining stars that seemed to glow just a little brighter from beneath its boughs.

"It's not yet midnight," I remarked. "And I'm not going to wish anyway."

He huffed out a laugh, walking into view. The shadows crept across him like dark tendrils with each step closer.

He smirked, "Glad you're enjoying the shawl."

I tugged it tighter around me. "Please tell me you didn't skip the entire party just for this?"

His expression darkened briefly before he flashed a deep smile, revealing his dimples. "Oh, I had other important matters to attend to."

Confusion flickered in my mind. "Important?" I chuckled. "What could possibly be more important than a party with plenty of ladies who—"

His lips pressed hard against mine, stealing my breath. He held my face in his soft hands and kissed me again. His intimate touch burned a hole in my frustration with an electrifying fire that consumed me until I couldn't breathe. A sudden flash of light seared through my closed eyelids as a sharp surge of energy stung my lips, tingling up into my mouth. In reflex, we pushed each other back, both with furrowed brows, hissing at one another at what just transpired. Bewilderment covered my mind as I touched my numb lips.

"What was that?" I cursed, angry at myself for letting my emotions take control. He touched his own lips when a loud snap bounced off the trees, echoing around us and quieting even the insects. We both jerked our heads towards the source, instantly on edge, knowing the warnings of the creatures that prowled at night.

He raised a finger to his lips, silencing me as we stood defensively, listening to any more unusual sounds. I strained to listen past the rustling of the stream from behind and the chorus of frogs. Another faint shuffle caught my attention, this time to our left. Cal heard it, too, his gaze shifting toward the source of the sound as the air around us grew thick with tension. The shuffle grew louder, almost clumsy, as I readied my stance. We stood still, listening. My heart thrummed in my ears when a pair of coppery-yellow eyes blinked once and then disappeared. The hair on my neck stood up, and my body pebbled with bumps down my skin. More movement arose, causing Cal to step back when a fawn emerged into view, nibbling on shrubs. The fear escaped my body immediately, returning my breathing to its natural rhythm.

"Scared of a fawn?" Cal teased, a mischievous grin playing on his lips. I shoved him away before walking towards the tree, settling down on the soft ground, and inhaling the earthy night air. Calum joined me, sitting close into my warmth.

We sat silently for a moment before he spoke. "I—" he hesitated. "I needed to know."

I looked at him with irritation in my eyes. All that firey passion moments ago had faded, turning into anger and guilt.

"Know what, Cal?" I demanded sharply.

He looked at me, almost saddened, yet his golden eyes still showed bright amidst the dark world around us. "Your lips, Eliah. Your lips on mine."

I stilled as my anger fueled—only another *toy* to play with. I gritted my teeth, fighting off my girlish emotions. I *wouldn't* let myself fall for him, ever. He wasn't capable of giving me the happiness I yearned for, and I couldn't remain. I refused to spend my life here in his shadow.

"Don't you dare place me as a piece in your game, Calum," I snapped. "I will never play."

I looked up at him, despising myself for *enjoying* his soft lips, which turned into a playful smile. "You couldn't bear the thought of *one* girl not swooning for you?" I hissed, scaring a few birds out of their nests. I wrapped the shawl tighter and stood, walking farther away from him.

We stayed there in silence, listening to the quiet music of the woods as I let my anger settle into the kernel of light within me.

"Why did you bring me here, Cal?" I asked, breaking the silence at last.

His eyes turned somber as he looked at me, his smile fading. He scuffed his polished shoes and shoved his hands into his pockets.

"I know something, El. Something that I—I couldn't live with myself if I didn't tell you," he confessed.

I furrowed my brows, waiting for his explanation.

"Do you remember the Leonardian War? After King Tyran's reign."

My thoughts flashed back to the history lessons with the scrawny professor who Jesri insisted Cal and I endure. One lesson stood out more than the others about the massacre directed by King Leonard. Thousands of Magics perished. The profound sadness of that realization had brought me to tears that night as I wrestled with the horror of an entire race being destroyed and, henceforth, forgotten.

I shook my head. "Only the massacre," I said, my voice trembling with the weight of the memory.

His brow furrowed in concern. "The war started when corrupted Magics summoned something," he explained, his tone grave. "They were seeking something dangerous. After the summoning, hundreds of other—" he paused, glancing around cautiously. "Creatures appeared. King Leonard rallied several neighboring armies to hunt them down, exterminating anything with even a trace of magic—no longer trusting those with such abilities."

My mind raced through the books I had read earlier, remembering reading something about the Spellcasters and their archaic plans that failed. "These...Magics, were they called the Spellcasters?" I whispered, feeling a sense of apprehension, as if speaking their name aloud might conjure them.

His eyes narrowed in surprise. "Yes, how—"

"Jesri's library," I interjected. "I was looking for information about the King's Match." I continued, detailing my search and how it yielded nothing further.

"You found this in Jesri's library?" he questioned.

I nodded, causing him to caress his jaw in thought.

"What is it?" I asked, eager to leave the darkening woods, now chilled by a brisk wind.

"The existence of the Spellcasters has been erased from most historical records, and if any text were found, it could be punishable by imprisonment or death."

My brows shot up in shock and confusion, sensing Calum felt the same way.

Sensing he didn't want to question his uncle, he continued. "The Kings were determined to ensure that no one would attempt such actions again since their failures led to something terrible."

"What do you mean, terrible?"

"That's all I know. Something terrible occurred following whatever evil magic the Spellcasters attempted," he recounted.

My mind spun with unanswered questions, the pieces refusing to align. The Kings had been deceiving us. But for what purpose besides us Mundanes who yield no magic? It doesn't make sense.

"Where did you come across this information?"

His demeanor shifted to one of seriousness. "This afternoon, I overheard Sir Alder mention the War with Jesri and Darius. I couldn't make out everything, but it seems the evaluation Sir Alder wants you in might involve creatures or some animal. They discussed the need for a cage."

My heart stopped, realizing what Jesri meant about taking the evaluation down. But what was its link to the War?

I stood up and staggered away from our tree, my mind swirling with questions. What *creatures* were they discussing? What animals? The last evaluation involving animals left me ill for weeks after a rabid dog bite paralyzed half my body.

I closed my eyes, feeling a surge of fear and anger course through me.

"Why tell me?" I snapped, struggling to contain the rising anger that threatened to overwhelm me. His eyes glazed over as he stood up against the thick trunk. "Why?" I rasped, feeling like a pawn in his game.

"To better prepare you," he said flatly, his temper rising.

"Evidently, that's what Levon is for," I spat.

His stature shifted at the mention of Levon to something mimicking disgust. He rolled his eyes before palming his face and stroking his hair back. "Can you not believe me when I say I'm trying to help you?"

I gritted my teeth, clutching the lavender shawl tighter in my cold hands. "Why?" I ordered. "Why does Jesri think I can do this? Or that I will?" I inquired, feeling pressure build up in my throat. "Why does he hate me?"

His face softened, realizing my terror. Despite my efforts to deny my fear, deep down, fear held me tightly, slowly squeezing the air from me as I secretly wished for our wretched tree to answer my pleas.

"El," Calum murmured, drawing me closer to him. I tensed, irritated at his attempt to soothe my fearful heart and regain control. I reluctantly let him stroke my hair, not having the energy for another fight.

I knew that this outcome would happen. That I would be sent away to use my abilities in whatever form was needed. I just wasn't prepared for...*this*.

"I don't know, El. I don't understand why Jesri thought you would be the one to do it," he confessed, a hint of jealousy coloring his words as he broke the silence.

I pulled out of his embrace, leaving me cold. Of course, he would be jealous. Calum was kin to Jesri, and I was nothing more than a pawn heading towards my demise.

Overwhelmed by a torrent of questions and emotions I wasn't ready to confront, I turned to walk away, but he caught my hand.

"Stay," he pleaded. "Please, El."

7

Every part of me yearned to flee, to find peace somewhere far from here. But his pleas, like a siren's call, tugged at the threads that still connected us. Despite all of Calum's flaws, aside from Aoife, he was my only friend, and the thought of finding comfort in his arms made me push past my fear and resentment. I couldn't let go of what might be our last moment together, so I stayed. He held me close as we gazed up at our tree and the stars twinkling through its branches. The soft, cool moss beneath us became our bed for the night.

"What do you think the tournament will be?" I asked, snuggling in closer to his side as the night grew colder.

"Something exciting enough to make Jesri say yes," he mocked, readjusting himself and pulling me tighter.

We sat silently for a moment, the gentle breeze whispering through the leaves and the sweet scent of flowering trees filling the air as we inhaled the fragrant night.

"Where were you at the party today? You've never missed it before."

He smiled sincerely, exposing his dimples even in the starlight.

"With Lady Annabelle," he cooed with a chuckle.

I couldn't help but roll my eyes and push away from him, feeling like the *other* lady he would always run back to when things got rough.

"Hopefully, she quelled your appetite because you missed the best pastries Jesri has ever gotten," I said, stretching out my neck.

He started full-on belly laughing, sitting up beside me and ruffling out his hair. "Could you imagine Lady Annabelle in the tournament or one of your evaluations?" Calum chuckled, shaking his head.

"She'd probably try to duel with a fan," I replied curtly.

"Or faint at the sight of her own shadow."

"You're terrible," I said, nudging him playfully, a smile tugging at the corners of my lips.

"Ah, but you love me for it," he retorted with a grin.

"You wish."

"What was that earlier?" he asked, touching his lip and turning the conversation somber. My mind returned to the sharp sting that shocked both of us.

"I don't know," I stopped, shaking my head, genuinely puzzled. "Maybe if you didn't have such a magnetic personality, the moonbugs would stay away."

He grinned, raising an eyebrow. "Are you saying I'm irresistible?"

"More like trouble."

"Well, they do say the best things in life come with a bit of trouble," he replied, laying back on the ground and pulling me with him.

I couldn't stop my laugh, which echoed through the trees.

We fell silent, listening to the nocturnal insects sing, until his breathing gradually slowed, indicating he had drifted off to sleep. With a nudge, I roused him, and together, we retraced our steps back to the estate, both wrapped snugly in the shawl. The wind had grown stronger, chilling the damp air around us as we quickened our pace.

Upon reaching the estate, we bid each other goodnight and went to our separate rooms. I fell asleep as soon as my head hit my pillow, only to be abruptly awakened by Aoife's cheerful voice as she drew back the thick curtains, flooding the room with warm sunlight. A groan escaped my lips as the sun touched my face.

"Oh, you have always been one for the dramatics," Aoife teased, perching herself at the edge of my bed. "You didn't train all night again, did you?" she remarked, gesturing to my clothes, which were still on from the night before.

I shifted my weight onto my right elbow, raising myself to face her. "Oh, no," I responded flatly, annoyed at being woken so early. What time was it, anyway? I managed fine on minimal sleep, but today, my mind and body rebelled against the lack of it.

"Jesri expects you at breakfast as soon as possible, and then it's off to warm up for your final evaluation," Aoife said with urgency in her voice.

I sat up, blinking against the sunlight filtering through my window, noticing the large, daunting gates being assembled outside. A knot formed in my stomach as I suppressed a rush of thoughts about what the potential *creatures* might be.

I palmed my eyes, releasing a sigh of frustration. The echoes of last night's conversation persisted in my mind like murky water, stubbornly refusing to fade away. With a groan, I determined to push the thoughts aside and focus on succeeding in today's evaluation.

Yet, my mind refused to obey and wandered aimlessly to thoughts about the Spellcasters, the innocent Magics, and the deceit taught for hundreds of years. It all was much too confusing to comprehend.

"Well, aren't you a cheery one this morning?" Aoife remarked, laying out clean training attire by my feet. "Come on now, don't make Jesri upset at the both of us."

I scooted off the bed, landing on the cool wood floor. Rubbing my eyes, surely red from little sleep. I slid off my clothes from the night before and quickly slipped on a new pair of black pants and a dark green top, lacing my boots up while Aoife combed my knotted hair.

"I can finish here, Aoife. Thank you," I said, yawing and beckoning her to leave.

"You'd best get down there on time, Eliah. And be careful with that arm of yours," she said with a wink. "Good luck, my dear. I know you'll do wonderful."

She hurried out the door, knowing she had a hundred and one things to do before lunch.

I quickly braided my hair, letting it fall down my back, and followed suit. I went down the staircase and nearly reached the door when voices echoed from the dining hall. My boots squeaked with the sudden change in direction as I turned towards the source, recognizing the familiar tones of Jesri and Calum conversing.

"Happy Evaluation Day," Jesri said, buttering his biscuit with jam as I entered the room. The dining decorations were cleared, leaving the large room feeling empty, like Jesri's cheery welcome. Calum greeted me with a smile, his eyes were also red from little sleep. I approached the table and took my usual seat next to him, scanning the room for any sign of Levon.

Jesri noticed my confusion. "Levon is preparing for your test," he explained, taking a bite of his biscuit, causing crumbs to scatter onto his plate. "Hurry and eat," he urged, gesturing towards my plate with cold eggs and a small, stale biscuit.

I took a bite, grimacing at the wetness that should not come from cooked eggs, and swallowed it with a glass of water. Calum stayed silent as he watched me gulp down the food, pausing to eat his extravagant gravy with onion-laced biscuits, toasted to perfection that made my mouth water. I shot him a reassuring look, silently urging him not to worry.

I stood up abruptly, not caring for the hard biscuit nor wanting to spend more time in Jesri's presence than necessary.

"Eliah," Jesri called out, halting me just before I reached the foyer, my emotions teetering off the edge. "*Do not fail me, girl.*"

His voice sliced deep, dripping with repulsion. Within an instant, my body ignited with anger, fizzling through my veins like a wildfire that was impossible to contain. His words seized me, taking hold of every blood cell, every vein, and thread of control, refusing to succumb to his entitlement.

The room buzzed with a sharp, metallic twang that sent my senses into overdrive while an overpowering fear crashed over me like a wave. I heard Calum shift, the chair scraping as he stood, his voice firm as he shot back a retort to his uncle. Jesri's response was a light, mocking laugh, followed by the sound of feet shuffling across the slick ceramic floor with pebbles crunching beneath them.

I clenched my fists, digging my nails into my palms as the pressure in my ears intensified. My body trembled, rooted to the spot, until Calum's gentle touch on my shoulder pulled me back, reminding me of where I was.

Calum clasped my hand, gently urging me forward, though his words were muffled. My feet shuffled hesitantly as waves of anger and fear thundered in my ears, swirling my mind into a chaotic storm of emotions. Suddenly, a sharp pain stabbed through my head, spreading in ripples that left my hands and legs numb. I could no longer tell if I was standing still or moving, only feeling the warmth of the sun on my face before I surrendered to the comforting embrace of darkness.

• ✦ •

My eyes snapped open, and I was blinded by a brilliant light, which soon softened into the gentle shimmer of sunlight filtering through the trees above. Groaning against the pounding in my head, I sat up, feeling a wet cloth slip onto my lap. I took a deep breath, feeling the hollow ringing in my ears fade into the soft songs of birds and insects. I blinked to see Levon sitting against a tree, his attention shifting over my body with palpable concern.

"Are you alright, my lady?" Levon's voice sounded distant as I fought to recover my senses.

I rubbed my face, feeling a rough texture scrape against my cheek. When I pulled my hand away, I noticed dried blood smeared on both hands and caked under my fingernails. I shook my head, trying to piece together what had happened.

"Eliah?"

I snapped my eyes back to his voice, forgetting he was there. "I'm...fine," I replied quickly, and surprisingly, I meant it. Despite everything, I felt okay, just a bit disoriented.

His eyes shifted to my bloody palms, and he stood. Worry covered his face.

"What happened?" he whispered with conviction.

I shook my head again, shrugging. I didn't know what had happened, still feeling the lingering pain within my skull. I looked back up to Levon in silent question.

"I saw you collapse in Calum's arms as soon as you stepped outside. I rushed over to help, but Calum wouldn't say what happened and only stayed silent while he carried you here," Levon explained, gesturing to the damp cloth in my lap. I picked it up and scrubbed away the dried blood from my hands.

"All I remember was being angry and—" I halted, recollecting the vivid details of my surroundings: Calum's breathing, Jesri's knife slicing into his food, and...fear, so much fear. "The test," I said, changing the subject. "Did I miss it?"

Levon laughed heartily, tilting his head back. "Your first worry is about the test?" he chuckled again. "Jesri really did instill resilience in you."

I bit back my tongue, letting the words roll off. Jesri did *nothing* to instill that. He was only there to punish.

"Did I miss it?" I asked again, sharply.

He shook his head. "No, my lady. You weren't out very long."

I twisted to stand as Levon reached out a hand, but I quickly backed away.

"I'm fine." I turned back to the estate, walking anywhere besides Levon's bright eyes.

"Eliah, be careful with yourself." His voice filled with sincerity.

I glanced back with a curt nod, hastily walking away and shaking away the murky fog that still held my mind.

I stepped into the open courtyard, where the tall fence loomed overhead, supported by sturdy wooden posts. Darius and some of his men, clad in green training cloaks, shared a laugh while pointing high to the fence's edge. Changing direction, I went to the back of the estate to catch a breath.

I turned the corner of the estate's plastered walls and adjusted my pace as the terrain sloped downward, forming a gentle hill that leveled out further below. In the distance, the shimmering sea caught the sunlight, its surface sparkling like a vast expanse of jewels. White sails could be seen, roaming freely. I inhaled deeply, relishing the humid air that sunk deep into my lungs.

I concentrated on breathing, inhaling, and exhaling slowly, trying to regain my composure. *What was that?* It felt like life had momentarily vanished, leaving behind only a profound sense of fear...fear unlike any I had ever known.

I stretched my arms and neck, letting the sun soak deep into my tanned skin. Closing my eyes, I concentrated on clearing my mind, letting the chirping birds and the distant yell of voices fade into the distance, and refocused on my lungs expanding and compressing—in and out.

Quickly, I opened my eyes, deciding to find Cal before warming up and letting my mind wander over what might happen in that cage.

I walked through the side door into the servant's quarters, where the maids quickly curtsied before hurrying off. The scent of warm butter filled the air, leading me to the freshly baked rolls. I couldn't resist snatching one, savoring each warm bite as the rich butter melted on my tongue. Continuing, I rounded the corner to the stairwell and began my ascent.

I jogged up, leaping across two steps and then back, focusing on balance and control as I tried to warm up my legs and lungs. The strain left me panting for air when I reached the top.

The back foyer was unusually quiet as I approached the staircase leading to our rooms. Murmurs drifted from a distant hallway, hushing as my shoes squeaked against the ceramic tiles. Just as I reached the other staircase, a hand grabbed my arm, yanking me back.

"*What are you doing*?" Jesri barked, his eyes filled with venom. I freed my arm and stepped off the stair, forcing my anger down. "Get out there. *Now!*" He pointed toward the courtyard, his voice commanding as he quickly ascended the stairs and blocked my path, leaving me no choice but to comply.

I clenched my jaw and rolled my eyes—not caring what the punishment would be.

Fine. I'll find Cal after.

I turned around and stomped away, hoping to annoy Jesri even more with the scuff and squeak of my shoes. I could hear him grunt with frustration as I walked back outside.

Darius was waiting by the fence opening with Levon at his side, talking about something in the notebook he carried. They saw me approach and fixed their stance.

"Feeling better, my lady?" Levon asked, closing his book.

I nodded. "Yes," I paused. "Though, I'd feel better if you could share any tips *besides* survival."

Darius glanced my way with a sly smile, raising his brows toward Levon. I shifted my weight onto my left leg, folding my arms across my chest in waiting.

Levon smiled. "What is it you say, Darius? Prepare for the unexpected?"

Darius chuckled, adding, "Trust your gut and be quick."

I pursed my lips. "Thank you for stating the obvious," I said, annoyed. I began to move around the fence, only for Darius to step in front of me.

"You know the rules, Eliah. No snooping," Darius said, treading carefully to avoid provoking my anger. "You'll find out soon enough."

I exhaled sharply—*fine.* Turning on my heels, I ran in the opposite direction, landing a solid punch on Darius's arm as I dashed past. His playful protest echoed after me, but I was too preoccupied with quelling my mounting fear to listen.

8

I perched high in the tree's thick foliage, anxiously awaiting the starting whistle. My fingers absently brushed over the cold, golden whistle Darius had given me, feeling its smooth surface as I replayed his words in my mind:

"Prioritize your safety above all else. You've got one hour—act fast, stay sharp, and take the three of them out. Wait for the signal to begin. If you're in danger, use the whistle to stun them. We'll be at the entrance, waiting."

I adjusted my bow and the trio of daggers strapped to my thigh, squaring my shoulders as I settled onto the branch. My stomach churned, but I forced myself to focus, sifting through possible scenarios of what they'd throw at me besides dogs. I tried to recall anything from my history lessons that might offer a clue to any creatures. It had to be something—

The signal rang out, echoing across the sky and stopping my breath. I swallowed my fear and leapt into motion, squatting low on the branch. Shouts rattled in the distance before ferocious growls slashed through my focus, coiling my stomach. I froze, gripping the tree trunk tightly, recalling the calming techniques Darius had drilled into me before any training began.

Inhale, exhale.

Inhale, exhale.

My breathing narrowed, turning back into its silent rhythm. Whatever that was, I didn't like the sound of it.

Another set of snarls and shouts echoed off the trees.

You've got one hour—act fast, stay sharp, and take the three of them out.

Centering myself with a sharp breath, I quickly assessed the width of the nearby tree and judged it suitable for my plan. After securing my bow, I pressed my back against the trunk, took another deep breath, and sprinted along the sturdy branch, launching myself into the air.

The collision with the next tree knocked the wind out of me. I instinctively clawed at the rough bark, scraping my hands as I desperately searched for placement. My bow rattled against the overhanging branches, throwing off my balance.

The snarls grew louder, more feral, and ravenous. Ignoring the pain, I pushed forward, jumping from one tree to the next, each leap drawing me closer to the spine-chilling growls.

My breathing became labored and frantic—inhale, exhale.

My mind returned to the last time Jesri evaluated me with dogs less than a year ago, and I failed miserably. There were six of them, and one with a feral infection that left me bedridden for weeks. I barely managed to knock it unconscious before it could tear me apart. That evaluation had plagued me with nightmares for weeks.

A sudden crunch to my right jolted me back to the present, followed by a low growl that sent icy shivers down my spine. *You've got one hour.*

I forced my fear deep down and steadied myself against the trunk, gazing toward the source of the sound.

A streak of white fur darted out of sight so swiftly that if I blinked, I would have missed it. I narrowed my eyes, tracing the path of the fur, and steadied my breathing. Embracing the trunk, I shifted to lower branches, aiming for a better view.

I landed softly, ensuring the leaves didn't quiver under the sudden change in my weight as I crept out further, testing the branch's sturdiness before scanning the area and sitting down, coiling my legs beneath me. It was eerily silent, except for the birds that chirped in the distance and the muffled laughter from the men waiting for me to finish.

I unslung my bow, swiftly drawing an arrow and letting out a sharp whistle, hoping to entice the creatures to come to me rather than hunt them down. I did it again, scanning the area for any movement or disruption.

Nothing.

I suppressed my anger and started to sheathe my arrow when a guttural growl shattered the silence beneath me. In an instant, searing pain shot up my leg as I saw large claws dig deep, scraping against my flesh and splattering hot blood on its white coat as the beast fell back to the ground, taunting me.

My scream pierced the air as my grip slipped on my bow, and I watched in terror as it plummeted down beside the beast. With a swift motion, I pulled my legs up and leaped to the branch above, clutching my bloody and torn leg. Letting out another anguished cry, I glanced back and locked my eyes with the creature. Its large yellow eyes peered deep into mine. I had never seen anything like it—a creature resembling both a wolf and a bear, moving with deadly silence unlike any other animal. Its once-white fur was now matted, and a sticky gray, and its eyes held an intelligence far beyond any ordinary dog I had faced.

It snarled, exposing its rotted sharp teeth. My heart pounded, adrenaline flooding my veins as instinct took over. Before I even inhaled, my hand was already moving, hurling my longest dagger straight into its eye. The beast dropped instantly, letting out a frantic screech as it clawed desperately at its face.

One hour.

How in Tyran am I supposed to take out *three* of these?

I quickly scanned the area, and before I could stop myself, I leaped down, landing hard on the ground and feeling the pain from my calf sting insufferably as blood oozed out. The smell of the beast overwhelmed me with surprise as I grasped hold of my bow with shaking hands.

It was still moaning and clawing at its eye as I let my intuition take over. I quickly backed up and lunged atop it, reddening its rough fur with my sticky blood. I dug my heels into its side, ripping out chunks of fur, trying to hold on as it thrashed beneath me. I shoved my bow string over its narrow head and pulled up against its neck as it snarled loudly, rumbling my body. It clawed for me as I squeezed my thighs against its frame, stinging my leg and bubbling out more blood. I held tightly to my bow in one hand before swiftly yanking the dagger out of its eye.

Blood sprayed, splattering onto my face as I quickly sheathed the dagger right before the creature started running violently, almost bucking me off. I yanked hard on my bow, hoping it wouldn't snap, and steered it toward a large boulder.

I sucked in a breath, unable to brace myself as it smashed with a sickening crunch, throwing me up and over before I smacked hard onto the ground. The air escaped my lungs, leaving me gasping with rapid coughs.

I shifted over to my side, swallowing any air I could and allowing my lungs to readjust as more pain cracked at my bones. I looked down at my left pant leg sliced open, revealing the four claw marks that would have me stumbling for who knows how long. I cut one of my sleeves off, hurriedly tying it around my bloodied leg, hoping it would stop the bleeding for at least a little.

One hour.

I struggled to lift myself, gauging how much weight I could put on my injured leg and grunted in frustration. Spotting a few of my arrows scattered nearby, I quickly retrieved them, limping over to where the unconscious beast lay.

Its breathing was labored as its eye bubbled out blood that coated its matted fur. I choked down a gag before another snarl erupted dangerously close. Whirling around, I pressed against the white beast, swiftly scanning my surroundings before feeling for my bow still hooked over the lifeless beast's head.

Another sickening growl reverberated through my bones as I frantically took hold of my bow and tugged hard. The other beast's snarl was wet and guttural, drawing more fear into me.

I calculated my steps toward the nearest tree, seeking an advantage, but deemed it unfavorable considering my worsening leg and the risk of becoming a target.

I swiftly scanned the area once more, unable to locate the second beast, as I continued to tug the bow free. Its head was at an obscure angle, lodging the bow between it and the boulder.

Frustrated, I grunted, urgently assessing my options with only arrows and daggers as a looming dread began slithering up my spine. Shifting my gaze to the right, I caught sight of two ghastly yellow eyes that sucked the air out of me. It was akin to the white beast but bigger and cloaked in fur as black as midnight, absorbing all light. One eye bore a slash, amplifying its already horrifying appearance into something grotesque and nightmarish.

It licked its teeth, drooling as it began stalking toward me slowly, snarling deep. I clung tighter around the bow, praying for help.

Terror gripped my chest, tightening with every heartbeat, like a spider weaving its lethal web around me. A trembling breath escaped me as I strained harder against the bow, each pull amplifying the icy dread threatening to paralyze me.

It crept closer, inch by inch, its eyes locked on me.

A curse slipped from my lips as fresh blood began to seep down my leg, my makeshift bandage already soaked through.

Inhale.

I leapt, scrambling up the lifeless beast with a frantic urgency. I twisted its head with a forceful shove, trying to tug the bowstring off that now scraped against the jagged boulder. A wet snarl blared close as I locked eyes with those horrid yellow eyes hurtling toward me with an alarming speed.

"*Tyran!*" I cursed in desperation. "*Please!*" My cries pierced the dense woods, sending birds scattering into the sky. Fear consumed me entirely as I shut my eyes tight, summoning every ounce of strength to yank my bow free. With a jolt, I flung backward, crashing to the ground behind the white beast, my bow clutched tightly in hand, now dripping with sticky blood. Without hesitation, I thrashed about, frantically retrieving several arrows scattered in the fall.

The beast advanced, just a few steps away; its foul smell mingled with the coppery scent of my blood. With desperate speed, I nocked multiple arrows, letting out a scream of pure determination as they shot into the beast's face. A sharp yelp tore from its throat as it staggered, but its momentum carried it forward, crashing into me with brutal force.

I cursed as the impact sent me skidding across the ground, the beast's massive body rolling over me. Pain exploded in every part of my body, its weight crushing my chest while its claws raked across my arm. Blood poured from my leg, pooling beneath me as dizziness clouded my vision. I could feel warm blood trickling down my face, the world spinning around me as I fought to stay conscious.

The beast quickly got up, thrashing its head violently and clawing at the arrows lodged in its snout. One stuck in its slashed eye while the others pierced its throat and mouth. I scrambled back toward my bow that lay a few feet from me.

It noticed the movement and snarled at me, quickly slashing out. I rolled sharply away as its large paw struck the ground, inches from my head. Swiftly, I pulled out my long dagger, realizing my others were scattered with my arrows in the crash, and scanned the area for my other two before another claw came crashing toward me. Instinctively, I held the dagger prostrate as its large maw slammed into it, stabbing straight through and spraying me with its ghastly blood. It yanked its paw back and clawed out again, barely slicing into my arm before I dodged away. Its angered roared, piercing my ears with a ring.

My body shook at the deafening roar, adrenaline surging through me as I forced myself to my feet, every step a jolt of pain. I stumbled toward my bow, gritting my teeth with each agonizing movement. Just as my fingers closed around it, a more thunderous and fearsome roar echoed from my left, stopping me cold.

I spun around, bracing for another attack, but what I saw left me breathless. This new beast was unlike the others. Its fur gleamed with a golden brown hue, streaked with rich golden-coppery oranges, and its massive frame bore more resemblance to a majestic wolf than the grotesque creatures I had just faced. Its eyes were a mesmerizing mix of bright coppers and golds, and shone with an unexpected gentleness that made me hesitate.

The jet-black beast snarled, its gaze locking onto me with a chilling, silent claim of ownership. My breath caught as the golden creature responded with a deep, menacing growl that reverberated through my chest. It stepped forward, placing itself between me and the black beast as if to shield me. The air crackled with tension as my heart pounded in confusion.

In a blur of movement, the black beast lunged, its fangs gleaming with deadly intent. It struck the golden creature with ferocious speed, sinking its teeth deep into its side. A blood-curdling yelp escaped the golden beast's snout, and my heart lurched in fear.

Frantically, I reached for the golden whistle around my neck—only to realize it was gone. Panic seized me as dread settled in my gut. With a desperate prayer on my lips, I tightened my grip on the bow and bolted, pushing my shredded leg to its limit and sprinting away as fast as I could.

As I fled, the clamor of battle behind me intensified, claws scraping against the earth and teeth clashing in a flurry of violence. The heat of their massive bodies bore down on me, just feet away. A sharp snap followed by a pained yelp cut through the noise, forcing me to glance back.

I quickly scooped up more arrows, nocking them with trembling hands. The golden beast had its jaws locked onto the black one's throat, blood staining its coppery fur. I released the arrows in a flurry, not caring for precision, just desperate to keep them at bay.

Within seconds, the fight escalated into a savage brawl. Teeth snapped, saliva sprayed, and guttural growls echoed around me, turning my insides to sludge. They barreled toward me like cannonballs, each trying to overpower the other in a frenzied race to reach me first. The ground shook with their ferocity, and I could feel the vibrations in my bones, my heart hammering in sync with the relentless violence.

I ran harder than ever. My lungs, legs, and body screaming against the strain. I felt my blood rushing down my leg, pooling into my boot as a numbness overtook it, tingling down into my toes just as I reached the tree. I began climbing as fast as possible; my nails split against the bark that splintered into my palms.

A torrent of guttural snarls echoed behind me as the black beast broke free and lunged at my legs with its bloody maw.

Its claw caught onto my left boot, pulling me down and taking my boot off completely. I hung on, kicking frantically, and forced the broken arrow deeper into its eye.

It yelped out again before the other beast jumped on its back, biting hard into its neck, its blood coating its teeth. They fell back with a sickening snap, seeing the black beast's head slump lifelessly in the massive beast's mouth.

I got to a branch and began hoisting myself higher and higher, wholly out of range of the golden beast that dropped the black beast at the base of the tree. It began roaming around under the tree, limping and whimpering out. Blood covered its golden fur with two of my arrows protruding from its back. I nocked another arrow, letting it fly into the beast's side. It roared in pain before it limped and fell to the ground.

I took a staggered breath, struggling to gather my thoughts as panic and fear churned inside me. I pushed the pain down and focused on the motionless golden beast lying before me.

There's no way that arrow took it down.

Still, I nocked another arrow, just in case, and released it. The arrow struck its neck, and the beast let out a soft, pitiful whimper that made a pang of guilt twist in my chest.

I shoved the feeling aside and settled onto the branch, focusing on my breathing to steady my racing heart.

Inhale, exhale.

My entire body trembled as the adrenaline drained away, and I became aware of the blood dripping from my head. I touched the gash on my hairline, pressing down to stop the bleeding.

I needed to get back to the gate, uncertain how much time had passed.

Pushing aside the fog creeping into my vision, I wiped away the blood that threatened to blur my sight and began my descent. My muscles screamed in protest as I slid down the trunk, finally jumping clear of the black beast that sent my leg barking in protest.

The golden creature lay several feet away, its breaths coming in slow, ragged gasps.

A strange sensation washed over me, urging me to aid the creature.

No. Absolutely not.

The creature's labored breathing persisted, only stirring my heart more. With a reluctant groan, I began to shuffle my way toward the beast, leaving a trickle of blood in my path.

As my hand made contact with the beast's soft fur, a surge of unexpected emotion flooded through me. In that moment, the apprehension that had clouded my mind dissipated, replaced by a profound sense of connection to the creature and an intuition of its inherent goodness, which seemed to radiate from every fiber of its being.

I moved fast, yanking out the arrows in its back and side as blood poured out but clotted unusually quickly. I did the same to the arrow in its neck as it stirred slightly before its breathing settled.

I stood, watching momentarily, holding my breath as if I could give it to the beautiful beast, hoping it would somehow make it out of these wretched lands and be free. My heart wilted before I slowly limped away.

I trudged on in a deep limp, not knowing what way to go but forward.

Only one more step.

Only one more—

A blistering pain pulsed through my head, ringing like canon from a warship. Across from me, Darius' men lounged against the gate, their laughter contrasting against my agony. I tried to call out, but my voice emerged hoarse and feeble. Every step I took worsened the swelling in my leg, and each movement sent a sharp sting through my body.

My eyes were beginning to stick closed from the blood that was now drying, leaving me looking like something straight out of a horror book Calum and I used to read as children.

"Look!" I heard someone say as my head continued to ring.

Only a few more steps.

My breathing and heart pounded harder, drowning out everything else and clouding my mind in a haze of noise. My legs gave out, and I collapsed onto the ground, my bow skittering away from me. I heard Darius shouting orders when warm, strong arms lifted me up.

The world around me was a blur of sound and motion, but I focused on the soft repetition of my name, whispered urgently in my ear.

And, for the second time today, I let the darkness pull me under.

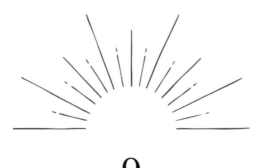

9

A radiant light materialized before me, urging me to pursue its luminous path. It danced with a kaleidoscope of golds, violets, and orange hues, weaving a mesmerizing tapestry of colors. Its gentle whispers carried sweet melodies, soothing the turmoil within my heart. As the light intensified, it pierced through the darkness, forming a shimmering doorway. Its core gleamed with such brilliance and purity that I had to shield my eyes from its radiant glow.

Eliah.

It whispered, softly enveloping me in its ethereal embrace. I reached out, gently touching its radiance as it spun around me, spiraling into infinity, illuminating everything in its path like a spiral of gold. Tears streamed down my cheeks as I basked in its comforting warmth, feeling the hope and longing I had always sought.

I allowed the light to envelop me, its graceful movements intertwining with my own as I danced with it, my hands trailing through its tangible essence. Abruptly, searing pain stabbed me, unbearable and consuming. I crumpled to the ground, the warmth and light draining from my body, leaving me cold and empty. The once-gentle light now trembled violently, its radiant hues twisting into a dark, cruel shade of red, staining everything it touched.

My scream echoed into the void as I reached desperately for the flickering brightness, battling against the destructive darkness. Haunting wails and screams pierced through the air, their chilling presence intensifying as I tumbled downward into a new doorway overflowing with nightmares and malevolent energies that thrashed. Its abyssal jaws consumed me, dragging me deeper into its depths, far, far away from the gentle light. A static, wailing noise consumed me entirely, scraping my own light from me until my anguished cries faded into the dark abyss.

— ◦ ✦ ◦ —

I bolted upright, instinctively reaching for the dagger at my thigh, but found nothing except a tight bandage. Panic surged through me as I stumbled over something, sending me sprawling to the ground with a thud. My head smacked on the wood floor, causing a sharp groan to escape my lips. A moment later, the door flung open, rattling its frame, as quick footsteps clipped close.

"Eliah!" Aoife yelped, seeing me in a heap on the ground.

I sighed deeply, another groan escaping my lips as I felt the stiffness and soreness ache within my body.

I'm safe and in my room.

With a grunt, I attempted to sit up, only to find my foot tangled in the bedsheets. Aoife hurried over, swiftly loosening the fabric and gently guiding me back into bed.

"Please, don't tell me you were considering getting up like *this*," she urged, gently settling my legs onto the bed, prompting me to slump into the welcoming embrace of my pillow. My head churned with a dense fog, but I clung to the reassurance that I was back in the safety of my room.

"I...I had a nightmare, I think," I murmured, my voice uncertain. The dream lingered in my mind, its reality hauntingly vivid and leaving me overwhelmed and confused.

"Let me take a look at your leg," Aoife insisted, casting a frustrated sigh that hinted at her irritation towards Jesri for allowing me to do such an evaluation. Wrinkling her brow with concern, she unwrapped the cloth tightly wound around my calf, extending to my lower thigh. I hadn't realized the wound had reached so high. Another bandage was wrapped around my arm, wrist, and head.

"How long have I been out?" I asked, sensing a slight throbbing in my head where the bandage covered the cut above my brow.

"Almost two days, my dear," Aoife answered softly.

"*Two days?* Did..." I hesitated, my words faltering. "Did I complete the task in time? Is the golden beast—" she hushed me, carefully rewrapping the bandage and tucking the bedding around me.

"Let's begin with getting you some food, shall we? You've lost a considerable amount of blood, Eliah," Aoife advised, with a concerned expression. "A healer will return around noon to administer more blood if necessary." She fixed me with a stern gaze. "And for my peace of mind, *please* take things slowly!"

She gave me a soft kiss on my cheek. "I'm very relieved you're awake." She ran out the door, fetching me food. The mere mention of it rumbled my stomach.

I sighed, staring at the blotched ceiling, my mind consumed by thoughts of the dream—the fight of light and darkness. I shifted my gaze to my arms, noticing dark purples and browns speckling them, leading up to a larger splotch on my right collarbone, barely visible beneath my white nightgown.

A soft yet firm knock came at my door. I shifted to a seated position, clearing my throat. "Come in."

The door creaked open, and Levon stepped inside, his attire suggesting he had just woken up himself. His brow furrowed in concern, a sentiment I rarely witnessed from anyone besides Aoife and occasionally Cal.

"My lady," he greeted, bowing low before moving towards the foot of my bed. He hesitated for a moment before speaking again. "Aoife told me you were awake. You had me extremely worried," he admitted.

I quickly adjusted, sitting up straighter and pulling the covers slightly higher, feeling exposed in my nightgown.

"I'm alright, truly. Just...out of sorts." I held my breath, not sure what to say.

"I'd be honored to have you join me, Eliah. At my estate, I mean...if you accept," he interjected, stumbling over his words, which seemed out of character, given his usual composure.

"I passed then?" I asked, not fully believing I did.

"You completed it well within the hour," he paused. "However, Jesri, as you know, is quite particular about order, and...well, he's under the impression that you didn't, given that *I* carried you out."

The memory of strong, comforting arms enveloping me flashed vividly in my mind, his voice echoing my name like a lifeline, tethering me back.

"Of course, Jesri would assume such idiocy. He'd prefer to see me bleed out for the remainder of the hour than offer assistance," I remarked bitterly, not caring if he told Jesri. He let out a low chuckle, but it quickly faded. "Thank you, Levon. For helping me once more that day."

He smiled with a nod. "If you accept the offer, I'll inform Jesri, and we can depart whenever you're ready." He hastened towards the door, appearing noticeably uneasy in my private chambers. Pausing just before exiting, he added, "I'm glad you're awake." With that, he slipped out before I could respond.

Although Levon appeared closer to my age and exuded a quiet charm, his presence still evoked the same unease I experienced around Jesri, who wanted power, wealth, and control.

Brushing aside the thought, I nestled deeper into the pillow, my mind churning with all the possibilities of leaving, *actually leaving this place.* A twinge of excitement nestled deep into my heart, carrying me off to a deep sleep.

"No more sleeping."

I felt a gentle pat on my feet and blinked at the warm, inviting light.

"Eat," Aoife insisted, setting a tray before me filled with a feast fit for a queen. My mouth watered at the sight of the sugared plums, savory pastries stuffed with an array of greens and sweet ham, and *warm*, delicate eggs. I wasted no time devouring it all, savoring each bite and reveling in the lavish flavors.

"Oh, slow down!" Aoife teased, her laughter infectious as she took a bite of a sugared plum. Giggles escaped me effortlessly with each delightful taste.

Whether it was thanks to Aoife's persuasive skills or Levon's, I couldn't say, but one thing was sure—Jesri would *never* permit me such food, *especially* after a *failed* evaluation. I couldn't help but feel delighted, imagining Jesri's likely frustration.

I finished off the last bite with only crumbs left. My stomach, now uncomfortably full, churned with a sudden onset of nausea. I flopped back in bed as a genuine smile lined my lips. A rush of excitement coursed through me, imagining a world beyond the confines of Jesri's estate. Recollections of adventures shared by Jesri's friends and Calum's parents, who had fled to the distant East Ulvery Sea, flooded my mind. What had once felt like an unrealistic dream now seemed within reach. Despite the upcoming training with Levon for the Match, no one cares to tell me about it. The prospect of leaving behind these yellowed walls fills me with hope.

"Aoife, help me get dressed, will you? I'd like to get some fresh air."

She gave me a look before helping me rise from the bed, grounding me with a comforting sense of normalcy. I couldn't help but wonder if I truly needed the help, considering how surprisingly well I felt despite the lingering discomfort in my leg and small thrum of pain in my head.

Aoife helped me into a pale yellow dress with sheer sleeves adorned with delicate blue flowers along the hem. Wearing the dress felt rejuvenating as if declaring to Jesri and Levon that I could exceed their expectations and be more than just a pawn in their game.

She wove my hair into a long braid down my back and helped me slip into my shoes. Despite anticipating whatever this new adventure held, I couldn't help but feel a pang of sadness at the thought of leaving Aoife behind. Her gentle demeanor and motherly kindness had always comforted me, making her feel more like family than I had ever considered Jesri or even Calum to be.

My thoughts drifted to Cal, and the memories of our time together under the wretched wish tree flooded my mind. I knew I would miss him too.

"Aoife, have you seen Calum around?" I inquired, finding it odd that he had yet to visit. But then again, I should expect nothing less from him. I cleared my throat, hoping to dispel the swirling thoughts.

"I saw him briefly yesterday after breakfast but not since then," she replied. I nodded, forcing my expression into one of unconcern. Standing up from the vanity, I linked arms with her. "Care to take a walk with me?"

After walking a few laps around the gardens, Aoife decided it was time to return and attend to her other duties, encouraging me to rest. Feeling a slight ache in my leg, I agreed it would be wise; plus, I wanted to continue my search in the library to calm my growing anxieties about the impending departure and find more information about why Levon and Jesri were discussing the Leonardian War.

My heels clicked against the freshly polished floors as I entered the library. The air was thick with dust, and the scent of mildew was evidence of pages left unread for years. Enjoying the solitude, I relished the quietness of my thoughts. The shelves towered high and wide as I went to where I had left off, reading a book containing information about the Spellcasters.

Approaching the shelf, I noticed the book was missing, along with several others nearby. Furrowing my brows, I wondered who had been rummaging through them.

I reached for one of the last books on the shelf, its corroded red cover and gold binding catching my eye. I twisted it over reading the title: *The Dark History of Leonardian Trials.* Pausing momentarily, I noticed that the book appeared relatively clean compared to the others nearby, suggesting somebody had recently read it.

As I turned the page, a sense of foreboding gripped me, causing me to unconsciously hold my breath, knowing the illegality of such contexts. Each page turned felt like a step deeper into a dark abyss of history. My fingers hesitated, yet continued to flip until they randomly landed on a page detailing a gruesome massacre where thousands of men, women, and children perished in flames.

The words on the page seemed to sear into my mind. With a sharp intake of breath, I slammed the book shut, squeezing my eyes closed to banish the haunting images from my mind. Clutching the book tightly against my chest, I pivoted to leave, only to hear the swift approach of footsteps echoing through the silent aisles.

In a panic, I grabbed several other books from nearby shelves, hastily attempting to blend in with the library's ambiance and conceal the illegal book. But in my haste, I collided with someone emerging from an adjacent aisle, sending the cascade of books tumbling from my grasp. Each one hit the floor with a resounding thud, echoing the weight of the unsettling knowledge contained within the book's pages.

"Apologies!" the footman exclaimed, taking a step back in surprise. "Lady Eliah, forgive me. I didn't realize you were in here."

I relaxed the tension in my shoulders as I bent down to retrieve the fallen books, still holding onto *The Leonardian Trials*. He stooped down to assist as I swiftly snatched a few, hiding the book beneath them.

"Not to worry. I wanted to read some of my favorites before I leave."

He handed me a few books with a quick smile before bowing slightly. "Enjoy your reading, my lady," he said, promptly striding past me. Seeing a footman here, especially one with a specific purpose, struck me as odd. He didn't look familiar either. I found myself staring at his retreating figure, trying to place where I might have seen him before, but nothing came to mind.

Gathering my books, I began to walk away when I noticed him turning down the same aisle I had been in. Confusion clouded my thoughts before a sickening feeling crept over me, urging me to hurry. With a throbbing limp, I quickened my pace, tiptoeing out of the library and into the foyer.

"My lady?" the footman's voice rang out, his footsteps clipping closer.

I stopped in my tracks, feeling the weight of inevitability settle upon me. Turning back, I forced my expression into a mask of serenity. "Yes?" I replied coolly, pausing for effect. "I don't recall us being properly introduced."

"Malcolm, my lady," he stated, his tone eager. "May I have a look at the books you're carrying? I seem to have misplaced a particular one."

My heart lurched. Why would a footman be interested in *The Dark History of Leonardian Trials*? Anger and fear bubbled within me, wishing I possessed the sharp wit of Calum.

"I doubt you'd find the...romance I'm reading to your liking," I retorted, starting to walk away, quickening my pace.

"Wait!" His hand closed around my shoulder, sending a jolt of pain shooting through my bruised collarbone. I let out a curse, pulling away. "Forgive me, my lady. I...I didn't..."

"Don't you ever lay a finger on me again, Malcolm, or I'll hunt you down like I did to those beasts!" I spat, my words dripping with venomous anger before I reined it in. His face paled, and his attempt to regain control was evident in his scrambling demeanor.

"Eliah," Calum's voice echoed from the balcony above, instantly quelling my anger. The footman stiffened, standing at attention. I bit my cheek, turning to see Calum descending the stairs. "Leave us, Malcolm," he ordered with an eerie forcefulness. I cocked my head, puzzled by Calum's formality with the footman.

The footman nodded and scuttled away, his footsteps echoing in the distance. I waited until I heard the back door close before succumbing to the pressing annoyance of Cal's disappearance.

"Where have you been?" I paused. "What's going on with you?"

A smirk danced on his lips as he tenderly kissed my hand. "I'm relieved to see you're alright, Eliah. Truly." He enveloped me in a gentle embrace, mindful not to cause further pain. Yet, I couldn't shake the feeling that...he wanted to. "And nothing is wrong," he whispered.

Stepping back, I didn't reciprocate the embrace.

"What's going on?" I demanded, folding my arms in tighter around the books.

He chuckled, a wicked gleam flickering in his eyes, reminiscent of Jesri when he hatched a mischievous plan. "I've stumbled upon something I believe could spare you from this Match," he whispered.

"What kind of information?" I countered, eyeing him warily as he moved closer and reached for my hand again.

"Eliah, what if *I* took your place so you could remain here, safe and sound, until I returned?"

"What?" I blurted out, his proposal catching me completely off guard. "You can't be serious?"

"Or what if I found someone else?" Desperation colored his words, his breath tinged with urgency. "Please," he pleaded, his eyes shimmering with silver that had to be deceptive. "I can't...bear the thought of losing you like my parents."

He squeezed my hand, igniting a surge of anger within me.

No—NO!

This is rightfully mine. I've worked my entire life for it, and it was my key to freedom.

"No." I tore my hand free. Something about this all seemed uncomfortably wrong. "I know you want to make your uncle proud, but I can't *stay* here, Cal. I was trained for this, even if it leads me to my demise."

The longing that had adorned his face moments ago twisted into disgust. His jaw clenched as he glanced down at my books. *"I need you, Eliah.* And do you honestly think you'll come out victorious in this Match?" he scoffed. "Just look at how well you handled those beasts."

His words dripped with venom, piercing my heart. "You wouldn't last a day with Levon and his plans, but I can keep you safe!" he said, pointing to his chest.

Advancing towards me, he backed me against the wall. His eyes blazed with anger and desperation, a side of him I had never witnessed before, starkly contrasting his usual playfulness. He appeared weary, pained, and sad, as if he were grasping at straws.

I readjusted the books in one hand and pressed the other against his chest, attempting to push him back slightly and quell his rising fury.

"Cal, *you know* how I feel about this life. This might be my one chance at *actual* freedom, not just wishful dreaming." His eyes narrowed, piercing into mine. *"I have to do this,* Cal. I couldn't live with myself if I let *you* take my place," I said, my voice trembling as I tried to suppress the overwhelming emotions, realizing that I was truly marching towards my doom and taking all my dreams with me.

I slipped out from under his hand, which rested against the wall, and began to ascend the stairs to my room, refusing to look back.

"You know I'm only trying to protect you!" his voice sliced through the air in a low, hissing whisper, mingling with grief and anger. I forced myself to glance back, seeing tears staining his cheeks, yet his eyes burned with nothing but rage.

My fury surged through me, a searing heat threatening to consume me. I clenched the books until the bindings dug into my skin. *"I don't want your protection,"* I spat out.

The tension in the air crackled, the fire between us intensifying. Gritting my teeth, I locked eyes with him before continuing up the stairs, holding my head high despite the lingering pain with each step.

I slammed the door shut with a force that rattled the frame, locking it to keep him out. My heart pounded in my ears as I tossed the books onto my unmade bed, frantically scrambling to light the hearth, not caring that Jesri had forbidden it, even on the coldest of nights. Rules meant nothing now. I needed the fire. I needed something to burn as hot as my anger.

The spark caught, and the wood crackled as flames flickered to life, feeding on the air. My breath came in ragged gasps as heat surged in the room, letting it consume every rational thought. With a wild, reckless motion, I grabbed Calum's purple shawl and *The Dark History of Leonardian Trials* and hurled them into the fire as if they were poison I needed to purge. Seeing the words in the book burn as all those innocent Magics did.

The fire roared, devouring the book and shawl with a ferocity that mirrored my own. The shawl twisted and blackened while the book's pages curled and disintegrated, their essence reducing to ash that filled the room with a bitter, acrid scent. Soot clung to my yellow dress, smearing it with blackness, but I didn't care about the dress, the room, or anything else—I needed to see them burn. The flames' heat licked at my face as I watched it rage, begging to consume more as a twisted satisfaction brewed in the pit of my stomach.

I didn't need him or his protection.

All I wanted was the feeling of control.

10

The healer who checked my wounds assured me I'd be fully recovered by the week's end and removed the bandage from my head. Surprisingly, no blood transfer was necessary, and he marveled at how quickly I was up and moving, thanking my training for the agility. After he left, Aoife continued to scold me for building a fire in the room, which dirtied everything within. Since Jesri cut off the chimney, Aoife opened more windows to dissipate the smoke before Jesri found out, but it only seemed to circulate the sooty air more. Ignoring her protests, I quickly changed out of my dress and into my training attire, eager to clear my head.

"What are you doing?" Aoife asked, pulling at my training sleeves. "No, Eliah. You shouldn't train!" she protested, trying to stop me. I ignored her completely, shoving my feet into my boots and tying up the laces. *"Eliah!"* she huffed with a motherly displeasure. "Please, you need to rest!"

I pushed her out of the way, already feeling remorse for my actions—but I didn't care enough to stay. All I wanted to do was punch something, and if Darius hadn't put up a new bag, I'd find him instead.

I left the door open, racing down the back stairs, ignoring the ache in my leg with each pounding step. As I reached the bottom, the scent of musk from the sweat and rigor of Darius' men's earlier training sessions hit me. The training room lay empty, with the punching bag still absent from its usual spot. Frustration surged within me, and I couldn't contain my anger. I shouted out, the sound reverberating through the open space. I refused to suppress the fury; instead, I allowed it to consume me. Grasping a sword, I felt the coolness of the hilt in my hand as I struck out against the thick wooden beam, already scarred by numerous blade marks.

I slashed and charged, letting my anger guide me through the dance despite the rising pain and stiffness in my collarbone and leg. Frustration crackled off onto the blade with each forceful swing, urging me to play with it. The air around me turned metallic, prickling my arms with tiny bumps.

I cried out in frustration once more, slicing the beam again before I fell onto my knees, letting the sword rattle as it hit the stone. I clenched my hair, hyperventilating at the resounding grip of agony and despair that pierced a hole into my chest, my heart, and every fiber of my soul.

I sank to the ground, cradling my knees as tears streamed down my already sooty face. It felt like I was plummeting into that dark abyss of my dream, its inky blackness pulling me ever deeper into its grasp, with barely a faint glimmer of hope to cling to.

I brought this upon myself. I allowed myself to become too deeply immersed in emotions I couldn't manage, in dreams that would never be granted. No matter how hard I tried to pull or cut at the strings, I was still a puppet to them.

Calum's words echoed in my mind. How could I emerge victorious when all this was merely Jesri's cunning method to indirectly extinguish me, only to gain sympathy and admiration for himself while I suffered? It was all a façade—every aspect of it. Everything was orchestrated for Jesri's welfare, from the relentless training sessions to the senseless evaluations. It made me sick.

A brown, ruddy boot nudged my foot, signaling Darius's silent observation of my breakdown. Unmoved, I stayed curled up, indifferent to my undoubtedly wretched appearance—my face smudged with soot, scattered with minor scratches, and a prominent gash promising a lasting scar.

"Sulking on the ground like a child, hm?" Darius said, breaking the last tether of hope I clung to.

Gritting my teeth, I allowed the surge of anger to cut through me, but in my regret, I lashed out, inadvertently adding to the pain in my aching leg. Without thought, I swept my feet out, causing Darius to tumble to the ground, only to find me on top of him, ready to smash his head in. His quick reflexes intercepted my fist, yanking me back to the floor.

"*Eliah—*"

His voice was interrupted as I kicked back, knocking the wind out of him, and stumbled towards the daggers. With practiced ease, I flipped one through my hands. Anger surged through me like oxygen, igniting fierce flames within my blood and clouding my mind in a haze of fury.

He rose to his feet. "Fine. You want to dance?" he threatened, flicking his fingers toward me before settling into a defensive stance.

Enveloped in rage, I charged at him, propelling myself over his shoulder and twisted in his grasp as I tightly entwined my legs around his neck. Pain erupted in my leg, surging up into my hip as I threw my body back, pulling him down with me. We slammed into the floor in a chaotic tangle of limbs and rage, gasping for air to re-enter our lungs.

I tightened my grip on the dagger. He rose to his feet first, quickly seizing both my wrists and forcing me to stay on the ground. I kneed him in the groin, and he loosened his grip with a gasp of pain. Seizing the opportunity, I jammed my shoulder into his chest, shoving him off. I got to my feet and threw myself onto him, pinning him down.

"*Eliah,*" he rasped again, this time with a pang of sadness that my heart wouldn't let in—couldn't let in.

I flipped the dagger into my other hand, ready to slice through skin when he took hold of my leg, digging into my already tender thigh. I cried out, losing grip on the dagger that clattered to the ground. He got up, swiftly dragging me by my feet. I tried to get out and grab ahold of anything to prevent him from pulling me further.

"Eliah! Enough of this!" he spat as I twisted my body towards him with enough force to kick my strong leg free, smacking him in the face. He stepped back, blood dripping from his already crooked nose, and held up a hand.

My breathing heaved as I sat still. My eyes glazed, forcing the claws of my anger to calm and instead sent silent tears lining my eyes. Instant regret threaded through me like a roaring river, pulling me underneath. I moaned out in a whimper and sank to the ground.

He wiped the blood from his nose and smoothed back his black hair before returning to me. Despite my efforts, tears threatened to spill as he knelt down and enveloped me in his firm, comforting arms.

"Eliah," he whispered, calming my racing heart and unleashing the water-gates. "Don't cause yourself more pain before your journey even starts."

I sat immobile, trapped beneath his embrace, and sobbed. Emotions over-flowed, engulfing me until all I could do was inhale his familiar scent and allow him to cradle me like the father I longed for—the father who never left me in Jesri's grasp.

"Eliah, let this anger be the force to make you stronger. Don't let it control you," he whispered quietly and quickly between gasps of breath. "Whatever this Match will be, it will push you beyond what you have previously done. *Let* Sir Alder teach you. Let him be your guide so you can finally be free to be who you want to be. *Trust him, Eliah,*" he stopped, holding back his emotions.

He let go, forcing me to look at him as he held onto my arms. "I tried Eliah. I tried to testify for you, but Jesri has his ways. *Don't let him win.* Be your own person and win this damned Match." His eyes blazed with compassion, evoking memories of my childhood, of him simply being there, supporting me, nurturing my strength, and even sneaking me candies. "You are capable of extraordinary things, my girl."

He held me a little longer as I let the raw emotions simmer off, feeling the dwindling fire deep within me burn to a sizzle. He helped me to my feet as I embraced him again, this time holding him tight around his neck.

"Thank you, Darius."

Thank you for being the father I always longed for. For never letting me go. For being there when I needed it.

I swiftly let go and walked away, not wanting to meet his eyes again before more tears would crumble me whole.

11

I n the days leading up to my departure, time seemed to blur together as I eagerly anticipated escaping this place and being rid of the Archenon men. I packed the few dresses and training clothes Jesri permitted me to bring, endured his stern lectures on proper court etiquette, and meticulously cleaned every corner of my room before he allowed me food.

I took a long look out my window, imprinting the colorful woods in my mind, hoping that wherever I went, I could feel as at *home* as I did when its vibrant beauty embraced me.

Below, the hustle of servants and guards I had grown up with lined the estate walls, prompting me to depart.

I descended the stairs and stepped out the estate doors, greeted by welcoming voices. Levon stood beside his ebony carriage, caressing his bay mare, nodding briefly at me before conversing with his footmen. I took a deep breath, the humid air filling my lungs and propelling me forward with readiness.

Against the wall, Darius stood tall, clad in his usual training leathers. He embraced me tightly before heading off with his men, leaving no trace of the blunt emotions I knew he was holding back. He gave me a wink and nod before Aoife threw her arms around me, crying into my hair.

"Don't forget me," she sobbed with a tease. "Be brave, my dear." She held my shoulders, her gaze piercing. "You're going to do amazing things, Eliah!"

I blinked back tears, thanking her for everything. She released me with a gentle pat on my cheeks before I approached Calum, standing tall and noble.

Although my anger towards him had subsided along with the tears shed after the quarrel with Darius, an unspoken tension lingered between us.

I had only caught glimpses of him throughout the week. He never allowed me to speak before slipping away, veering down another hallway, or leaving before dawn to avoid me.

I could sense that he was aware of the book I had burned, particularly after Jesri uncovered the makeshift fire in my room, causing a commotion for all to hear. Calum's response was uncharacteristically muted—he neither demanded an explanation nor offered one himself. His silence, a departure from his usual demeanor, left me bewildered and on edge, the uncertainty gnawing at me like an itch I couldn't scratch.

However, the only words I heard from him were behind the closed doors of Jesri's study two days ago as they argued over my departure, etching a relentless memory in my mind.

"It's unwise to let her out of our sight with everything happening! Why send her now? And with him!" Calum's voice boomed, causing the wall I leaned against to tremble.

"Enough, boy!" Jesri's voice thundered, reverberating through the halls and halting even the servants in their tracks. "We had an agreement! What's done is done, and I will tolerate no further discussion."

Calum cleared his throat, drawing me back to the present.

"My lady," Cal said, bowing and lightly kissing my hand. He swiftly straightened up and released my hand as his jaw tightened, glancing at Levon and then Jesri. Resentment burned in his golden eyes. Perhaps he, too, wanted to be free.

"Goodbye, Calum," I paused, lifting my head high, refusing to let myself cry for him. I began to speak, but before I could, he swiftly enveloped me in a hug, holding me tight and absorbing every last scent of me. I surrendered to his embrace, easing my tension.

"I'm so sorry," he whispered with a sob before releasing me and quickly retreating into the estate. I stood there, sifting through our memories together, every game, every laugh, and every argument, feeling good to let them go. To let go of every illusion and unfulfilled promise.

With determination, I walked past Jesri without a glance. Taking Levon's hand, I allowed him to guide me into his carriage, settling onto the plush, velvety seat with enthusiasm. I watched the two exchange words before Levon entered, sitting across from me with a smirk.

The sun was at its peak, casting a discomforting heat inside the carriage despite the open windows. I was thankful Aoife insisted I wear the plain white dress, which concealed my features and looked more like a nightgown, yet its elegant, silky material helped to alleviate the discomfort.

As the carriage tugged away, a flurry of butterflies stirred in my chest, tinged with emotions. Jesri walked inside as Aoife took out her white handkerchief, waving it frantically overhead as tears streamed down her face, mirroring my own. I returned her wave, feeling a rush of emotion swell up inside me as I saw her fade from view.

As we neared the gate, Darius and the other guards greeted me with bright smiles and salutes. Darius broke rank to bow swiftly, his smile now streaked with tears. As we passed through, they all broke formation, waving goodbye before closing the gate.

I kept my eyes fixed on the estate for as long as it remained visible, watching it shrink into a distant memory on the horizon. Despite the pressing tears, I willed myself to remain composed, determined to show strength even as my heart felt heavy with leaving behind everything I had ever known and unsure of what the future held.

I turned from the window with a deep breath. Levon was absorbed in a book, sitting regally in his white tunic and knee-high boots. I quickly glanced away, feeling uncomfortable being so close to him, and shifted my knees to avoid touching his. We sat in silence for what felt like an eternity, the quiet stirring my nerves.

Looking back out the window, I could no longer see the glittering sea. I wondered if I would ever see it again—or anything familiar, for that matter. A sense of dread replaced my earlier excitement as countless questions flooded my mind.

Why did Jesri do it? Why barter me to Levon for a *Match*? Why was Cal acting so...distant? And how did this tournament connect to the Leonardian War and those Spellcasters?

Nothing made sense.

I grunted in frustration, massaging my temples to quell the relentless questions and swirling emotions.

Levon glanced up from his book, an eyebrow arched. "Is something troubling you, my lady?"

"Do you have more riddles for me, or do I have to beg to find out what this Match is about?" I demanded, irritation lacing my words.

His gaze drifted downward, and he closed his book with a soft thud. "Every year, King Thealor, like his ancestors, hosts mini-tournaments, spanning from dancing and jousting to baking and winemaking. All purely for pleasure," he began, his smile dimming. "But every few years, he announces a Match—where individuals blessed with talents, such as yours, are called upon."

"Talents like mine?" I scoffed, my voice wavering. "I'm not sure I would call it talent."

"What you have goes beyond talent," he murmured softly, his eyes locking onto mine with a sincerity that made me pause.

I narrowed my brows and laughed, a brittle sound. "Then what might these *talents* help me with in this Match?"

"Perhaps that's another part of the riddle you'll need to solve," he mused, his tone gentle but enigmatic, a faint smile hinting at a deeper knowledge he wasn't ready to share.

I stared at him, stone-faced and annoyed, but my resolve was crumbling. Letting out a long sigh, I decided I wasn't ready to beg...yet. "Where are we now?" I asked, trying to keep my mind from wandering.

He kept his grin, looking out the window. "It looks like we're still in Fern-wen," he noted, briefly meeting my gaze. "We should reach the Desrin border in a few hours, where we'll stop at an inn." He stretched out his legs, which now rested on the edge of the bench I was sitting on. "Did you bring anything to keep yourself occupied?"

I curtly nodded, recalling the book I had stashed in my satchel that sat at my feet. Glancing out the window once more, I resisted the temptation to reach for it, knowing from past experience that focusing on a book while moving could lead to motion sickness, and I was not keen on spending the next few days in a smelly carriage.

Levon straightened up, returning his attention to his book.

"What are you reading?" I inquired, eager for any distraction to quiet my racing thoughts about the Match.

"Some war tactics that would likely bore you," he replied. I folded my arms, holding back a snarky retort.

"Planning to go to war anytime soon, hm, *Sir Alder*?" I asked, growing irritated by his presumption.

He chuckled. "I wish, *Eliah*."

I sat up straighter, taken aback by the comment. "Truly?" He looked up at me with amusement and nodded. I shook my head in continued disbelief. "Enlighten me then," I commented with more sarcasm than intended.

A grin played on his lips as he lowered the book. "About war tactics?" His voice resonated with the carriage's movements, purposefully evading my ques-tion. "You'll find out soon enough."

"No, why the desire for war?" I pressed. He furrowed his brows, the smile vanishing from his lips.

"Perhaps a tale for another time," he replied, lifting his book once more and returning to his reading. I rolled my eyes, shrugging off the dismissal.

I inhaled and bit my tongue, remembering Jesri's voice in my head about behaving. Slowly exhaling, I rested my chin in my hands, leaning against the window, and pushed aside my frustration.

As we journeyed on, the vibrations from the uneven path beneath the wheels reverberated through the carriage. The vibrant hues of the woods gave way to a sea of lush greenery, with towering pine trees and unusually thick trunks stretching as far as the eye could see. In the distance, mountain ranges emerged, their peaks obscured by clouds looming ominously close, obscuring our view as we approached.

I glanced back at Levon, who was now engrossed in writing something down in his notebook and couldn't help but notice his charm. His tunic draped effortlessly over his sculpted shoulders, revealing glimpses of his hazelnut skin beneath. My eyes traced the contours of his chest, following the rhythm of his breath. I observed the movement of his scarred hand, noticing how his fingertips had turned black from the charcoal stick he was using. His eyes shimmered with a sense of adventure, which I had always longed for, and I hoped this training might fulfill.

"Enjoying the view?" he teased. I snapped out of my trance and turned to look out the window. I struggled to swallow my embarrassment, but my neck and cheeks betrayed me, flushing with each jolt of the carriage wheels.

"I am," I replied softly before clearing my throat. "It's quite different out here." I caught the hint of a playful grin on his lips as he closed his notebook and retrieved a cloth to wipe his blackened fingers.

"The world is much bigger than those pretty woods of yours," he remarked.

"They were never mine," I muttered.

His smile dimmed. "Perhaps not, but they were a sight to behold." I dared a glance at him, and his emerald-blue eyes sparkled in the setting sun, deepening the color of my blush.

I cleared my throat in an attempt to clear my mind. "I'm ready to see what else the world has to offer," I said, and I meant it.

Leaning forward, he rested his elbows on his knees as the fabric of his open shirt exposed more of his chest. Sensing my gaze, he flashed me a sly smile and locked eyes with me. "I believe the world is ready to meet you."

—— ⋅ ✦ ⋅ ——

I wasn't aware that I had fallen asleep when I was quickly jolted awake after Levon tapped his shoe against mine rather forcefully. My neck was stiff and pulsed with pain as I tried to move.

"We are almost to the inn," Levon said, holding back a grin. I looked out the window to see that the sky had dimmed to a dark violet color, with only the setting sun as our guide.

"Did I sleep long?" I asked, rubbing at my neck and stretching back my shoulders.

"No, although—" his lips turned up. "I was about to throw you out with that horrid snore you make."

"I do not!" I snapped. He only laughed, not giving me any indication if he were serious.

We were no longer in the thicket of trees but on a vast open landscape, embraced by rolling green hills and valleys dotted with the twinkling lights of nearby towns and scattered mountains in the distance. Seeing several settlements clustered together made the world feel more tangible, reminding me of my small place within it.

The horses trotted down a winding hill and approached the inn, which had large wooden posts with vines that roped around each one. Though the inn was much larger than I was expecting, it was homely, and as soon as we stopped, I quickly jumped out of the carriage, excited.

"Do I need to remind you of your role as a lady?" Levon teased, a playful glint in his eyes. "I hope you'll conduct yourself accordingly, especially when we dine with the king," he added, waving off the footmen and declining the use of a stepping stool.

"Conduct myself?" I countered, folding my arms with an animated pout. "You mean I can't stroll around in my training gear, taking out my frustrations on anything that crosses my path?"

Levon chuckled. "Tempting as that sounds, perhaps save it for the training grounds," he suggested. "And no one *should* be themselves around the king," he quipped, flashing me a cautious smile as he took my arm, leading the way towards the inn. Suppressing the urge to fire back a witty retort, I allowed him to guide me inside, exchanging a glance as we crossed the threshold.

He pushed open the large wooden door, and a wave of warmth greeted us. A plump woman carrying a basket of mixed vegetables paused mid-stride. "Oh, welcome! What can I do for you?"

"We'll need a few rooms for tonight," Levon replied, gesturing as the two footmen entered with our belongings.

"The only rooms I have left are with two beds," she said with a shrug, her gaze lingering on my arm linked with Levon's. Hastily, I released his arm and stepped back, realizing she assumed we were a couple. I was about to correct her when Levon spoke up.

"We will take them. Thank you, Madame—" he stopped, waiting for her name.

"Oh! Tyran, no. Only Mrs. Bestrum," the woman said, with her cheeks flushing. She walked over to a small table at the far end of the wall and grabbed two silver keys with a red ribbon on each. "Here you are," she said, placing them into Levon's hand. "Upstairs on your left. You can pay once you leave," she stated, hurrying with her full basket.

"Thank you, Mrs. Bestrum."

He pivoted, scooping up the bags, and gestured toward his footmen, who promptly fell into step behind us as we ascended the stairs. The wooden floor groaned under our weight, and distant voices and laughter reverberated through the corridor as we passed several doors, finally arriving at ours. Levon set the bags down with a thud and handed a key to one of the footmen, who swiftly disappeared into their own room carrying bags. Then, Levon slid our key into the lock, pushing the door open to reveal a stale room devoid of the cozy atmosphere downstairs. The two beds were cramped and uncomfortably close, with only a small stand between them, adorned with a solitary lamp. There was no bathing area, no vanity, no armoire.

"Levon, if you insist on lecturing me about proper conduct, may I remind you that we're sharing a room?" I remarked, gesturing towards the cramped space, clenching my jaw in frustration. Calum would be livid if he found out about this arrangement.

"Would you prefer to sleep in the carriage, my lady?" he retorted, his tone tinged with annoyance.

"What about—" I started, searching for an excuse. "What if I need to relieve myself during the night?" I trailed off, a pang of realization hitting me at how entitled I must sound.

He gestured down the hall and briskly entered the room, depositing my trunk on one bed and his on the other. Then, he stepped back out into the hall where his footman waited.

I closed the door with a resounding thud. How was I supposed to navigate this with him? I suppressed a groan, recalling Darius' advice to control my anger.

Fine. This was to be a new experience, a new...I hesitated, uncertain of what lay ahead besides potential disaster. Squashing the thought before it could spiral further, I made my way over to the bed.

Sinking onto the thin mattress, it groaned under my weight as I unraveled my braid. With a sigh, I slipped off my boots and kicked them underneath the bed. Stretching out my legs and arms, I massaged my tight neck and shoulders, still bearing the bruises from the evaluation.

As I stood up to move my trunk to the floor, the door swung open once more, revealing the two footmen with more of our belongings in tow. They piled the cases high into the corner before scurrying off as if afraid of my presence.

"Hungry?" Levon reentered the room, balancing two bowls of steamy stew, accompanied with a hearty roll.

"Yes!" I exclaimed, my stomach protesting loudly at the delicious aroma emanating from the food. Levon handed me one bowl before settling on the bed opposite me, the old mattress creaking with each movement.

"Why do your footmen seem to be afraid of me?" I inquired, sinking back onto the bed and sampling the stew. Surprisingly flavorful and spicy despite its less-than-appetizing appearance.

"You're the charming and quite attractive lady they've heard about for months," he said, taking a bite.

I sat there, a mixture of confusion and frustration evident on my face. "What do you mean?" I pressed. Levon remained silent, opting instead to shovel stew into his mouth while stealing nervous glances in my direction. "Levon," I demanded.

He finished his meal and set the bowl down on the small table between the beds. "Jesri is quite the storyteller," he remarked, reclining on the bed with his feet dangling off the edge.

If I could only strangle Jesri right now, I would. His mastery lay not in truth but in weaving webs of deceit, and I could only imagine the elaborate tales he had spun for Levon.

"I'd wager he painted me as the epitome of desirability, destined for greatness, yet claimed my life in Fernwen was much too mundane for someone of my *talents*," I began, my voice thick with bitterness. "He likely bribed you to whisk me away, to toughen me up for whatever this Match may be, and parade me before the king like a prized possession—all so Jesri could revel in the glory and earn respect within the Royal household." I paused, taking another bite of my meal.

Levon propped himself up on his arm, his gaze piercing as he studied me intently. He parted his lips to speak, but I interjected before he could utter a word.

"Hm? Was that not correct?" I challenged. "Perhaps he paid you handsomely to whisk me away and parade me before the King's Court, all so he could swoop in as the heroic rescuer of his damsel in distress? Hoping that by showcasing his efforts, he would earn admiration from those around him, who would then urge him to stay, forge alliances, or resort to whatever means necessary to paint himself as the hero!"

Levon shook his head, a hint of amusement dancing in his eyes. "You certainly have a vivid imagination, my lady." Levon's emerald gaze bore into mine, unwavering and steady. "Don't let yourself get upset over crushed flowers, Eliah," he advised, his voice calm but firm. "Your emotions are written all over your face, in your body language. Don't let it show."

I rolled my eyes in annoyance, utterly defeated. This anger, an unwelcome intruder, seemed to hold me in its grasp with unrelenting force.

"Then what *did* Jesri tell you, Levon?" I inquired, my words dripping with sarcasm.

"He simply claimed he had a beautiful young lady in need of a better life," Levon replied calmly, his demeanor unruffled despite the storm brewing within me.

I clenched my jaw, fighting back the urge to hurl my bowl across the room, channeling all my frustration into maintaining control, remembering Darius's words to trust him.

A better life?! If he truly wished for me to have a *better life*, then why subject me to such cruelty for as long as I have been breathing? I scoffed bitterly, realizing, once again, it was all just a façade.

"I don't believe you. Why else would Jesri allow you to take away his prized possession unless he also stood to gain something? You two had an arrangement, and I'm merely the pawn in your little game," I retorted, rolling my eyes and gritting my teeth, struggling to contain my anger.

Levon's demeanor softened, a hint of sympathy creeping into his expression. "He could be rash at times—" he paused, holding up a hand as I laughed bitterly.

"He *was* exceedingly cruel to you, Eliah. And while it's true that we have an arrangement, I assure you that you will be looked after in my care. I did not enjoy watching you suffer. Not even a *prized possession* merits such harsh treatment. You have my word, Eliah. You will be cared for, and you will succeed."

His words extinguished the flames of anger burning within me. I sat there, rendered speechless, simply staring at him before nodding in gratitude and silently finishing my stew. I yearned for a better life—one where I could shed the label of an orphan and thrive with strength and resilience.

He broke the silence. "So, you've never ventured beyond Fernwen?"

"No," I admitted, pausing briefly. "I've been to town on special occasions, but I was never allowed to venture beyond Fernwen." Except for that one time when

Jesri permitted Calum and me to ride to the Western Sea Port for important business matters in his carriage. I couldn't help but chuckle at the memory, recalling how I ended up getting sick and decorating the carriage with the contents of my stomach. Jesri was furious, and he never allowed me to ride in his carriage again after that incident.

"Was there a reason?" he asked quietly.

I shrugged my shoulders. "Jesri likes to keep his possessions close..." I trailed off, suddenly aware of the irony in my words, given that he was the one forcing me to leave.

"Well," he leaned back, his head resting against the wall. "The world is vast—much bigger than you might imagine. It's a place of contrasts, Eliah. Not every garden or flower is in full bloom; shadows linger in even the brightest places. But there is also light, goodness, and beauty amidst the darkness; you just need to look for it."

I nodded, eager for the new adventure that awaited, yet unable to shake the feeling that darkness still clung to me like long, spidery fingers that pulled me deeper into its web. It was as if the echoes of my dreams were warning me, whispering secrets I couldn't quite decipher.

12

O ver the next two days, we traveled through a blur of cities, lush foliage, towering mountains, and quaint inns that took my breath away.

Levon and I scarcely exchanged words since our first night at the inn. The silence between us felt palpable, especially considering we shared a room, and all I had was a tattered nightgown that left little to the imagination. Levon left the room to give me privacy, but the awkwardness grew when he returned and found me hiding under the thin covers that smelt of mildew. As he clicked off the light and settled into his bed, I could sense his eyes against my back from across the room.

I found myself unable to sleep and was up before dawn, longing to discard the constraints of my nightgown. Quietly, I tip-toed through the darkness, clutching my clothes from the previous day, and hurried to the bathing chambers to change. After my return, I was greeted by Levon's warm smile, accompanied by a bowl of steaming broth. He had already finished his meal, slipping past me with his footmen in tow.

We left before dawn broke and continued in silence, giving me time to collect my thoughts over the next two days. Levon's mention of darkness sent my mind spiraling with questions about the Spellcasters and the haunting shadows in my dreams. I hoped Levon's library was extensive, given how he always kept his nose in a book, and my first question would be the whereabouts of his library.

Upon arriving at Levon's estate, which was surprisingly larger than Jesri's, I was immediately struck by its vastness. Nestled against a mountainside, it was enveloped by a dense forest of towering pines.

The estate exuded a charm that made it feel like a noble home. Its architecture was a unique blend of elegance and strength, with golden accents that caught the sunlight and sparkled like precious gems. The sprawling structure boasted high-arched windows, intricate carvings, and a roof that shimmered with gold. Balconies protruded at intervals, offering stunning vistas of the expansive landscape below.

From the estate, gazing southward, one could take in a panoramic view of the town, a bustling hub of life. This view, far from the isolating estate, added a sense of connectedness, making one feel a part of something bigger, a vibrant community that thrived beyond the estate's serene borders.

The meticulously maintained estate grounds were stunning. Pathways wound through lush gardens filled with vibrant flowers and well-manicured shrubs. Fountains adorned with statues of fictitious creatures gushed crystal-clear water, adding a soothing melody to the quaint environment. The air was filled with the intoxicating pine aroma and the blooming flowers' fragrance.

Before Levon could help me, I hopped out of the carriage and walked inside, completely awestruck at the beauty. My boots clicked against the opulent, polished floors as I saw the massive library on the far left of the door.

His library was extensive, with towering shelves extending far and laden with countless books of all shapes and sizes. Its grandeur was evident in the polished floors and the orderly arranged dark wood shelves, untouched by even a hint of dust. It starkly contrasted Jesri's cramped, suffocating library; this space felt expansive and inviting as if urging visitors to immerse themselves in every page.

I approached an older woman with silver streaks twisted throughout her dull brown hair. She was sorting through some papers with a stack of books at her side. She glanced up at the sound of my footsteps with confusion. I offered her a small smile, noting her gaze quickly shifting towards Levon's ebony carriage outside the window. Recognition dawned on her face with a smile as I neared her table.

"You must be Lady Eliah!" Her voice, though crackling, carried warmth.

I nodded and offered a small curtsy. She emerged from behind the desk in a pale blue gown, appearing almost gray in the lighting.

Extending her hand, she said, "I am Madame Katherine Hannel. Apologies, I was so consumed with my studies that I hadn't heard you arrived."

"No apologies are necessary. We did just arrive," I explained, my voice faltering. Her expression changed to confusion. I quickly added, "It was a long journey, and I had much on my mind. I am hoping you might help me with my search?"

"Oh, of course. What are you searching for?" she inquired, her curiosity evident.

I opened my mouth, then quickly shut it, remembering the consequences of containing information about the Spellcasters. Her large brown eyes waited. "Could you direct me to the wars over the last few hundred years?" I quickly asked.

Her brows shot up, and she caught herself with a laugh, clearly surprised by the question. "Any specific war you're interested in?"

My mind drifted back to the book about King Leonard I had burned, and I wished I had read it instead, yet I was unsure if I would have been able to imagine those innocent Magics burning like the book.

"I am to learn new battle techniques and hope to utilize some of them once Sir Alder attempts to challenge me. I heard that the Leonardian Era was to have contained several great warriors?" I improvised the made-up fact, hoping I wouldn't catch her too off guard. Her brows knitted together in deeper confusion but managed a tight smile. With a slight nod, she gestured for me to follow and led me to a column of books in the far back corner of the library.

"This wall here is where you might find most of the histories of war during that era and this column here," she said, pointing to the far right end. "Is where you might find specific war techniques and battle strategies."

She smiled and waited for me to say something, but I only nodded in gratitude before walking away, feeling her gaze pierce through my lies. I made sure I was out of her sight before I went searching. The books were old and tarnished from use. I ran my fingers over the backs, scanning for anything related to King Leonard, the Magics, or any indication of the Spellcasters.

I heard footsteps echoing into the library when I found a book that looked more tarnished than the rest. It was a dulled-out brown book with black strappings not clipped into place properly. I picked it up, feeling the weight of its contents, and noticed it had no title. I began to open the pages when I heard Levon's voice echoing to Madame Hannel. Feeling like a child caught stealing pastries, I hastily returned the book to its shelf and hurried toward the section on battle techniques. Just as I was about to reach it, Levon rounded the corner of the bookshelf, catching me off guard; my shoes squeaked against the floors and caused me to stifle a startling screech with my hand.

"What in Tyran's name are you doing?" His brow was lined with sweat, and guilt washed over me. I realized he was probably unloading my things and more, but I pushed back the growing embarrassment.

"I—" I stopped short, not knowing what to say.

"I've been looking for you and was told you wanted directions to the library. Is this the first place you'd want to visit after never stepping out of Fernwen?" he breathed, folding his arms.

"I...had too many thoughts and wanted direction," I admitted.

"Direction?" Levon's brow arched, his gaze falling on the rows of books. "To war?"

I managed a petty smile.

He chuckled. "Well, I'm not sending you to battle if that's what you think." Suppressing another laugh, he took my arm and began guiding me out.

"What *is* it that you plan to do with me then?"

He flashed a subtle smirk, his emerald-blue eyes locking onto mine. "Things that are better left unsaid for now," he murmured quickly. "If I tell you, it will spoil the fun."

"The fun?" I mocked, growing irritated by his musings and hoping his *fun* wasn't anything like Calum's.

He replied with a raise of his brows, escorting me into the main hall.

It was opulent, with polished cream-marbled floors that stretched before us, reflecting the soft glow of the chandeliers above. A luxurious chestnut rug lay in the center, adding warmth to the expansive foyer. To our left, the grand staircase curved gracefully, its ornate railing beckoning me to feel its soft lacquer.

The walls were adorned with vibrant landscape paintings, each meticulously placed to enhance the cozy ambiance of the space. Rich hues of green and gold popped against the cream-colored walls, adding a touch of elegance to the grandeur.

In my rush to locate the library, I overlooked the welcoming atmosphere of the home—a sharp contrast to the somber ambiance of Jesri's estate.

"Your home is beautiful," I remarked, admiring the wall of paintings.

"I hope it will be satisfactory so that, one day, you might also call it home," he replied with a smile. "Come, let me show you to your room."

We climbed the stairs, granting us a view of the floors below, revealing the house's spacious design. From there, we could observe the main floor and dining area, to another small passageway that hugged the openness of the main hall. We went down the first hallway, closest to the stairs. The walls were creamy white and decorated with dark, warming wood doors and banisters. We passed a few rooms filled with plants while another seeped musty air, furnished with leather chairs and a dark mahogany table buried beneath stacks of papers.

We reached the far end of the hallway, where an expansive window covered the entire end wall, exposing an immaculate landscape of greenery that begged me to explore.

"This is your room," Levon said, opening the door and allowing me to walk inside. I couldn't stop my jaw from dropping as I absorbed the room I imagined fit for a queen.

The bed was large enough to fit several people, with fluffy white covers and gossamer drapes that flowed to the ground with grace. The light, gold-speckled walls made the room sparkle, complimenting the two large crystal windows that let in a dazzling, warm light. A gold-painted vanity and armoire sat on one side of the bed, with a smaller dresser on the opposite. An oversized loveseat sat near one of the large windows next to a small white table stacked with books.

"Calum said you enjoyed reading, so I made sure there would be enough books for you to read. Though it seems you may be more interested in war techniques rather than the lyrics I brought you."

A laugh bubbled out, "I do indulge in both."

He smiled. "Your things should already be set in place with your dresses there," he said, pointing to the armoire. "And your new training attire, along with other things in the dresser."

He then walked over to a side wall with a door that slid open. "And this here is your private bath. So that you may relieve yourself during the night." He winked, and I felt a blush of embarrassment rise.

I walked into the bathing chambers to see a large clawfoot bath with a luscious ivory rug. I swallowed my excitement, but Levon captured it and smiled at me, flashing his pearly teeth.

"You're free to enjoy yourself as you like, my lady. I have a meeting here shortly that I must attend, but after, I can show you around if you'd prefer. Training starts first thing tomorrow, and dinner will be served at six."

With that, he left the room, leaving me in awe, struggling to process his words as I marveled at the opulence around me. I had never experienced such luxury before; this room was truly fit for a queen. Whatever deal Jesri had made and whatever scheme he was up to, it might be worth it, if only for this.

———— + ✦ + ————

I awoke the following day well before dawn. The sky was still a dark grey, layered with mist, giving the landscape a wintry appearance despite the advancing spring. The towering pines pierced the sky like spears, and the grass still wet from the morning dew.

I stretched, marveling at the absence of any aches and pains from a proper bed and the calmness of a full stomach. My toes curled in the silky sheets that hugged me gently and provided warmth. Excitedly, I bounded out of bed and went to the bathing chamber to change the bandage on my leg. Surprisingly, my leg was practically healed, leaving only faint marks behind, so I decided not to replace the bandage. Only a few bruises remained on my arms, blending into my tanned skin like sunspots. The one on my collarbone had nearly vanished, too, leaving only a faint yellowish tint behind.

I washed up and wove my hair into a simple coronet. Though not as elegant as Aoife's craftsmanship, it sufficed. During dinner, Levon remarked that there were no lady's maids or valets to assist in getting ready. He explained how he never believed in such notions and grew accustomed to handling things himself due to some undisclosed history he failed to mention. I assured him it wasn't inconvenient and admitted I looked forward to handling things independently. Besides, I couldn't imagine allowing anyone else besides Aoife to assist me.

Clad in my new black and green training attire that hugged me in all the right places, I crept out the door and down into the main hall, waiting for Levon and his instructions to wait. The paintings along the walls still shimmered in the dim light of dawn. One painting, in particular, held me spellbound. Its brushstrokes danced with a multitude of colors, seemingly pushing back against the scorched edge of darkness surrounding the painting. It depicted a vibrant riot of colors bursting forth from the canvas, as if engaged in a fierce battle.

"Ready?" Levon's voice startled me, echoing loudly in the expansive hall. I turned to find him dressed similarly to me, wearing a long, tight black shirt accentuating his hazelnut-toned form, dark green pants, and tall black boots laced up to his calves. "We will take it easy today," he continued. "Two laps around the estate, and then back for breathing techniques."

He strode out the door before I had a chance to think. The brisk air stung my exposed hands as I hurried to catch up with him. "Keep pace with me," he said as I reached his side.

He began with a jog and I matched his pace. The cool air ripped through my throat and lungs like a knife. I wasn't used to running in higher climates, and Levon noticed my breathing stammering.

"It will take time to acclimate. In through your nose," he said, pausing to catch his breath. "And out through your mouth."

We ran along the grassy terrain as the sun began peeking overhead, turning the sky a brilliant blue. There was more of a variety of trees than the pines I saw out the windows, and though they weren't vibrant with color, they were still beautiful. We ran onto a gravel path that led into the trees, enveloping us in the mist.

"Keep an eye out," Levon breathed. "There are prowlers that lurk in these woods."

I only nodded, making a mental note to ask what type of animals he meant, and went back to focusing on my breathing. We emerged on the other side and descended the hill toward his towering estate, seeing the bustling town shimmering in the distance. His house looked majestic amidst the trees and the rising sun, casting a golden light on each tinted shingle. It seemed fit for a king to reside in such splendor.

We looped the far end of the estate covered in grassy hills and began again. By the end, we both were panting, gradually slowing our pace to a walk. The sun was now fully radiant, warming my body and forming beads of sweat on my brow.

"You're good at keeping steady, even with your injured leg. How are you fairing?" Levon asked, taking deep breaths in and out as he rested his hands on his hips.

"Fairing well enough to keep pace with you," I quipped.

He flashed his teeth with a shake of his head and stalked in front of me, slowing his breathing even more. "In through your nose." He breathed in. "And out through your mouth."

I followed suit, inhaling and exhaling for several minutes before fully calming my breathing, feeling refreshed as if I had just woken up for the day.

"Good. Now, remember that in any situation—especially with that temper of yours—" he stopped short as I shoved his arm. He promptly snatched my hand and pulled me closer to him, his grip firm. "*Especially* with that temper," he added with a tease before letting me go.

I pushed away, my anger crackling like static within me. I forced it to stop, focusing on my breathing; I recalled what Darius taught me long before Levon could claim he knew me.

"Is that all you've planned to teach me? How to *breathe?*" I scoffed, folding my arms.

"I plan to teach you how to focus, to gain control over your thoughts and maintain your mental clarity when other...*forces* might want to disrupt and invade your clarity," he said, striding past me toward a sunny spot shimmering through the trees.

I narrowed my brows, "Invade my clarity?" I huffed. "Like you haven't already done that?" I mocked.

Tyran, please tell me this isn't what I was trained to do all my life. If that's all he plans to teach me, then Jesri is in for a loss, yet perhaps that wasn't a bad thing.

He only shook his head and laid down on the plush grass, making a pillow of his arms. I stomped over towards him, lying down beside him. The grass was cool against my back, barely damp from the warming sun. I squinted to see the blue sky overhead and waited, breathing in and out.

His voice cracked against the silence, "Focus on how your body feels. How the grass slides underneath your neck, how the sun kisses your face. Feel those emotions of yours, the ones buried deep within your soul and allow them to live freely without a cage. Tell yourself that you are safe, that fear is not a part of you. That you are at peace."

I adjusted my body, honing in on the rise and fall of my chest and the annoying itch that suddenly appeared at the center of my back. I shrugged it off, concentrating on the breeze that rustled through the tall trees, bending and swaying to a rhythm of serenity.

Inhale, exhale.

My breathing slowed as I focused on the tingle of my fingertips against the smooth grass. The pulse and flow of my heartbeat thrummed within my skull, the emotions that pulsated with color deep within me. I closed my eyes and focused on the red-darkness of my eyelids and the flutters of light that danced from the ripples of the trees.

I took a deep breath in, smelling pine mingled with decomposing wood, the earthy scent of the rocky trail, and Levon's clean scent. I focused on his rhythmic breathing, in and out, as my mind began to wander, tracing the dance of shadows across my closed eyelids.

Streaks of golden light twisted and tugged against my emotions, filling me with a warmth that pricked the tips of my ears and down to my toes.

My surroundings blurred, melting with my breath and wandering thoughts that drifted like the sea's tides. The earth beneath me pulsed with vibrancy as if I'd drawn my first breath after a lifetime of drowning. My fingers stung with lively energy, urging me to dig deeper into the soft soil. Clumps of earth clung to my nails, infusing me with newfound vigor. Feeling drowsy from the run, I was tempted to surrender to the gentle embrace of sleep.

The dappled light filtering through my closed eyelids played in shades of gold, swirling and pulsating with my heartbeat.

I fixated on the crimson hues that began dancing over the luminance of the sun above when suddenly, a burst of brilliant light flooded my closed eyes, momentarily blinding me.

Recoiling, I clenched my eyes tighter as the pulsating abruptly stopped, leaving a chilling stillness in its wake. A peculiar chill swept through the air, raising the hairs on my neck and arms. My senses heightened, transporting me back to that sinister dream where the shadowy claws ensnared me, dragging my soul into the abyss.

The rhythm of my heartbeat intensified, pounding against my chest like a stone. I struggled to summon the peaceful image of golden light, begging it to lift me from the engulfing darkness. Yet, the shadows tightened their grip, dragging me further into their abyss.

My breaths grew erratic, stuttering in a desperate attempt to find solace.

Inhale, inhale.

Exhale, inhale.

A surge of redness flooded my vision, scraping my core with a blazing fire that choked me. Frantically, I clawed into the earth, desperate to grasp the sensation beneath my fingers.

"Eliah!"

The claws dabbled up my spine. Up my arms—

"*Eliah, wake up!*"

Wake up.

El-i-ahhh.

The velvety voice slithered over me, like spoiled blood melting on my tongue, coursing through me like thick tar, and binding my pulse to its command.

Pain erupted in my chest, thundering through my ears in a deafening clamor of frenzied fear. A jolting surge of electricity pulsed through me, coursing through every fiber of my being, convulsing me in a static of fear, darkness, and crimson hues.

Unable to breathe, a brilliant flash of light seared through me, dissolving the tar-like grip and flooding me with warmth and relief as golden hues washed over the blood.

My eyes snapped open, blinded by the sudden brightness. I shielded my face, hesitant to close my eyes again, while the full sensation of my body and senses flooded back to me. Sweat lined my back as panic set in, and I bolted upright, colliding with something solid.

"Eliah, stop!" Levon's deep voice flooded my ears, steadying my racing heart. He pulled me into an embrace, allowing me to hear the steady rhythm of his heartbeat. "Eliah, you're safe. You're okay."

I gasped for air against his chest, forcing my eyes to stay open...to see, but struggled to focus on anything but the overwhelming brightness. I felt his arms shift, lifting me into the air.

It all felt too real, too overwhelming.

Eliah.

The claws, the darkness of my dream. Whatever it was—it knew me.

13

A blinding headache continued to pulse at the base of my skull, but I pushed it aside as a healer examined every inch of my body, testing my patience.

"Levon, truly, I'm fine," I spat out, irritation coating my words. I watched him pace back and forth while the healer finished an unsuccessful diagnosis, merely guessing at the cause of my convulsions. I rolled my eyes dramatically. "I'm fine!"

I stood up, spun around, and began waving my arms, trying to convey my truthfulness and dismissing whatever had just occurred. But deep down, I couldn't shake off the fear and confusion that gripped me.

Earlier on the lawn, as I had gradually regained my senses, I found myself lying there, frozen in a haze of fear and confusion, unable to articulate the strange sensations coursing through me. It felt as if my very being was under attack and if something or someone was intimately aware of my thoughts and feelings.

The underlying feeling of being watched, of something knowing me deeply and thoroughly, sent chills down my spine. I couldn't shake the eerie sense that I was no longer alone in my own mind, and the fear of the unknown gripped me tightly, making it hard to breathe. But the feeling intensified, churning my stomach until I retched last night's dinner over Levon's black boots. His eyes were the only thing that helped pull me out and return me to whatever reality I was in.

"Keep an eye on her," the healer cautioned, eyeing Levon with a knowing look. His balding head spotted with sun-induced freckles creased. "If another episode happens, you might want to reconsider—" he hesitated, his gaze shifting to me through his spectacles.

I narrowed my eyes at both of them, feeling a surge of anger.

"Thank you, Chayler," Levon acknowledged quickly but sternly, as if he knew the healer on a personal level, as he began escorting the man out.

I watched them through the glass window as they exchanged a few more words before Levon returned. Confusion and frustration clouded his face, dimming the brightness of his eyes.

"Why didn't you tell me?" he snapped, running his hand through his hair, concern etched in his eyes.

"Tell you what?" I shot back, my patience thinning.

"About these...episodes."

"Levon, I assure you that you don't need to reconsider. I don't know what just happened, but I'm fine!" I insisted, and I meant it. "I've been through and seen a lot worse. I've never had that happen before." He looked at me flatly, clearly not believing a word I said. "Truly, I'm okay."

He stood there, scrutinizing me, searching for an explanation beyond my own. His features softened, but his jaw remained tense, and his fists clenched, betraying his growing worry. After a long, heavy sigh, he extended his hand.

"Come, let's wash up and go have some fun."

+ ✦ +

After freshening up, I slipped into a new gown I had found hanging in the armoire. It was a creamy white with quarter-inch sleeves and delicate scalloped edges. The snug bodice flattered my form, tapering just below the knee. The skirt was layered with shimmering tulle, intricately plaited to swirl gracefully with every movement. With my hair left cascading down, I made my way out the door.

My headache became dull, slowly easing its claws while a growing fear persisted with each passing moment. The vision, or thought—whatever it was—danced throughout my mind on its own accord. I struggled to push it away, but it stubbornly embedded itself deeper, staining my memories with its inky darkness. A chill ran down my spine, hinting at something deeper, something more menacing unfolding within me.

I inhaled, trying to shake the dark feelings.

Levon was in his study a few doors down, shuffling through a stack of misplaced papers. He wore a dark tunic with a navy blue sash wrapped around his waist, the rich colors complementing his hazelnut skin. As he looked to me, his teeth gleamed brightly, his smile so infectious it made me suppress a grin of my own. The warmth in his eyes and the crinkle of his smile softened the intensity of his earlier concern.

"Ready?" I asked, stepping into the study, twiddling my thumbs nervously. Levon finished organizing a few papers before extending his arm.

"You look lovely, my lady," he said with a playful twinkle in his eye.

"Thank you," I replied, feeling a flush of embarrassment rise to my cheeks. Compliments from men were not something I was used to.

He nodded with a smile as we walked down the grand staircase and out to his waiting carriage.

The ride was swift, and when Levon instructed the footman to halt just outside town, a surge of excitement coursed through me. Stepping onto the rocky pathway leading into the bustling streets, I was instantly enveloped in the vibrant energy of the place. The only experience I had gotten close to something like this was the parties Jesri threw, which were often enough that I truly didn't mind not going into the markets. Yet, this was completely different, with various smells, colors, views, and so many different people who didn't know my history. And there were no judgmental stares to contend with.

We passed by a line of carts filled with peculiar fruits and spices, which made me want to linger a little longer and touch the rough edges and patterns painted on each cart.

Voices echoed off each other like thunder, and money was passed back and forth like a secondhand. Laughter bubbled up from every corner and wiggled its way into my heart—like butterflies dancing through the swarm of people in all shapes and forms.

Levon chuckled, drawing me towards a nearby cart laden with delectable treats. The array of puff pastries, bonbons, chocolates, truffles, and tarts on display immediately seduced my senses. Levon exchanged a few coins with the cheerful vendor, selecting an assortment of sweets before handing me an elderberry tart. Its rich flavor sent my taste buds into a delighted frenzy.

He led me from one cart to another, each offering a unique array of goods. At one, vibrant flowers caught my eye, their colors so vivid and unfamiliar that I struggled to find the words to describe them.

"Levon!"

We halted and turned, spotting a tall man pushing through the crowd towards us. Levon's grin widened at the sight of him.

"Edmon!"

The two embraced, clapping each other on the back like longtime friends. My heart tinged with a surprising surge of jealousy for his easygoing life, with friends and people who admired him for simply being who he was.

Edmon stood almost a foot taller than Levon, lean and lengthy. His ruddy brown hair kept falling into his face, adorned with a scattering of freckles that mirrored those on his forearms and hands.

"I didn't know you were back already," Edmon said over the bustling crowd.

Levon grasped my arm, pulling me into the conversation. I fought to keep my footing, feeling my cheeks flush with embarrassment and irritation rising within me. I flashed a strained smile, hoping Levon would sense my subtle frustration.

"Allow me to introduce Lady Eliah."

Edmon's smile widened as he offered a brief nod. "It's a pleasure to meet you. I've heard tales of your bravery already."

I willed myself to remain composed, hoping my cheeks wouldn't betray me, and silently wished Levon hadn't spread stories about me to *everyone* he knew.

"How lovely to learn that I'm so well-known already," I remarked, shooting Levon a sarcastic grin. He chuckled and tightened his hold on my arm.

"Join us for dinner tonight! I'm certain Lady Eliah would love to hear of your tales," Levon stated with a smile.

"It would be my pleasure, but Ma's been keeping me busy with lists since I returned," Edmon replied, holding out a long parchment covered in tiny handwriting. "Preparing for the start of the courtship parties," he added with a touch of sarcasm, patting his chest and fluttering his eyes.

Levon's smile widened. "Invite her and Mel to join us then!"

Edmon gave him a knowing look. "We both know how that would turn out. Perhaps after the preparations are done."

Levon nodded, patting him on the back. "Good to see you again, Ed."

"Keep out of trouble with this one, my lady," Edmon teased as he walked away with his long list in hand.

Levon shook his head, chuckling, and pulled me closer as the crowd grew busier.

The way Levon carried himself around Jesri's estate seemed a world apart from the Levon who greeted Edmon, and I couldn't help but view Levon in a new light. My mind traced back to when he claimed to have been a *guiding light* to men he had worked with.

How had he gone from that position to the one he was in now, and with an estate like that? I had underestimated him, assuming he was similar to Jesri and Calum, knowing Jesri wouldn't associate with someone as low class as Edmon, and the thought unsettled me. Levon defied my expectations of men, and I couldn't help but chuckle at my flawed perceptions.

He continued guiding me toward another line of carts and more people waving handkerchiefs, hats, spoons, and a dozen other things to buy.

As we ventured further, the crowd gradually thinned, and we found ourselves navigating stoned walkways, powdered with dirt and dust that caught in our throats.

A large fountain lay at the open center yet ran dry with decaying coins turning to rust. Doors could be heard opening and shutting, while carriages and horses could be heard off in the distance trotting along. We walked past a large window with a gorgeous emerald gown stuffed for presentation. My eyes expanded at the silkiness of such a dress, reminding me of the gown I now wore.

"Thank you for the dress," I expressed, tucking back strands of hair that danced in the sudden breeze. "I don't remember when someone got me a gown other than to be a showcase item."

Levon's smile faded, turning somber. "I plan to buy you many more, even if your eyes are the only ones that see them."

"No. That's not what—"

"It is already in the works," he said, cutting me off.

I smiled, unsure how to thank him for such kindness and not wanting to continue the conversation.

He cleared his throat. "Shall we?" He extended his arm.

We proceeded until we arrived at a small café with two weathered tables basking in the sun. Levon opened the door, and a bell chimed softly. Aromas and warmth enveloped us, stirring my appetite.

"I hope you're hungry because Mrs. Bleel's cuisine is exceptional."

I nodded, excited to eat somewhere other than within the confines of Jesri's glamorous dining room.

He brought me to an open window with food on display, where a few lingering people were sitting lazily at the few open tables behind us. Levon quickly ordered food before we sat at a table closest to the door.

Levon glanced out the open windows, seeming off from his previous joyful presence.

"I have to meet with someone to take care of something," he said, rising from his seat. "The food will be out soon. Please don't wait for me to eat. I'll be back shortly."

With that, he left the room, leaving me alone to contemplate his sudden departure. It dawned on me that this entire outing might have been arranged so he *could* meet with someone. I couldn't help but notice the shift in his demeanor after the healer's visit, and I prayed it wasn't concerning me.

The room fell into a hushed silence, broken only by the soft clinking of the cutlery as a generous plate of boiled potatoes, roasted dove, and creamy vegetables was placed before me. The rich aroma filled the air, but my mind was too preoccupied to appreciate it fully, noting that only a plate for me was served.

14

The past two weeks passed in a haze of relentless training. Each morning, well before sunrise, we set off on grueling runs, pushing ourselves harder every day to beat our previous times. Levon had drilled into me the importance of mastering the breathing techniques, insisting they were even more crucial than combat skills. At first, I didn't see the point, especially in terms of my emotions, but in the thinner air of the higher altitude, I felt the difference—they steadied my movements and kept me sharp during weapon training. Each exhale fueled my strikes, making them stronger and more precise as I tapped into my sharpened senses, doing my best to remain in control.

When I had free time from the usual grind, I turned to archery practice. It felt like a breath of fresh air—a chance to focus purely on refining my aim and form without the pressure of competition or expectations of Jesri weighing me down.

Since Levon preferred to handle tasks more independently, he requested that I help with food preparation and cleaning, which was surprisingly enjoyable. He also rolled up his sleeves to pitch in alongside his staff and help prep the food or clean up after supper.

It was strange but heartwarming to see how closely he worked with his staff, unlike Jesri's, who were always afraid of making a mistake.

It felt almost surreal like any day I might wake up back at Jesri's estate, stuck in forced conversations with people who resented and admired me because of Jesri and Calum's status. I could almost feel the exhaustion creeping back, the same kind that had once driven me to burn out. It was hard to believe that Levon's behavior was normal for these people, and it made me realize just how much I had been robbed—robbed of any sense of goodness.

As we washed and dried the dishes after another delicious meal, Levon observed my slumped shoulders. He had a knack for noticing things, particularly regarding me.

"May I inquire why you're scrubbing so vigorously?" His tone carried concern. I glanced at his forearms, each movement delicate yet powerful as he dried the ceramic plates.

"I don't understand," I paused in my scrubbing and faced him. "Why aren't you like Jesri? Or Calum? Or any other arrogant men who hold me in such low regard? Why are you so kind?"

His emerald-blue eyes glowed in the kitchen's dimness, illuminated only by a few lanterns. He grinned, prompting me to roll my eyes before resuming scrubbing. Abruptly, he reached out and took my hand, compelling me to stop.

"Most *men* are not like them."

I drew in a breath, unsettled by the multitude of unanswered questions swirling in my mind. Jesri's involvement with someone like Levon didn't add up.

"I need answers," I murmured, pulling my hand away from his, the sensation of soap lingering on my fingers. "Please."

He exhaled, glancing at the remaining few people tidying up in the kitchen. Setting down a plate, he reached for a towel to dry our hands. "Elise, could you finish up for us?"

A blonde woman nodded graciously, offering a smile as we headed back upstairs.

I looped my arm through his as we ascended the tight spiral staircase to the main floor, guided solely by the lamp he held. The dancing flame cast unsettling shadows on the walls, and I couldn't shake the feeling of unseen eyes watching our every move.

"There are things I still cannot say. But ask me, and I'll answer—" he glanced down at me, "—based on the question."

I nodded as he led me to the main stairs and into his study. Papers still lay scattered across the mahogany table, his notebook open with charcoal nearby. Hastily, he closed it before I could catch a glimpse. Two large leather seats and a smaller table between them, adorned with an empty crystal glass, welcomed us. He gestured for me to sit as he settled into the other chair. The room was filled with aroma, a blend of sandalwood and citrus, making me wonder if he spent more time here than in his own room.

"Why are you and Jesri friends?" I asked, the words coming out harsher than I intended.

"I wouldn't call us friends, but rather partners—"

"For work purposes?" I interjected.

He hesitated, then nodded. "Yes."

"Why? Why would you choose to work with him?" This time, my words dripped with venom, each syllable laced with bitterness.

"It's not that simple," he lamented.

"Not simple?" I scoffed. "You have a choice. You get to decide!" I stood up, my fists clenched as I struggled to contain the swift and intense surge of anger. "I don't understand why you want to take my freedom and do this Match and be *working partners* with Jesri. I...I can't wrap my mind around it. You're too kind for something like that...aren't you?"

"Eliah, calm down. Remember the breathing techni—"

"*Calm down*?" The words tasted metallic on my tongue, shaking me to my core with every breath. Instantly, I regretted uttering the words, feeling childish and feeble.

Why couldn't I control myself?

Frustration surged through me, and I didn't want to continue this conversation anymore. I went for the door, yanking it open only to have it slammed shut, barely missing my fingers.

I hissed out and turned around to find him looming over me, his arms pressing against the door on either side.

"Control it," he spat. "Don't let it overpower you, or *you will fail*, Eliah."

I tried to push him away, but he stood firm and immovable.

"I didn't come here for you to lecture me about my *anger,*" I hissed.

He backed away. "I *work* with Jesri because I believe you are the key to something crucial, and I *chose* to work with him to get *you* out." He pointed a finger at me as his nostrils flared in anger.

I stared at him, dumbfounded.

All of this was for some worthless beliefs he held about *rescuing* me? I scoffed. I am not a damsel in need of saving. I clenched my fists, feeling my anger rise.

"A key?" I sneered. "A key for what?"

"You wouldn't understand," he snapped.

"Then help me understand, Levon! I'm tired of being kept in the dark. Help me understand—"

"I can't!" he exclaimed, his voice rising, silencing even my breathing.

We stood in silence for a few heartbeats, feeling the tension swell between us.

"Can't, or won't? They are two *very* different things," I murmured. He stroked his hands through his hair, his sleeves still rolled up from cleaning, and shook his head. "What are you not telling me?" I sat back down on the seat, trying to make sense of *everything*. *"Why* this Match to begin with?" My voice flooded with desperation.

"Eliah," he sighed, rubbing his temples as he settled beside me, his scarred hands in plain view. He glanced up, meeting my eyes. "I'm not *kind,*" he paused. "I've done things—dark things—that I have to live with," he stopped again, his gaze becoming heavy. "Some things are best left in the past, Eliah. But this *anger*—you don't realize how quickly it can take over, turning everything good inside you into something dark. I've seen it happen to myself, and I don't want you making the same choices I did."

His words hit me like a punch, and my mind flashed to the Spellcasters and the massacre of all those innocent Magics. I swallowed hard, almost choking on the weight of his confession.

I hadn't expected him to be so honest. He was clearly trying to make amends, to be better—that explained his work in the kitchens and his kindness to his staff. But that didn't mean he had the right to dictate my life or control my choices and emotions.

I placed a hand on his arm, noticing how the light in his bright eyes had dimmed, replaced by a hollow look of regret.

"Levon, you're not here to be my protector. Your job is to train me for the Match, not shield me against things that *might* happen. What I need right now is to know what this Match truly involves," I breathed, matching his heaviness. "I have to win—It's my only shot at breaking free from Jesri."

He stared at me, absorbing my words in silence before taking a deep breath. I pulled my hand back and stood up, the anger still boiling inside me, ready to explode. "I need to know what I'm up against. You can either tell me or I'll figure it out myself." I turned, yanked the door open, and slammed it shut behind me, frustrated that my room was so close to his study—I needed more space to cool off.

The uncertainty weighed heavily on me, stifling and relentless. I was desperate for answers, even though I knew they might reveal truths I wasn't ready to confront.

—— + ✦ + ——

I needed air. I needed to get out and take control of my life, even if only for the evening, and explore the town on my own terms. I waited until his footsteps faded down the hall into silence before I changed into my training attire. Opting for a long black top and brown pants, I slipped one of the daggers I had stolen from training earlier into my boot as I tied the laces. After securing a satchel, I flung open the immaculate curtains to reveal a full moon illuminating the shadowy grounds below.

The sky was an inky black, dotted with dozens of shimmering stars and constellations, looking down at me with indignation for what I was about to do.

I cracked the window open, feeling a cold gust of wind rush in, sending shivers down my spine and raising goosebumps. Hastily, I searched for an overcoat and found one at the bottom of the armoire. It was patched with leather and lined with rabbit fur, instantly warming me up as I slipped it on.

I walked back to the window and looked over the glen, where tall trees framed the path leading to the town. In the distance, the lights glowed softly, hinting at the lively activity beyond.

I glanced down, assessing the distance and my footing before making my move. Gripping the window frame, I carefully lowered myself onto a narrow ledge, just wide enough for one foot. The thrill of rebellion surged through me with each cautious step.

At Jesri's estate, such recklessness would have been unthinkable. Darius's men patrolled the grounds so vigilantly that slipping out unnoticed seemed nearly impossible.

A smile tugged at the corners of my lips—Levon, on the other hand, was much less of a worrier.

I descended smoothly until my footing faltered, leading to a sudden fall. I managed to quickly grab onto another small ledge to slow my descent before dropping in a heap on the ground. Coughing for air, I quickly recovered and brushed myself off. With a grin threatening to escape, I started my run toward the town, containing the laughter that bubbled up inside me.

The cold air and high elevation stung my throat with each breath but propelled my legs and arms to move faster. The dirt beneath my feet crunched loudly against the stillness of the night as the moon illuminated my path. Tears streamed down my face from the cold, and the uncontrollable giggles from rebelling urged me to run faster.

With arms outstretched, I twirled, letting the gentle wind lead the way.

I came to a halt, crouching down to catch my breath. As I covered my mouth to stifle my giggles, I couldn't help but reflect on the freeness. With Jesri, it took all of my control not to defy him, to assert my independence, and to prove that I was not his to control. I allowed him to believe he held sway over me, allowed him to perceive me as his prized possession, all the while knowing that my liberation was inevitable. I would never return to that life, never to be his pathetic ward.

A sudden rustle to my right jolted me into silence, halting my laughter and leaving me breathless. I immediately scanned my surroundings, my heart pounding as I recognized how vulnerable I was on the long, rocky road. The darkening sky and dense trees surrounding me seemed to close in, intensifying my sense of how utterly alone I was.

My thoughts returned to Levon's warning about the prowlers from our first run together. He had never given specifics about what might be lurking in the shadows, but the vague fear he had instilled was enough. The dread in my chest grew sharper, and I felt a surge of panic. I had no intention of staying around to find out what dangers lay hidden in the darkness.

Drawing my dagger, the skin on my neck pebbled as another flurry of movement rustled behind me. Regret flooded me—I should not have done this. How utterly foolish of me.

A deep snarl reverberated from the ground to my left, sending a shiver down my spine. Every fiber of my being urged me to flee, and my heartbeat echoed loudly in my ears. I crouched low, regulating my breath to silence and sharpening my senses. With cautious steps, I advanced, straining my eyes to pierce through the darkness of the thicket.

What in Tyran was *I thinking*? I huffed, annoyed at myself. I *wasn't* thinking, that was the problem.

As more movement stirred behind me, branches cracked loudly. Whirling around, I extended my leg to steady myself. The rustling of several bushes and branches revealed that I was vastly outnumbered.

The movements quickened, accompanied by the menacing sound of snarls and the snap of saliva. My thoughts returned to the beasts in my evaluation, realizing they made a similar noise that made my skin crawl. Clutching the dagger tightly, I prepared to flee or fight.

A growl lashed out to my side, exposing a leathery black feline animal with talons and teeth like daggers, already dripping with blood. My stomach heaved, ready to expose tonight's dinner.

I stepped back, quickly looking in my peripheral vision, only to see another one pounce out behind me. I slowly stood back up, hoping to look taller than I was.

Their jet-black bodies contrasted sharply with their milky-white eyes, suggesting blindness. Despite their stature, standing just below my shoulders, they crept with a vengeful determination on their six powerful legs—six, not four. My swallow stopped in my throat.

"Tyran," I swore under my breath.

Why would these *things* be so close to the town? I stopped my thoughts as a fearful spark ignited, making my mouth dry. Within an instant, two more jumped out, all four circling me like a hawk narrowing in on its prey.

Inhale.

Before thinking longer, I cried out, slashing my dagger and cutting one right in the eye before it pounced on me. Its weight crushing me as its talons tore through my flesh. I screamed out in pain, frantically slicing my dagger into anything it came in contact with.

A sticky warmth pooled on my chest, sending me into a frenzy of emotions as my arm burned in pain. I quickly saw the others stalking back and forth, watching.

My dagger made contact, as did its claws, sending us both roaring in pain. The fire within me erupted, slicing through my darkness like sharp nails. It clawed at me relentlessly until all I felt was a fiery burn.

I screamed, allowing the pain, the warmth, and the flames to consume me until I felt like stardust. Abruptly, a bright light flashed, momentarily blinding me as a weight lifted from my chest and my fingertips burned with searing pain that was bitter cold.

My eyes snapped open to see the creatures scattered several feet away, two of them unconscious as more began to creep out of the forest line.

I went to wipe away the sticky blood coating my eyes before one caught me by the boot, dragging me towards the forest as another clamped down on my left arm. Pain engulfed me, blurring my vision as I kicked and screamed with every fiber of my being.

A frenzied fear consumed me as I slashed away, one strike after another. A deafening screech reverberated through the thicket as the creature faltered at the noise.

I wiped my eyes in time to see an arrow lodge deep into the animal's throat above me, coiling and spewing black blood onto my chest. Another arrow whizzed past, lodging into the animals on my right and left, then to the one dragging me by foot.

Some scattered away, yelping, but were only replaced by more of them. I stumbled to my feet, feeling blood running down the entirety of my being. I looked for the archer as more arrows buzzed past, lodging deep into each animal, ready to pounce. I felt weak, unable to defend myself with the small dagger that wanted to slip from the warm blood in my hand.

A tall figure emerged from the thicket of trees, swiftly releasing arrows with lethal grace. His dark brown cloak billowed at his side, the hood casting shadows over his face. The air resonated with the twang of his bowstring and the agonized cries of the beasts as they fell, one by one. With the tip of his bow, he sliced through the creatures as though they were mere butter, scattering them away until only their echoing cries were heard in the distance.

I swallowed hard as I clutched my bloodied arm, noticing he also took a deep, steadying breath. As fast as it happened, it had ended.

Awkwardly, I stood, feeling my dagger threaten to slip from my grasp. I glanced down to see my coat torn into pieces, revealing tattered remnants of my shirt beneath with a sizable gash running down my leg and pooling blood into my boots. My satchel was nowhere to be seen.

I blinked away stars, struggling to regulate my breathing and stand upright with the engulfing pain threatening to overtake me in my leg and arm.

The man seized my bloodied arm, wrenching me towards him.

"What were you thinking?!" His voice carried a roar of rage as I tried to yank my arm back in pain, but his grip was unyielding; his figure dominated over me as he examined my shaking arm. "You could have been killed!"

He bared his teeth, releasing my arm with a forceful shove, and muttered curses under his breath. He pulled back his hood and palmed his eyes as anger and loathing radiated off of him.

Stepping back, I hissed as a surge of pain splintered up my leg. His head snapped in my direction, worried about my hiss as I stood dumbstruck by his beauty. His eyes were amber, gleaming like molten gold, outshining even Calum's gentle light-golden brown gaze. They held a vibrancy, an intensity that seemed to pulse with life, drawing me in with an irresistible temptation.

Some of his shoulder-length hair was pulled back, revealing his straight and stubbled jawline and muscular neck. He stood a few feet taller than me and felt...familiar. I took another step back, forgetting my leg, and stumbled back.

He was at my side in an instant, grabbing my arm firmly. "Can you walk?" he hissed, his voice urgent.

I tried to yank my arm away, but the sudden movement made my head spin and my vision blur. "I didn't...need saving," I gasped, struggling to clear the haze of dizziness and feeling a flush of embarrassment creep across my cheeks.

Awkwardly, I began shuffling back toward Levon's estate, keenly aware of how ridiculous I must have looked. I hoped he would disappear into the trees as quickly as he had appeared.

Behind me, I heard a frustrated grunt as I wobbled. The pain in my leg and arm threatened to overwhelm me as I forced myself to keep walking. When I glanced back, I saw him striding after me, his bow slung around his chest. I stopped abruptly. "I *still* don't need saving. *You can leave,*" I snapped.

He continued forward, stopping right in front of me. Without a word, he thrust a small jar that looked like salve into my hand. "I think you do," he growled, then swept me up into his arms, his clothes becoming stained with mine and the creature's blood. He walked forward, leaving me seething with a mix of rage and humiliation.

15

The man carried me to a nearby stream, keeping watch as I attempted to wash away the dirt and blood that coated my hair, neck, hands, and clothes. The water stung my skin, intensifying the chill as the night grew darker. He demanded I lather my bleeding wounds with the salve he shoved in my hands. Its sting surpassed even that of the icy water, but it sealed my wounds almost completely, leaving me speechless as I saw my skin stitch together.

He spat at me to hurry as he nervously continued to scan the surrounding area.

Rising swiftly, I brushed past him, each step heavy with a dull ache as I headed back onto the dirt road toward Levon's estate. Despite my fervent curses, each one aimed at driving him away, he remained stubbornly at my heels, as relentless as the biting wind slicing through my soaked clothes.

"Okay, thank you for that interesting salve and for rescuing me, but I'd rather not a stranger to follow me home. Now, leave!" I snapped, my anger boiling over, but he merely scoffed, his smirk infuriating me further.

"Not a chance," he shot back, his defiance sparking a surge of rage within me.

I grunted in frustration, sensing that fiery ember of irritation burning deeper inside. As we rounded the bend, the expansive glen of Levon's estate came into view, illuminated by the soft glow of lanterns scattered about. It stood in stark contrast to the darkness we left behind.

I quickened my pace as I crossed the grass toward my now-closed window, glowing with a faint light within. Dread filled my heart, knowing I had been caught.

The man abruptly clutched my good arm again, dragging me towards the front entrance. I cursed at him, attempting to break free. "What's *your* problem?" I sneered.

"*You are,*" he snapped, baring his teeth, and continued to pull me, forcing my boots to skid across the gravel. He dragged me up the smooth steps and seized the large knocker on the door, banging it against the hefty oak doors. The sound echoed through the estate, awakening everyone in its path.

"They're asleep!" I spat, wriggling my arm out of his grasp.

"As should you be!" he said through bared teeth.

He finally released me as the door swung open, revealing Levon, several men, and guards behind him. Levon's eyes widened in a moment of shock, first taking in my stained and bloodied clothes, then paling as he noticed the man standing beside me, also covered in my blood. The silent exchange between them spoke volumes, leaving me to wonder if they knew each other. When Levon's gaze shifted back to me, it carried a chilling intensity.

"Emil, take Eliah up to her room," he hissed to the guard at his back. "Have Saasha clean her up. Stand guard at her door until I arrive," Levon commanded, his voice billowing with outrage.

Emil moved forward, seizing my arm and pulling me into the home as if I were a child. The seething anger radiating from these men only fueled my fury. Despite the pain throbbing through my body, I resisted, my feet scraping against the polished floors.

"I can walk on my own!" I snapped, feeling Emil's grip tighten, undoubtedly leaving bruises on my arm. But he let go, shoving me forward. Glancing back, I caught sight of my rescuer glaring daggers at Levon, his face twisted with rage against the candle-lit entrance. Levon's gaze met mine, his eyes cold as he turned back to my rescuer, his hands clutched and shaking.

The laughter and freedom I felt had long dissipated, replaced by a heavy sense of dread, knowing I had squandered any chance at freedom.

Embarrassment flushed my cheeks, adding to the redness of my bloody face. I averted my gaze, walking with Emil trailing behind me.

+ ✦ +

Dressed in my new nightgown, courtesy of Levon, I anxiously awaited his arrival. Saasha silently departed after helping to clean and patch up the remaining wounds the salve couldn't cover, leaving me to ponder the forbidden magic it seemed to contain.

As the night wore on, exhaustion set in, turning my eyelids heavy. I never intended for this...*chaos* to happen. I rubbed my eyes, wallowing in self-loathing.

The door creaked open, accompanied by a gentle knock. Levon stepped in, his demeanor no longer angry but rather tired and defeated. As I began to apologize, he raised his hand, silencing me before I could continue to speak.

"Do you comprehend the gravity of your actions tonight? Do you *realize* what could have happened to you?" His voice, though cold, carried an undercurrent of concern as his eyes burned with judgment. "Eliah, if you want to leave, you can. I *won't* restrict your freedom. But please, for Tyran's sake, *inform me*. I realize our previous conversation may have fueled your anger, but you must *think* before you act."

All I could do was look down, feeling embarrassment burn through me. I clenched the covers, trying to think of something to say, but nothing came—nothing I could do to atone for what I had done. I knew I was foolish for even taking the first step out the window and acting out of anger.

"How am I supposed to defend myself when you don't tell me anything?" I shot back, my voice rising with anger.

He stepped closer, running a hand through his hair. "Those creatures you encountered are called Miehjas, and I warned you there were prowlers—"

"Not prowlers that kill!" I retorted. His fists clenched as I raised my voice.

"It's late," he countered, evasive once again, though his voice tinged with urgency as he moved beside the foot of my bed. I huffed in frustration, struggling to contain my emotions as he continued. "You have no idea how terrified I was when I returned to your room and found your window wide open. *Knowing* the Miehja were out there. I—" he stopped abruptly, his voice catching in his throat before he composed himself.

"I immediately shouted for my men to wake up, grabbing weapons and praying that you were still unharmed. Then, when I heard the knock and saw you covered in blood," his words trembled with emotion. He cleared his throat and straightened his white tunic, his demeanor a mix of concern and resolve. "We'll discuss this further tomorrow. Rest now, and please *don't ever do that again.*"

He stalked back to the door, swiftly blowing out the candle, engulfing me in darkness and leaving me at a loss for words. Too many questions swirled in my mind, but I struggled to articulate them as I grew tired. I sank back into bed, gazing up at the smooth ceiling, searching for patterns among the bumps and faded spots, but found none, much like everything else in this place.

Turning over, I tried to expel thoughts of the Miehja, Levon, and his sorrowful eyes. Yet, the memory of my rescuer, with his broody demeanor and burning eyes, lingered, haunting my dreams and filling me with an unsettling sense of dread.

+ ✦ +

I awoke only after a few hours of sleep, surprised by the absence of any marks or blemishes from the Miehja attack—as if it had all been a nightmare. Shaking off my confusion, I hastily dressed, anxious to meet Levon for my morning run. Racing down to the entrance, I paced, rehearsing several apologies in my mind and scolding myself for my foolishness. His footsteps approached against the silent morning, and I forced myself to stand tall and fake interest in the painting hanging nearby.

"Stop pretending you're enjoying that, and let's go."

My eyes widened in surprise while my heart dropped with dread. I whirled around to find my rescuer from the previous night standing before me. His expression was filled with disdain as if appalled by my presence. He had forgone his cloak, revealing attire of brown leather, with weapon straps adorning his legs. A dark brown tunic accentuated his chestnut shoulder-length hair, fully pulled back in a tight knot. His amber eyes still blazed with an intensity that pierced into my soul.

I tried not to flinch at his gaze, pursing my lips. "What are *you* still doing here?"

A smirk formed on his lips, creasing his tan skin as he folded his arms over his chest, puffed with pride. "I'm here to ensure you don't do anything idiotic *again*." His last word came out with a bite, foretelling that if I did, he would rip my head off for it. "And to train you *properly*."

"I didn't realize you were a nanny," I retorted, mirroring his folded arms and stance. He rolled his eyes at me before turning and walking out the door, the same one he had brought me to just several hours earlier.

"Don't make me drag you again...*Eliah*," he mocked, waiting for me by the open door. Rage surged through me, crackling the air with intensity. I waited for it to erupt and tear me apart completely.

He merely grinned, stepping aside, and waited for me to move. With a heavy breath, I quivered with irritation as I advanced toward him. Wherever Levon was, he better have a very good explanation for this.

"Why would I *ever* go anywhere with you?"

"Why would you ever go anywhere *without* me?" he smirked, before grabbing my arm again and dragging me outside.

"*Let go!*" I hissed, struggling to break free of his tight grip.

He finally released his grip as we reached the path leading to the back of the estate, heading toward the armory. The morning felt colder than usual, and our breaths were visible in the chilly air, rising from our lips like wisps of smoke.

He continued towards the weapons, striding with an air of superiority as if he were some self-appointed king. I couldn't help but roll my eyes and spit with disgust. He embodied the same self-absorption that Jesri and Calum bled. Too full of themselves to give a care about anything but—

"Is sulking *all* you're capable of?" he jeered, glancing back at me as he halted beside a barrel of weapons. He yanked out a large sword, tossing it between his hands to test its weight and balance. His arm muscles flexed under its weight.

Suppressing my anger, I stormed over to him with heavy steps. "I don't train with strangers. And all I know is that you could be an imposter, misinforming me about whatever—" I cut myself off, realizing it might not be wise to disclose the Match with someone other than Levon. Folding my arms, I watched as he approached, his every move dripping with sarcasm.

"It's a *pleasure* to meet you, my lady," he said, bowing mockingly. As he straightened up, he advanced toward me again, causing me to instinctively take a step back. "I'm Kaizen—there, now we're acquainted," he added, his voice lowering. "Now grab a sword," he growled.

"Tyran, please, help me not to kill him," I muttered under my breath; my lips pursed tightly as I marched toward the barrel.

Ignoring the swords, I grabbed a Footman's Mace instead. Its top was adorned with a row of uneven spikes that ran down into its center. Balancing it between my hands, I tossed it back and forth, mirroring Kaizen's earlier actions with a hint of disgust.

He narrowed his brilliant amber eyes at me, and I matched his stare and forced my face to remain impassive, hoping he wouldn't notice my discomfort.

Kaizen strode toward me, plucking the tip of his sword with a grin. "Fine, let's see what you can do with that," he taunted.

Before I could think, he struck, the mace reverberating against my arms. I stumbled back as another blow hit, causing me to lose my grip. In an instant, the mace went flying, and he held his sword up to my throat.

"Dead," he hissed, standing mere inches from my face. With a forceful push, he thrust me back. "Again."

He walked out and around, assuming a defensive stance with his sword held overhead. Anger struck at my heartstrings like a haunting melody, humming deep within and urging me to ignite into a fiery rage. I forced it down, remembering Levon's words and breathing techniques. *I am in control.*

Retrieving the mace, I swung it back and forth, letting the heavy metal pull me with it. He was unnaturally quick, I will give him that. But his condescending attitude needed to stop, along with that infuriating smirk. Gritting my teeth, I squared my shoulders and met his gaze head-on.

I struck first, throwing my entire body into the swing and slamming the mace into his sword with a resounding crack. He stepped back, retaliating with another strike, but I managed to defend myself and counter with a kick. My foot connected with his leg just before he stomped down to catch it, but I was too quick for him, so I lashed out again.

This wasn't a dance; it was a battle. Both of us unleashed the rage within, each blow resonating with fury. With each thunderous clash, the earth trembled beneath us, echoing like a stampede.

I struck hard, forcing him to stumble back. He smirked at me, arrogantly pushing back the strands of his hair before casually dropping the sword to the ground and rolling up his sleeves. With a flick of his fingers, he taunted, "Show me what you can do...orphan."

The fire within me surged, melting my insides and igniting like lightning as I let the mace drop. With a primal cry, I lunged towards him, letting the wind take my feet as I jumped into the air.

My fist slammed into his cheek before he could even finish speaking, sending shock waves up my arm with a sting. I delivered another storm of punches to his arm and ribs, but he expertly evaded several blows. With a forceful shove, he pushed me away, landing a strike on my side that left me gasping for air. Stumbling backward, I quickly dodged his next attack, sensing him holding back and further fueling my frustration. In a swift motion, he swept his leg out, catching hold of my foot and sending me crashing backward in a heap. My face collided with a nearby rock, sending my vision spinning.

He pounced on top of me, crushing the air from my lungs as he grasped my wrists in one strong hand above my head and pinned his knees into my thighs. His other calloused hand closed around my neck, squeezing gently.

"Dead again," he breathed into my ear. I shifted my leg from his, my knee ready to strike his groin, but he quickly grabbed my thigh, pushing it down. "Definitely dead," he growled. I spat at him, feeling foolish as I squirmed in his grasp.

"Kaizen!" Levon's voice pierced through the rage swirling inside me.

Kaizen smirked, lifted one leg, and released my hands. Without thought, I slammed my fist into his handsome face and shoved him off, spitting at him once more.

He fell back with a grunt, chuckling as he slowly rose to his feet. His eyes glinted with amusement as his hand touched his red cheek, mirroring my throbbing knuckles. I stood up, preparing to throw another punch, but Levon's hand gripped my shoulder, forcing me to face him.

His crystal eyes shimmered with rage as he tilted my chin up to examine my face. I could feel a bruise forming and swelling around my eye from the rock, but I was too consumed by anger to care. I quickly shoved Levon away and turned back toward Kaizen, who was still disturbing the peaceful morning with his laughter.

"Are you out of your mind!?" I hissed at Kaizen, storming toward him as he proceeded to clap with amusement.

"Well done, Eliah," he breathed. Standing just a breath away, he stared down at me. "You wouldn't last through one round." Stepping back, he turned to Levon, who was now seething with rage. "And there's no way in Geisha I'll allow it."

Levon gritted his teeth, his jaw fluttering as he stared at Kaizen with the same intensity.

My stomach churned, burning my fingertips and turning the air metallic. I could taste it on my tongue and sensed that Levon and Kaizen might have felt it, too, judging by their backward steps and side glances at each other.

I grasped Kaizen's tunic, feeling his breath against my face. Oh, how I longed to shatter every bone in his pretty face.

"*You know nothing about me!* And you, of all people, do not get to choose what I do!" My fury surged through me, pulsating with every heartbeat. I could feel it thickening the air around us, enveloping us in my seething rage.

Kaizen took a step back, gently prying my hand from his shirt. His gaze shifted towards Levon, who stood there pale, his eyes blazing with ice.

"I won't. It's too dangerous," Kaizen declared, his voice edged with firmness.

He turned back without waiting and stalked to the barrel, stooping to retrieve the sword and slammed it into place.

I felt an overwhelming urge to keep punching something, to scream, to cry with rage as I watched him stalk away.

Levon's touch on my hand effortlessly brought me back to reality. "Eliah..." his voice trailed off, laden with frustration.

"No!" I shook off his touch. "I don't want him training me, Levon. I'm sorry I left last night—but look at me!" I faced him now, extending my arms and gesturing to the whole of me. "I'm *fine!* I don't need protection; I *need you* to teach me how to win this Match that you're *determined to keep a secret!* You saw how easily he took me out."

I stopped and palmed my face, heaving in a breath, trying to calm my racing mind, which only began spiraling downward.

"Eliah, Kaizen is a different breed—"

"I wasn't looking for comfort," I snapped. I turned back towards him, seeing his jaw clench as he glanced at Kaizen's figure rounding the other side of the estate. "Why can't you tell me?" I yelled, scaring off any peace left.

"*Because I don't know!*" he shot back, matching my anger and running his fingers through his unkempt hair. "Do you have any idea how infuriating you are?" He turned away, cursing under his breath as he rubbed his face in frustration.

I stood there with my arms crossed, demanding more explanation.

He looked back at me, his frustration evident. "I'm serious when I say I don't know," he trailed off, his expression growing pale. "There have only been a handful of Matches in his lineage, but each one is always different, always a surprise until right before, and always deadly."

My throat closed up, but I held my head high.

I scoffed a laugh. Why else would Jesri send me here if not to be rid of me and gain something? The realization hit me hard, and the weight of my repressed emotions seemed to press down on me, intensifying with his confirmation that he didn't know.

"Thank you for sharing what you know," I said, my voice strained but steady. "And...I apologize for what happened last night."

"Don't. I would do the same in your situation," Levon cut in.

We stood there in tense silence for a few moments before I broke it.

"Who is Geisha?" I asked.

He looked at me with shock and confusion. "What?" he retorted quickly.

"Kaizen, when he said he wouldn't allow it?"

He looked down and away, shaking his head. "I don't know. But I have much to do today, so let's hurry with our run."

He began jogging away, leaving me with the sinking feeling that he wasn't telling the truth.

16

I sat alone in my room during lunch, hoping the sunlight streaming through the tall pines outside would offer me the same tranquility cascading through my windows. Yet, my mind was anything but calm, swirling with relentless questions and uncertainties. I reached for a book from the stack Levon had given me, hoping to find solace in its pages. But no matter how hard I tried, my thoughts kept gravitating back to the impending Match, the mysterious Spellcasters, and Levon's cryptic mentions of the *key* I was to him and the stranger who had intruded on my training.

I let out a grunt of irritation, slamming the book closed and feeling the soft, worn spine against my calloused fingers. I had less than an hour before I was scheduled for supper prepping duty with Elise and Saasha, and I silently welcomed the prospect of their company.

Setting the book back on the side table, I grabbed my plate and took it down to the main hall, where I put it on a table before the library.

I peeked into the immaculate room, noticing that Madam Hannel wasn't in her usual place behind her desk. Quietly, I hurried to the back corner she had initially directed me to on my first day here. I never had the opportunity to explore these shelves alone, even after spending much of my free time in the library, assisting her in sorting through books and papers in hopes of uncovering anything related to the Spellcasters. Yet, my efforts always fell short.

I trailed my fingers along the rows of leather-bound books in varying shades. Starting from the far left end, I searched for any title of King Leonard, but nothing immediately caught my eye. Disheartened, I selected a few volumes and leafed through their pages, but my search seemed hopeless. Returning the books to their places, I repeated the process with several more, only uncovering details about historical dates, royal lineages, conquered territories, and military campaigns. With each passing book, my enthusiasm wilted, worn down by the tiny print on every page, until I found an old leather-worn book that looked like it was barely holding together. I leafed through the worn yellow pages to see creatures—terrifying monsters, scribbled throughout.

I turned the page to reveal a grotesque creature, its deformed body towering over the page. It looked as though it had been pieced together from shards of bone and sinew that hadn't fused correctly. The head was lopsided, with eyes of different sizes and rows of jagged teeth dripping with saliva. I shivered as I took in the unsettling image, then glanced down to read the description.

RANKHOR
CREATION: *UNKNOWN.*
INHABITS: *UNKNOWN.*
CLAWS ARE ABLE TO INSTANTANEOUSLY INJECT POISON AND HAS ACIDIC SALIVA. EYE SHOTS STUN THEM ENOUGH TO GET AWAY.

I turned another few pages, each revealing more grotesque monsters that would undoubtedly haunt my nightmares. One in particular made my skin crawl: Skinners. They appeared almost human but were skeletal and unnaturally elongated, with arms that were disturbingly long and twisted. Their bodies were a patchwork of misshapen skin, bubbling grotesquely over their thin, bony frames. Obsidian eyes stared out from its hollow-like sockets, and a gaping mouth stretched wide in an expression of pure horror. A black, tattered cloak billowed behind their lanky forms, and a sharp dagger gleamed menacingly at their sides. The sight of them was enough to make my blood run cold.

DARK MAGICS KNOWN AS SKINNERS

***CREATION:** XALDRUK—THE FOREBEAR OF ZEPHARIMS*

***INHABITS:** UNMARKED TERRITORY, PREMTHIAM, AND MORE UNKNOWN REGIONS.*

SKINNERS ARE DARK MAGICS WHO DELVED TOO DEEPLY INTO DANGEROUS ANOMALIES FROM XALDRUK, TRANSFORMING THEM INTO THE LIVING DEAD. THEY EARNED THEIR NAME FOR THEIR GRUESOME PRACTICE OF SKINNING THEIR VICTIMS ALIVE AND SEWING THE SKIN ONTO THEM-SELVES. ACCORDING TO LEGEND, SKINNERS SKIN THEIR VICTIMS IN A DESPERATE ATTEMPT TO FEEL WHOLE AGAIN.

Approaching footsteps echoed on the polished floors, snapping me out of the horrifying trance as I slammed the book shut, feeling like I might summon them just by reading it. I swiftly shoved the worn leather book back in place and took it as my signal to retreat to the kitchen.

I began rounding the corner, trying to clear my mind of the horrid images of the monsters. Gently touching the cool surface of one of the shelves, I became aware of Levon and Kaizen's voices resonating within the library. Standing rigidly, I held my breath as their quiet voices grew louder as they walked near. I quickly returned to the opposite shelf, hoping to conceal myself.

"This is—"

"Insane?" Kaizen interjected, his annoyance palpable. "I fail to see *any* silver lining in this situation, Levon. *She's isn't doing it,*" he spat.

"What other choice do I have?" Levon hissed through clenched teeth. "If we pull her out, the king's eyes will be on us—on *her.* Jesri will demand her back and take her straight to the Onyx Mar—"

Their voices abruptly ceased as another pair of shoes clicked across the floor.

"Oh! Pardon me," Madame Hannel's voice interrupted.

"No need to apologize, Katherine; we were just leaving," Levon responded warmly.

As Kaizen and Levon's footsteps faded into the main hall, I realized I had been clenching my fists.

Why was Kaizen so desperate to control what I did? And where would Jesri take me?

With my teeth clenched, I slipped out of the library. Fortunately, Madame Hannel was preoccupied with some documents, averting her attention and allowing me to slip by unnoticed. I swiftly grabbed my plate off the table and descended the spiral stairs into the kitchen.

— • ✦ • —

My hands dripped with soapy water as I struggled to push back my hair while scrubbing the last ceramic plate from lunch. Wiping my wet hands on a nearby towel, I glanced over to see Saasha and Elise diligently at work. In muscle memory, their hands quickly dried and chopped ingredients in dinner preparation.

Over the past two weeks, I'd gradually let my guard down around Saasha and Elise, finding solace in their company, and felt genuine excitement whenever we gathered for meal prepping. Unlike the other women I'd known back home, who seemed intent on tearing me down or using me to further their agendas, whether it was getting closer to Jesri or Calum.

I returned to the table and grabbed a knife, joining Saasha and Elise in cutting up the remaining vegetables.

"How did you end up joining Levon's staff?" I inquired, a smile playing on my lips.

"I was found, much like you," Elise replied, completing her final chop of a carrot. "Levon saw something in me and offered me refuge. He gave me a sense of belonging and security when I needed it most, and I owe him more than words can express." Her smile held a hint of something deeper, leaving me curious about the untold chapters of her story.

She often kept her soft blonde curls draped in front of her face to conceal the long scar that ran from the side of her eye to her jaw. Despite her efforts to hide it, there were moments when she would absentmindedly push her hair back, revealing the mark.

Whatever trials she had endured, the resilience in her blue eyes spoke of kindness.

After drying the last plate, Saasha sat in a heap and bit into an apple. "I, on the other hand, asked for the work."

She chewed through her words, driving me to chuckle at how unladylike she was right now and how much I wished I had the strength to be like her.

She was the complete opposite of Elise, with raven-black hair, freckles covering every inch of her dark skin, and seafoam eyes that made me miss the sea salt air.

"Since I had a few useful talents, he decided to give me a chance," Saasha explained, a hint of gratitude in her voice as she savored another bite. "Joining Sir Alder's household was a dream come true for me. Who wouldn't be thrilled to work for someone respected for their kindness?"

Elise chimed in with a nod, her eyes reflecting a similar sense of appreciation.

Then why in Tyran would he associate with Jesri or Kaizen, for that matter? I was unable to comprehend the reasoning behind it.

"Have either of you ever met Kaizen or know if he's been on the estate before?" I inquired, seeking some clarity.

They both shook their heads, mirroring my bewilderment.

"Though Sir Alder is a kind man, he is quiet and keeps to himself," Elise remarked, sliding the produce into a boiling pot of water.

"He's quite the charmer if I do say so myself," Saasha remarked, finishing off her apple and dabbing her hands on her apron.

We all chuckled, diverting our attention to the plucked and cleaned chicken on the table. Saasha swiftly pivoted toward the warm bread oven, sliding in another batch of fluffy dough to rise.

While Saasha tended the bread, I joined Elise in seasoning the chicken.

"Eliah, can you get me the dried lemon, pepper, shallots, and tarragon from that cabinet over there?" she asked, expertly cutting the chicken apart.

I nodded and walked to the cabinet filled with jars of dried spices, the overpowering aroma filling the air as I opened the door. I quickly found the lemon, shallots, and pepper, placing them on the table below. After moving several more jars aside, I found the tarragon, marked with a small dragon scribbled on the label. I brought the spices over to Elise, holding out the tarragon.

"Why does this one have a dragon on it?" I asked as she finished washing her hands and began spreading the lemon and pepper over the chicken.

"It's referred to as the 'little dragon' because of the bite it gives. It's quite the flavor," she explained, finishing the seasoning before placing the chicken in the blazing coal oven.

I nodded, marveling at how much I didn't know about the nuances of preparing such wonderful food.

Together, we carefully lowered the rest of the vegetables into the boiling pot of water, the spices mingling with the rich scents of our cooking.

The kitchen was not as extravagant as Jesri's, but it was comforting with its glowing candlelight's and expansive windows that reflected a cozy warmth. The walls were lined with the same golden stone as the estate's exterior, while its floors were dark-stained wood that mimicked the tabletops and chairs. Several cabinets held spices, produce, nuts, hard cheeses, and anything you could think of that lined one side of its wall, tempting me to take a bite out of some dried berries.

"We may have watched you this morning, and you must teach us how to throw a punch like you did," Saasha exclaimed, leaning casually against the table.

I felt my cheeks flush at the attention. "I'm not sure I quite won that fight," I stated, embarrassed they were watching my outburst from this morning.

"Nonsense, you held your own," Elise reassured me, pulling her hair back forward as she spoke.

I chuckled lightly, sitting beside the long table as we waited for the food to cook. "I can show you much more than that if you'd like?" I offered with a smile, a warmth spreading through me at their kindness.

They both nodded in agreement before Elise spoke up. "I'm sorry for all you've had to endure, Eliah. I can't imagine the weight of your responsibilities. But seeing how adept you are at handling yourself, I have every confidence you'll succeed in the King's Match."

My throat tightened uncomfortably at her praise and realization of how much everyone seemed to know about my past *and* the King's Match, especially considering I had only recently learned of it. Granted, Jesri had kept most things from me to show dominance.

"Thank you, Elise," I murmured, the gravity of her words settling heavily on my shoulders. Saasha gave me a wink. It was the same knowing wink she had left me with after helping me following the Miehja attack, a silent gesture of support. My heart filled with warmth at their kindness.

We heard footsteps descend the spiral stone staircase, and we all turned to see who approached.

"Lady Eliah?" the tall, rosy-cheeked footman called from the bottom of the stairs. "You have a letter."

Glancing at the girls, I noticed Elise's bright smile and flushed cheeks as she looked at the footman. With a suppressed smile, I approached him, feeling joy at seeing Elise's fondness for him. He extended the letter, and as soon as I saw Calum's handwriting, a rush of longing swept over me. I snatched the letter away, surprised by my yearning to hear from him.

"Thank you."

The footman nodded before turning his attention to Elise and Saasha. "Afternoon, ladies," he greeted, prompting Saasha to continue cleaning while Elise waved.

"Afternoon, Aveal," Elise responded, her cheeks mirroring the rosy hue of Saasha's apple.

Suppressing a grin, I addressed them both. "I'll see you both at dinner?" I confirmed, receiving enthusiastic nods from the pair.

With that, I slipped past Aveal and hurried up the stairs, clenching the letter tightly.

Once upstairs, I hesitated at the main floor, feeling that Kaizen might be with Levon in his study, and I didn't want to run into him headed to my room, so I decided to go back to the library instead.

As I entered, Madame Hannel was engrossed in her paperwork, hardly noticing my arrival. I made my way to my usual corner, settling into the velvety red chair next to the stack of books I had been perusing during my stay.

I quickly tore the letter open.

MY DEAREST ELIAH,

FORGIVE MY DELAYED CORRESPONDENCE. UNCLE HAS TASKED ME WITH NUMEROUS RESPONSIBILITIES THAT ONCE FELL UPON YOUR CAPABLE SHOULDERS, AND I CANNOT HELP BUT FEEL REMORSE FOR NOT SHARING THE BURDEN WITH YOU SOONER. I DEEPLY REGRET NOT BEING THE FRIEND YOU DESERVED, AND I OFFER MY SINCEREST APOLOGIES.

As I read Calum's formal words, I couldn't help but stifle a laugh. His attempts at formality were endearing, though transparent with his silly games that I somehow found myself missing. I shook the thoughts away and kept reading.

I MUST CONFESS, I DID NOT ANTICIPATE THE PROFOUND SENSE OF SOLITUDE THAT WOULD ACCOMPANY ME EACH MORNING WITHOUT SEEING YOUR FACE, NO MATTER HOW CUNNING YOUR DEMEANOR MAY HAVE BEEN.
STOP THE EYE-ROLLING.

I did stop mid-motion.

I TRUST YOUR TIME WITH SIR ALDER PROVES LESS DEMANDING THAN LIVING HERE. I HOPE YOU ARE SEIZING THE OPPORTUNITY TO EXPLORE THE WORLD WHILE YOU STILL HAVE THE CHANCE.

I'VE BEEN RESEARCHING ON MY OWN SINCE UNCLE WON'T TELL ME ANY-THING AND I'VE STUMBLED UPON FURTHER INFORMATION REGARDING THE EVIL MAGICS—DETAILS I BELIEVE YOU WOULD FIND INTRIGUING.

SUPPOSEDLY, THEY WERE PART OF THE MAGICS THAT WENT ROGUE, WANTING SOMETHING MORE FOR THEIR LIVES SINCE THEY KNEW THEY WOULD WITHER AWAY WITH KING LEONARD AND HIS SAVAGE WAR.

FABLE SAYS THAT THEY WENT TO LIVE WITHIN THE ADAUNTAS MOUNTAINS, WHERE EVEN THE MOUNTAINS BEGAN BOWING TO THEM—WHATEVER THAT MEANS.

I HAVE ALREADY SAID TOO MUCH IN A LETTER. I HOPE YOU'LL BURN IT LIKE THAT BOOK THAT MIGHT HAVE GIVEN US MORE DETAILS.

AOIFE TOLD ME TO GIVE YOU HER MOST PROFOUND LOVE.

I MISS YOU, ELIAH.

CAL

My heart swelled as I read his words, realizing how much I missed him. Memories of our time together, nestled beneath that wicked, faulty wish tree, flooded my mind. Despite my attempts to suppress them, those childish yearnings lingered.

Shifting my focus to the Spellcasters, I couldn't help but wonder how Calum managed to gather information on them. Perhaps it wouldn't hurt to ask Levon if he had any insights if he wouldn't punish me for asking due to its illegality. However, the excitement I felt moments ago was quickly overshadowed by regret and despair, knowing I *wouldn't* obtain more knowledge.

I stuffed the letter into my pocket and stormed towards Levon's study, praying Kaizen would be elsewhere. With a few hours until dinner, a walk through town seemed like the perfect way to shake off my overwhelming thoughts, hoping to pry more information from Levon.

Bounding up the stairs, I took them two at a time, lost in thought, when I nearly collided with Kaizen. He clenched my arms, swiftly catching my fall.

"*Careful,*" he growled, his grip tight with irritation.

I shrugged off his hands and shoved past him, refusing to acknowledge his presence. Striding purposefully towards Levon's study, I found the door closed. I raised my hand to knock—

"He's not here," Kaizen interrupted, his tone dripping with disdain, leaning up against the railing.

I clenched my teeth, willing myself to stay calm. Squaring my shoulders, I met his gaze head-on. "And where might he be?" I demanded, my voice tight with frustration.

"Out," he replied curtly.

"Out *where*?" I advanced towards him, arms folded defensively across my chest.

"Why does it matter to you?" he countered, his stare unwavering.

"Who are you?" I demanded, changing the subject and wishing he would just leave. He only mirrored my stance, stoned faced. I huffed out a breath, attempting to quell my irritation. "Just tell me where he is, will you? I have a question for him."

"You can ask *me* anything," he retorted, his steps matching mine as he closed the distance, adjusting a loose strand of hair escaping his half-bun.

I scoffed, rolling my eyes dramatically. "Oh, right! Because clearly, you answer my questions," I snapped, the sarcasm dripping from my words. I couldn't help but let out a bitter laugh before my expression hardened into a glare.

"That question was irrelevant," he sneered.

"Okay, well, how do you and Levon know each other? Obviously, you and Levon are very well acquainted to let you *stay* here and *train* me."

"Why do you care to know so much about me?" he taunted with a sly grin.

"I think I should if *you* are the one hiding in trees," I spat.

His lip barely tugged up as he let out a low grumble. "Levon and I have known each other a long time. But our views changed, and we went separate ways...until recently."

"Until recently?" I echoed.

He glared at me, refusing to elaborate.

I gritted my teeth, knowing I was getting nowhere. "Where is he?" I asked one last desperate time.

Kaizen's vibrant amber gaze turned fiery, and for a moment, I thought he might lash out. I braced for a brawl, but to my surprise, he relented. "He's at the market, meeting a friend. And you shouldn't be left in the dark about anything," he admitted, his voice unusually agreeable.

"Oh?" I mocked, not wanting this conversation any longer. I stormed past him, eager to escape his irritating eyes.

The daylight outside meant the Miehja weren't likely to be lurking about, and the idea of heading to the markets for some fresh air sounded much more appealing than sitting stuck in here *with him*. I walked past him and headed for the stairs.

"Now, where do you think you're going?" Kaizen's voice cut through the air as he trailed two paces behind me.

"Out," I replied, echoing his earlier tone. But before I could take another step, he grabbed my arm, pulling me back towards him.

"Not without protection, you aren't," he insisted, his grip firm and unyielding.

I hissed in frustration, forcefully pushing his calloused hand away. "I don't need *your* protection. Besides, the Miehja are not out this time of the day," I retorted, continuing down the stairs with him in reluctant tow.

"The Miehja are always a danger, day or night. And you *did* need my protection last night," he countered, halting my stride with his words.

I stopped abruptly, skeptical. "What do you mean they're always out? Wouldn't there be more...casualties if that were the case?"

Kaizen paused, weighing his words carefully. "The Miehja only attack what they perceive as a threat," he explained cautiously.

I scoffed, gesturing to myself in disbelief. "And I look like a threat?" I challenged.

He met my gaze evenly. "Apparently."

I shook my head in frustration and stormed out the door, heading straight for the narrow path where I was attacked just hours earlier. There were no signs of the incident on my body, making the whole situation seem utterly ludicrous. Kaizen's sudden appearance and his audacity to order me around as if he hadn't just materialized out of thin air—it all felt wrong. Something didn't add up...but deep down, I knew the only person who would give me any pretense of truth was the insufferable man now trailing behind me, back into the very woods where he saved me.

+ ✦ +

He trailed behind me in muteness the entire way, his silence only adding to my irritation. Yet, begrudgingly, I couldn't deny a slight sense of relief knowing he was there in case the Miehja decided to make an unwelcome appearance.

His steps were silently stealthy, prompting me to glance back several times to see if he was truly following. But he vanished without a trace once we reached the town, lifting an unwanted weight off my shoulders. Yet, I couldn't shake the feeling that he would continue to keep a watchful eye on me from a distance.

The market was noticeably quieter compared to the bustling scene on my first day with Levon. Vendors were slowly packing their stands for the evening, stowing away fruits, clothing, and trinkets. The air was thick with the scent of spices, teasing my senses and stirring my appetite.

As I strolled through the bustling market, several friendly faces greeted me with warm smiles. Each nod and wave filled me with a comforting sense of belonging. It felt refreshing to blend into the crowd, savoring the simple joy of being just another person among the vendors and shoppers. For a while, I was free from the weight of my background and the ever-watchful presence of my guardian. The lively chatter, the vibrant displays of goods, and the rich aromas of street food created a tapestry of normalcy that I rarely experienced. This brief escape allowed me to breathe easier, my steps lighter as I navigated through the market stalls.

I took in the array of colorful scarves, indulged in the aroma of ripe berries, and even sampled one without charge. My heart swelled with the excitement of new experiences and the simplicity of life here. Unlike the constant whirlwind of extravagant events at Jesri's estate, life in this quaint town allowed me to simply exist, free from the pressure of expectations. Despite my rigorous training sessions each morning, everything felt different, as if I were shedding the constraints of my past and embracing a newfound sense of self.

"Hello, dear one," a crackling voice called out as I passed a makeshift tent. I halted in my tracks, turning to see an old woman beckoning me over. Her toothless grin gave her mouth an eerie appearance, and my curiosity was piqued as she held up an unusual gem that shimmered with an otherworldly glow, its colors shifting in the sunlight.

"Do you believe in spirits?" she asked, thumbing over the gem. Her voice carried an unsettling undercurrent that sent a shiver down my spine.

My gaze snapped back to her, surprised by her sudden and unexpected remark.

The notion of spirits had never truly crossed my mind before. "I don't know," I confessed, feeling uncertain and needing to flee from her gaze.

"Come closer, child. Let me show you the treasures that seek you," she urged, her voice quivering as her hand trembled uncontrollably. The sparkling stone she held radiated with an ethereal light, casting an eerie glow over her weathered features.

I offered her a hesitant smile, finding her approach rather strange. "They're quite peculiar. Where did you come across such gems?"

"That, my dear, is a question that will die with me," she replied with a toothless grin, her words tinged with an unsettling sense of fear.

I glanced down at the table cluttered with an assortment of glittering jewels, their radiance contrasting sharply with the worn surface beneath them. Some gems shimmered with a captivating blend of gold, pink, and blue, while others boasted the regal hues of copper and sapphire.

"I haven't seen you around here before. Visiting or new to town?" The woman croaked.

Struggling to tear my gaze away from the captivating gems, I offered her a hesitant smile. "Visiting," I replied tersely, a sense of unease settling over me in response to her piercing stare.

"Who?" she pressed, her scrutiny growing more intense with each passing moment.

I hesitated, feeling a knot form in my stomach as I carefully weighed my words. "Just a friend," I finally managed, my voice strained and feeling a need to escape. "I don't have any money, but thank you for letting me look at your—"

"Eliah? What are you doing here?" Levon's scolding voice shattered the tense atmosphere with a feeling of relief despite his disapproval, which hung heavy in the air like a thundercloud on the brink of bursting.

I gave Levon a tentative smile, quickly averting my eyes from the gaze of the old crone. "I've come to get some fresh air."

Levon's glare bore into the old woman before returning to me, his expression a mixture of concern and frustration. Behind him, Edmon stood like an imposing figure, a silent sentinel guarding our every move. Levon seized my arm and guided me away into a secluded corner, his grip firm with agitation.

"Are you mad?" he hissed.

"I thought you said you wanted to help me be free. Did you not?" I retorted, frustration bubbling beneath the surface as I met Levon's gaze with defiance. He massaged his forehead and released my arm with a resigned sigh.

"It *was* only last night you showed up bloodied and torn at my door. Can you not stay put?" he pleaded, his tone tinged with exasperation as he looked around.

"Stay put?" I scoffed, unbelieving. "Levon, I've stayed put my entire life." There was a fleeting flicker of realization in his eyes, but it vanished as quickly as it had appeared. "And don't worry—"

"He's here?" Levon interrupted, his voice sharp with concern.

I halted, surprised by the sudden fearfulness that flashed in Levon's eyes, his gaze darting anxiously through the crowd.

"Yes, he walked me here," I replied, my confusion evident in my tone. Levon noticed and sighed with frustration, turning towards Edmon, who was conversing with a dark-haired woman nearby.

"Ed!" Levon called out, his voice carrying over the bustle of the market as Edmon bid farewell to the woman and made his way towards us, his hair swaying into his eyes.

"Hi there, Eliah," Edmon greeted, tipping his head in acknowledgment.

I offered him a curt nod and forced a tight smile.

"We'll continue another time, and you will join us for dinner next week," Levon declared, directing his words toward Edmon.

Edmon chuckled and nodded. "I'd better be off then. It's good to see you, Eliah."

Levon extended his arm, signaling me to take it, and began leading me out of the market. As we passed by others, his stance was unwelcoming as he cautiously scanned the area.

"Levon, what's going on?" I demanded, clutching his arm tightly, anger rising within me. "Please, no more secrets," I spat out, unable to contain my frustration.

He scanned the surroundings as we finally reached the narrow path leading to his home. "Fine, if you must know, I got word that Edmon knows what might occur for the King's Match."

I abruptly stopped, my feet grinding against the pebbles underneath. "Truly?"

He nodded, his expression grave. "He's got reliable sources, and they all seem to agree. King Thealor's been hauling in crates and cages filled with food and...wild animals."

"Animals?" I repeated incredulously, my voice dripping with disbelief.

"Yes," he muttered, his voice tinged with regret.

My mind returned to the nerve-wracking evaluation I endured with those ferocious beasts. No, it couldn't be.

"*When* did you find out about this?" I demanded, my anger bubbling up fiercely.

My question stopped him in his tracks, and I could see the guilt flicker across his face. That's why he insisted on that evaluation with those creatures. Would he have still taken me if I hadn't passed? Would the creatures be like the Miehja? Or those beasts? I didn't realize I had been trembling until Levon grasped my hands in his.

"Eliah," he cursed, his voice urgent, forcing me to meet his gaze. "Eliah, *don't be afraid.*"

"You knew from the start. You knew," I accused, my anger fueling every step as I marched forward, the crunch of the rocks drowning out the tumult of emotions raging within me. How? How could I have been so blind not to see it?

"Eliah, please," he implored, desperation seeping into his voice.

I heard the crunch of an extra pair of feet walking behind me, and my mind immediately flashed back to Kaizen's words: *You shouldn't be left in the dark about anything.*

I stopped abruptly, pivoting on my heels. I deserved to know—no more secrets.

"Who are the Spellcasters?" I demanded, my tone laced with anger and determination, thinking to ask about that book of monsters, but thought better of it. They were fables. They had to be.

Levon's eyes went rigid with fear, and he quickly glanced over to Kaizen, who appeared like a shadow and remained stone-faced as always. I squared my shoulders, placing a hand on my hip, refusing to back down. We still had an hour or two before dinner...I could wait.

The tension hung heavy in the air as the two men exchanged a silent conversation through their eyes, and Levon's complexion drained of color.

"Tell us what you know," Kaizen ordered, his voice cold and commanding.

After I shared my limited knowledge about the Spellcasters, Levon's expression morphed from bewilderment to fear and finally settled on anger. He grabbed Kaizen, demanding him away, and the two exchanged heated words, making the gravel pathway back to his estate feel even more ominous. My anger ignited, shaking me from the core and sizzling the air around me. I stepped towards them, intruding on their conversation, when Kaizen held up a hand, looking at me with an icy warning that sent chills down my spine, even as my burning anger flared within.

"*Breathe, Eliah,*" Kaizen's voice cut through the rage swirling inside me, placing his hand on my shoulder.

I heaved in through my nose, hating everything and hating the secrets. Hating these wretched men. Hating Jesri and especially hating Kaizen. I gritted my teeth, pushing my anger harder against the cold.

"*Then tell me,*" I hissed out, venom lacing my tongue.

Kaizen's grip tightened on my shoulder, pulling me away from Levon, who was now wide-eyed and just as angry.

"Kaizen, no. We can't," Levon demanded, but Kaizen's hold on my arm grew more painful.

I thrashed against him, struggling to maintain my balance as he shoved me to the ground with a vicious, taunting grin. I hit the gravel with a huff, feeling its sting as it bit into my palms upon impact. My lips peeled back, exposing my teeth, while the flames of rage roared deep, boiling my blood with steam.

"No, *orphan.* You are not ready," Kaizen rasped, his wicked smile endorsing my flames. I lunged for his neck, but before I could reach him, he grabbed hold of my wrists. He pushed me back again, taunting me like some annoying bug that wouldn't leave him alone.

"*Shouldn't be left in the dark about anything?*" I barked at him, my voice dripping with venomous rage.

He merely smirked in response, provoking me further. With a primal cry, I lunged forward, aiming a punch at his face. But he effortlessly sidestepped, leaving me stumbling forward, my knees and palms meeting the unforgiving gravel.

"You're far too slow, Eliah," Kaizen taunted, his voice dripping with derision. "Perhaps when you learn to fight properly, I'll consider enlightening you."

"Enough of this, Kaizen!" Levon's voice cut through the tension, his fury evident in the fiery glint of his turquoise eyes and worriedly looked around our surroundings.

I jumped up, fueled by a raging desire to tear Kaizen's face apart, but Levon intercepted, standing firmly between us.

"Eliah, *stop*," he ordered, gripping my arms with a strength that forced me to meet his gaze. His eyes softened in stark contrast to Kaizen's dismissive snort and prideful retreat.

I wanted to unleash a torrent of curses at him, to rend him limb from limb and rid myself of his presence. I never knew I could hate someone so intensely.

I ground my teeth, fury coursing through me, as Levon's rough hand grasped my chin, forcing me to face him. "Eliah, look at me," he urged, his voice cutting through the storm of anger within me as I averted my gaze. *"Look at me."*

I fought to rein in my anger, struggling to find my center amidst the tumult of emotions that seemed to take control.

This wasn't who I was.

With a frustrated grunt, I locked eyes with Levon. "If you're still going to hide things from me, I'm done," I declared, my voice a thunderous roar echoing through the trees. "I won't be part of this anymore. Why can't I have a choice, too?" I demanded, wrenching my arms free from his grasp, fully aware that no matter what I wanted, I had no choice in the matter.

Levon let out a heavy sigh, rubbing his temples in frustration. "I know, Eliah. I know," he confessed, his voice heavy with regret. "I want you to have a choice. I want you to be free," he insisted, his words carrying the weight of his sincerity. "I want you to know everything, but...you can't right now. It's too dangerous," he pleaded, his hands closing around mine with a desperate urgency.

"Please, trust me," he implored, his eyes dark with unspoken truths and burdens too heavy to bear alone.

I felt utterly powerless, trapped in a web of obligations and threats. There was no escaping the Miehja, no fleeing from Jesri's reach or this Match.

But something had to change. I had to play their game if I wanted to uncover the secrets veiled from me. I would submit to Kaizen's training, cease my constant questioning, and mold myself into the person they wanted me to be.

I would not bend or surrender my freedom. No matter the price, I was determined to shatter these oppressive chains and liberate myself, even if it meant confronting the wraith of death itself.

17

As three weeks slipped by, I found myself suffocating under the weight of compliance, each day pushing me closer to the brink. Levon was consumed with preparations for the Match and the impending dinner with the king, an event that filled me with more dread than the tournament itself.

And to my dismay, Kaizen had become an ever-present figure, infiltrating every aspect of my daily routine. The mere thought of working alongside him, especially when we had to clean together in the kitchens, filled me with repulsion. I held no desire to spend more time in his company beyond our demanding training sessions, which had escalated to levels far beyond anything I had experienced under Darius's watch.

Each morning unfolded with a relentless routine. Starting with a rigorous run alongside Levon, followed by an hour of breathing exercises, controlling my thoughts and emotions. After Levon departed for his other duties, my training continued with Kaizen, focusing on weaponry and defense. Both mentors pushed me to the brink of exhaustion, testing my limits until my body protested against the relentless strain.

Training with Kaizen delved deep into the core of combat, dissecting every aspect of a fighter's demeanor. From stance to gaze, breath to anticipation, we left no element unexplored in our pursuit of mastery. Frustrated by my lack of prior knowledge in close combat besides what Darius had taught me, I yearned for the guidance of books. However, Kaizen remained adamant that true wisdom came not from pages but from experience. His mysterious past only added to my intrigue, leaving me with more questions than answers about his origins and connection to Levon. With each elusive response, my resentment simmered, mingling with an insatiable curiosity that refused to be quenched.

Amidst the rigorous training regimen, Levon insisted on etiquette lessons, a task more taxing than the soreness in my muscles. I had assumed I possessed a decent understanding of etiquette, but each session unveiled the gaps in my knowledge, humbling me and fueling my determination to improve.

After enduring Kaizen's grueling workouts, I was promptly ushered to the ballroom, where Elise patiently guided me through the intricacies of posture, conversation, and social grace—where she learned them from Levon himself.

Levon, on the other hand, assumed the task of honing my dance skills, but not before insisting that I cleanse myself and don a gown suitable for the occasion. Thus, I kept them waiting, relishing in a luxurious soak in the opulent clawfoot tub, scrubbing away the grime and sweat that Kaizen had mercilessly extracted from me.

As the steam enveloped me in a cocoon of warmth, a gentle knock echoed at my door, interrupting my steamy indulgence.

"Eliah, please tell me you are not soaking in the tub," Levon pleaded through the door.

With a chuckle, I swiftly arose from the tub, dripping water onto the plush rug. I wrapped up in my robe and slid the bath door open, exposing Levon leaning against my bed frame. "Of course you were," he remarked dryly.

I flashed him a grin, releasing my braided hair from the confines of my robe. "You don't want me to appear clean and ladylike?" I teased sarcastically.

Levon chuckled, strolling over to my armoire. Witnessing him so relaxed since Kaizen's arrival had become a rare sight. I yearned for these fleeting moments when he let his guard down, reminiscent of our initial encounter or his visit after my last evaluation. That felt like ages ago.

"Today we are doing footwork, so you will be wearing these and full dining attire," he announced, holding up a pair of evening slippers with a low heel and extracting a corset, stockings, and a lavender dress that shimmered against the light.

I couldn't help but scoff. "You're serious?"

He grinned mischievously, placing the items on my bed. "Remember, you are a lady. Not some trained assassin rolling in mud. It would be nice to see you in something other than your training attire," he remarked with a hint of playfulness in his tone. "I'll get Elise to help you." He started for the door, readying to close it, before I called out to him.

He paused, his intense gaze fixed on me, and I felt the words choke in my throat. He flashed me a knowing smile before quietly shutting the door behind him. I released a breath I hadn't realized I was holding and collapsed onto my bed.

Our dynamic had taken a strange turn. In our private moments or when we danced, the world around us faded away, leaving just the two of us. Yet, as soon as reality intruded, those feelings evaporated, and we resumed our cautious dance, skirting the edge of a deeper connection.

It bothered me that he kept secrets and only stayed in the shallows. So, I stopped asking, not wanting the tension to return between us.

A soft knock interrupted the silence, and Elise entered with a warm smile. Her hair was partially pulled back, revealing glimpses of the long scar running down her face, a reminder of her past struggles. I couldn't help but feel a pang of empathy for her pain.

Sensing my eyes on her scar, she reassured me with a hint of irritation, "Don't fret about me, Eliah. I'm quite capable, you know."

"I'm sorry, I—"

"No need to apologize," Elise interrupted gently, her hand squeezing my shoulders reassuringly. "Truly. I've come to terms with the fact that this is who I am."

I returned her smile, genuinely pleased for her yet feeling a twinge of envy. "What happened? If that's alright with me asking."

She began lacing the corset, pulling tight enough to deflate my lungs. "I was raised in an impoverished home. My parents struggled to keep us alive, and my mother..." she paused, her voice heavy with sadness. "She did what she had to in order to put food on the table. My father passed away before I really got to know him."

With each word, her hands moved precisely, expertly lacing up the corset. "I was ten years old then and was out with my brothers, desperate to find something to eat—anything to keep hunger at bay. I thought I was fast enough, so I stole food from a cart." Her voice wavered as she recalled the painful memory. "I only remember hearing the crack of a whip and then searing pain as my eye swelled shut. My brother managed to get me home, but we couldn't afford a healer. So it scarred, creating a remembrance to always be honest."

She smiled timidly as she finished helping me into my dress. "Elise, I am so sorry you had to go through that. I..." My mind raced through the endless grief I had given myself for my own parents leaving. Yet I was fed, cared for, and given a bed to sleep in. My heart ached with guilt for my selfishness.

"Please, don't pity me. I am changed because of it. I've heard of your life, Eliah, and I am grateful for the life I've lived instead of what you have gone through."

Her words touched a part of me that I tried to keep disconnected from myself—something I didn't want to face yet. So I nodded and embraced her, hoping I might be as strong as her one day.

We strolled arm in arm into the ballroom, its opulence reminiscent of the dining area. Crystal chandeliers cast starry reflections against the dark walls and gleaming wood floors. Levon sat on a bench by the unlit fireplace, engrossed in a book, looking regal in his dark attire, and smiled, hearing the click of our shoes on the polished floors.

Aveal, the footman Elise had once blushed over, stood nearby with a few others. His face lit up as Elise entered, and she returned the smile with newfound confidence. She squeezed my hand before confidently striding toward him. I couldn't help but wonder what had shifted to bolster her self-assurance.

"You look lovely," Levon complimented, bowing and taking my hand. I glanced around to see several other lady's maids and footmen conversing, wondering why they were there too. Levon must have caught my apprehension. "Don't worry. No one will be watching you; they are too enthralled with their partners."

"You should have told me that *everyone* was waiting for me," I mumbled, hoping they hadn't been waiting too long. Levon only laughed and led me to the center as others followed suit. Delicate tones and beats from the pianoforte began to play, sending a rhythm of music echoing throughout the room.

"Breathe. You show your fear as much as you do your anger," Levon said, pulling me into him. "Just follow suit as if we were dancing at the Spring Harvest."

"That was different. I didn't have the king's eyes on me."

"But you'll have mine," he smiled.

My toes curled as his fingers intertwined with mine, and we swayed to the sound. Others followed, parting and swirling as if this dance was taught in childhood. I stumbled a few times on my feet, not remembering when I had worn heels. I counted the beats in my head, trying to remember the next move and parting to the twirl and partner exchange.

"Just let the music take you," Levon whispered against my ear as we nestled back close from a twirl. "Let go of the worry of making mistakes and simply be." His hand tightened around my waist, pulling me closer and sending a wave of brimming flames up my back.

He let go, taking hold of one of the lady's maids beside him, as I did with a footman. Levon's eyes never left mine as we parted and rejoined.

"Good," he said, taking my waist and hand. "Much better."

I couldn't help but roll my eyes before I tripped over his foot, forgetting the pattern. He caught me and flashed a wicked grin.

"Perhaps I spoke too soon," he teased as the music stopped and applause filled the room.

We danced several more rounds to different tunes, each seeming so effortless for everyone else. I didn't enjoy the feeling of appearing incapable in front of most of his staff, and I noted to tell him not to do that again.

After the last dance, cheers and laughter echoed throughout the room, and I couldn't suppress my laughter. Levon thanked everyone before fetching me a drink and, upon returning, sank beside me on the sturdy seat.

"Thank you," I said, taking a drink of water. "Where did you learn to dance like that?"

His eyes turned somber. "My mother," he replied. He looked at me, warning me not to press further, though he knew fully I would, and continued. "She was known for her art in dance and danced with me nightly. It became our little tradition before she moved on to the next world."

"I'm so sorry," I offered sympathetically, as memories of our first dinner together flooded back, along with Jesri's pointed reminder that Levon, too, was an orphan. "She must have really loved you to put up with your snobbery," I teased, hoping to lighten the mood.

He responded with a lazy smile and nodded. "She was a wonder."

I smiled. "How long ago did she pass?"

"A very long time ago. I was still young myself. She died from...a rare condition with no cure. It started with convulsions, leading to memory failure until she never woke up one day."

My heart sank as I recalled how terrified Levon had been during my first episode of convulsions after arriving here. I didn't understand why he had bothered to call a healer then, but it all made sense now.

Reaching out, I touched his arm, and he responded with a gentle squeeze. "I'm truly sorry, Levon. I can't even begin to imagine losing someone like that."

He shrugged, his muscles flexing under his tunic as he stood, gently pulling me up. "It was a long time ago, Eliah. I can barely remember her touch."

We walked out to the main hall and stepped out into the warm sun, the days were hotter now, dawning the start of summer.

"Still, I think it would be much harder to lose someone than not knowing them at all."

"That's not true," he interjected unusually quickly. "Your pain is as much a loss as mine. It still hurts."

I took a shallow breath, feeling the corset constricting against my ribs and making deep breaths impossible. I struggled to comprehend everything—myself in this absurd gown, escorted by a handsome man. Shaking my head, I tried to dampen the overwhelming emotions.

"Have you learned anything more about what the Match might entail?" I asked, trying to distract myself, no longer caring to maintain my façade.

Levon sighed, his expression troubled. "Not yet. Edmon's been preoccupied with the courting parties, but he should have more information by the week's end."

I nodded, battling the rising tide of fear. "And what about dinner with the king? How many contestants are there?"

He must have sensed my growing fear, for he squeezed my hand tighter, pulling me closer. Despite the sun's relentless heat on our backs, I found comfort in his warmth beside me.

"It'll be like any other dinner party Jesri threw, except I'll be there. And there are eight contestants, one from every region."

"Eight?" I muttered, struggling to draw in a breath against the corset. "I overheard that it's nearly impossible for anyone to secure a spot in these. How in Tyran did you and Jesri manage to get me in?"

He drew a breath. "I used to work for King Thealor, Eliah—"

"Work for?" I interrupted, unbelieving. "What do you mean you *worked for*? You said you worked with people who went to taverns? Not the king."

He chuckled, his laughter echoing through the open air. "I worked among his Royal Army, alongside drunkards who did frequently visit taverns."

Seeing the silent plea in my eyes for more details, he relented. "I was young when I enlisted in the Royal Army. It was a demanding environment, but it provided unparalleled access to information. I worked my way up, eventually handling private assignments from the king himself." His gaze turned distant as if haunted by memories. "As I've said before, I've done things I'll forever regret and will always carry the scars," he added, flexing his fingers.

"But how did you get out?"

"After completing numerous personal assignments for the king, he grew...agreeable, granting me the freedom to choose my own path. And so I chose this, freedom from his regiment. I wanted to *help* rather than take, and I yearned for my mother to be proud of her son. And so, this," he gestured towards the surrounding trees and estate, "was my parting gift from King Thealor."

My jaw fell open, stunned into silence. It all clicked into place. Why else would Jesri befriend a man like Levon unless he had influence with the actual king? No wonder Levon's estate was fit for a king himself, adorned with rooms of pure gold. How else could a mere *Sir* have so many connections within the Kingdom?

Levon's laughter broke through my thoughts, and he took my hand. "I wanted to tell you from the start, but I knew it would sour the relationship we were forming, especially after you spoke so *highly* of Jesri," he teased. "I could never find the right moment, and I sincerely apologize for not being completely honest—"

"Then why?" His eyebrows narrowed in confusion. "Why do it? Why put me in?" I asked.

He let go of my hand as his face turned dark. I suddenly wished I hadn't asked the question, unsure if I truly wanted an answer.

He heaved in a breath. "Because...after all I did, all the horrible things that I've done, and after hearing your story from Jesri, the only way I saw a sliver of freedom for you...was this."

My heart sank and burned passionately, raging with bubbling anger that pricked my tongue with copper. "How long?" I hissed out, struggling to force the anger down. Every inch of me that wanted his warmth was long gone. "*How long* were you working with Jesri?"

He took a step back, sensing my growing rage. "A while," he said, cutting his thoughts short.

My mind raced back to those first days when Jesri turned more malicious after my failed acceptances of suitors and handlers. He forced me to train with

Darius until I bled on the stone floors, until I vomited from exhaustion day and night, until I was beaten and bruised.

I was still *so* young and naïve, even before I had my first bleed. The parties Jesri threw started to become toxic, with people looking at me with even more hesitation, ladies snickering, and calling me hurtful names, which Jesri made sure I knew.

I sucked in a breath, trying to register everything, trying to calm the tumult of emotions.

Soon after the decline of suitors, Jesri had returned home from a longer-than-usual business endeavor, unusually happy. He even treated Calum and me to a feast fit for the kings, with every pastry imaginable hinting at celebrating something that would go down in history. Only then did he make my training harder and became more demanding, saying he would only show me to another suitor once I was ready.

It couldn't have been because of Levon. Could it?

The sensation of flames licked at my fingertips, amplifying every sound until it felt like the world was closing in on me. I clawed at my corset, desperate for relief, desperate to breathe.

It was all his fault. Every bit of it. He was the one who drove Jesri to madness, provoking him with unrealistic ambitions for a mere child. If he hadn't made that deal, perhaps I'd be living a more normal life with a guardian who didn't push me to the brink or force me to do unspeakable tasks.

Levon reached for my hand, compelling my searing gaze to meet his. The intensity of my surroundings surged as I felt the blood rush to and from Levon's palm up into his beating heart. Heard the birds soaring to our right, the insects chattering and buzzing beneath our feet.

"*Eliah, look at me.*"

My heart stuttered, roaring to be able to *breathe.* The sun pressed down on me, blinding me with thoughts of reddening darkness with its long, spidery legs to take me whole and pull me down, down, down.

"*Eliah!*"

I couldn't stop my fingers from burning, feeling like it seared my flesh right off. The metallic twang rushed up my nose, stabbing right into my brain, sending the raging flames within me bursting out.

All I could do was scream and scream and scream before those long, spidery fingers dragged me down, cutting off my air supply and leaving me in a heap on the ground.

18

I was trapped in an unending whirlwind of gold, black, and crimson hues, so vivid they seemed to seep into the depths of my soul, distorting my perception of reality. Thoughts scattered like distant echoes, and each breath felt like a beacon in the darkness, betraying my presence to unseen forces.

Crouching amidst the shadows, I wrestled with the oppressive mist that seemed to ensnare the very essence of my being, pulling me along an unfathomable river of fear.

Golden sparks cascaded around me, lighting the darkness with their celestial glow. Each pulse and spark sent a surge of energy through me, electrifying my senses. But as the radiant display continued, a darkening crimson crept in, weaving sinister threads that whispered haunting nightmares and long-forgotten memories that I didn't want to surface.

The thunderous roar of the clouds echoed overhead while red lightning crackled through the air like fiery spiderwebs. In the distance, towering mountains loomed like jagged spikes, casting a shadow of dread over me. Each peak was capped with snow, contrasting sharply against the encroaching darkness that swirled threateningly, dancing in a frenzied horror illuminated by bursts of lightning. A chill raced down my spine, leaving me paralyzed with fear.

I struggled to move and break free, but invisible fingers gripped me tightly, pulling me deeper into the abyss until the golden light was swallowed whole.

19

My eyes snapped open to a bitter, biting cold that engulfed me. Gasping for air, I found myself face-to-face with fiery amber eyes hovering over me. I jerked upright in pain, my hair plastered to my face and chilled with ice.

"Geisha, bless me." A voice rasped as two strong hands took my face. I coughed and sputtered, slowly realizing that Kaizen crouched before me, not those bloodied mountains.

I pushed him away instinctively, though regret flooded me instantly, and I found myself slumping into his arms for support.

My body throbbed with burning pain, a fiery ache coursing through me, yet I felt as if I had plunged into a frozen chasm, shivering uncontrollably. Gasping for air, I noticed the absence of the suffocating corset constricting my ribs. Grasping for reality, I blinked slowly, seeing my torn dress and corset lying beside me, leaving me only in my wet petticoat and skirts clinging to me.

Instinctively, I tried to cover myself before feeling the comforting embrace of a warm cloak draped over me. Clutching it tightly, I trembled violently as my teeth chattered, sending echoes of cold reverberating through my skull.

"Breathe," Kaizen whispered softly, his hair brushing against my face, tickling my nose as he lifted me from the ground, my own weight feeling overwhelming. I struggled to focus, clinging to the steady rhythm of his heartbeat.

"Levon," I rasped, trying to recollect what happened. Where he went, where—where I went. "Levon?" I slurred.

Kaizen only hushed me as I tried to force myself to look out, but my head lolled to the side as his sturdy hands wrapped around my shivering body. I heard the shift of the door and the click of his boots on the tiled floors, bounding up the stairs.

"Ka—" I began, but he cut me off sharply.

"Save it, Eliah."

Pain. Every step he took, every pounding beat in my head, was excruciating. Even breathing felt heavy, each blink and swallow laden with discomfort. I focused on his heartbeat and scent—a blend of old leather, cedar, and bergamot. Despite his vigorous daily activities, he smelled surprisingly fresh.

A door clicked open, and he gently laid me on my plush bed; his warmth receded, leaving me shivering beneath his cloak. I mustered the strength to lift myself slightly, straining against the ache as the sound of running water filled the room.

"What happened?" I whimpered, the words barely escaping my lips. I clenched my teeth in a useless attempt to still the chattering; my limbs trembled with an unnatural cold sweat. Closing my eyes, I sought refuge from the growing ache pulsating through me, each fiery wave of pain crashing over me like a relentless tide, leaving me utterly vulnerable and hollow. As if my soul was being taken from me with each shallow breath.

"Geisha," he cursed. "*Eliah, stay with me!*"

He shouted something down the hall, but the words blurred together in my hazy mind. I forced my eyes open again, wincing at the harsh light that flooded the room, catching sight of Kaizen striding back toward the bath. His back was bare and slashed with scars—four circular ones that looked more recent and battered down his back, side, and neck. He pivoted, rushing back to my side, removing the cloak, and crouching low, sliding off my stockings and heels before he pulled me close to him, warming my body against his hot skin.

"Kaizen," I managed to choke out, my voice barely a whisper.

"Hold onto me," he begged.

With all my strength, I held onto his neck, slumping into his sturdy chest as he began fumbling with the strings of my skirts. He lifted me slightly and removed my skirts before taking me into his arms and gently lowering me into the steamy, hot bath. My petticoat clung to me like a second skin, leaving nothing to the imagination.

He raced out of the room, leaving me to sit in the comforting warmth that enveloped every inch of my body. I shifted, positioning myself so only my back was exposed as shouts reverberated from the hallway and hurried footsteps shuffled back and forth. Closing my eyes, I willed my thoughts to silence, but the searing pain continued to shoot through me, sending icy-hot waves cascading down my skin.

"Oh my," came a gentle voice next to me. I turned my head to find Saasha kneeling beside me, holding a towel. "Let me take this off," she urged, pulling at my petticoat and lifting it over my head just as Elise rushed in, followed closely by Kaizen.

"She's ice cold. We need to heat the water," Saasha declared, holding onto my shivering arm.

"Saasha, go help Levon; I brought up your kit," Kaizen commanded urgently, his voice laced with worry. "Elise, go make some hot tea and prepare her bed."

"No," I breathed. "My head," I mumbled weakly, hearing feet shuffle away. The water began to warm, enveloping me in a soothing heat that again dulled my senses. My shivering ceased, and I allowed myself to slump further into the tub; with my back to him, I felt his bright amber eyes searching.

Soon, footsteps approached, accompanied by the clinking of a tray.

"Here's the tea and a robe," Elise said softly.

"Help me lift her out," Kaizen's voice was hoarse. I tried to protest, to tell him I wanted to stay in the bath a little longer, but no words formed as arms lifted me out and wrapped me in the robe. He gently laid me in bed, pulling the covers over me as a click of a spoon clinked against china.

"I'm going to Levon. Make sure she drinks the whole of it." His footsteps could barely be heard, as the only indication of him leaving was the door closing shut.

"You heard him, Eliah; drink," Elise said.

I felt the cool porcelain touch my lips as a citrus warmth cascaded down my throat. I let her pour me another and another until I was warm and comfortable, feeling the weight in my eyes drag me deep into the inevitable.

———— ⋅ ✦ ⋅ ————

I awoke to a startling screech that rumbled throughout the room and bounced off the walls, only increasing with sound. I covered my ears only to find shackles on both my wrists and ankles that burned with any movement. It was so dark I could barely see the silhouette of the chains holding me as awareness shot through my chest. *Where* am I?

I was no longer in bed but somewhere with stone flooring and walls. It was damp, with water dripping off in the distance. The cool breeze drifted in, swirling the murky air that smelled of mildew and urine, chilling me to the bone.

I yanked on the chains, their metallic clang echoing into the depths of the room or cell I found myself in. Panic surged through me like a wave, trampling any sense of calm as I yanked on the chains again and again. Not caring about the sticky blood that now dripped from my wrists or the pain that inevitably forced me to stop.

It was too quiet, too dark. I blinked, hoping my eyes would adjust, but my ragged breathing was the only tangible thing in the suffocating darkness. Another horrifying screech pierced the air, followed by the crack of a whip and distant shouts. I had to be somewhere in the estate, but—

Slowly, the door creaked open, casting a faint sliver of light into the oppressive darkness, revealing more than just the shadows of my own fears. I held my breath, pressing myself against the wall, hoping to blend into its cold embrace, the shackles digging deeper into my skin.

A dark figure emerged from the doorway, suffocating the air around me and freezing me with terror. It approached with an unsettling grace, tall and imposing like a man yet moving with the fluidity of smoke until it halted just a few feet away. The darkness seemed to pulse and writhe around the figure as if it were a part of it.

I blinked repeatedly, straining my eyes to discern more than just the figure's outline. Ice seemed to crawl toward me, raising tiny bumps on my skin and causing uncontrollable shivers. The man advanced, drawing nearer and nearer until he stood only a few feet away, while the frigid air around me felt like shards of ice slicing through my every breath.

Another screech pierced the air from the open door, causing the man to pause and turn toward the sound, waiting. Without hesitation, I thrust my foot into the air, the chains scraping against the stone floor as I swung them toward his feet.

My heart stopped and began beating too fast as the chain passed through him as if he were nothing but a shadow. Fear scraped down my mind, causing me to tremble more than the cold.

The man turned to face me, cocking his head to the side, baring his teeth amidst the encroaching darkness emanating from him like tangible liquid, flowing and crawling toward me. I tried to scream, but no sound escaped as tendrils of the shadow wrapped around my neck. Their slick, icy touch paralyzed me, constricting and cutting off my airways as its spidery touch taunted my lips, prying my mouth open. Desperately, I clawed at them until my hands were restrained by my chains, leaving me helpless as they lifted me off the ground.

No, no, no. Please!

The man stalked toward me as white speckled my vision, ready to pull me under into oblivion. Its icy tendrils clawed into every crevice of my being, seeping into my mouth, ears, and nose, violating my senses and scraping against the fragile walls of my mind, releasing an unfathomable torrent of terror.

"Hello," the man whispered, sending razors down my exposed body. His smile was a sinister promise of torment. *"I've been waiting for you,* Eliah.*"*

20

My scream pierced the oppressive silence, reverberating until my voice faltered into a hoarse rasp. Refusing to confront the chaos, I kept my eyes shut tight against the onslaught of sounds—shouts, scrapes, and a persistent tugging against me. With every fiber of my being, I'd fight and claw my way out from the suffocating grip of darkness, even if I became a part of the darkness itself.

"Eliah!"

"What's the matter with her?"

"Eliah, open your eyes! Look at me."

No. No. No. It was all wrong; the shadows were too loud, whispering and taunting me, ripping me open and apart.

"El! Look at me!"

El. That—that voice.

"El, please!"

The darkness constricted around me, dragging me into its embrace as I struggled against its suffocating grip. Desperately clawing, I finally felt something solid beneath my fingers. Something warm.

"El, open your eyes." The soft voice pulled me back to that wretched tree of comfort—of home.

I forced my eyes open, blinded by a cascade of light that seared my pupils. I recoiled but felt the comforting embrace of warm, solid arms encircle me.

"Shh. You're safe now. You're okay," he murmured soothingly, his fingers gently tracing my cheeks as he drew me nearer, his touch tender against my hair. Blinking against the brilliance, I finally managed to focus on his soft, golden eyes lined with silver. "El," he breathed, holding me tightly.

"Cal?" I rasped, my mouth dry. I pushed him away slightly, desperately seeking his gaze for confirmation, for the grounding touch of reality. "Calum? H-how?" I cried out, pulling his tunic and nestling into his chest that thumped hard and...beating.

This is real.

I sat cradled in his arms with my tears flowing freely, staining my cheeks with salt until my body trembled with the force of my sobs. His reassuring whispers against my ear were my lifeline in the gloom until, gradually, my cries subsided into shaky breaths.

"You're safe," he repeated, his fingers threading through my hair with a tenderness that eased the ache in my chest. He held me until my frantic heartbeat steadied into a familiar rhythm.

As I finally gathered the strength to open my eyes again, he gently moved me to face him. His tousled hair remained, but there was a newfound maturity etched in the stubble along his jawline and a subtle heaviness in the depths of his gaze.

"How...how are you here?" I managed to choke out, my voice breaking the heavy silence.

I glanced around, seeing the soft golden hues dancing in the sheer curtains as sunlight streamed through the window. I was in my room.

It had all been a dream. Every terrifying moment was just a figment of my imagination. I rubbed my wrists and then my neck as if trying to physically banish the lingering remnants of the darkness that had tormented me. The whispers echoed in my mind, still haunting me.

He chuckled softly, but his words sent a shiver down my spine. "What? You don't want me around? Even after *that* emotional meltdown?" His attempt at humor fell flat, and I shot him a glare, my head throbbing with my distress.

I wasn't in the mood for games.

His smile faltered as he pulled back, a strong crease forming between his brows as he looked at me like he'd never seen before. He opened his mouth, then closed it before shaking his head and looking down. He cleared his throat, smiling oddly, which sickened my stomach. "Jesri got word that something had happened and sent me on the road the same night. You had us all worried. Especially now," he confessed. "Tell me, what happened?"

I struggled to find my voice, my thoughts a tangled mess of confusion and unease. "What...what do you mean you got word?"

"Levon sent a letter," he explained, his tone somber. "Saying there had been an accident, unsure if you would be able to continue. Jesri...was furious."

My mind flashed back to my last conversation with Levon outside, unsure of *what* happened. "Where is he?" I rasped, needing water.

"Levon?" he huffed, not caring to conceal his jealousy with the roll of his eyes. "This was all a mistake, El. You're coming back home with me."

"What?" I croaked, my throat tight with disbelief. "No. I... Jesri would never allow it. I don't want to go back, Cal. You know that."

"You're delusional, El. Look at yourself! Barely two months here, and you end up in a coma," he spat out with anger in his voice. "The two of them wouldn't even let a healer look at you. It doesn't make sense."

"A coma? How long was I out?" I retorted, pushing him away, my frustration mounting.

"A little over a week."

"A week?" I blurted out. It couldn't be. "*Where's Levon?*"

"Maybe consider cleaning up before you start interrogating," he taunted, attempting to divert my attention.

I glanced down at myself in my new nightgown. Memories flooded back—the bone-chilling cold, followed by the enveloping warmth of a steaming hot bath. And Kaizen...he had carried me. His back was painted with scars.

"Where is—"

"*No*," Calum interrupted, holding up a hand. "Stop talking and go freshen up. I'll fetch you some food." With that, he rose from the bed and exited the room without another word.

I released a heavy sigh, blinking against the blinding cascade of light that flooded the room and feeling stiff and disoriented as I remained seated. Groaning in protest, I attempted to move my neck and arms, eventually summoning the strength to swing my feet off the bed and stand up. Every muscle in my body screamed in protest as I stretched, the ache seeping into my bones. With a determined effort, I shuffled towards the bathroom, mustering the will to turn on the tub faucet.

It felt as though I had been unconscious far longer than a week, and the mention of food only intensified the gnawing ache in my stomach, tempting me to overcome my soreness and venture downstairs to fetch it myself.

I shed my robe and closed the bath door behind me before sinking into the warm tub water with relief. Gripping the lavender and rose-infused soaps, I scrubbed vigorously, coating every inch of my skin and hair in the fragrant foam, hoping to banish the weight of the invisible manacles that still bound my wrists and ankles with its icy sting. I held my breath and submerged, letting the shadow's tendrils dissolve along with all the noise, replaced by the watery ambiance of my beating heart.

I sat up, inhaling air as water rushed over the full of me, rinsing the soap from my hair and body.

I heard the click of my room door opening, accompanied by the inviting aroma of food that instantly set my stomach rumbling. Hastily, I jumped out of the bath, grabbing my robe to cover up before drying off. Sliding the door open, I found Calum standing there with a tray laden with various foods—fruits, bread, cheeses, meats, nuts, and a generous glass of water.

"Eat," Cal commanded curtly, placing the tray on the table by the window. His impatience was evident, and he kept eyeing the door with irritation. But I was too famished to dwell on his mood.

The aroma of the food enveloped me as I sat on the plush chair beside the table, stirring my senses and driving me to devour it with an almost primal urgency. With each bite, I felt a sense of liberation, as if I were escaping into a world where only the flavors mattered, driving me to eat and eat until the pain subsided.

I was aware of Cal's watchful eyes as I shoveled food into my mouth. But despite his presence, the food tasted divine, each bite a symphony of flavors that danced on my tongue, offering a temporary rest from the turmoil.

Once the tray was emptied, I gulped down the entire glass of water, feeling refreshed and satisfied. Leaning back, I released a hefty sigh of contentment.

Calum chuckled, his bright smile revealing his dimples. "What happened to those impeccable manners of yours?" he teased, joining me by the window where the whispers of summer breeze stirred the muggy air in the room.

He clasped my hand, his thumb tracing comforting circles over my knuckles. "You had me very worried there, El. I'm glad you're awake," he confessed softly.

I responded with a shrug, avoiding his gaze as I swept my wet hair over one shoulder and looked out the window. Memories of our last civil conversation, back on my founding day, flooded my mind, but I pushed them aside, forcing a small smile as I met his warm eyes.

His brows knitted together again before his eyes abruptly widened with uneasiness and concern. He scanned my face with furrowed brows. I quickly looked away, feeling a knot in my throat.

"Tell me what happened?" I asked, eager to dispel the strange tension that hung between us.

"Tell you? How about you tell me?" he retorted, releasing my hand and settling onto my bed with a frustrated sigh. "No one around here seems to care about giving me the truth about the accident." I shot him a glare, but it only seemed to amuse him further. "Fine, Miss Demanding."

"Calum," I interjected sharply, my voice filled with irritation.

He let out a heavy sigh. "All I was told was that you had fallen while walking with Sir Alder and then started having these...convulsions?" His gaze lingered on me, "And apparently, it's not the first time?" he stated with a hopeful flicker in his eyes as if he expected me to offer some clarification. But I could only glare back at him, my frustration bubbling to be set free.

"But that doesn't quite explain what happened to Sir Alder," he continued, a note of irritation creeping into his voice. "They said you pulled him down with you, but it just doesn't make sense. Are you absolutely sure you don't remember anything?"

My heart sank at the mention of Levon. None of it made *any* sense. All I could recall was the suffocating darkness, the creeping tendrils of shadows, and the struggle to breathe in that cursed corset.

I shivered, willing myself to stay grounded in the present.

"No, Cal," I replied, my voice tinged with frustration and confusion. "I don't remember anything."

He released a frustrated sigh, rising from his seat and casting a resentful glance towards the door. "They're all eager to see you. Finish getting dressed, and I'll be waiting downstairs," he muttered, his tone heavy with annoyance. With that, he headed towards the door, again leaving me empty and overwhelmed with unanswered questions.

"Cal," I called out. He stopped, barely turning toward me at the open door. "It's good to see you," I said hesitantly. His lips turned up, and he glanced over his shoulder to give me a wink before he closed the door. I let out a breath and walked toward my armoire.

Quickly dressing in my underthings, I pulled out a cream-colored tunic that hugged my body, woven with threads of silvery gold that caught the light. Slipping into dark brown pants adorned with several pockets, I grabbed a brush from my vanity and began the task of untangling my stubbornly knotted hair. After weaving it into a braid that fell down my back, I finished lacing up my tarnished boots and sat at the vanity.

I took a long, hopeful breath, yearning for things to return to normalcy, for a chance—my thoughts abruptly halted as I caught sight of my eyes in the mirror. I blinked repeatedly, rubbing them in perplexity. Instead of their usual gray-blue hues, the rims emitted an unusual light brown that faded into a muted yellow and then into a vibrant green. The colors seemed almost otherworldly, reminiscent of the constellations I gazed at during sleepless nights, similar to their distant lights that shimmer with an ethereal glow.

I blinked again, frustration coursing through me as I forcefully rubbed my eyes, hoping they'd return back to their normal gray-blue.

I am delusional. My mind is playing tricks on me.

With an abrupt movement, I thrust myself out of the chair and yanked open the door, stomping down the hall and the stairs onto the polished floors below. The voices echoing from the dining area only fueled my annoyance, spurring me to hasten my steps as I reached the main front doors. I was not interested in conversing, especially when wrestling with unanswered questions myself.

With a surge of anger, I shoved the large doors open and stepped outside, immersing myself in the warmth of the sun and the soothing caress of the passing breeze that rustled through the trees.

Inhale, exhale.

What's going on?

Rubbing my eyes again, I made my way towards the running path that Levon and I used to run nearly every morning before Kaizen's arrival disrupted our routine, leaving me to run alone with him, always trailing behind like an unwanted shadow. I pushed aside the irritation, trying to regain my focus as I turned into the incessant chirping of insects and the soothing sway of the trees.

"Nice to see you on your feet again." A deep voice interrupted, jolting me out of my thoughts and into a defensive stance. I clenched my teeth, not in the mood for talk, *especially* with him—always there and endlessly following. "Trying to escape, hm?" Kaizen mused.

Forcing the irritation from my voice, I turned towards him. He was in his usual attire with his hood on and a bow slung over his back. "Anything to get away from you," I retorted before continuing forward in a jog. He followed and kept pace with me.

"What a pleasant *thank you* from someone whose life I've saved again, *orphan*," he breathed, his smirk betraying the irony in his words.

"Don't call me that," I snapped, no longer bothering to hide my disgust as I tried to bolt down the path into the woods. But before I could go further, he

quickly grasped my arm, yanking me back to him. I hissed at his hold and yanked my arm away as he turned and stood in front of me, blocking the path. My gaze drifted to his bruised hands; the patches of dried blood were stark against his skin.

"What *would* you like me to call you then?" he taunted, his voice barely above a murmur, taking a deliberate step closer. His arms folded tightly across his chest, concealing his hands as if to shield me from the sight of his wounds.

I stood my ground, looking up at his burning amber eyes, unwilling to break his stare. He stepped closer, closing the gap between us and hollowing out my chest.

"Lost your voice?" he grumbled, leaning in so that I could feel the heat radiate from his body. My heart pounded and pulsated throughout me like a fiery wave. "Perhaps you can tell your *brother* I don't bite," he whispered, his lips barely brushing the shell of my ear and sending chills down my neck. He pulled back and nodded toward the back window of the estate where Calum stood, watching.

"He's *not* my brother," I countered, stepping away and trying to find a change of subject. "What happened to your hands?"

His eyes narrowed, a smile curling on his lips. "Is the orphan worried about me?" he teased, his voice dripping with mockery, igniting anger to swell within my chest.

"*Don't* call me that," I spat, my glare sharp enough to kill.

He chuckled, tilting his head. "Well, you never told me what to call you."

"I don't want you calling me *anything*. Now move, or I'll—"

"Or you'll what?" he stepped closer, closing the space between us until I could feel the heat of his breath. "Fight me?" His gaze bore down on me with anger, taunting me. "Remember how well that went last time?"

My teeth clenched as rage surged through my veins like molten lava.

"Get. Out. Of. My. Way." I hissed, my hands balling into fists.

"Make me," he whispered with a deep growl like this was all a joke to him. Before I could stop myself, I lunged, slamming into him with all my fury. We hit the ground hard, and I straddled him, my fist connecting with his jaw, sending a jolt of pain up my arm.

He laughed, his eyes gleaming with amusement. "You look good up there," he mused, his words stoking my rage even further. I swung again, but he caught my hand mid-air, and before I knew it, he twisted us around, pinning me beneath him. His weight pressed down on me, his grip like iron as he trapped my arms above my head and his legs immobilizing mine.

Kaizen licked his swelling lip, a dark grin spreading across his face. "You never learn, do you?" he taunted, his hair falling into his face, his hood now down.

"Get off me," I hissed through gritted teeth.

"I'd rather not," he purred, his grin turning feral and his eyes gleaming with a sickly pleasure.

I dug my heels into the rocky ground, struggling to break free, but before I could, Kaizen was suddenly yanked off me.

"Get off of her, you prick!" Calum roared, his voice seething with rage, his upper lip curling in disgust. He crouched down to help me up, and though surprised by his sudden anger, I accepted his hand in shock.

Kaizen got to his feet, his fury radiating like the sun, scorching everything in its path. The tension between him and Calum crackled in the air as they locked eyes in a deadly stare. Calum took a step forward, and I quickly placed a hand on his chest, pushing him back.

"Cal, stop," I ordered, my gaze darting to Kaizen, who was glaring at Calum with a hatred that seemed even deeper than what he held for me. I raised a hand to him, stepping between the two of them. "Cal, go back inside," I urged, trying to calm him down and not wanting him to get hurt.

His golden eyes met mine, and I silently pleaded with him to let it go. The tension in his chest softened as he clasped my hand over his heart, pulling me closer to him.

"You're coming with me," Calum commanded, wrapping an arm around my back, his grip firm as he tried to lead me away. I resisted, struggling against his hold and desperate for a moment to *breathe*—to get away from everyone.

"Get your hands off her!" Kaizen growled, his voice like thunder as he stepped forward, his anger rippling through the trees around us.

Calum halted, his hand dropping from my back as he turned to face him. Without hesitation, Calum lunged at Kaizen, slamming him to the ground. His fists rained down, each punch fueled by raw, unbridled fury. It was as if Kaizen was letting it happen, a twisted smile playing on his lips between the blows. Panic surged through me as I lunged at Calum, my nails scraping at his arms and shoulders as I screamed for him to stop. As much as I despised Kaizen, I didn't want to see him torn apart like this.

"Calum!" I screamed again, but he shoved me back, sending me stumbling to the ground in a huff. That moment of distraction was all Kaizen needed as his eyes met mine in a rage. With a powerful kick to Calum's chest, he sent him sprawling to the ground, gasping for breath. Both men quickly got to their feet, their rage like wildfire and ready to consume everything.

I scrambled to my feet and threw myself between them with outstretched arms. "*Enough!*" I shouted, my voice echoing through the trees. My gaze flicked to Kaizen—his lip was split, and a dark bruise was already blooming on his cheekbone.

"Who in Tyran are you?" Calum spat with anger, standing up straighter as he brushed the dirt from his tunic and stepped protectively beside me, not knowing that Kaizen would never hurt me.

Kaizen let out a low, mocking laugh. "I could ask you the same question," he sneered, the air crackling with tension. He touched his bleeding lip, then spat on the ground with disdain.

Calum's jaw tightened, his fists clenching. "Because she came here, you think you can just show up and own her like some *pet*?"

Kaizen's expression darkened, his gaze locking onto Calum's with deadly intensity. "And you think you're the puppeteer controlling all the strings here?" He narrowed his eyes, "She's not yours to control."

Calum's temper flared, and he took a step forward, his voice low and threatening. "Say that again, and I'll make sure you regret it."

Kaizen leaned in slightly, his tone dripping with defiance. "Go ahead, try. But we both know how this ends, and it won't be you coming out on top."

"Both of you, stop this!" I shouted, shoving Calum back with all the force I could muster, still feeling rather weak from being in a *coma* for a week. "*Go, Cal!* I'll be right behind you," I hissed, pushing him again, desperate to defuse the situation.

Calum resisted, his gaze locked onto Kaizen with a burning hatred until he saw the plea in my eyes. With a frustrated growl, he rolled his eyes and turned away, gritting his teeth as he shot Kaizen one last glare before stalking down the path.

"What the hell?" I snapped at Kaizen, who had closed the distance between us with deliberate steps. "You *knew* he was watching," I accused, my voice trembling with a mix of fury and frustration. I could see right through his intentions, the way he played the situation to provoke Calum—to provoke *me* like he always did.

Kaizen straightened, his posture confident as he took another step closer, his presence almost suffocating. "Go on," he rasped, his voice low and rough. "Levon's waiting for you." His words were a dismissal as if the whole confrontation had been nothing more than a game to him. He turned his back on me and stalked into the forest, his movements fluid and unapologetic.

I clenched my fists, my nails digging into my palms as I watched him vanish into the dense bramble of trees. Every fiber of my being wanted to scream, to lash out at all of this, but I forced myself to hold it together. With a deep breath, I turned and headed toward the estate, dreading to have Levon *and* Calum in the same room. And worse, facing Levon after whatever happened between us.

+ ✦ +

I heard Calum's voice echoing off the floors before I turned the corner into the dining area. I found him raking his fingers through his hair, Elise seated at the table in a muted red dress, and Levon gazing out the window with his back to me.

"Eliah!" Elise rasped as our eyes met, her face emitting a wave of confusion before she came in for an embrace. "We were all so worried. How are you feeling?"

I gave her a smile. "Fine, truly. I feel fine." It wasn't a lie. Physically, I felt strong, as if I could run for miles. But mentally, I was drained and apprehensive about whatever had happened between Levon and me, and now knowing that I was to meet the king within the week.

Cal eyed me wearily before looking at Levon, who stood frozen before the large window. I gave him a hesitant nod, still feeling uneasy after what transpired and feeling all too much like he *was* here on watch duty for Jesri, pulling the strings.

"May I have a moment alone with him?" I murmured, addressing Elise and Calum, with my gaze shifting towards Levon. Elise nodded, offering me another quick embrace.

"I'm so relieved you're awake," she said, squeezing me tightly before hurrying away, leaving Calum to regard me with apparent disapproval. I shot him a pointed look, silently conveying that I had managed perfectly well without him thus far. He only raised his eyebrows in response, looking me up and down as if to say, '*Really?*' before brushing past me to follow Elise.

Suppressing my annoyance, I forced myself to stride towards Levon, suddenly feeling awkward in the lingering silence.

"Are you going to continue gawking at Kaizen, or should I leave?"

"No," he quickly replied, his head turning slightly, revealing only a glimpse of his warm hazelnut face. "Please, I—We..." he faltered.

We lingered in silence, the weight of unspoken words hanging heavy between us. Unable to bear it any longer, I stepped forward and grasped his muscled arm.

He didn't resist as I tugged on the sleeve of his white tunic, coaxing him to face me. My breath caught in my throat as I beheld the left side of his face, marred by bruises of varying shades. Some had begun to fade into a sickly yellow, while others retained a deep, angry purple hue. A small stitch traced along his jawline, and his once-swollen eye now blazed with redness, starkly contrasting his vibrant eyes.

He reached out to me tentatively, but I instinctively stepped back, a mix of shock and concern flooding me. I brought a hand to cover my open mouth, struggling to find the right words to express the tumult of emotions swirling inside me. I felt a wave of guilt, knowing I had done that...somehow.

"It's that bad?" he somberly teased, easing some of the tension burning inside me.

"Levon," I rasped, my hand twitching as if to reach out and touch his face, but I stopped myself, recoiling at the reality of what I had done. He swiftly grasped my hand in his own. "I did that to you," I whispered, unable to meet his gaze, overwhelmed by the guilt and regret that washed over me.

His calloused fingers brushed against my knuckles while his other hand gently tilted my chin upwards.

"Look at me, Eliah," he urged, his voice carrying a mix of command and desperation. I resisted, keeping my gaze fixed downward, feeling increasingly guilty.

"Eliah, look at me," he repeated, his grip on my chin tightening, compelling me to meet his gaze. Reluctantly, I raised my eyes, locking onto his brilliant gaze. His eyes widened as he scanned my face.

"You scared me," he confessed, a faint, sorrowful smile playing on his lips. His words pierced through me, stirring up a whirlwind of pain and sorrow. "I wasn't sure how long I could go without seeing your eyes or hearing your voice," he admitted, swallowing hard.

I shuddered, averting my gaze and taking a sudden step backward. He let his hand fall to his side as I shook my head in disbelief. His words from our walk echoed in my mind—this was his doing, and I couldn't ignore it. He bore the responsibility for all of this.

Sensing the change in tension, he shifted on his feet, teeth gritted in frustration. "*Eliah*... I had to do what I did to get you. If I hadn't—" he paused, locking his gaze with mine, the silver flecks in his eyes seeming to burn brighter. "Something else would have, and I couldn't bear that thought."

"But you could bear the thought of me possibly dying in this Match that you agreed to?" I snapped, the tension escalating as my anger simmered beneath the surface. "And what do you mean by something else?" I spat, knitting my brows together.

He rubbed his jaw, shaking his head in disbelief.

"What?" I lamented, frustration lacing my words. "You asked me to look at you, and I am. Perhaps for the first time, I'm truly seeing you." I took a deep breath, attempting to rein in my anger. "I'm sorry for this," I said, gesturing to his face. "But you cannot expect me to be fine with knowing you were the cause of all my pain. You were the one who betrayed me to Jesri. You orchestrated this entire ordeal. *I was just a child, Levon!* You took what little I had left and gambled it away for some lucrative ambition of a haughty Lord and never once spared a second glance for the child left bloodied in the training match." I stopped, huffing out a deep, seething breath that thundered inside me, reminding me to collect myself, my anger, and my all-too-loud voice now echoing throughout the room.

"I don't expect your forgiveness, nor do I want it," he muttered, his voice barely audible over the roaring rage in my ears. "But I do expect you to fulfill your purpose." He met my gaze with an intensity that sent a jolt of fury coursing through me. "And I will not apologize for doing what I did."

My breath caught in my throat, igniting the simmering rage inside me, urging me to unleash all the pent-up anger I had spent a lifetime suppressing onto him. I clenched my fists, gritting my teeth, and poised to strike out like we did that first day before I felt a warm, familiar hand on my shoulder, pulling me back—pulling me back into that life of submission, where I only obeyed, where I sat and listened, waiting for that wretched tree to make my dreams a reality.

One where he did pull all the strings.

Tears welled up in my eyes even before I saw the pain reflected in his own eyes. He quickly strode past me and out of the dining room, his footsteps a mere whisper against the ornate polished floors. Calum's hand tightened on my shoulder, seizing the opportunity, and pulled me into an embrace.

"Let's go home, El," he murmured into my ear, his words leaving me stunned and still grappling to comprehend every rutting thing. "I miss you. I can't bear to live without you by my side. Let's run away. Anywhere. Everywhere." He cupped my face in his hands, his breath mingling with mine. "I'll go wherever you lead. Just take me, and I'll follow. You shouldn't be here with these fools."

My heart swelled at his words, Levon's, and everything I was never meant to have. Believing that perhaps darkness was the only thing I was ever destined to feel—a never-ending stream of shadows that consumed me and my bleak life.

With a heavy breath, I pushed him away, knowing his game.

"No," I breathed, my hand still resting on his chest. He cocked his head, scowling at me, his frustration palpable. "A part of me will always love you, Calum, but I'm done. What you have to offer is something I could never accept." I knew that staying with him would only leave me vulnerable to Jesri's venomous schemes, coiling me back into his grasp and make me his puppet forever.

He grabbed my chin, his grip firmer than before, and forced me to meet his gaze. His eyes blazed with an intensity that mirrored the turmoil in my own heart.

"El, *please*," he begged, desperation creeping into his voice.

"You should go," I uttered, my grip tightening on his wrist until he relented and let go. "Give your report to Jesri. I'll finish what I started, but tell him I *won't* be coming back."

The words tasted bitter on my tongue, knowing it meant leaving Aoife and Darius behind and possibly never seeing them again. But I couldn't return, no matter how much it pained me. I couldn't.

He stood there, tall and composed, taking deep breaths to quell his frustration.

"*So be it*," he relented, roughly kissing my forehead before turning to leave. His footsteps echoed loudly against the floors, each step cracking my soul deeper into the awaiting darkness, begging me to finally collapse.

— • ✦ • —

The following day, Calum left without so much as a goodbye. Another bitter ending, but deep down, I knew it was for the best. Shifting on my feet, I unleashed my frustration on the training posts Kaizen had set out in the estate grounds, each blow landing with a satisfying thud in the open air. We said nothing of our previous encounter with Calum, and I was grateful. I wanted to forget it—forget it all.

I let out a frustrated huff, rolling my neck and squaring my shoulders as I prepared for another round of punches. "Control it," Kaizen spat, his tone cutting through the air like a blade. "Use those emotions to drive you, not to lose control."

I shot him a defiant glare, his cheek still swollen from yesterday, but looked less bruised...somehow. "Feeling up to getting punched today?" I snarled, delivering another jab and cross hook at the post with all my might, splintering the wood and splitting open my skin. Again and again, I unleashed my fury, each blow fueled by the raw intensity of my emotions, until both knuckles were bleeding, staining my wraps with their crimson hue.

"Enough!" Kaizen's voice thundered, but I paid him no heed, lost in the primal satisfaction of inflicting pain. "*I said enough!*" He finally intervened, grabbing my arm before I could deliver another lethal blow, peeling my skin right off.

I threw my arm back, shaking off his hold, and swung my other arm right for his side, knocking the wind out of him. He only grinned, a low chuckle of amusement escaping him, fueling my anger.

"Why don't you tell me why *your* hands were scabbed over yesterday?" I spat at him, throwing another blow to the side, only to have him block it like a viper, clutching onto my bloodied hand.

"I'm not particularly fond of talking to anyone with emotions they can't hide," he replied coolly, his tone aggravating me further.

I stood up tall, ripping off the bloody wrappings. "No? Well, what about me being left with unanswered questions?" I retorted, echoing his own response to my inquiries the day after meeting him.

He shook his head as if forcing himself not to answer and quickly grabbed a sword, tossing me one before weighing another in his hand and stalking away from the posts.

I huffed, raised the sword, and followed him.

"Let's see if you can still keep up with me," he challenged, swiftly lunging and striking my blade, reverberating into my arm.

We danced in battle play, dodging and striking. I watched his chest rise and fall before deflecting a deadly blow that he aimed at me repeatedly. Though a bit of stiffness crept into my body, I shook it off like shedding a dress and bounced back with renewed mental sharpness and strength. Perhaps all I needed was a week's worth of sleep to feel...alive.

I saw a moment of hesitation and struck; he barely dodged my sword and grinned.

"Better...for an amateur," he sneered, igniting a fierce anger within me. I lunged forward, turning in a swift motion and striking his blade with all my might. The resounding clang echoed through the misty morning, silencing all living things around us.

I focused solely on my breathing, remembering the breathing techniques Levon had been teaching me and letting it become the rhythm of my vigor as I felt the fiery rage inside me intensify.

I jutted my foot out, disrupting our dance as Levon had done on my first day. He managed to catch himself before I could unleash my fury upon his sword.

We came to an abrupt stop, both frozen in place with our swords shaking against each other. A sly smirk played on his lips, and his hair fell, covering his cheeks as he dropped the sword.

I took a deep breath, attempting to regain control over my breathing, and brushed back the strands of hair that had fallen from my braided crown. "Are we done here?"

His jaw flexed, his fingers tensing in unison before he released a long, irritated sigh. "No. Levon's prepping for the departure and asked me to ensure you remember your *etiquette.*"

For a beat, my heart deflated, knowing he didn't want to see me. But then, a surge of conflicting emotions washed over me, leaving me uncertain if I could even bear to face him myself.

"First, I'll never dance with you, and second, I can't picture you being refined enough for it," I snapped, my irritation evident as I turned sharply toward the estate.

"I believe you already have," he mocked, quickly grasping the sword from my hands and shoving it into the barrel.

I couldn't help but roll my eyes, flexing my hands; my knuckles stung in the open air as I proceeded forward. His footsteps trailed behind me, their crunch on the grass only adding to my annoyance.

"Wrap your hands, or Levon will kill me for letting you sully his home in *your* blood," Kaizen demanded, throwing me a roll of the same tape I wore when fighting.

"Hm, perhaps that's not a bad thing," I retorted, slowly wrapping my hands back up. When we reached the foyer inside, I could hear him heading off in a different direction, and I breathed a sigh of relief.

After freshening up, I hurried down to the kitchen, hoping to persuade Elise to take over dancing duties from Kaizen and to express my gratitude for everything they'd done. As I descended the stairs, I found Saasha slicing potatoes and Elise bending down to retrieve something that had fallen. Other members of the staff were busy cleaning or baking. Despite the kitchen being stationed below, the heat was sweltering even with the windows open, making me cough amidst the steam and fragrant fumes of the cooking food.

"Eliah!" Elise chirped, running toward me and embracing me. Saasha gave me a smile and a shrug, stopping mid-chop.

"Need help?" I offered, stepping into the bustling kitchen.

"You can cut those onions; I've been dreading it all day," Saasha replied with a hint of sarcasm while Elise joined her with a large bowl.

I furrowed my brows at the sight of the piled vegetables, spices, and meat on the table. "Are we expecting someone?" I asked, gesturing towards the abundance of food.

"Sir Alder is throwing a grand feast for tomorrow. He's invited several courtiers and friends!" Elise exclaimed with excitement, a surprise considering her usual demeanor. My expression fell at the thought of a dinner party with Levon's acquaintances, especially before leaving for the king.

"A party?" I echoed, my voice barely concealing my distaste for such gatherings. Pushing aside my feelings, I grabbed the onions and a knife, ready to lend a hand.

"I was joking about the onions, Eliah," Saasha clarified, her expression mirroring my initial concern before softening into a warm smile that seemed to say, *I'm glad you're okay.*

"No, I insist. You both have done so much for me, and I've only been the Lord's snotty orphan everyone expected me to be." The pungent aroma of the onions intensified in the steamy room, stinging my eyes like tiny daggers. I blinked back the tears and chopped through them as swiftly as possible, determined not to lose a finger in the process.

"Eliah, no one has ever thought that of you. We know your monsters," Elise said softly, stepping closer to me. "We were so worried," she paused, her voice trailing off as if playing out the scene in her mind. "Levon was *terrified*. We all were."

I kept chopping, my movements becoming more mechanical as tears blurred my vision, each blink intensifying the burning sensation. Levon didn't seem terrified or relieved that I was awake, nor did Kaizen. The only one who seemed genuinely concerned was now miles away, venturing towards those once vibrant trees that would now be fading into a usual green hue.

I released the knife, allowing it to clatter onto the table as I stumbled toward the now-empty basin, needing a moment to collect my burning eyes.

Saasha chuckled, taking my place and chopping the rest of the onions. I rinsed my hands and splashed water on my face, letting out a sigh of relief. "Truly,

Eliah, we're glad you're okay," Saasha stated, the onion seeming to have no effect on her. I clenched the rag in my hand, feeling unworthy of such worry.

This was a mistake; I shouldn't have come down here. "I'm sorry," I muttered softly before trudging up the stairs, each step feeling heavier than the last. Before I rounded the corner, I heard Levon's voice down the curved hallway, which led to a small ornate sun room that was too small for any chairs or tables.

"It's there," Levon said barely above a whisper.

"We can't let her continue—" Kaizen's deep voice hissed.

"We have no choice!" Levon spat and abruptly stopped as I stepped onto the last step.

I stopped, waiting for him to continue conversing, but he didn't as he met my gaze. He nodded toward Kaizen and walked down the hall, strutting past me, offering a fleeting, sad smile as he walked out the door.

Kaizen stopped beside me, and I shot him a scowl, grunting in annoyance before reluctantly following him toward the ballroom.

"I don't need you reporting my every move," I retorted, growing increasingly irritated by his presence and tried to push aside the uneasiness stirred by the words I overheard.

The only response was the subtle rise and fall of his muscled back, accompanied by a dismissive shake of his head before we entered the ballroom. Taking a string, he deftly pulled his hair back into a low bun, then glanced at the footman seated at the pianoforte, waiting for our arrival. As the footman looked up and sat straighter, he began to play a simple melody.

Before I could retreat, Kaizen firmly gripped my arm, drawing me closer to him.

I held my breath as my hand rested on his, the other lightly grasping his sculpted shoulder, trying to understand the familiarity of his hand in mine. Subtly, I attempted to increase the distance between us by arching my back and shifting sideways. But his smirk widened, and he pulled me closer, refusing to allow any space between us.

His breath tingled up my neck as his feet guided mine with precision, ensuring no gap formed. We danced like that through the song, his hold unyielding until he finally released me into a twirl.

My feet stumbled as I tried to regain my balance, but he swiftly pulled me back into him.

"You seem to be enjoying this," I retorted, looking away toward the door, silently pleading for the song to end or for Elise to come save me.

A low noise rumbled in his throat as he quickly let me go, abruptly stopping right before the song ended. Another tune started, but I refused to continue, wanting to wash myself of his infuriating touch, and he didn't resist.

"Why is Levon hosting a party?" I snapped, unable to let the question settle longer.

He raised his brows, his gaze piercing as it swept over me. "Why do you think?" he sneered before turning away as if my question was beneath him.

I lunged forward, grabbing his tunic to halt his steps. "*Why?*" I demanded through clenched teeth. "So I can be paraded around like some *trophy*?" I fumed.

"He did it to protect you, Eliah. Because he cares," Kaizen countered, his voice edged with frustration. "But maybe that's something you're incapable of understanding."

"He did it to protect *himself*, clearly something you fail to comprehend," I shot back, my frustration bubbling.

His amber eyes blazed with indignation, a tangible flame that made my heart stutter with trepidation. But I refused to back down, meeting his gaze with equal intensity, determined to stand my ground.

Before I could storm away, he grabbed my arm, yanking me back with a force that made my teeth clench. He opened his mouth to say something, then shut it abruptly, gritting his teeth, and stalked past me out the door.

Glancing back at the footman, who seemed frozen under my gaze, I sighed and continued out. The soft strains of music followed me all the way to my room.

I had a sinking feeling that this dinner would unfold much like the one where Jesri blindsided me with Levon. And once again, I felt utterly unprepared.

21

The next day unfolded like any other, but with an undercurrent of dread that lingered until Elise knocked on my door, holding out my dinner dress, which she said Levon had selected. It was a soft green silk adorned with shimmering gold tulle that cascaded along the skirts and climbed up the bodice like a constellation of the heavens. Thin straps embellished my shoulders with golden caps that trimmed the top.

Elise clipped a golden jewel into the right side of my hair before finger curling my hair, letting the locks cascade down like a flowing curtain.

"Elise, I apologize for running off yesterday. I...I've never been great at making friends," I confessed as she curled my ends.

"We understand, and we're always here for you. I'm happy to see you're okay." She squeezed my shoulders, offering a reassuring smile. "You look beautiful."

I glanced back into the vanity. "Thank you for everything. You must be a Magic to make me look this good," I complimented with a smile.

We shared a laugh, but it left me with a hollow feeling in my chest, reminding me of similar conversations I had with Aoife. I made a mental note to write to her before bed tonight to tell her everything, although I was sure Calum had already filled her in on the details.

I turned back to my reflection as Elise finished the last curl. My eyes sparkled like a brilliant green constellation against the shimmers of my dress, while the charcoal liner and dusty pink lips softened my tan skin. "Thank you," I whispered as she helped me into the nude heels that Levon had insisted I wear.

"Oh, these men are in for a delight," Saasha remarked, opening the door and settling onto the bed. I chuckled, uncertain how to act under the scrutiny of unfamiliar eyes.

"Do you know why we're having this dinner?" I asked, eagerly hoping it *wasn't* to parade me off.

The two of them shrugged in unison, shaking their heads. "Sir Alder enjoys lively company, and I'm sure he wants his friends to meet you before you head for the King's Court. The more people on your side, the better," Saasha explained.

"Why?" I asked, unsure why I needed people on my side or why I had to pretend to be someone I wasn't.

"A bigger wager for the contestants?" Elise faltered. "I wish I knew. But...come now, Sir Alder said I need to get you to his room by six."

She tugged my arm, pulling me off the chair, as Saasha followed suit, intertwining their arms with mine. We passed his study and the stairs, heading to the west corridor and balcony. It wrapped around the library below and led to several doors and various hallways I had yet to explore.

"His door is at the end. Good luck," Elise said, kissing my cheek while Saasha squeezed my hand.

I watched them until they rounded the corner and went out of sight. Pushing down the thrum of dread poking through the calm, I approached the dark mahogany door. Knocking, I heard a shuffle of feet, and then the door swung open, revealing Levon shirtless and frozen, his eyes grazing me as if he had never beheld such views before.

I smiled tightly, trying to push down the rising awkwardness, as he stepped aside and allowed me to enter.

The click of the door closing behind me echoed through the room. I glanced around, taking in the neatness of his space, with its gold and teal accents. A cobalt rug lay beneath his bed while a leather lounge chair sat nearby. The far wall was adorned with shelves of books, some resting on a small desk nearby. Turning back to him, I avoided meeting his gaze, focusing on his face, which was almost completely healed.

His features were marred with bruises only a few days ago, and they had seemingly vanished. His vibrant eyes furrowed, catching my sudden surprise.

"Elise came in, and," he breathed out, striding to his armoire, "powdered my face—made sure it wasn't noticeable. I couldn't be hosting a dinner with the guests to leave with that gossip," he mused as if nothing was unsettled between us.

"She did an excellent job," I remarked, holding my breath.

He turned back to me, taking hold of a white tunic, his eyes sliding up me again.

"She did, indeed." He pulled the shirt on, quickly buttoning it up. "Forgive me, I didn't realize it was already six."

I gave him a forgiving shrug, walking toward the bookshelf. My heart still racing with uncertainty.

I ran my hand over the spines of the books, waiting until he was fully dressed before turning back to him, not trusting my thoughts or eyes. Across the floor, I heard a shuffle of movement as I continued my survey of his personal library.

My hand slid over a familiar-looking book with black strappings. I traced the spine, recalling the first day I arrived at the library and my previous encounters. I pulled it out, seeing the cover tarnished from use. Unclasping the first latch, I was stopped by Levon's hand over mine.

"I'd rather my personal journal remain *personal*," he teased with a smirk, taking the book away and clasping it shut.

He was lying. The tension in the air was suffocating, thick with unspoken resentment and awkwardness.

Straightening my back, I forced a strained smile as he extended his arms, his cuffs unbuttoned. He cleared his throat, "Help me with this, will you?" His request sounded hollow but sincere.

Suppressing a sigh, I complied, assisting with one hand and the other. His touch felt like a branding iron against my skin; I sucked in a breath. The atmosphere grew even more uncomfortable.

"Eliah," he breathed, his voice heavy with regret, his eyes searching mine as he grasped my hand. "I was unkind to have treated you as I did the other day and all the days following."

His gaze dropped to our intertwined hands, a fleeting moment of vulnerability. "I don't know how to earn your forgiveness, but I'll keep trying. I hope one day you'll trust me. I'll make things right...and perhaps it will all make sense one day."

His words tumbled out, but the sincerity in his voice only stoked the fire of my anger.

Trust? I scoffed inwardly. The word landed in my gut like a punch. There was no trust here. Our entire relationship was built on a foundation of secrets I wasn't allowed to know. Only empty promises of *one day*.

"When I was asleep, I saw things I can't describe. It felt real, *too real,* and for the first time, I truly *felt* fear, Levon...and I was fearful for my life," I confessed, gripping his hands tighter, searching desperately in his bright eyes for some kind of understanding. They seemed so distant, so unreachable. "I was scared to die, knowing that I never had the chance to truly live."

I sighed heavily, feeling the weight of my words pressing down on me, and continued. "Let's not pretend anymore, Levon. I don't want to keep playing this role. I'm not fearless or heroic by any standard, and I know you truly cannot trust me enough to give me any source of information. You're keeping secrets from me." I released his hands, gesturing towards it with frustration. "I don't know if I'll ever be *able* to trust you."

The hurt in his eyes cut more profoundly than I expected, and I turned away, striding towards the door, unable to bear the weight of the emotions swirling between us.

"Your dream," he demanded abruptly, his tone tinged with urgency. "What was it?" The image of the shadowy figure flashed through my mind, the icy grip of chains tightening around my wrists and ankles.

"It was just a dream," I replied curtly, meeting his gaze head-on. "You should focus on getting ready."

"Later, then?" he asked.

I walked to the door, not caring to meet his eyes. "The guests are arriving, and the host shouldn't keep them waiting," I said, opening the door.

He sighed, rubbing his temples in frustration before stooping down to lace up his shoes and don his dark blue overcoat. But I stormed out before he could finish, my anger simmering with escalating irritation.

———— + + + ————

The clatter of voices and the scent of food filled the air, drowning out the urge to yell in frustration.

"*Eliah,*" Levon hissed, his footsteps echoing behind me. "Eliah, stop."

I skidded to a halt, knowing there was nowhere to run. I straightened my back and sharply turned to him, folding my arms.

"*What Levon?*" I sneered. "Stop so I can go on with your little schemes and lies that you so fully parade in front of me?"

His face was a mixture of confusion, anger, and despair, mirroring my own.

"I'm tired of this *act,* complying and conforming to *your needs when no one tells me a bloody thing!*" I raged, trying so very hard to keep my voice low. "You're a coward," I rasped, beginning to walk away.

"From the moment I witnessed your fiery spirit in that wretched dining room Jesri never let you eat at," his voice quivered with raw emotion, stopping me in my tracks once again. "To the time I found you bloodied after your evaluation or your ruffled hair after waking up next to you in the inn—I knew," he stopped, holding back his emotions. "You have been more than I could have ever imagined." His confession was raw and vulnerable.

"I've made mistakes, Eliah. Horrible things that haunt me every waking moment," he confessed, his voice heavy with remorse. "But I'm trying. Trying my best. All I've ever known is heartbreak and duty. I'm trying to forge a life my mother would be proud of, to honor her memory, and to give you the freedom you deserve."

He gave an airy, frustrated laugh, palming his eyes. "If being desperate for redemption makes me a coward in your eyes, then so be it."

His words stirred a whirlwind of emotions within me, a tumultuous storm of doubt and longing. Darius's last plea echoed in my mind, urging me to trust him and embrace his guidance—a choice that held the promise of freedom, of finally becoming who I truly wanted to be.

I pressed my fingertips against my temples, attempting to quell the rising tide of doubts and fears that threatened to overwhelm me.

Taking a deep breath, I locked eyes with Levon, finding a storm of emotions mirrored in his gaze, reflecting the turmoil raging within me.

"How can I trust you," I whispered, my voice barely audible over the tumult of emotions swirling within me. "When you keep me in the dark about matters that shape my life?" The words hung heavy, burdened with unspoken pain and betrayal.

His expression darkened as he glanced towards the festivity in his home, the noise of his guests a jarring contrast to the heaviness of our conversation. With somber steps, he approached me, a solemn aura enveloping us like a blanket of mourning.

"Tomorrow," he promised, his voice thick with emotion, uncertainty shadowing his features. "I'll show you." His breath hitched, betraying an uncertainty that seemed to gnaw at him.

I glanced towards the clamor of voices, the laughter, and the music serving as a stark reminder of the façade we were forced to maintain. With a heavy sigh, I nodded, I could endure the charade for one more night. But come tomorrow, the truth would be laid bare, and I would finally have the answers I so desperately sought.

We walked silently as he guided me down into the main foyer, where voices echoed with a resonance that seemed to freeze my heart in its tracks. The magnitude of attendees hadn't quite dawned on me until now.

A footman acknowledged us with a nod as Levon tightened his grip on my hand, leading us forward with a determined stride.

With a gentle push, he swung the doors wide open, revealing the resplendent dining room. It was a spectacle of elegance, filled with what seemed like a multitude of guests adorned in exquisite gowns, sharp suits, ornate hats, gleaming shoes, and gloved hands. I swallowed hard, summoning every ounce of courage to hold my head high as a sea of eyes fixated on us, washing over us like an overwhelming tide.

Clapping commenced as Levon's eyes wrinkled with joy, raising his hand to stop the cheering.

"My friends!" His voice rang out, starkly different from moments before and brimming with a joy that seemed to brighten the room, happiness I hadn't seen since Spring Harvest.

"It is an honor to be graced by the presence of each of you tonight! To stand by me in my endeavors, in my life's journey, and," he paused, his gaze tender as he turned towards me with sincerity in his emerald-blue eyes. "My queen," he muttered, loud enough only for me to hear.

Caught off guard by the unexpected statement, I felt a rush of warmth flooding my cheeks, rendering me speechless and flustered. The room erupted in applause as we made our way around the grand table towards our designated seats at the head.

Amidst the gathering, I spotted Edmon conversing with the captivating lady from our encounter at the market, a moment that now felt like a distant memory. A young girl sat beside him, accompanied by an older woman whose silver-streaked hair framed a face filled with gentle curiosity. The young girl's eyes met mine with an endearing innocence that softened my nerves.

I squeezed Levon's arm, remembering to breathe as the delicate fabric of my gown swayed gracefully against my shoes with each step forward.

"You do look like a queen, Eliah," Levon's warm breath brushed against my ear, igniting a cascade of conflicting emotions within me. His words, though flattering, only served to deepen the turmoil swirling inside.

"I'm still mad at you," I muttered, my gaze fixed on my shoes as I struggled to maintain a mask of composure.

"Good, that means you're being you," he quipped, his tone playful yet tinged with a hint of regret.

In response, I couldn't resist digging my nails into his forearm, a feeble attempt to convey my frustration. He chuckled softly, effortlessly evading my grasp as he pulled out a chair for me. Reluctantly, I lowered myself into the seat, acutely aware of the weight of strangers' eyes observing.

"Let's enjoy ourselves tonight; we can do introductions later. For now, let's eat," Levon announced, his voice breaking through the uneasy silence as the servants filled the room and began to serve the lavish feast.

Aveal, at the helm, placed each dish with practiced precision, the table adorned with tantalizing delicacies. The aroma was irresistible, tempting me to shovel everything in my mouth simultaneously.

The evening unfolded, and the room buzzed with activity as guests eagerly helped themselves to the luxurious spread, passing plates, platters, and utensils laden with food amidst a chorus of laughter and animated conversation.

Seated beside me was a man of striking appearance, looking slightly older than Levon, his ebony skin contrasted with his silver hair and vibrant green eyes.

With a friendly smile, he extended a platter filled with an assortment of pastries my way. "Levon mentioned your fondness for sweets, and I always say it's best to start with the delicious things first rather than end with them," he remarked, his voice warm and welcoming yet foreign with a thick roll that sounded like he was from the eastern continent.

I couldn't help but laugh as I accepted the platter, selecting a few powdered pastries, and passed it over to Levon, who responded with a wink of acknowledgment.

"I'm Casmir," the man introduced himself, extending his hand across the food-laden table.

I shook his hand, noting the surprising softness of his touch, reminiscent of Elise's gentle embrace. "Levon has spoken highly of you. It seems everything he said is true," he added, helping himself to another plate piled high with meats while Levon nudged me teasingly.

"Casmir has been by my side for as long as I can remember. But be warned, he's quite the talker," Levon teased, earning a playful glare from Casmir as he handed me the plate of meats.

I couldn't resist the temptation, sampling each dish before more made their way around the table. Across the room, Edmon caught my eye and waved, prompting the young girl beside him to follow suit with an enthusiastic gesture. I returned the wave with a small smile, feeling Levon's reassuring hands gently resting on my lower back.

"You're doing great," he murmured, his words offering a moment of solace amidst the chaos of the evening. Ignoring his praise, I continued to eat, my stomach protesting against the onslaught of food and my dress silently pleading for mercy.

"Tell me, Casmir, what's it like to be friends with Levon?" I asked as the lady seated beside him rested her arm on his, awaiting her own introduction.

Casmir cleared his throat, a knowing glint in his eyes. "It's quite the adventure, I'll give him that," he chuckled before turning towards the radiant woman beside him. Her complexion was creamy gold, and her brown hair framed her face in soft waves that barely brushed her shoulders. Her almond-shaped brown eyes sparkled with warmth as she extended a graceful hand towards me. "This is Admearin, my wife," Casmir introduced with a fond smile.

"It's a pleasure to meet you, Lady Eliah. You're even more beautiful than Levon described," Admearin complimented, her words etching a shy flush to my cheeks as I shot Levon a pointed look. He smiled but remained engrossed in conversation with the lady to his right.

"Thank you, Admearin. Although I must say, Casmir here is a fortunate man to have such beauty by his side," I replied, attempting to deflect the attention away from myself.

"A beauty but with a temper," Casmir interjected between bites, earning a playful swat from his wife and a roll of her eyes but causing a warmth to flood into my own.

"Men," she muttered before turning her attention back to me. "But thank you, Lady—"

"Just Eliah is fine," I interjected, taking a final bite of the orange-infused pastry filled with sweet cream.

She offered a warm smile. "Eliah," she echoed before returning to her own plate while the lady beside her whispered something in her ear.

We all finished eating, wishing our clothes would expand over the fullness of our bellies.

Levon rose from his seat, a glint of anticipation in his eyes. "Now that we're sufficiently satisfied, let us move to the ballroom for some dancing and wine," he announced, prompting everyone to rise in unison, offering their gratitude to the nearby footmen as they made their way out of the dining room. Edmon lingered nearby, accompanied by the enthusiastic girl and the gray-haired lady, their presence triggering memories of our initial encounter.

"Hello, Eliah. Levon," Edmon greeted with the warmth of a towering oak. "Allow me to introduce my sister, Mel, and my mother, Cleola."

Both women offered graceful curtsies, their smiles revealing gleaming teeth.

"Nice to meet you both," I replied with a polite nod.

Levon shifted, embracing Cleola and Mel in turn. "It's wonderful to see you both," he exclaimed, but Cleola's sharp eyes caught sight of Levon's powdered face.

"What happened to you?" she exclaimed, her maternal instincts kicking in as she examined Levon's face with concern, her fingers trying to brush away the powdered façade.

Levon chuckled, his arm wrapping around me. "Training happened," he remarked, pulling me closer, his touch sending a warm flush to my cheeks.

Cleola shot me a playful glare, her eyes twinkling with mischief. "Good, he needs a good beating every once in a while," she teased, prompting a surprised laugh from me as she and Mel followed Edmon into the ballroom.

"And here I thought your only friends were Edmon and Kaizen," I remarked, the latter's absence suddenly weighing heavily on my mind. "Where is—"

"He has other matters to attend to," Levon stated with a smile.

Slowing my pace, I allowed Levon to enter the ballroom ahead of me, taking in the simple yet elegant decor adorned with strings of flowers cascading from the ceiling. It lacked the opulence of Jesri's gatherings, but it possessed a quiet charm sufficient to infuse the evening with a touch of grace.

Levon tugged on my arm, guiding me from one individual to the next. We mingled with people from all corners of Creos and even some from the Eastern Continent. Among them were sun-kissed figures, freshly returned from vacationing in Kleads, while others were Artisans, Merchants, or Publicans. It was a breath of fresh air to interact with such a diverse array of individuals and to encounter people beyond the confines of Fernwen or Jesri's tightly woven network of connections, where all I was ever known as was the *orphan* girl.

After greeting every last person, I collapsed onto a plush couch and took a long sip of the strawberry-lemon wine. Sitting up straight, remembering my etiquette, I surveyed the room, my gaze landing on Levon, who had shed his dark blue coat, leaving it draped over a nearby chair. In the background, the footman from earlier played the pianoforte, setting the backdrop for the lively chatter that ensued. More footmen entered, bearing trays of wine and an array of pastries.

Amidst the commotion, Admearin caught sight of me, the click of her red heels punctuating each step as her sparkling red gown billowed behind her.

"How are you holding up?" she inquired, taking a sip out of her glass, wreathed in her red lipstick, and settled beside me.

I responded with a shrug and a half-hearted smile.

"Well, you seem to be handling it better than I would," she remarked, shaking her head. "Meeting all these people, all at once? No, thank you." She took another long swig of her wine.

"I prefer to observe rather than be the center of attention," I admitted, watching as she finished her drink.

She nodded in agreement. "I despise parties and only attend for Casmir's sake. That man could talk the ear off a statue if given the chance." We shared a laugh as we observed Casmir engaging a group of men, his animated storytelling leaving no room for other conversation.

"I'm glad to know I'm not the only one," I smiled.

With a nudge and a graceful adjustment of her tight dress, she prepared to rise. "Perhaps when Levon and Casmir are distracted doing their duties, you and I can go exploring."

"I'd like that very much," I replied earnestly.

She squeezed my hand affectionately before standing. "I should go rescue those poor men; their ears are probably close to bleeding out," she quipped with a playful grin. After a few steps, she turned back towards me. "It's truly an honor to meet you, Eliah. Levon speaks highly of you, and now I can see why," she added before walking off to the group of men, leaving me to ponder her words.

I shifted uncomfortably in my seat, pretending to take sips of wine and longing to shed the confining dress to indulge in a hot bath.

Levon's gaze met mine, a silent question lingering in his tilted head before he excused himself from his conversations. He crossed the ballroom floor with purpose until he reached me, hand extended.

"Care for a dance?" he asked, his tone hopeful.

"No," I retorted, batting my lashes.

"Then what do you care for?" he mused.

I shot him a sharp glance, caught off guard by the unexpected question. "Why should anything I care for matter to you?" I muttered, aware of the prying eyes that had turned in our direction.

"Because you matter to me, Eliah," he asserted softly, his hand reaching for mine.

Reluctantly, I allowed him to pull me to my feet, aching in my unforgiving heels. I followed him onto the dance floor, acutely aware of the eyes of those around us.

"No one else is dancing," I lamented as he pulled me close, his hand slipping to my waist.

"Then let's give them something to look at," he said, a grin tugging at his lips, drawing me closer to him.

Trust him.

I forced a smile as Levon guided me through the dance. The chatter around us gradually faded as more couples joined in, including Edmon and Jeane, the pretty lady at the market, and Admearin and Casmir. We moved with the music, synchronized with the others, twirling and stepping in harmony until the music came to a lyrical stop, met with a round of applause as more guests joined in for the next dance.

"You're stunning," Levon whispered, his words soft against my ear as he dipped me.

"Don't think flattery will sway me from being angry with you," I countered sharply.

"No? And here I thought a little flattery and some good pastries would do the job," he remarked.

"Perhaps if you weren't so lacking in certain areas, you'd have more admirers beyond superficial things," I taunted as we parted, skillfully rounding the couple next to us before rejoining, his hand placed a bit lower than before.

"And what would it take?" His voice was a whisper against the backdrop of the rising crescendo, sending shivers down my spine and igniting a flush in my cheeks. I sucked in a breath as his hand trailed up my back, leaving a trail of warmth in its wake.

"The truth," I murmured before stepping back, leaving him standing alone amidst the other couples who ended their dance with affection. All I wanted was a drink to cool my reddening cheeks and to escape these tumultuous feelings that danced within me.

As the party drew to a close well into the night, everyone departed with tired, red eyes, yearning for sleep. I could barely muster the energy to climb the stairs to my room before collapsing onto the bed, still fully clothed.

Hours later, I awoke to find my feet aching, still cramped in heels. In the darkness, I kicked off my shoes and shimmied out of the dress, relishing the soft embrace of the sheets as I settled into bed. With a sigh of relief, I unclipped my hair, allowing it to cascade around me, before succumbing to the warm embrace of sleep.

———— ⁺ ✦ ⁺ ————

"Eliah?" The sound of my name jolted me awake, and I was greeted by the warmth of the sun filtering through the window. I rubbed my eyes, adjusting to the light, to find Saasha gathering my dress and shoes into a large tote placed at the foot of the bed.

"Sorry for waking you, but you have a long journey ahead and haven't even packed yet," she explained softly.

"Journey?" I croaked, trying to find my voice.

"You're to leave for the King's Court," she said, questioning.

"Today?" I asked, sitting fully upright, feeling a heavy weight press into my chest.

"No one told you?" she inquired, knitting her brows together.

I rubbed my eyes again, blinking back against the light. "No, no one told me," I muttered, feeling the full weight of leaving bearing down upon me. I sat up and shifted off the bed.

Realizing I was only in my underthings, I hurried to the dresser and swiftly donned a pair of dark green pants and a black top.

"Thank you for waking me. I didn't intend to oversleep," I apologized, quickly weaving my hair into a coronet.

"Don't worry. Most of the staff did, too. We *all* celebrated last night," Saasha reassured me with a smile, deftly packing several of my clothes and dresses into the tote. I hastened to lace up my boots before assisting her with items from the vanity and dresser.

"What does one wear in front of the king?" I murmured, my gaze lingering on the dresses hanging in my armoire.

In a few days, I would be dining with King Thealor, a man I knew so little about besides the endless comments from Jesri, who constantly raved about his Court.

My mind returned to King Leonard and the Leonardian War, where all those innocent Magics were slaughtered. I hoped that I wouldn't be facing that same evil in the eyes of a descendant of a man who destroyed an entire race.

"Anything you wear will be perfect," she said. "I'll finish up here; Levon needs you and is waiting in his study."

I nodded my thanks as I walked to his study. Through the crack of the door, I saw him and Kaizen engrossed in something on his desk. With a soft knock, I pushed the door open.

The two straightened as I stepped in.

"Seems like you had quite the night," Kaizen remarked with a mischievous grin.

"Too bad you didn't," I retorted.

His grin wavered as Levon chuckled and gave him a playful pat on the back. "Can you make sure the carriage is prepared?" Levon instructed, nudging Kaizen toward the door. Kaizen huffed away, his footsteps heavy with irritation.

"Why *didn't* he join us last night?" I inquired again.

"He was patrolling. The Miehja have been acting up," Levon explained. My mind flashed back to the sight of dried blood on Kaizen's hands as he disappeared into the whispering woods a few days prior. "But don't worry, we've stationed guards to keep watch. No harm will come to anyone in my home," he reassured me.

I nodded, hoping his words held true.

He swiftly gathered the papers strewn across his desk, carefully bundling them into a leather satchel. With a quick motion, he tucked his charcoal and rag inside as well. "I promised to show you the truth. Let me stash these in my room, and I'll meet you in the foyer," he said, flashing a reassuring smile before slipping out and heading down the balcony walkway toward his room.

Left alone, I couldn't suppress the mounting unease about the truth I was about to confront. Feeling that it was something I might not be prepared to face.

22

I paced back and forth, anticipation mounting with each hurried step as I waited not only for Levon but also for the foreboding journey to the King's Court.

I glanced out the large crystal windows, seeing several maids and footmen bustling about, carrying food baskets to our totes and trunks. Kaizen conversed with two burly guards, gesturing toward the distant mountains, their nods implying agreement.

"You look more like yourself in those clothes," Levon's voice startled me, and I spun around to find him descending the stairs. "But I must admit, you were breathtaking in that dress last night."

I shook my head, attempting to conceal the rose creeping up my neck and suppress the turmoil of feelings churning in my stomach. With a sigh, I walked toward him as he extended his arm, praying he was finally going to give me the truth.

He guided me toward the long hallway to the small sunroom but stopped at a large painting that occupied more than half of the wall. A stunning ebony-skinned lady with long brown hair was caught mid-twirl, her dress flowing behind her in an elegant cascade of dusted sparkles. Her closed, smiling eyes gleamed brightly, reflecting the familiar face guiding me.

I had never taken the time to admire it or notice its beauty and...familiarity.

"Your...mother?" I breathed. He gave a shallow nod, a brief smile mirroring the lady in the painting. "She's beautiful."

"She was," he said with sadness.

I lifted my eyes to meet his despite the shadow of her presence lingering in his mind. He offered a quick smile and released my arm, running his hand down the side of the golden-rimmed frame. A latch clicked, and he gestured for me to step back. With a fluid motion, he swung the painting open, revealing a small wooden door, its surface recently polished. I gave him a questioning look as he pushed the door open and guided me inside before closing the painting behind us.

The air grew cold and murky as we descended the spiral stone staircase, reminiscent of the one leading down to the kitchen. The only illumination came from faint glows emanating from bits of broken crystal and glass embedded in the walls, reflecting the sunlight or perhaps the luminescence of moonbugs—I couldn't discern which. Yet, the effect was undeniably magical. It felt like we were traveling through stardust, the passageway speckled with countless shades of blue that shimmered and flowed around us, creating an ethereal, otherworldly atmosphere. The light danced on the stone steps, casting a gentle glow that guided our way, transforming the descent into an enchanting fable.

"What is this place?" I rasped, struggling to contain my wonder.

"A part of me that I hold very dear," he replied, his gaze locking with mine as we continued our descent.

His eyes seemed to shimmer more vibrantly than they did in the sunlight. He must have sensed my amazement, for he flashed me a playful smile as we reached the bottom step. The room enveloped us in a radiant glow emanating from swirling shards of luminous stones that seemed *alive*.

A towering stack of books and scrolls stood along one wall while a grand tarnished mirror adorned the opposite side. Its reflection danced off the stones and illuminated the entire space with captivating brilliance.

Another shelf held an array of trinkets and oddities, slowly gathering dust. At the center of the spacious alcove, a large stone jutted out from the surrounding rocks, cradling a shimmering copper box so snugly it seemed inseparable, like a mother holding her child.

"What's that?" I asked, pointing at it. The sight was unlike anything I'd ever seen—the flowing electricity of the box drew me in, tempting me to twirl as Levon's mother had.

"Something I hope will one day see the true light again," he responded cryptically.

"You're speaking in riddles," I remarked, feeling annoyed. "I thought you were going to tell me the truth," I stated, folding my arms.

He responded only with a pearly grin before leading me to the mirror, which was far grander than it initially appeared. Its frame was intricately adorned with silver threads resembling vines, and tiny crystals glowed the same blue as the fragments surrounding us.

"Look. What do you see?" he prompted.

I gazed at my reflection, noticing that my eyes almost mirrored the brilliant blue hues surrounding us and that I appeared leaner and healthier for the first time in my life. My dark auburn hair seemed to radiate with greater intensity, its reds swirling—

"Am I supposed to see something?" I interrupted, growing irritated.

"Look deeper," he urged, stepping up close behind me. I resisted the urge to lean into his warmth, especially considering the chill of the air down here, visible in the wisps of my breath. He closed the distance between us, his hand lightly resting on my forearm as he looked into the mirror. He leaned into my ear. "Find what you do not see," he whispered, his breath caressing down my neck, sending pulsing waves of heat cascading through me, unsure how to feel standing this close to him.

I peered deeper into the tarnished mirror, acutely aware of his proximity—so close it was intoxicating. His hand slid down into mine, and I couldn't help but notice the faint remnants of yellowing bruises on his face, now fading into mere whispers of the incident I still couldn't understand.

However, his eyes shone brighter than ever, mirroring the same vibrant hue as the blues around us and somehow—somehow...like mine, *glowing*.

I blinked to dispel the confusion, then swiftly turned towards him to meet his gaze. His eyes still reflected the swirling blues of the room, though not as vibrant as they appeared in the mirror. Glancing back at the mirror and then returning my gaze to him, I noticed the stark difference.

His lips curled into a subtle smile, barely revealing his teeth, and it dawned on me just how close we had become. I sucked in a sharp breath, feeling the heat spread across my face, neck, and ears.

"You see it," he whispered, his grip tightening on my hand.

"I...I'm not entirely sure what I see," I admitted, my gaze sweeping over the shimmering blues within the small alcove. "What is this place? And please, spare me the riddles."

"This place is made from everything that reminds me of home," he replied softly. "I made it solely on my own."

His mother's face flashed in my mind, her image mirroring the sparkling patterns surrounding us, reminiscent of those on the painting. The vibrant hues of the paint were unlike anything I had seen before; a place like this must have cost a fortune.

Shaking my head, I stepped away from him. "And how is this," I asked, gesturing to our surroundings. "Supposed to reveal the truth to me?"

He looked down, swallowing hard before clearing his throat.

"Eliah, when I called you my queen last night, it wasn't to prove a point to my friends. *You are my Regina*," he confessed, quickly inhaling a sharp breath and turning his back to me. His gaze was fixed on the mirror with a somber expression.

"I first saw you in a market by the Fernwen seaside. You looked sick," he paused, recollecting the memory with sadness. "And so thin," he continued, running his hands through his short hair before facing me again. "Your hair was tied back in a long braid, and you wore a white floral dress that was far too big. You stumbled over your feet. You clung to Calum, pleading for him to stay as he and Jesri left you alone by the carriage while they traversed the markets cavorting with pleasure." He settled his rising voice as his jaw fluttered with an anger I hadn't seen before.

"You kept your head down, swaying as you nervously twisted your dress between your fingers. Your eyes were swollen from crying. You stayed by the carriage, wiping your face," he paused, a subtle smile crossing his face as if the memory of me still vividly played in his mind.

"Once they were out of sight, you straightened your shoulders and left the carriage, slipping away before the footman could notice. Wiping your tears away, you transformed into someone resilient and headstrong. I trailed behind you to the beach, where you kicked off your boots, burying your feet in the sand, inhaling the salty air eagerly. You absorbed everything around you—the view, the sounds, the soft sand underfoot. Your hair fluttered in the wind as you started twirling, just as my mother always did. You danced and splashed, matching the rhythm of the rise and fall of the sea foam, and laughed for joy," he smiled, looking up into my eyes, sending my heart swirling with emotion. "You brought a smile to my lips for the first time in ages."

He approached me, gently clasping my hands and tracing his thumb over my knuckles. "I was still in the royal guard back then. Life wasn't easy, but I knew—I knew I *had to find you*. Someday, somehow, I would meet you—help you. Ensure you never had to shed tears for whatever unpleasantness Jesri or Calum brought upon you."

A glint of silver shimmered in his eyes as he cupped my face in his hands, prompting my own tears. "Eliah, what I did...I had no choice," he faltered. "Once I realized it was Lord Jesri in the tavern that night, I couldn't bear the thought of losing you." A solitary tear trailed down his cheek that he quickly brushed away as he fought back the emotions.

"At first, Jesri believed me to only be a boy, being only in my late teens and crudely dismissed me until he saw the royal insignia on my uniform. He was apologetic and bought me a drink, where he then drunkenly confessed everything to me—every detail of his degrading treatment of you, his intention to sell you like a commodity to all those hungry powered men, with hideous plans and expose you to who knows what horrors. So, I took action. I made sure he agreed to let me train you once you were ready, and I dangled the bone, letting him know I was leaving the Royal Guard and was looking to be in a similar business. I divulged what the king had revealed about hosting a Match unlike any other, and it sent Jesri drooling," he gritted his teeth, his jaw fluttering.

"It kept him tethered to me as he insisted on information, hungry to know when things would be ready. I attempted to intervene early, proposing to train you. Still, he refused, wanting himself to be the one who taught and trained you, in hopes that it would attract enough attention for the king to notice. He grew hostile towards my persistence, so I ceased and maintained a mask of cooperation," he paused abruptly, his fist clenching.

"I *never* anticipated the capacity of his cruelty towards you, and I deeply regret not finding a way to retrieve you sooner, to liberate you by any means necessary. But I saw no alternative," he confessed, tears streaming down his face, mingling with mine as they fell onto the cold, unforgiving stone floor. "I wanted nothing more than to confront him, but I had to continue to play the part and maintain the illusion of being the partner he believed me to be."

We stood there in silence as my heart trembled, gazing into his eyes, which brimmed with regret and sorrow. I tried to summon the memory of dancing by the sea, but it was overshadowed by the rush of thoughts stirred by his story—by the *truth*.

"I don't let people know about my past," he murmured softly, his voice carrying a vulnerability that tugged at my heartstrings. "I don't let them glimpse the shattered pieces inside of me. To see the struggle it is to piece myself back together just to navigate this world that was never ours."

His hand, still cradling my face, tightened gently as he drew closer, his breath warm against my skin. "But you, Eliah...Sabene," he paused, on my middle name, his eyes turned somber. "You are not just anyone. You *are* my queen, now and forever, and I would be honored if you'd have me."

Tears flowed freely down my cheeks as my heart expanded with a turmoil of feelings that rippled through me unchecked.

"Why me?" I breathed, leaning into his rough hand.

He met my gaze, his touch gentle as he brushed away the tears from my cheeks.

"Because I made a promise long ago," he began, his voice a whisper carried on the weight of sincerity. "A vow to be a good man, to protect, to show kindness, and I have traversed every mountain, every valley, desert, and continent to ensure it."

We gazed at each other and felt the despair of our desires to simply be who we were—without acting or having the shackles of others' dreams weighing us down.

More tears flowed freely, a poignant reminder of how deeply I yearned for the naiveness of childhood, where the belief of being loved and remembered was unquestioned.

He gently brushed away my tears, his touch soothing the rawness within. "I never knew my parents, and I've harbored resentment towards them for it. They made me believe that from the very start, I was nothing and would amount to nothing. Jesri reinforced that belief, and Calum...he never fought for me," I lamented.

I let out a frustrated exhale. "I accepted what was handed to me because I convinced myself I deserved it. No matter how much it angered me, I played the role I was expected to play. Always performing, always striving to please, and never truly being able to be who I—what I—" My words faltered, lost in the tangled web of uncertainty and longing.

His confession had stirred something deep within me, a confusing mix of hope and fear, anger and desire. It was as if all the emotions I had suppressed for so long came rushing to the surface, overwhelming me. I felt my chest tighten, my heart pounding with disbelief and yearning. The weight of his words, calling me his queen, was almost too much to bear. How could I ever *be* loved?

My mind raced with memories of all the times I had doubted myself, all the moments I had felt unworthy. Yet, his words chipped away at the walls I had built around my heart, threatening to expose the vulnerable core I had kept hidden for so long. Tears welled in my eyes, and I fought to keep my composure, unsure if I was ready to let someone in completely.

Levon lifted my hand to his shoulder while his other hand clasped mine, drawing me close.

We swayed together in silence, moving as the glowing river of colors surrounded us. With only the sound of our intertwined heartbeats, I found solace in his embrace, a moment of rest from the turmoil within.

"My mother used to say that the music of dance could soothe the mind and soul," he murmured softly.

His touch ignited a fire within me, warming my heart as it spread beneath my skin. I felt the strength in his hand on my back, the roughness of his calloused fingers against mine.

Leaning in, he pressed his forehead against mine, and in an instant, all the anger, hatred, and resentment I held for him melted away, replaced by a newfound understanding, a shared truth.

"I hope one day you'll discover yourself, Eliah," he whispered, his voice tender and sincere. "And perhaps your parents *did* wish the best for you. Maybe the circumstances they left you in were better than their own."

Sadness flickered within me, and I was unwilling to accept such a notion. Yet his words planted a seed of doubt, a tiny glimmer of hope that perhaps there was more to my story than I had ever dared to imagine. That I was more than all this. But how could anyone want me if even my own parents, the people who are supposed to love you unconditionally didn't even want me?

"*I* want you, Eliah Sabene," he declared huskily, drawing me closer as his hands encircled my waist.

I lifted my gaze to his, confused about how he knew just what to say, and took a deep breath, the cool air filling my lungs, its crispness a stark contrast to the heat of my racing heart. My mind raced between the desire to believe his words and the fear of what that belief might bring.

Could I trust him? Could I allow myself to believe in his words?

The warmth of his touch stirred a desperate yearning for connection and truth within me. I longed to trust him, but the weight of past betrayals and the haunting memories of twisted truths held me back, leaving me vulnerable. His eyes, filled with intensity and sincerity, seemed to promise a different future—one where I could finally be who I truly was.

We paused our swaying, the energy between us crackling like sparks dancing in the vibrant glow surrounding us. His touch sent shivers down my spine, burning a trail of warmth along my arm that seemed to set my skin ablaze. My cheeks flushed, the heat spreading to my neck and ears as his hand traced a delicate path up to my jawline.

"I don't know if I'm worth wanting," I breathed less than a whisper.

A tender smile curved his lips, his gaze unwavering as he gently lifted my chin. "Eliah," he murmured, his voice brimming with sincerity. "You're worth every journey across oceans and worlds, every moment until this one. You're worth it all."

My breath hitched as our breaths mingled. His thumb traced my lips, shooting stars into my vision as time seemed to pause. He looked down at my mouth, then back into my eyes, silently pleading, yearning. Flames surged through me, stinging my ears and cheeks as if they were alight with fire that melted away all logical sense.

He cradled my face in his strong, callused hands, each rough edge telling a story of his past sorrows and desires, all centering on me. His beautiful eyes blurred together as his lips brushed mine, setting my entire being ablaze with a fire much different from how I felt with Calum.

In an instant, his touch turned rigid, the tenderness replaced by a sudden tension that gripped his frame. With a sharp intake of breath, he swiftly pulled away, dropping his hands as his gaze darted towards the stairs with an urgency that set my heart racing.

I followed his line of sight as my eyes locked with Kaizen's, who was radiating fury and seemed ready to attack.

23

"What in Giesha is your plan, *Levon*?" Kaizen's words slashed like a whip, cracking the once passionate air, each syllable dripped with venomous derision.

In an instant, Kaizen was at my side, his fingers like iron claws, as he seized my arm and thrust me toward the stairs. But before I could react, Levon intercepted him with angry determination.

"Take your hands off her," Levon growled, tearing Kaizen's grip from my arm and shielding me behind his towering frame. "I've had *enough* of your help. *Go,*" he said, pointing back to the stairs.

Kaizen puffed an airy laugh filled with mockery. "*You know I can't do that,*" he hissed between clenched teeth. "You'll end up being the one to kill her before the others get a chance."

My gaze snapped to Levon, whose expression hardened in response to Kaizen's threatening words.

"Others?" I demanded, stepping out from behind Levon's protective stance, my voice trembling with urgency. "What do you mean, *others*?"

"You will, Levon. It's *forbidden*. Remember *your* place," Kaizen spat, taking hold of Levon's collar. The room's cool blues morphed into searing oranges and reds as if reflecting Kaizen's simmering anger.

"*I don't care.* I've waited long enough and won't waste my time any longer," Levon countered, forcefully pushing Kaizen's hands away.

"You don't care?" Kaizen snapped with enough hatred I took a step back.

The two of them snarled at each other with venom, having that silent conversation within their eyes. Levon's jaw clenched, and with purpose, he turned toward me, reaching out for my hand. But I hesitated, retreating and watching the once tranquil blue ambiance erupt into a tumult of fiery hues, painting the room in shades of crimson and gold as if they reflected the feelings in the room.

"The truth, Levon," I interjected, looking back to him and suppressing my confusion and rising fear. Kaizen scoffed as a smug grin spread across his face, crossing his arms over his chest. He shot Levon a challenging glare, silently daring him to speak.

Levon's jaw tensed, his eyes flashing with a mixture of anger and frustration as he locked gazes with Kaizen. "I thought we were on the same side," Levon seethed, his voice tight with suppressed emotion.

"We are, but I think it's time she knows *the truth*," Kaizen replied, his tone heavy with brooding intensity. Levon bristled, puffing up his chest with irritation.

"This is *my life* you're both toying with. *No more secrets*," I rasped out, my frustration simmering beneath the surface. Despite my wish that Kaizen had never intervened, a part of me was grateful for the potential knowledge he might bring. "*No more.*"

Levon stood there looking in shock and anger. Kaizen growled lowly, waiting for Levon to answer.

"Eliah," Levon began, his voice strained with hesitation. The vibrant scarlet hues of the crystals surrounding us began to soften, returning to their tranquil blues. "Eliah, you're being..." His voice faltered as he fought against the truth with sorrowful eyes.

"Say it," I demanded, my voice quivering with fear.

"That day at the markets, when you asked about the Spellcasters," Levon continued, each word heavy with dread. My blood ran cold at the unexpected mention of them. "They are just as malicious and evil as you feared. And..." he paused, the truth catching in his throat. "They're *hunting* you."

He instantly held my arms, anchoring me as my limbs went slack.

"Hunting?" I breathed; my mind spun with a whirlwind of dread and endless questions, suffocating as if the air itself had been sucked from my lungs.

"We won't let them touch you, Eliah. I swear," he vowed, his words a flicker of hope in the abyss of my terror. He clung to my hands. My heart pounded in my ears, drowning out all else as he pressed on, his voice dripping with desperate urgency.

"Their leader, he feeds on the fears of our souls," Levon's voice quivered with horror and disbelief, each word heavy with the weight. "They all infiltrate minds, dreams, and even the earth beneath us. I didn't want to believe it during our breathing exercises, before your evaluation, or when you wouldn't wake up after our encounter," he said, gesturing towards his barely bruised face. "Or with the Miehja attack..." His voice trailed off, his gaze distant as if haunted by the memories.

"Before Creos' civil war between the Magics and the Mundanes, the Spellcasters were once ordinary...Magics, wielding their abilities for good, or so many thought. Rumors spread about certain Magics delving too greedily into their powers and breaching boundaries that should have never been crossed. From their leader, they birthed a darkness that twisted their magic into something horrific that should have never existed in time or here in this realm," he paused, looking towards Kaizen. "This was the beginning of the Cataclysm." I narrowed my brows, trying to remember ever hearing of the Cataclysm in any of the history lessons Jesri demanded I take, but none came to mind.

The two of them glanced at each other again, having that annoying silent conversation with their eyes before Levon continued.

"King Leonard foresaw the devastation these Spellcasters would bring and attempted to contain the threat through tests and trials. But when the people rebelled, Creos plunged into civil war, starting the Great Cataclysm in more than just..." he stopped, quickly glaring at Kaizen. "More than just this world, and therefore, King Leonard had no choice but to eradicate all Magics for the safety of his Kingdom and his people."

"Peace reigned for years here in this world," he said as if he could recall being in such times. "Until a group known as the Onyx Market arose—a group of bounty hunters targeting those few individuals whose lineage possessed magic, and branding them as threats to society. Falsehoods spread like wildfire, and bounties were placed on any leads to a Magic, leading to countless disappearances in the dead of night for a wealthy sum. Even those innocent souls, devoid of any magic, vanished without a trace," a single tear slid down his cheek, which he quickly wiped away.

He drew in a sharp breath, his fists clenching with anguish.

"When I was in the Royal Guard, I had no option but to obey orders and follow these rumors to see if they were true."

The air thickened, turning the tranquil blue hues into a torrent of dark purples that seemed to swallow the room, mirroring the same turmoil within me. Instantly, I regretted almost kissing him, regretted coming here, allowing him to train me and lull me into submission.

I stepped back, speechless, feeling the tendrils of darkness from my dreams cling to my mind as if it were simply making itself comfortable.

"Eliah," Levon said, reaching out. I yanked my arm back from him as anger sliced through me like a tidal wave.

"*Are you still on that mission?*" I snapped, now shaking with anger. The mere suggestion that *I* could possess any trace of magic ignited a blaze of indignation within me.

His eyes darkened, the air around us crackling with an intense amber glow, swirling with fiery reds, scorching yellows, and gleaming golds. We swiftly turned our gaze to the shimmering crystals, the room pulsating with tension.

"I told you *I left that years ago*," Levon anguished, his emotions rising.

"*Then why*? Why are the Spellcasters hunting me?" I spat, the words bitter on my tongue.

Kaizen answered before Levon could interject. "All we know is that the Spellcasters have never stopped hunting for what they want most: immortality and power, and they'll stop at nothing to chase even the faintest whisper of a lead."

Fear began clawing at my insides. "What makes them believe I hold anything of value?" I pressed, forcing my voice to remain firm despite the tremble in my limbs.

Levon interjected, "Before dinner yesterday, you mentioned a dream. What was it?"

The memory of the shadowy figure flashed vividly in my mind, causing me to reflexively clasp my wrists, still feeling the icy touch of the manacles. Levon and Kaizen looked at me expectantly, waiting for me to elaborate.

"After...whatever happened," I began, gesturing towards Levon's face. "I believe I wasn't able to wake because I was trapped. Trapped in a cold...dark cell, chained to the ground like some kind of wild animal. There was so much fear and darkness that it felt tangible, as if it *knew* who I was and where to find me."

I released a shaky breath, trying to push away the memories of blood-curdling screams and the haunting image of the shadowy figure with its long, spider-like fingers wrapping around my throat. Unconsciously, now clutching at my own.

"A dark figure knew me by name," I stuttered, not wanting to relive it further, fearing what it might mean.

Kaizen went ridged as Levon huffed angrily, staring at me like they had seen a wraith.

Kaizen interjected. "With their leader, the Spellcasters found a way to fabricate neural pathways through hellish anomalies in their magic—the things that connect everything," he paused, disgust and anger radiating from him like the color surrounding us. "They have found something within your mind—the slightest of memories you had as a child, something you witnessed, or something that caused a rift they could see through for their filthy desires."

"You're telling me *they* are causing these...tremors—these dreams?" I said, barely above a whisper.

"The dreams, yes," Kaizen said as the two of them nodded, sickening my stomach. I stepped back, trying to take it all in. My breath caught in my throat as I attempted to swallow, but my mouth went dry as fear crept in like tendrils of darkness, swirling my mind with confusion. I clenched my fists together to stop the trembling.

"If you still have a warrant to silence these rumors," I mocked Levon before turning my gaze to Kaizen. "Then what is *your* role in all this?" I ordered, coiling my anger and trying to understand any of this.

Levon clenched his teeth, a glint of remorse flickering in his eyes.

"To protect you," Kaizen stated flatly.

I couldn't help but emit a hollow laugh, feeling utterly numb. "But you're both, somehow, on the same team?" I mocked again, glaring at Levon.

"That's *why I left,*" Levon snapped, holding my gaze angrily. "I didn't know what all those secret missions would entail, but I *had* to do my duty. For more reasons than you could *ever* understand."

Kaizen gripped Levon's arm, backing him down, as my hands shook with anger.

Levon shook off Kaizen's hand, his focus sharpening on me. "I'm not looking for pity, Eliah," he declared, his voice edged with bitterness. "Every day, the choices I made haunt me, but they were necessary for the greater good. I acted in service of the essential objective, regardless of the consequences. And I intend to honor my promise to her," he nodded towards the stairs, where his mother's portrait hung. "No matter what, I won't allow anyone to harm you. I swear it," he vowed, his tone resolute.

I absorbed his words, trying to steady my emotions amidst the creeping fear that the Spellcasters had *infiltrated* my mind. They were not merely a made-up bedtime story to scare a child into submission but a real threat skulking in the shadows.

"Then what about the King's Match?" I demanded, releasing my grip on my emotions and searching for truth in his emerald-blue gaze.

"We proceed as if nothing is amiss. We will be safest within the King's Court, and I have allies who are keeping me informed," Levon replied.

"How long have you known the Spellcasters created these...pathways in me?" I pressed, my tone sharp with accusation.

He met my gaze wearily. "Not until after your first evaluation," he confessed quietly.

"Were you *ever* planning on telling me?" I demanded.

"Would you have believed me if I had told you sooner?" he retorted. "You barely trusted me, assuming me as arrogant as Jesri."

"You're not disproving that point," I seethed, feeling the pulse of the amber glow in the room resonating within me, leaving the air thick with tension.

Kaizen cleared his throat. "We need to leave, it's a long journey to the Creaic Gap, and we shouldn't be out after dark," he stated, his gaze shifting to Levon with a silent warning.

Levon nodded his agreement as Kaizen ascended the stairs. Leaving us trailing after him in uneasy silence.

"Why subject me to this tournament then? Won't participating make me an even bigger target?" I hissed, looking at Levon with sunken shoulders. "You claimed you had no choice; let me make one." Desperation lined my voice.

"Eliah, I...I can't," he replied, his voice strained. "There's too much at stake to pull you out now. Jesri would demand your return, and who knows what he'd do to you next. And if the king knew, he'd send even more scrutiny your way." His desperation was evident as he took my hand, his eyes pleading for understanding.

"As far as we know, *no one* knows you're the one the Spellcasters are targeting with their mind-scraping. Casmir told me that the Onyx Market is in disarray trying to identify individuals, but they're hitting dead ends. The 'Casters aren't divulging any information to the hunters this time, and we fear the reasons behind their silence are bigger than we can comprehend."

"Casmir?" I replied softly, not believing that friendly silver-haired man to be a part of such schemes. "And how do you plan to protect me against all this?"

His hand trembled as he halted me on the stairs.

"We'll protect you, no matter what it takes. I won't allow anything to harm you ever again," he swore, squeezing my hand tightly. "We hope that if you become champion, the king will deploy his forces to safeguard you, grant you freedom, and it will all be worth it."

"*But why?* Why me?" I whimpered, the words escaping before I could stop them. "Why protect me when you've slain so many others?" Instantly, I regretted my words as I saw the hurt in his eyes turn to smoldering anger.

"Because without you...life itself would cease to exist," he muttered, turning away, ascending the stairs, and disappearing through the door. I stood there, breathless and confused, still wondering why. An immovable fear began to gather in my mind and heart as I stood there, uncertain if I should be grateful for finally receiving answers.

+ ✦ +

I emerged from the secret alcove, determined to maintain a façade of strength despite the fear coursing through me. I refused to succumb to it. Whatever lay ahead, I was determined to face it head-on. Even if it meant risking everything, I was prepared to fight for my freedom.

After quickly eating a light breakfast, I said my goodbyes to Elise and Saasha, not allowing my emotions to spread further, and hurriedly went outside, soaking in every last ounce of this grand estate, the tall evergreens I'd grown to love, the glimmering views of town off in the distance, but having a foreboding feeling that I wouldn't see it again.

Levon conversed with several staff members at the carriage door while Kaizen sat as the coachman, holding the reins as the horses pawed impatiently. I thanked the people lining the estate, appreciating their well-wishes, before taking Levon's hand. He helped me into his sleek, velvet-lined carriage, the rich fabric and polished wood gleaming in the afternoon light as my stomach turned leaden with worry.

He began to close the carriage door, but a palpable discomfort hung around him. "I'll be with Kaizen until we reach the Creaic Gap, where we'll stop at an inn. We hope to arrive at the King's Court by sundown tomorrow," he explained, managing a faint smile before bidding farewell to the others and clicking the door in place.

"Levon," I began, catching him through the open window before he could join Kaizen. "Thank you."

He looked down, not meeting my eyes. "I might be beyond redemption, but I'm simply trying to improve. That's all I have left." His words carried a weight of regret and determination, revealing the depth of more sinister things happening.

He stepped from view and hopped onto the driver's seat, rocking the carriage before the horses moved and propelled us forward.

I wasn't sure whether to be thankful for the peace or upset. I sighed, annoyed at myself for being frustrated with him—frustrated by his unsettling past, the orders he shouldn't willingly have followed and every painful detail I was unprepared to hear. Perhaps I should have remained in ignorance.

I rubbed at my eyes, hoping to dispel the tumult of emotions as we entered the woods where Kaizen first found me, bloodied and a mess. I prayed that that would be the last time I'd ever encounter the Miehja.

I inhaled the sweet pine scent mixed with the dry dirt rising from the carriage wheels.

Inhale.

Exhale.

The world was *much* bigger than I could have ever thought possible, and the problems deadlier than I imagined.

The shadowy figure flashed before my eyes, my name like claws on its tongue. I shivered, pushing the image away.

"They feed on the fears of our souls," I muttered to myself, the weight of those words settling heavily in my chest.

I sucked in a sharp breath, feeling the carriage sway beneath me, a physical reminder of the uncertain journey ahead.

"I am afraid," I admitted quietly, the truth hanging heavy in the air.

—— · ✦ · ——

The dense trees gradually gave way to gentle, rolling hills and valleys and vibrant cities bustling with life. As I watched the bustle beyond, I couldn't help but think of what I might never encounter again—tasting Mrs. Bleel's savory dishes, savoring the fragrance of exotic spices, hearing the giggles Elise might exclaim after a stolen kiss or Saasha's cheesy grin.

I hadn't anticipated missing Desrin as much as I did. I never thought I'd find solace beyond the confines of Jesri's elegant estate. Yet, I was undeniably mistaken, and the fleeting taste of freedom felt liberating.

However, with each rhythmic thud of the carriage wheels against the stone road, propelling us northward towards a court I wanted no part of, that sense of liberation slipped further from my grasp. Towards an uncertain future, with a king and his ridiculous Match to feed his court's appetite, or toward demise with the Spellcasters and the Onyx Market.

I scraped at my nails and tugged at my hair and sleeves, growing increasingly impatient and desperate for answers. I yearned to talk, to distract myself from the mounting tension. Grabbing the book from my satchel, I read through its pages until it became unbearable to look down for another moment. The memory of the light breakfast I shared while conversing with Elise and Saasha churned in my stomach, threatening to resurface.

Leaning against the window's opening, I focused on calming my breath, quieting my racing thoughts, and soothing my restless soul, anything to distract myself.

I sat up straight, irritated as Levon's secret alcove breached my mind. I replayed the sensation of his lips against mine and what it meant. Butterflies fluttered in my stomach, but I forcefully pushed the image away, shaking my head to rid myself of the thought.

How could I be infatuated with him, of all people? One who is working with Jesri but is...kind? One who desires my freedom but makes no move to get me out of this Match? How could I let myself feel these emotions when all my life I've only ever been told to hide them and push them down, to believe that all I was good for was as a weapon? But no matter how hard I tried, the butterflies didn't dissipate; they only made my heart flutter more intensely.

Touching my lips, I let out an exasperated breath, forcing my thoughts to quiet. Determined to focus on the present and not get tangled in emotions I had no business exploring, I settled against the window, counting the sparse trees that passed by before I drifted off to sleep.

The carriage lurched to a sudden stop, jolting me forward. Grunting in frustration, I caught myself on the velvety seat opposite, then sat up and peered out the window. The carriage swayed from side to side until Levon came into view, adjusting his dark tunic after hopping down. He walked to the door and pulled it open.

"We wanted to stop and stretch our legs for a moment," he explained, extending his hand wrapped in a black leather glove.

I accepted it, quickly smoothing my hair and wiping my face, hoping I didn't appear too disheveled from sleeping. Stepping out, I relished the sweet, lush scent of the surroundings. We found ourselves amidst an ocean of open fields and tall, swaying stalks, with a large mountain looming in the distance. Inhaling deeply, I rolled my shoulders and stretched my neck, glancing up to see Kaizen standing atop the carriage, surveying the fields.

"We're safe," Levon quickly added, noticing my frown. I managed a curt nod before he gestured for me to join him at the back of the carriage, where he opened a box filled with leathered fruit, nuts, bread, and dried meat. He grabbed a handful of everything and handed some to me, tossing more up to Kaizen, who caught it effortlessly.

"How close are we to the Creaic Gap?" I inquired.

"About another two to three hours," he replied, clearing his throat before taking a bite of bread and meat. I followed suit, taking a few bites, surprised by how hungry I was, and quickly finished the handful he gave me.

"I'll join you inside if you don't mind," he asked, his eyes glinting in the full sun. I gave him a slight nod before he whistled up to Kaizen. "Let's head out; I'll sit with Eliah," he called out to Kaizen.

Kaizen looked at him knowingly and hopped down to his driver's seat, taking the reins in his hands. Levon opened the carriage door and helped me inside before the carriage lurched forward, carrying us away and across the swaying green sea of hills.

"I'm surprised by how open it is out here," I remarked, still gazing at the rolling hills, attempting to break the awkward silence.

"King Thealor prefers these lands for farming," he said with a smile, gazing out at the green expanse. "You'll miss the openness here once we pass the Gap."

"Is it busier than the town?" I asked, not sure how anything could be more chaotic than that. He nodded, prompting my mind to wander to visions of the King's Court.

Awkwardness hung heavily between us as we sat fidgeting, each waiting for the other to initiate more small talk. He cleared his throat, opening his mouth as if to speak, but then hesitated, opting to glance out the window again, admiring the sense of freedom beyond.

"I apologize for my comments earlier. It was a lot to handle all at once," I confessed, feeling the weight of my admission. "But thank you for telling me the truth." The sincerity in my words conveyed my gratitude for finally being given clarity after years of uncertainty, even though the weight of it scraped my heart.

He looked at me, his expression surprised, his mouth slightly agape and eyebrows raised.

"Is the Lady Eliah apologizing to me *and* thanking me?" he teased, shifting slightly closer to his seat across, a hint of amusement playing on his lips.

"Don't expect me to hand them out freely," I retorted, narrowing my eyes. The tension eased as we shared a brief moment of lightness.

"*I apologize* for leaving you with questions," he confessed, his voice full of remorse. "I didn't want to share the reality when we didn't fully understand it ourselves. When we first met, it took every ounce of my soul to keep silent about the tournament and the evaluation. Jesri was worried you would act out. He forced me not to say anything, threatening to cancel his deal, and I'd risk losing you...again." His head hung as he clasped his hands and leaned forward on his legs.

"I couldn't risk losing you," he continued, his tone softening with admiration. "You were so much stronger than Jesri led on. Fearless, determined to fulfill your dreams to obtain freedom, no matter the cost. You were far more formidable than the girl I remembered against the seaside." His words carried a mix of awe and affection.

A flush of red spread across my cheeks as I cleared my throat, trying to quell the rising feeling. "Do you have any more details about what this Match might involve?" I asked, hoping Edmon had provided more information.

His expression turned blank. "No, it became too risky, and we didn't want the king to trace it back to us. Especially since he's obsessed with surprises and has been known to imprison anyone who spoils it," he explained, his voice tense. Taking a deep breath, he averted his gaze and started to tap his foot nervously. "I'm sorry," he stammered. "For everything. I didn't know what else to do to grant you freedom...to keep you safe."

I hesitantly touched his arm. His eyes met mine, forcing me to retract my hand. But understanding washed over me—realizing his promise to his ailing mother, vowing to be a good man, but becoming ensnared in the evil and misery of the world. Yet, he found his own path to freedom and tried to help others find theirs—people like Elise, Saasha, and me. I offered him a sad smile, observing the weight of his choices bearing down on him. It made me wonder if not all men were inherently malicious, as Jesri had often claimed.

"I do vow to protect you, Eliah. Always," he declared solemnly as he took my hands in his. His expression softened as he gazed into my eyes. "I pledge my life to you and will honor that promise. Bitter words and a fiery heart mean nothing if not from you. I am not easily broken; know I am yours now and forever."

My breath caught in my throat as he glanced at my lips, igniting a flurry of emotions that danced down my body. Irritation bubbled within me, frustrated at myself for craving the touch of his soft lips. Yet, there was a newfound sense of *freedom* in being desired by someone as flawed as I was. It dawned on me that my brokenness could be the very thing that someone might cherish fully, unlike the fleeting infatuation I had with Calum.

I wished I could go back and tell my younger self that good things were on the horizon, urging her to hold on a little longer. The label of an unloved, forgotten ward didn't define me entirely—it was just a fraction of who I was. Beyond my scars and past traumas, I *was* desirable, and this realization filled me with hope and empowerment but frustrated me with the longing to be touched by him.

"I'm still upset at you," I taunted, breaking the growing silence.

"It wouldn't be you if you weren't," he smiled, letting go of my hands and leaning against the carriage wall.

The sun shone through the carriage, casting shadows across his face as we rode on through more fields of green. His face was still marred with yellowing bruises along the small scar barely visible under his jawline.

"What happened?" I asked, causing him to cock his head in question. "To your face, I mean," I said with a swallow.

His jaw fluttered as he glanced back out the window. "One moment, you were yelling at me; the next, I was in my room with Saasha stitching me up." He turned to look at me, a tight smile on his lips. "Believe me, I've been through much worse."

"Did I do that to you?"

He only stared at me, slightly shaking his head but not answering.

A hard lump formed in my throat as I tried to force down the gnawing fear from their tales about the Spellcasters and bounty hunters.

We rode in silence as awkward tension filled the air, drowning out all the noise from earlier.

He cleared his throat, "Did you always enjoy pastries?" he asked rather abruptly.

I couldn't suppress my laughter quickly enough at the unexpected question. "Well, as you know, Jesri was never keen on letting me indulge in anything delicious. So I had Calum sneak me sweets, then Aoife joined in too, knowing Jesri had enough and wouldn't notice they were missing."

He smiled fondly, "My mother and I used to walk to her favorite pastry shop every Saturday before she fell ill, and I think that's why I fell even harder for you at the Spring Harvest Celebration because of your love for pastries."

"Oh?" I teased, feeling the blush creeping back up my cheeks and flutter into my heart. "And here I thought you were too drunk on the wine?"

He grinned, "Or perhaps too drunk on the notion that I was finally with you?"

My heart pattered, and the churn in my stomach turned into butterflies, blushing my cheeks.

He looked up at me with a chuckle, "You hide your emotions very well," he mused, crossing his foot over his knee.

I couldn't help but suppress a grin. "Well, if you didn't say such things, perhaps I wouldn't have to."

We shared a chuckle, the tension between us melted away with each passing moment. His gaze turned tender as he looked back at me, putting his leg back down and leaning forward.

"I mean it; I am yours now and forever, Eliah," he declared, his hand finding mine on my knee, sending a shiver of warmth through me at his touch.

He moved closer, intertwining our legs. "You'll never wrong me, Eliah," he whispered, his voice a soothing balm to my racing heart.

24

The Creaic Gap was more daunting than I had imagined. Its jagged gray cliffs jutted into the air like towering pillars, merging into the carved-out mountains still capped with snow. The fading light seemed to cling to the fog swirling in the air as the clouds loomed overhead, refusing to break formation around the Gap. The chill in the air intensified, coursing through me with a shiver. I exhaled slowly, stretching my legs one last time before we set off to find the inn that Levon had said was hidden within the mountain itself. The entire landscape felt stifling as if the atmosphere was thick with the same dread enveloping me.

The bright oranges and pinks of the sunset finally succumbed to the elements, giving way to an inky sky. To the right of us was a sea of farming fields that stretched on for miles, broken up by scattered large trees that blew in the breeze. To our left was the towering mountain carved out to form a jagged wall.

I took a deep breath, the cooling night air sharp in my lungs, and felt grateful for the long sleeves I had opted for.

"We shouldn't be out this late. Let's get moving," Kaizen grumbled, walking past me and climbing into the driver's seat.

Levon helped me back into the carriage, and we rode along the tall wall, passing a few inn outposts gleaming with lanterns as the sun faded further, turning the sky a deep indigo. Only the light of our lantern guided us now, casting an eerie glow that illuminated the fog swirling around us before we finally came to a stop.

"I need to go let them know we're here to open the carriage entrance. I'll be right back," Levon said, stepping out of the carriage and vanishing into the darkness. The carriage remained still, and knowing that Kaizen was still with me brought a sense of calm. I watched the line of lanterns flicker on the wall through the window, casting shadows against the large wooden door Levon walked through.

The carriage swayed, and the door slammed open, startling a curse out of me as Kaizen gripped the sword at his hip.

"*Move. Now*," he hissed, extinguishing the lanterns. Fear gripped my heart, compelling me to stay close to him. He clutched my arm, guiding me until we were between the carriage and the horses, who also stood frozen, their ears twitching, listening to whatever Kaizen had sensed.

"What is it?" I whispered urgently. He clasped my mouth with his calloused hand, his face inches from mine as his vibrant amber eyes scanned the surroundings.

I slowed my breathing and strained to hear what he had detected—a series of eerie clicking noises that slithered and swayed against the chirping of crickets, which stopped intermittently. My heart pounded in my ears as I searched his wide eyes for answers.

We stood frozen as the clicking grew louder, the rustling moving closer until a sharp click sounded to our right, only mere feet away. Kaizen let go of my mouth and shoved a dagger into my hands.

"When I say run—"

Laughter erupted from the mountainside as a cascade of lights broke through the darkness, blinding us, indicating the inn opened the carriage opening. The clicking instantly stopped, vanishing along with the shadows.

Levon came into view, standing frozen, looking to Kaizen's unsheathed sword and then to my fearful eyes. Several large men behind Levon approached the back of the carriage and took our trunks. I stepped back from Kaizen, forcing my trembling to subside and finding my breath again. I quickly placed the dagger behind my back and regretted not wearing my leathers.

Levon paced towards us, exchanging a worried look with Kaizen. Kaizen subtly nodded, and stepped forward, gripping the reins, and led the horses and carriage toward a large opening that had appeared in the mountainside, with stalls and other carriages stowed within.

I steadied my breathing as Levon peered into the darkness, guiding me to the front door of the inn. He kept a constant watch over his shoulder, keeping me close until we were safely inside. The door closed firmly behind us, sealing out the night.

Inside, the warmth and light were a welcome contrast to the cold outside. Levon's breathing was ragged with fear and anger, drowning out my thoughts amidst the chatter, the clinking of dishes, and the smack of cards.

I turned to find several groups gathered around tables, laughing and enjoying themselves. They guzzled down golden liquid, played cards, and savored their meals. My stomach grumbled at the enticing aroma of food, prompting me to move closer, hoping to ease the tremors of fear within me.

Levon reached for my hand and pulled me into a quick embrace, breathing in as a shuddering breath escaped his lips. "Eat first, then we'll talk."

I nodded as he led me toward a pale-skinned man with a beard as dark as night.

"Well, isn't it little Alder all grown up, yet somehow still looking as youthful as the first day we met," the man said, grabbing two large wooden plates and walking back to the large stone oven, where several pots and pans were simmering. The warmth and rich smells filled the air, thawing my frozen fear. We both managed to smile.

"And isn't it little Jucam all grown up, looking more like an old man with that beard?" Levon replied with a tease, which made the man full on belly laugh. He returned with the plates, setting them down before us, piled with delicious food, which made my stomach ache with hunger.

"How long has it been? Mam's been so upset you never returned and has waited every fall and winter for you," he said, scratching his beard.

Levon's smile became genuine as he shook his head. "A few years. I wanted to come back, but plans changed," Levon stated, glancing at me.

Jucam's raven eyes skimmed me and smiled.

"Eliah, this is Faren Jucam, owner of this fine inn and the best cook around," Levon said.

I gave him a tense smile and a curt nod, trying my best not to glance back at the large wooden door, praying it was strong enough to hold whatever was out there. Levon squeezed my hand, bringing me back to the present.

"Nice to meet you, milady." Jucam pushed the plates forward, "On the house. Just make sure to tell Mam hi before you leave, or she'll have my hide."

Levon laughed in agreement and nodded his thanks. He took the two plates and guided me toward an empty table farthest from the door. He pulled out a chair for me and then sat down himself.

"Eat first," he reminded me, touching my shaking knee.

Inhale.

I took a bite, hoping my grumbling stomach wouldn't attract attention, and was hit with an explosion of flavor that instantly distracted me from my fears. The lemon and onion potatoes, seasoned with some exotic spice, danced on my taste buds while the juicy roast warmed my belly and soul.

Levon laughed, breaking me out of my trance.

I covered my mouth, still chewing. "This is amazing."

"Jucam was in the Royal Cookery before he left to come here," Levon explained.

"I'm sure King Thealor was not happy about that," I remarked, taking another juicy bite of the shallots mixed with fiery greens, perfectly spiced.

"He wasn't. But Jucam became a father, and the king knows the importance of family," Levon said before taking another bite.

"The king?" I said, sneering slightly. "I don't know if I ever thought King Thealor to be a family man."

He only laughed as we both finished off our plates with satisfaction. He wiped at his lips with his thumb, a gesture that sent a thrill of butterflies bounding in my chest. I found myself unable to meet his gaze, instead wringing my hands with the urge not to reach out and touch him, refusing to allow myself to harbor such *feelings* for him. But deep down, I knew that he was nothing like Jesri or those pompous men, that he *was* kind, and he was trying the best he could to help me obtain my dreams no matter what bind he was in.

I stood. "We've eaten."

He nodded and grabbed the plates, walking back toward Jucam to express his thanks before returning and taking my hand. He led me down a long hallway lined with moss and scattered doors, stopping at one deep within the mountain. The cold air sent a chill down my spine as he opened the door. Kaizen was sitting on the large bed at its center, eating his share of the savory food. He seemed unbothered and continued with his meal as we entered.

Levon let go of my hand and locked the door behind us. I scanned the cool, stone room. Our trunks sat at the far end of the wall, where a narrow hallway led to another small room with a single bed. My surprise surpassed the novelty of an inn carved out from a mountainside, and I was impressed by the decent accommodations.

Levon walked to a closed door on the right and opened it with a smirk. "It looks like you're blessed and will be able to relieve yourself during the night," he teased, a faint echo of our first night at that inn weeks ago. Despite the tension in the air, I managed a weak smile.

I brushed off the awkwardness, noticing Kaizen's confused face, and walked toward the smaller room on the left, glancing inside.

"I don't know if I should be called blessed with a potential *bounty* on my head, let alone the Spellcasters *hunting* me," I remarked, the weight of my situation settling heavily on my shoulders.

"We are safe here," Levon retorted, his voice carrying a hint of defiance, while Kaizen finished off his plate with a stoic expression. I shot a glare at Kaizen, demanding answers.

"We are," Kaizen reiterated, his tone unwavering.

"What was that outside?" I snapped, still looking to Kaizen, waiting for an explanation as my heart pounded with anticipation.

Kaizen took a deep breath. "I believe it might have been a Breva, but I've only heard of their lore," he said, wiping his mouth. Levon's expression grew pale as I awaited further explanation.

Rising from the bed, he moved with a sense of purpose, setting his plate near the door as his cloak trailed behind him with regal elegance. "They're blind," he explained, his voice carrying a hint of urgency, "and rely on echospotting to navigate. It allows them to sense objects and blend into their surroundings. If I hadn't been on edge and noticed the subtle slithering, I might have mistaken the clicking sounds for insects."

I tried to push the horrifying image out of my mind. "Are they similar to the Miehja? Are these creatures bred by the Spellcasters?" I asked, wrapping my arms around myself for comfort.

"The Miehja are bred to kill," Kaizen paused, his gaze flickering to Levon before continuing. "The Breva are bred to capture and report. They attack by striking with a poison, paralyzing you and slowing your heartbeat to barely a breath while they swallow you whole and slither back to deliver their report." His voice darkened. "But whatever you do, do not let one take you. *Run away as far and as fast as you can.* Because if they take you—" he stopped abruptly, shaking his head, unwilling to entertain the thought.

Bile coated my throat as I shivered at the thought of one of us being attacked—taken. "The Spellcasters know where we are then?" I whispered, feeling a chill run down my spine. Levon came beside me and squeezed my hand in silent comfort, though it felt more like an apology.

"I suspect one was lurking nearby and caught your scent," Levon replied with a hint of disgust. "We'll have to be on high alert as we pass through the Gap."

"My scent?" I echoed, a knot of fear forming in my stomach.

Kaizen nodded gravely. "Each neurological pathway holds a scent and can serve as a beacon to...specific beings. And since you've already had dreams through the 'Caster's anomalies, they have most likely identified your scent or aura to their creatures." His words sent my mouth dry as fear crept over me, feeling disgustingly exposed.

"Perhaps now," he said mockingly, his gaze drifting to where Levon's and my hands were clasped together as his face turned angry. "You'll finally start fighting instead of hiding." Anger surged within me, and I shot him a glare that could cut through steel, confused at his abrupt change. "But perhaps that would never be in your nature."

I struggled to swallow, feeling the weight of his words pierce through me, knowing that all I'd ever done was live in submission.

Levon glared at him as Kaizen walked to the other room, forcefully closing the door behind him. I forced the growing anger laced with fear down as I sat on the bed, holding my head in my hands. The bed shifted to the right of me, and Levon's body slid next to mine. His warmth was tangible in the cool room.

"I've been so naïve, Levon," I confessed bitterly. "Maybe it would have been better for me to wallow in self-pity at Jesri's estate—forever a pet to him. I didn't know that the world was this...evil."

His hand shifted onto my back, stroking lazy fingers down my spine, but his touch brought me no solace.

"*Don't wish for that*. You're not naïve; you've just been kept in the dark, like everyone else," he explained, his voice tinged with sympathy.

"How do *you* know all this?" I shot back, frustration bubbling up within me. He looked at me with haunted eyes as he flexed his scarred hands. I palmed my eyes in exasperation, leaning into him as fear and anger churned within me.

A metallic twang sliced through the air, jolting my senses. Levon snapped his hand back as if stung, his eyes ablaze with an emotion I couldn't quite decipher.

"Eliah," he began cautiously, holding up his hands and rising from the bed. "Calm down."

The world seemed to spin as the metallic scent of blood invaded my senses, setting my nerves ablaze with rage and fear. My vision blurred with fury, my mind clouded by irrationality.

"*Calm down*?" I scoffed, the laughter ringing hollow as I relished the surge of anger coursing through me like wildfire. The door swung open, revealing Kaizen with a dagger at his side. His amber eyes burned with intensity, but

I refused to cower under his gaze. Instead, I met his fiery stare with a snarl, allowing the wrath within me to ignite like a storm of dark, icy flames.

The world tilted with agonizing pressure as the coppery surge of rotted blood stifled my nostrils and pulsed through my veins. I blinked, trying to reconcile myself, as a pit deep within me boiled and retracted as if afraid. I tried to swallow, but my mouth was as dry as the desert. Fury speckled my vision and muddled my fearful mind, instantly snapping my control to succumb to the irrational, moving my body.

"Stand down, *orphan*," he taunted as a wicked smile crossed his lips. Levon's bright eyes dimmed, brimming with anger at Kaizen, but he backed against the side wall.

"Kaizen, no, not here!" Levon ordered, yet no words came from his mouth.

I cocked my head with confusion but before I could think, a torrent of shimmering rage surged through my veins like a relentless inferno threatening to consume me whole. Despite my efforts, I could only choke a twisted laugh through clenched teeth as the seething anger roared within, fighting back against an oily presence that invaded my core. I grappled with the rage pulsating throughout my body like suppressed ripples. A chilling pressure bore down on me, worming its way deeper into my skull as it surged through me with an unyielding force, compelling me into submission and driving the tendrils of darkness deeper into my shaking soul. I struggled to breathe as my body seized.

"At least I'm broken enough to realize I'm nothing more than an orphan!" I snapped, seeing right through his rugged and dark stature.

Kaizen only clapped and grinned, sickening my soul even more, and relished with each tormented part of me.

I wrestled with the relentless pressure, struggling to fight back with each surge of force that threatened to overwhelm me entirely. With a snap, the tumultuous storm of darkness engulfed me, unleashing a torrent of memories that tore through my mind like a tempest.

I saw the cruel lash of Jesri's whip and felt the sting of his malicious words searing into my core. The relentless training, day in and day out, the hunger gnawing at my insides as I pushed myself to the brink. The self-hatred, the doubt, the excruciating pain that I buried beneath layers of determination, driving myself forward through sheer force of will.

Each failed test of the dagger and setback absorbed the torment of my wretched soul, fueling the flames of my fury. Nights drowned in salty tears, my body bruised beyond healing, my once untouched hands now calloused and scarred. Rumors, like poison, coursed through my veins, clotting my blood with each passing memory, each reminder of my past.

It seemed endless, the relentless flood of memories, each one a painful reminder of my past, my agony, my fears for parents who never returned. The bitterness welled within me, fueled by the resentment I harbored towards that wretched tree that never granted my childish wishes but seemed to heed the golden-eyed boy I adored time and time again. He was everything I was not—carefree, confident, everything that stirred up jealousy in my pathetic, wretched life.

A waste.

A sudden flash of light shattered the darkness of my thoughts, and I found myself back in Jesri's study, barely feeling the plush rug beneath my feet as I hung my head, the bruises on my arm throbbing in protest. My face burned from the recent confrontation, the echoes of Calum's voice reverberated off the closed door, his desperate pleas and cries filling the room.

"It was my fault! She didn't do it!" His voice grew more frantic with each passing moment, the sound of grunting and hurried footsteps drawing nearer. "Uncle, please. No!"

The door crashed open, and Jesri's piercing gaze bore into me, stealing the air from my lungs. I averted my eyes, focusing on the plush rug beneath me, my fingers absently tugging at the torn fabric of my shirt from the branches that had broken my fall.

Without warning, Jesri seized my arm, dragging me roughly from the chair and toward the door. Tears welled in my eyes as his grip tightened, sending waves of pain shooting through my injured arm. I glanced back at Calum, his eye swollen shut, with his face marred with scrapes mirroring my own. He collapsed to his knees, his cries echoing through the room.

I'm sorry, Calum mouthed as Jesri dragged me out the door. I noticed the line of staff watching, their faces numb with worry as he took me toward the foreboding woods, now frosted over with a bitter cold that had swept through, causing the humidity to amplify the cold air surrounding us.

He threw me into a bush that further bloodied my already pained body.

"Jesri, please," I gasped, trying to contain my trembling that would only cause more punishment.

"When I *expect* you to be a part of my house, I *expect* you to keep all the rules," he hissed out through gritted teeth. His anger radiating like a warm fire on the cold ground. The sun was darkening against the murky clouds as small wisps of air puffed from each breath.

"I'm sorry—"

"Sorry doesn't cut it, you foolish girl," he howled, sending the birds flying away. I sucked in a sob wishing I could fly away with them. "You sleep here for the night—"

"I'll freeze," I whimpered.

"Make that two." He took hold of my chin, rippling the pain deeper. "I don't want to see your pathetic face on my grass until then. And don't make me regret this— I need you *alive.*" He shoved my face to the side and left, leaving frozen steps in his wake.

I shuddered in the cold, tears freezing on my cheeks until my well of sorrow ran dry, leaving me hollow beneath the ebony black sky dotted with bright stars. Gathering what little strength I had left, I forced myself to find the tree, my only solace. I steadied my chattering teeth against the damp air and stumbled forward, heedless of lurking creatures that might see a vulnerable girl as easy prey.

I stumbled onto the cold, mossy ground beneath the wishing tree, desperate for it to remember—a plea not to forget the pathetic girl too angry to follow the rules.

"*Please,*" I begged, collapsing against its trunk, overgrown with gnarled roots that stuck up and shielded me from the cold. "*Please.*"

The air stirred, swirling frost before me as a blinding light hissed out, shooting skyward and raining shimmering sparkles around me, thawing my frozen, aching body until I fell into a deep sleep, only waking with a warm wool blanket over me.

I jolted back to the present, a snarl escaping my lips. I struggled to shake off the icy chill gripping me, feeling as though I was staring out of my own eyes but somehow locked deep inside. Memories flashed by, some forgotten or forced into oblivion until now. Exhausted, I returned to the present, a blinding pressure building within my head.

Worried amber eyes came into view, and instantly reignited the anger, my hands curling as I was lunging for Kaizen, no longer in control of my body. My fingers wrapped around his tanned throat and squeezed as hard as I could. The veins in his neck bulged as his eyes flickered with darkness.

I screamed, but no sound emerged, and I fought against my own hands, desperate for them to release their grip. Levon was on me in seconds, tearing at my arms, his voice joining mine in frantic cries to stop. Kaizen's amber eyes were bright with concern as he grabbed my fingers, attempting to wedge his own between mine to break the hold.

I wailed as pain shot through my skull, sending my vision spinning with dizzying intensity. An oily blackness crept up my spine, suffocating me. The familiar sensation of spidery fingers wrapped around my throat, squeezing until a loud snap echoed in my ears, jolting me back to reality. Agony erupted from my fingers, radiating up my arm and side. I fought against the darkness with a violent thrash, clawing for control as my vision slowly returned.

Kaizen's worried eyes met mine, and realization struck. I abruptly released my grip, feeling guilt flood in as pain radiated through my trembling hand. Levon pulled me away, and Kaizen coughed, clutching his neck as he leaned against the wall, struggling to stand. I collapsed to the ground and sucked in a breath, seeing my little finger dislocated and jutting out at an odd angle.

"*Kaizen, enough,*" Levon warned, shoving him harder against the wall and pinning him there. "*Enough.*"

A tense exchange of silent words passed between them before Kaizen shoved Levon off.

"Remember *your* place!" Kaizen hissed, pushing away from the wall and slamming the door to the small room shut, the sound echoing off the stone walls.

I closed my eyes, letting my heart swell back into my soul and drive the memories away.

Inhale.

Exhale.

"This is going to hurt." I felt Levon's hand take my dislocated finger as I grounded myself on the cold stone floor.

Inhale.

"One, two—"

I yelped, quickly stifling the cry as more pain jostled up my arm. Levon wrapped a small bandage around the injured fingers, then lifted me onto the bed, holding me close as the tears fell. I let the fear, the pity, the hatred, and the anger consume me until darkness overtook everything.

———— + ✦ + ————

"It is attainable, Xaldruk," the oily voice hissed, barely audible, as the surrounding darkness pulsed, sending tremors through the earth. The mountains trembled, and the rivers roared in response.

Cheers erupted from below, their echoes bouncing off the blood-stained sky.

"Good," the shadowy voice snarled.

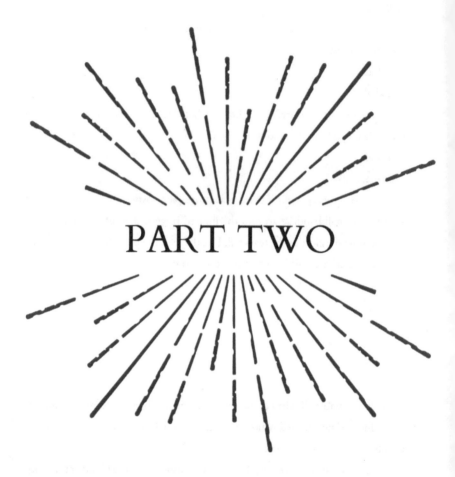

PART TWO

25

I woke to the gentle rhythm of Levon's chest moving beneath me, his arms still wrapped around me, warding off the chill of the night. I rubbed my tear-stained cheeks, feeling the weight of exhaustion settle over me as I shifted against the stiffness in my limbs. Levon shifted as I sat up in the darkness, wondering how long I had been asleep. A faint yellow light filtered in from under the hall door, casting a soft glow over my surroundings.

I slipped off the bed, the cool stone floor grounding me as I navigated the darkness towards the privy. After securing the door and swiftly attending to my needs, I emerged to find Kaizen standing mere inches from the door. His hand shot out, muffling any startled sound that threatened to escape my lips. His eyes blazed with an intensity that seemed to pierce the dimly lit room. After releasing me, he gestured for me to follow silently. He disappeared into his small room, waiting for me to enter before closing the door, plunging us into a cloak of impenetrable darkness.

A slash crackled as a flame materialized, illuminating the room as Kaizen set down the oil lamp, casting eerie shadows over his features. His leathers, cloak, and tunic lay discarded on a chair, revealing a muscled chest adorned with several scars, each a testament to a past battle. One scar, jagged and deep, led down to his left hip, disappearing into his pants.

I quickly shifted my eyes up and around the room as he grabbed his tunic, sliding it back on and closing the distance between us. His features blazed with worry, an unfamiliar expression in those usually harsh eyes.

"Eliah," Kaizen said urgently, his eyes intense. "There's more at stake here than this rutting tournament, so listen carefully or risk succumbing to the darkness and losing more than your chance at freedom."

I stared at him, wide-eyed and unsure how to react.

"Levon will hate me for telling you all this, but you need to know," he sighed, rubbing the stubble on his face with worry before pulling me away from the door as if afraid Levon might overhear. "With the neural pathways established, the Spellcasters are able to use their twisted abilities to manipulate minds," he continued. "They can tear apart and connect to pathways within *your* mind, turning you into a puppet. They're able to do this through the very fabricator of the universe called the Ethereal—magic, if you will."

I inhaled sharply, my mind flashing back to earlier, feeling so hollow and buried deep within myself. "I thought," I paused. "I thought I was going crazy," I muttered, recalling Kaizen's amber eyes darkening under my chokehold.

"They exploit your weaknesses. Show you everything you despise about yourself and rummage through your memories like a drug," Kaizen said, his gaze steady. "Only a conflict of pain can disrupt their control," he said urgently. "So, when you feel it happening again—*and it will*—you must let it happen to, first, *understand it.* Focus on what it feels like, how it moves within your mind, and how it scrapes through your thoughts. For when it happens again, you'll be able to fully grasp it and channel your anger towards it to crush its head." He looked over me as fear entered my heart.

"So, I need you to clear your mind," he whispered. "They can take a step into these connecting pathways through your fear, so *command* your fear to dissipate. It can have no place in you. Remember the breathing techniques Levon has taught you: *You* control your emotions. *You* control what you feel."

I took a sharp breath, trying to make sense of all this, and feeling rather odd that Kaizen was *helping* me rather than beating me down.

He glared at me, his eyes practically glowing in the dark, as I quickly nodded, steadying my heartbeat and convincing myself that I wasn't afraid.

"Do you feel any tangible fear?" Kaizen asked, his gaze piercing as if he could read my thoughts.

"I...don't think so—"

"Are you afraid?" he pressed, his tone urgent. "I need you to guard yourself and fight back. Even if you *are* afraid, you *must* fight back—"

"*I am afraid,*" I admitted with a hiss, lifting my chin with determination. "You are hearing yourself, aren't you? All of this is absolutely insane!" I hissed, my anger spiking.

Kaizen's eyes narrowed as he realized how close we were and took a step back. Fear and anger intertwined deep within me, feeling consumed by a battle of lies and secrets that had been hidden from me for far too long. The inside of my core burned with a determination to prove him wrong, to prove the fear wrong.

"Control it, Eliah," he snapped back. "Because *that* will be all you have left."

———— ✦ ————

I racked my brain, replaying Kaizen's short but critical commands repeatedly. A sick feeling gnawed at me as I clasped my hand around my throat, the phantom shadow of the figure's grip lingering with each breath of cool air slicing through my lungs. I ran up and down the long corridor, the inn's single hallway stretching for miles. Door after door, I kept running, unable to sleep, unable to let myself feel or think too much about what had transpired.

When you feel it happening again—and it will—you must let it happen.

The maggot, the pressure. It was real and ready to brand me into submission, waiting for me to fail and to fear.

I pushed harder, letting the weight of my body ache against the pull of my legs with each thrust and bounce.

Control it, Eliah, because that will be all you have left, his words echoed in my mind.

Inhale, exhale.

The ache in my mind begged for more distraction while my lungs and legs begged me to stop. I hit the main foyer, gulping down air as the cool mountain stone licked my face with each breath. A few drunkards were slumped in scattered chairs, twitching in their sleep.

I turned and began walking back to the room, inhaling deeply to let the sharpness of the air dispel my thoughts. My heart slowed to its normal rhythm, faster than before, and I stood with a newfound confidence to take control of my life how I saw fit.

Finding our door, I pushed it open just as Levon swung it open from the other side.

His eyes went wide, and his clothes were in disarray. "*Tell me* when you feel like taking a run for the night when things are—" he started, then stopped abruptly, shaking his head. "You don't know how terrified I was waking up, and you were gone."

I wanted to retort with bitterness, knowing he'd be even more terrified when I began the tournament, but I held my tongue, feeling the desperate need for sleep weigh heavily on my body.

"I couldn't sleep."

He rubbed his face, fatigue evident in his eyes. "Get some because you won't have much of it soon," he said, retreating into Kaizen's room, firmly shutting the door behind him. I clenched my jaw and reached the privy to wash up.

Splashing my face with cold water, I scrubbed away the traces of fear and exhaustion as best I could with the standing washbasin. Hastily changing into a fresh set of clothes, I placed Kaizen's dagger within easy reach, and I crawled under the covers and closed my eyes, but sleep eluded me; my mind too noisy with anxious thoughts.

"Why did they show me that memory?" I grunted into the pillow, frustration seeping through my voice. I forced myself to still, battling restlessness as I focused on each breath. Counting seconds, I urged my mind to stay disciplined, wishing I had taken Levon's breathing training more seriously, especially if Kaizen said my life depended on it. But before I could continue my count, sleep overtook my body.

A soft tickle traced down my arm, and I jolted awake. My dagger was instantly in hand as Levon backed away, his hands raised in surrender.

"You must stop startling me," I groaned, replacing the dagger on the bedside table and flopping back onto the bed.

"How else was I supposed to wake you?" he mused, adjusting his tunic with a smile playing on his lips. I rubbed my eyes and sat up.

"Well, you must refrain from it when I'm asleep," I rasped, my tone sharper than intended.

He chuckled softly. "We should leave as soon as possible to arrive by sundown tonight. I let you sleep as long as I could." His hand reached for mine, but I hesitated, causing him to withdraw his hand and take a deep breath. "I'll meet you at the entrance. I need to see Jucam's mother before we leave. Kaizen's preparing the carriage and will meet you."

With that, he exited the room, taking out the last trunk of our things. I rose from the bed, gathering my hair into a braid, slipped on my shoes, and exited the room, ensuring the dagger was securely tucked into my boot.

Kaizen was eating at a table by the hearth in the main foyer. I approached him, scanning the room to note the absence of the previous night's drunkards, replaced by new faces.

He caught my eye and nodded towards Jucam, who was bustling behind his table. "He has food ready for you. Hurry and eat. We should have left an hour ago," Kaizen snapped as if our conversation last night had never happened.

I sighed, rolling my eyes as I approached Jucam, who quickly spotted me and greeted me with a bushy smile. "Morning, milady. Let me get you your food."

Returning his smile, I thanked him sincerely. "Your cooking is excellent."

Embarrassment tinted his pale cheeks. "The pleasure is all mine to give," he replied with genuine gratitude. He handed me a plate laden with fried meat and eggs, with a creamy vegetable sauce simmering over the whole of it.

I nodded my thanks and walked back toward Kaizen, who was now standing with his empty plate. He brushed past me, "Stay put until I come back."

I shot him a glare in response and settled into my seat, not bothering with the pretense of eating like a lady. Instead, I dug into the breakfast with eagerness. By the time Kaizen returned, I had finished my meal and watched as he laughed with Jucam. It was a rare sight to see him look genuinely happy.

He caught my eye, and his laughter and smile dwindled. He redirected his attention to Jucam and resumed their conversation as I collected my empty platter and walked over to them, returning it to Jucam and expressing gratitude for the delicious meal. Jucam smiled warmly, but Kaizen's expression returned to its usual seriousness.

Kaizen motioned for me to follow as we headed through the large stone doorway into the open fields, where I prayed a Breva wasn't lurking. The sun was now bright against the soaring Gap, dispersing the fog and leaving no place to hide except for the endless fields to the south. The carriage was loaded, and the horses stood ready for the last leg of our journey.

"Do you still have that dagger on you?" Kaizen questioned, pulling his leathers tighter, about to hand me another one.

"Is that even a question?" I rebuked, watching him unsheathe another slightly longer dagger with a small ruby pommel, the gem looking as mysterious as those from the lady back in the market. Its handle was interwoven with threads of golden vines that wrapped around to the steel, which was jagged and gleamed with a peculiar silver.

I lost my voice, remembering this very dagger—the same one wielded by the man who saved me from those men at the tavern where Calum had taken me for *fun*. Realization struck as I shot my eyes back up to Kaizen, taking in his stature, his hair, and his hand. Memories of that night flooded back—how his thumb had gently rubbed over my knuckles, the way he took out all those men with lethal grace. He was...worried, so unlike his brooding self now.

I knitted my brows together. "It was you," I muttered, looking back down at the dagger and then up at him, struggling to believe it myself. He cocked his head to the side, puzzled. "You were the one who saved me from those men at the tavern."

He maintained his usual stony expression, only blinking before shoving the dagger and its sheath into my hands. "I don't know what you're talking about," he said, opening the carriage door and forcing me inside. I didn't resist as confusion clouded my mind.

Why was he there? *That* wasn't a coincidence.

I continued to examine the dagger, its tip so sharp that it drew a small trickle of blood from my finger as I pricked myself. I set the dagger in my lap and clutched my hand.

Just then, the door swung open, revealing Levon's bright smile and snapping me back to the present.

"Ready?" Levon's voice broke through the tension, and I swallowed hard, offering him a nod, not believing I was. "I'll be up top until after the Gap," he informed me before closing the door and sealing me inside the carriage.

With a jolt, we set off, the wheels rolling along the towering gray wall until we found the Gap's opening where the fog lingered, swirling around the wheels as we ventured in. The carriage grew colder as the day faded into a watery light, eventually succumbing to a murky darkness. The echo of the wheels on gravel reverberated off the walls, creating a deafening hum. In the distance, the end of the Gap appeared as a mere sliver of light, teasingly close yet seemingly unreachable.

I watched intently out of both windows, feeling as if oily, dark eyes were watching our every move, counting each second and every breath. My heart thudded loudly inside my head, drowning out the hum of the wheels as fear tightened its grip on my heart.

Control it.

Inhale.

I gripped the radiant dagger, running my fingers over the pommel repeatedly when a spike of anger scorched my insides with a sudden intensity as I thought back to Kaizen's broad back, bumping the disgusting liquid Calum got me onto my back. To his stealthy silhouette slamming into those grimy men like a moth attracted to light.

Why was Kaizen there?

I gritted my teeth with anger when a piercing screech suddenly tore through the echoing thrum of our carriage's wheels, bringing us to a staggering halt. Kaizen and Levon muttered something that echoed off the Gap's walls as I tightened my grip on the dagger.

"Eliah."

I whipped my head towards the other door, exhaling a jagged breath. The carriage lurched forward faster than before, and Levon's voice shouted from above, accompanied by banging against the roof. Kaizen hissed something too faint for me to hear over the ruckus of the carriage against the echoing Gap.

The carriage surged ahead again, throwing me back into the seat as another screech pierced the air close to my left. I braced for impact, clutching the dagger tightly as arrows whizzed past, followed by a roaring shriek that froze my soul. I pressed my hands to my ears, trying to drown out the cacophony as the carriage tossed me around, hurling forward faster. The thunderous beat of hooves against the wall drowned out all other sounds, blurring my surroundings into a chaotic blur and leaving me feeling helpless. Kaizen and Levon's voices were lost in the chaos as more screams echoed behind us.

"Eliah." The voice hissed again, dreadful and menacing.

"NO!" I shouted as a clawed paw, black as death, struck the side of the carriage, sending the carriage careening to the side before hitting back down. Another arrow whizzed by, finding its mark with a scream.

I pressed my face against the window, witnessing the black creature crumple with an arrow embedded in its eye. A Miehja.

"Faster!" Levon's voice pierced through the chaos, accompanied by the sharp crack of reins against the front mast. The fog began to disperse as several arrows flew past, their watery light casting eerie reflections from the Gap's end. "We're almost there."

The vibrations from the wheels rattled my body as we propelled forward in eerie silence, broken only by the clamor of the carriage wheels. The light dispelled the oily, dark feeling as swiftly as it had come.

A patting sound came from the roof. "We're safe," Levon gasped out, his voice tinged with lingering fear. "We're here."

The carriage gradually slowed as we reached the Gap's end, basking in the bright light. I released a long breath, still clutching the dagger as I leaned closer to the window, trying to get a glimpse at the court Jesri never stopped talking about, and hoping another black paw wouldn't appear.

Navy and gold flags billowed in the soft wind as several guards clad in the same color formed a protective barrier at the entrance, standing stoic with large shields and swords strapped to their hips. A few held extended poles blocking the long billowing road northward toward the city, which was breathtaking.

Towering, glimmering buildings sparkled in the sun's rays, casting a rainbow of hues across the rolling, clipped-to-perfection landscape. The sky seemed to mirror the vibrant scene below, swirling with clouds that danced in response. I could see the castle far in the distance, looming like a pointed mountain.

The carriage halted, and I felt it sway as Levon emerged into view, clapping some men on the back with a wide grin, continuing to converse.

Two guards approached the carriage, one casting me an unsettling grin that sickened my stomach, remembering the men at the tavern. Remembering Kaizen being my rescuer once again.

I swiftly averted my gaze, feeling exposed and praying they would let us pass before whatever animal attacked us in the Gap came stalking, unsure why it hadn't already.

With a creak, the door swung open, and Levon's smile wavered as he settled into the carriage, taking a seat across from me. My eyes implored him for answers, but he simply shook his head, holding the door ajar. "Go up top. A change of scenery might help clear your mind."

I furrowed my brows in question but refused to stay sitting any longer, feeling like a doe headed toward the slaughter. Perhaps I could *help* up top or do anything other than sit.

I gave him a curt nod and got out, feeling the cool air from the dark Gap nip at my bones, begging me to run to the golden city and the sun's warmth. Anything out of the murky grasp of whatever was lurking in there.

My foot found purchase, and I hoisted myself up. Kaizen's eyes were still turned back to the Gap, even though he started moving forward as soon as I sat down. The guards parted for us, and it took all my effort not to look back, too, fearing that whatever had been chasing us was watching.

"I suppose you won't tell me what happened back there unless I beg?" I said, my voice barely audible over the clatter of wheels on stone.

"Begging would be nice," he taunted with a devilish grin. I narrowed my eyes, unamused, knowing he would tell me.

"Why aren't the Miehja still attacking?" I asked.

"More of them surround the Gap to keep threats out, and they're not attacking because I put an end to it and *you* controlled it," he stated matter-of-factly.

I sat in shock. "I *controlled* it?" I shook my head, "And how am *I* a threat?"

"Your emotions. Don't you remember anything I told you last night?" He then eyed me up and down with a grin tugging at his lips. "And I'd say you're a threat."

My expression turned sour, feeling rather irritated at his bluntly stated fact, even though I'm grateful he tells me things. "To you, I will be," I challenged and held tight onto the seat's bar. I breathed in, waiting several moments before asking, "I know it was you at the tavern. Why were you there?"

He eyed me again, his jaw flexing. "I should be asking why *you* were there?" he questioned, through narrow eyes but didn't deny it this time.

"Thank you," I muttered, feeling those disgusting men's hands still on me. Yet still unsure what to think.

He curtly nodded and turned forward, whipping the reins and commanding the horses to move faster.

I turned to the view, embracing the spectacular wonders of the city hidden behind the surrounding mountains that flared with colors.

The large spired castle loomed in the distance. Its cobalt spires sparkled against the bright sun, now beating down on us and warming my bones thoroughly. A sea of homes, buildings, markets, and shelters in all shapes could be seen as we descended into the valley, hearing the hum of chatter, carriages, and animals surrounding us.

I couldn't help but smile at the immense difference between life at Levon's or Jesri's to this. Each structure was unique, a testament to the vibrant life that thrived here.

Kaizen breathed an airy laugh.

"What?" I challenged harshly.

He only shook his head as we rounded a bend to see a market larger than Levon's entire town, stretching far and wide with thousands of goods sold by shouting sellers. A whirl of smells hit me like a wall.

The horses plodded off towards a bend close to the mountain's edge while the tall, spired castle dominated our view, standing tall even in the distance. No wonder it would take us an entire day to get through this mess.

I swallowed, realizing that I would soon face the king—the man Jesri had always idolized and raved about. The man who Levon worked for. The man whose lineage killed off thousands.

I swallowed again, calming my roaring flames, and determined not to obliterate the very court itself. For damning my life with this lofty Match that might bring me to my demise, but also my potential freedom.

We continued for several miles, the rhythmic clatter of the carriage wheels accompanying our thoughts. I gazed at the colorful buildings and bustling crowds, watching the sun arc across the sky until Levon tapped the roof, signaling our stop. Stepping out onto the worn, stony ground, he gestured ahead.

"I'm sure we can all use a moment to stretch our legs. There's a bakery not too far from here," he said, his smile infectious. I glanced at Kaizen, who merely gave a curt nod of agreement and urged me to follow Levon as he waited.

Stretching my legs, I took Levon's hand as he led me through the winding streets. Each one offered sights and smells I had never encountered before, tempting me to indulge in its delights.

We rounded several corners, brushing past a throng of people walking in every direction, and finally stopped in front of a tiny shop lodged between two tall buildings. It looked less like a bakery and more like a forgotten place no one cared for. A sign hung crooked at the door, reading: *Tazina's Bakery.*

"Jucam is the best cook, but Tazina is the best baker with sweets grand as your imagination," Levon said, pushing open the weathered door, its bell chiming as we entered.

As soon as we stepped inside, the tantalizing aroma of freshly baked cookies enveloped us, tempting me to devour every treat in sight. The space was cozy and inviting, with a rustic wooden table and two chairs tucked to the side. A bright glass display showcased an array of delectable delights, each confection more tempting than the last.

"I'll be right there!" called a voice from behind the closed door at the back. Just then, a hazelnut-skinned woman with vibrant green eyes and intricately beaded hair emerged, balancing two large trays of sweets with practiced ease. Her eyes lit up as she caught sight of Levon.

"*Levon!*" she exclaimed, quickly setting down the trays and crossing over to embrace him. "It's been ages. How have you been? I've meant to visit, but things have been so hectic here," she chattered while Levon nodded in agreement. After releasing him, she gave his arms a squeeze before turning her attention to me, her gaze warm and welcoming.

"And who might this be?" she inquired with a hum.

"Eliah," I replied before Levon could introduce me. "I'm guessing you're Tazina, with the best sweets around?"

They both smiled at me, and she extended her hand. "What an honor to meet such a strong woman. You'd better be keeping Levon in line—he needs it," she teased, giving me a wink as she returned behind the counter. I couldn't help but smile as Levon smirked in agreement.

"Now, what suits your fancy?" Tazina asked, gesturing to the mouth watering array of treats.

Everything. Everything suits my fancy.

She must have read my mind, for she said, "How about a bit of everything? I've got several fresh batches in the back that need to be eaten today, and I'm sure your friend will want some, too."

With that, she disappeared into the back, the door swinging shut behind her.

"She knows Kaizen?" I whispered.

"She knows I'm always traveling with someone," Levon replied.

"And that someone couldn't have been me?" I remarked, feeling a twinge of irritation. He squeezed my hand and leaned back against the counter, a pearly grin spreading across his face.

"You do ask too many questions," he smirked, reminiscing about our first meeting and my endless barrage of inquiries. I rolled my eyes, and he squeezed my hand again, sending a rush of warmth through my veins.

Tazina emerged with two gray boxes and handed them to Levon. "On the house, just make sure you stop by often. I miss our chats—" Before she could finish, a person walked in, the bell cutting her off. "I'll see you two soon!" She turned toward the man as we walked out with a wave.

"Chats, hm?" I said, opening the box to reveal pastries Calum would have killed for. I took one out, covered in red chocolate and flaked with a drizzle of cream. My tongue sparked with joy at the sweet taste, and I had to restrain myself from grabbing another.

"She came to help in the kitchen several times for one of the many parties King Thealor threw, and I was to be her escort home," Levon explained before biting into a golden crispy bun dusted with powdered sugar.

We continued our walk, devouring most of the pastries and laughing off the fearful impending uncertainties. As we approached the carriage, Kaizen looked devilishly annoyed. He eyed us, instantly taking the box from Levon and finishing the remaining bite-sized pieces. I held back my laugh, knowing how odd it was for Kaizen to act normal rather than his annoying broodiness.

I sat back in the carriage with Levon as we trudged on while the sky faded into a warm orange, welcoming the night with grace. I couldn't stop staring out the windows, pointing and gawking at the sight. How incredible the structures, the people, and the sweets had been. Perhaps the township wasn't as dreadful as I had imagined, solely because of Jesri's relentless obsession. Yet, deep down, I knew that anything associated with Jesri's dreams often led to trouble.

26

The castle stood before me, a grandeur beyond my wildest dreams. Its size alone was enough to take my breath away, dwarfing even the towering Creaic Gap. Several spires reached towards the heavens, their peaks disappearing into the clouds. As we approached, I marveled at the walls constructed of cream granite adorned with intricate accents of blue and gold that would glitter in the sun. These same hues matched the guards' attire at the entrance, their breastplates, gloves, and belts gleaming in the sunlight.

Stepping through the imposing golden doors, I was in a vast entrance hall that seemed to stretch endlessly. My eyes widened in awe as I took in the opulent surroundings, feeling speechless in the presence of such splendor. Servants bustled about, their movements graceful as they welcomed us into the castle.

Every detail within the castle exuded an opulence and luxury Jesri would kill for. The high, dark-stained walls were meticulously polished and adorned with banners of rich gold, blues, and greens that hung with regal grace. Well-kept rugs, woven with a lustrous gray-blue hue, lined the outer walls, and the entire room was filled with hundreds of delicate jewels, crystals, and fancies that sparkled in the ambient light.

Levon's gentle touch on my shoulder pulled me back from my daze, grounding me into the present moment. I straightened myself, anticipation coursing through my veins as a servant guided us toward my private quarters. As we stepped into my room, I was awestruck by its grandeur, surpassing even the splendor of the castle entrance.

The lounging room greeted us with elegance, boasting a towering bookcase filled with literary treasures, a regal gold-painted table, plush cushioned chairs, and a magnificent blue and gold rug that beckoned one to sink into its depths. Moving into the bedroom, I marveled at its pristine beauty, where royal hues filled every corner, and the carpet felt luxurious beneath my feet, inviting me to sink my toes into its softness. A towering hand-painted partition sat by the large billowing windows, complemented by a large vanity and armoire, both painted with exquisite gold accents.

The bathing room mirrored the opulence of the rest of the quarters, featuring a plush rug that would cost a fortune alone, a porcelain clawfoot tub that promised indulgent relaxation, washing sinks for convenience, and a chamber pot discreetly tucked away. Overwhelmed by the sheer magnificence of my surroundings, I couldn't contain the bubbling amazement that surfaced. A wide grin spread across my blushing cheeks. This was more than I could have ever imagined: a haven of luxury.

"Did you live here, in the castle, I mean?" I asked, my fingers trailing along the soft pastel curtains that adorned the large crystal windows, which offered a breathtaking view of the surroundings.

"I stayed in the barracks under the castle, not as glorious, but still grand," Levon replied with a smile, his tone carrying a hint of nostalgia.

"Do you miss this?" I inquired, pondering whether I would feel a similar longing after the uncertainties ahead.

"No, not at all." I couldn't hide my surprise at his swift response, but before I could dwell on it, he gently took my hands in his own. "It's nothing compared to what I have now, but I would still trade it all to find you," he said, squeezing my hand and increasing my turmoil of feelings. Our moment was quickly interrupted as a maid entered the room. Levon dropped my hand and stepped back several paces.

"Welcome, Lady Eliah Archenon," the maid greeted, her voice trembling with nervousness. I nearly retorted, but Levon's warning, playful eyes stopped me, and I managed a strained smile. "And Sir Alder," she continued, regaining control over her voice. "The rest of the contestants won't arrive until tomorrow, so make yourselves comfortable until then. Explore and eat as much as you'd like. We are grateful for your presence and abilities to participate in the King's Match, Lady Eliah."

Several other maids entered the room, carrying baskets filled with fruits, pastries, trinkets, and oddities I didn't recognize. The head maid cleared her throat again. "King Thealor gives his gratitude." With a final curtsy, they all left the room, their footsteps making no sound on the polished floors.

I raised my brow to Levon, feeling disdain for the king, knowing he very well did *not* give his gratitude.

I let out a breath. "What now?"

"We wait until tomorrow. The king will want to meet you all personally at his feast and make you a spectacle at his Court."

"A spectacle? Meaning showing me off like a prize," I growled, biting down on my anger at the memories of Jesri doing the same to get what he wanted.

"Yes," Levon rasped, sadness lacing his voice. He opened his mouth, then shut it again but continued. "I...got word that Jesri and Calum will be attending. They should also be arriving tomorrow."

My heart sank into the depths of my emotions, burning within me like flames.

"I expected as much. I hope Jesri doesn't expect me to play his pet still and act as he desires. I'm no longer afraid to bite," I promised, letting my defiance color my words.

"I wouldn't expect you to," Levon replied, his smile widening as he backed away again as if refraining from further physical contact. He walked over to the basket of goods on the large table next to a vase filled with sweet-smelling summer flowers. "In agreeing to them attending, I requested that Aoife join."

I couldn't contain my smile, remembering how much I missed her. "Thank you," I said, watching him dip his head and continue aimlessly glancing through the basket of goodies. The air between us intensified as I felt a palpable sense of anticipation to be near him, feeling rather confused at such an emotion.

I swallowed, feeling those butterflies return and fluttering my heart to open—to let him in despite my past. Despite my brokenness. Despite *his* past and brokenness.

I had watched Levon; his smile was always genuine, and his actions were thoughtful and caring to those around him. Even though his past was as complicated as mine, he was still trying all the same. Trying to be a better man. Trying to help me gain my freedom though they were through completely idiotic paths.

I looked up at him and took a deep breath, unsure if I should step into this unknown territory.

But he had helped me to believe that I was more than a pathetic orphan; he desired my safety and wishes, and now he was ensuring Aoife would be by my side.

My thoughts were a chaotic swirl of confusion and longing. I had spent so long hiding my feelings; now, they felt impossible to ignore in this enormous room that felt all too small with him in it. The warmth in his eyes and the tenderness in his touch chipped away at my stubborn resolve, and the more I fought against it, the more my heart betrayed me, leaving me breathless and...yearning. Perhaps I didn't have to follow through with my promise not to let anyone in. And perhaps I was worthy of such admiration and that most men were not like Jesri and Calum. I saw the good in Levon; he was gentle, affectionate, and truly cared about my well-being, whereas Jesri never did.

I took in a long breath, feeling my fears fight back that this would all end like all my dreams ended, forgotten and non-existent.

My thoughts drifted back to our almost kiss at the estate. Grateful Kaizen broke it off because I was unsure if I would have been able to do it myself and unsure if these feelings were infatuation or real.

You'll end up being the one to kill her before the others get a chance. Kaizen's voice drifted into my mind, souring my mood as much as it did the first time he said it.

You'll end up being the one to kill her. What did that mean? Was it the Match? Or something else?

I cleared my throat as I watched him rifle through the basket. The butterflies in my stomach swirled into a frenzy, and I knew I was somehow falling for him *despite* everything. Despite Jesri, despite the Match, despite my fears. I was falling for him because he showed genuine concern and kindness, but I had to know.

"What did Kaizen mean when he said *you'll* be the one to end up killing me before the others do?" I muttered, not wanting to turn the air around us somber.

Levon turned back to me, his eyes meeting mine with a softness that made my heart skip a beat. His brows furrowed in confusion as he leaned up against the gold table.

He took a deep breath as he rubbed the back of his neck. "He was...referring to this," he said, gesturing to the room. "To the Match," he muttered, his voice going quieter.

I knitted my brows together, feeling indifferent to his answer but accepting it nonetheless, knowing he was trying to help me obtain freedom.

He slowly approached, closing the distance between us and pulsating my heart into a frenzy. "I'm sorry, Eliah. You know how I feel," he stated, his expression saddened. He looked up into my eyes as his hand reached out, gently cupping my cheek, his touch melting me, and his other hand took my own. "If there was any other way, I would take it. You know that, and I—"

"I know," I said, interrupting him. I knew his pain. I knew that he wanted my freedom as much as my own.

We stood there for a moment longer before he dropped his hands, yet there was an unspoken question in his bright emerald-blue eyes, a silent plea for permission that sent my heart racing with anticipation and fear of the unknown.

A warmth spread through me that was as terrifying as it was beautiful.

"You should blush more. It suits you," he remarked softly, his voice barely above a whisper, as if afraid to break the fragile tension between us. I let out a small chuckle, feeling the turmoil within me fizzle out as he took a step, taking my hand again.

Inhale.

I closed the gap between us without thinking twice, pressing my lips into his. A rush of sensations swept away all my worries, leaving only the crackling embers of desire in their wake and feeling a sense of freedom and control for the first time.

His soft lips sent a thrill of fire deep within my stomach as he took my face in his strong hands. I clenched his tunic, pulling him closer to me and feeling my legs weaken. Convincing myself that this was good and hearing Aoife's voice in my head that these feelings should be explored.

Our kisses deepened as if trying to capture every ounce of this before the inevitable separation of the Match. His lips parted and pressed into mine with more passion than the last as his hands moved down to my neck, just below my jaw. He abruptly paused, his breath warm against my lips.

"We won't be able to do this again until after everything is over," he murmured, his voice laced with longing and sadness before claiming my lips once more in a kiss filled with unspoken promises.

"I know," I breathed against his lips, mirroring his sadness, knowing that worse things might happen if we were seen together. Or if Jesri, Calum, *or* Kaizen found out.

With a tender, sad smile, he cupped my face in his hands again before his lips found mine with a fervor that left him intoxicated. As if he were waiting for this moment for a long, long time. I forced myself to melt into his embrace as much as he was melting into mine, holding tightly to the belief that this was good—that I wanted to embrace these feelings, and that I was worthy of love. That he really did care and that he wouldn't *kill* me as Kaizen had said. He had a dark past, but he was kind and trying to be better. He stated over and over again how he vowed to protect me, that I was his *Regina*—because he wanted me in ways that no one has ever wanted me before. He desired me as much as I desired to be loved.

As our kisses slowed and the world around us seemed to return, questions began to crowd my thoughts, each one heavier than the last and filled with nagging doubts, growing and twisting in the corners of my mind. Still, I clung to the idea that this was something to savor—a fragile, fleeting good—before the inevitable doom of the Match and the darkness beyond that could swallow everything whole.

———— ⋅ ✦ ⋅ ————

We spent the remainder of our day leisurely wandering through the impeccably groomed garden filled with fragrant flowers. Despite the looming dread of the upcoming tournament and concerns about Jesri, Calum, and the king, we maintained a light-hearted atmosphere with continuous jokes.

Levon mentioned that Kaizen was staying with a friend and would join us after everything was done. We discussed plans for the king's dinner, including how to present ourselves, practiced dance steps, and considered potential strategies for the Match.

"Have you heard anything more?" I whispered, referring not only to updates on the animals but also to any news about those searching for me.

"No, nothing on either front," Levon responded, his voice trailing sadly.

"When you first arrived at Jesri's, you knew I would face some type of animal in the tournament. That's why you tested me with those beasts, to see if I was capable," I remarked, more as an observation than a question.

He nodded. "I couldn't bear the thought of subjecting you to something so dreadful without truly knowing you could do it."

"So little faith in me?" I teased, allowing myself to lean into his side as we watched the sky transform into an aurora of swirling purples, blues, and pinks.

"It's not about faith in you," he reassured. "It's about my lack of faith in Jesri. I knew you had the strength, I just didn't want to expose you to more suffering."

Resting my head on his shoulder, I watched as lights flickered on, illuminating the garden grounds and allowing the symphony of chirping bugs and birds to continue their summer serenade. I inhaled his comforting scent, feeling it soothe my heart. I realized I could face whatever lay ahead, and for the first time, I knew I didn't have to face it alone.

We wandered back into the castle, where the king graciously arranged for us to dine in my quarters that evening. A lavish feast awaited us and threatened to overload my belly.

Sharing this intimate meal with Levon was a rare pleasure, and our bond was blossoming unexpectedly. We laughed throughout the evening, thoroughly enjoying each other's company for the first time, until we were practically doubled over.

When we finished, Levon began stuffing leftover food into the basket we had been given earlier. He asked me to do the same with my bag, stating that although he had made mistakes during his regiment, he would always try to help and be better with what little food he had. So with the basket and bag brimming with food, we ventured out into the streets, letting the ambience of lamp lights guide our way, distributing the food to those in need—the poor, the orphaned children, the widowed, the sick, and the homeless.

Beneath the canopy of twinkling stars, we turned a corner and encountered a red-haired woman, her anguished sobs echoing in the quiet night. Tears streaked down her dirt-stained cheeks as she clung to her two children, a small child nestled in her arms while another baby cried out in hunger. My heart twisted at the sight of their difficulty, and I felt a pang of empathy for their suffering. I approached her, my footsteps soft against the cobblestones, and knelt before her, offering the entirety of my bag.

Her gaze, a captivating blend of chocolate brown with flecks of green, met mine briefly before dropping to the bag in disbelief. She wiped away her tears with trembling hands, her expression a mix of gratitude. Beside her, the blond-haired boy clung to her side, his weary eyes filled with longing for sustenance. Unable to contain my emotions, tears welled in my eyes as the mother reached out and touched my arm, her voice choked with emotion.

"Thank you," she whispered with a heartfelt expression of pure gratitude. "Thank you."

I wished I had brought a blanket, a coat, or even a pillow—something more substantial to offer. Levon's touch on my shoulder pulled me from my thoughts, urging me to rise. The courageous mother and I held each other's gaze until I turned a corner and stumbled, overcome with emotion, collapsing into a puddle of tears.

Throughout my life, I had resented the path of fate that was laid out for me, yet I felt an overwhelming sense of gratitude at that moment. Despite my struggles, I was given warmth, sustenance, and shelter. I had never known hunger or homelessness, even if it was just a simple meal or a cold bed.

"Why? Why are there so many of them?" I cried out, wiping tears from my ruby cheeks, their warmth contrasting with the chill of the night air.

"Many have sought refuge here, finding it safer within the King's Court than outside," Levon replied gently.

He crouched down, enfolding me in his arms and lifting me again as a random foreboding feeling of fear began to worm its way back into my consciousness. Kaizen's warning echoed in my mind: *Control it.*

"How can a king bask in such luxury while his people suffer?" I hissed, a sour taste of indignation rising in my throat as I struggled to reconcile with the lavishness of my current rooms of his castle and the stark realities faced by his subjects here.

Levon held me close as tears streamed down my cheeks once more, the image of that tender mother's face and her struggling child etched in my mind. The other frail figures were too weak to lift the food to their lips, too feeble to offer a word of thanks or even steady themselves amidst their trembling.

"That's why I couldn't live here any longer. The first time I witnessed it myself, I was haunted by the knowledge of the suffering *I* was causing. I couldn't bear it any longer. I had to break free, help, and become a beacon of hope in this darkened world. And once I began, I couldn't stop until I had comforted every person I encountered," Levon confessed, brushing away a tear.

Elise's story echoed in my mind, knowing that he had seen her plight and welcomed her into a home. My heart ached with a mix of sorrow and remorse for harboring such deep-seated resentment towards his past.

"I'm sorry," I sobbed, my voice choked with emotion. "I'm so sorry you had to endure that alone." Remembering his own tale after losing his mother and joining the Royal Guard to find purpose, a family, and a belonging, until it wasn't. This kind hearted man had lived amidst horrors.

Levon simply kissed my brow and guided me back through the streets and into the glowing castle that held my fate and that of a haughty king sitting on his throne.

27

I awoke to the sound of curtains flying open and shards of sunlight piercing my closed eyes, jarring me awake with painful squints. A growl escaped my lips as Levon came into view, already dressed in a tight white tunic and long brown pants.

"Morning, my Regina," he greeted, kissing my forehead. I reluctantly sat up; my eyes were struggling to stay open, and I wanted to crawl back into bed. "Get up and dressed in your training attire. We're going for a run and some practice before the tailor arrives."

I shot him a confused look, my groggy mind struggling to process his words.

"A tailor?" I groaned, standing up and suddenly realizing I was only in my underthings. My face flushed red as Levon promptly turned around with a smirk.

I quickly reached for my pants and shirt, slipping them on with haste.

A devilish smile curled his lips as he looked over his shoulder.

"Don't you dare," I hissed as he turned back around right as I finished pulling my top down. I cursed at him, prompting him to step closer to me before quickly pivoting toward the lounging room.

"I'm not quite sure what I most enjoy you in," he purred, grabbing an apple from one of the side tables. He paused before fully exiting, "And yes, a tailor will be here to make you the grandest spectacle there ever was, though I'm not sure you could be quite as grand as you are in your nightwear," he teased, swiftly disappearing out the door right as my shoe hit the wall behind him.

The grandest spectacle.

A prize.

I inhaled deeply, letting the room's sweet scents of lemon and lavender calm my racing heart.

How was I supposed to face the king and thousands of others? How was I supposed to be something that I was not?

I walked over to the large golden vanity, running a comb through my tangled hair, evidence of my long and restless night. Salt stains marked my cheeks and neck as last night's haunting dream flooded back into my mind. My voice felt raw from repeatedly calling out to Levon, Kaizen, Calum—anyone to rescue me from the encroaching darkness that enveloped every inch of my cold, aching body.

I could still feel the phantom weight of the manacles on my ankles, wrists, and neck, the screeching and gurgling sounds echoing from the other side of the dark cell where I remained trapped. No shadowy figure could be seen, but its presence lingered; that thing—that creature with its milky white eyes snarling toward me.

I halted my thoughts before they could delve any deeper.

Control it.

Inhale.

It was only a dream.

Exhale.

A dream from *them.*

I hastily wove my hair into a messy coronet, a far cry from its usual neatness, but I welcomed the distraction to keep my mind from racing. I yearned to move, to run, to feel the weight of a sword in my hand or the impact of my knuckles against something solid.

I pushed the door open and found Levon seated at the large table, fiddling with the apple core. The lingering aroma of last night's dinner spices still hung in the air, a reminder of our late return well past midnight.

I grabbed a handful of blueberries, peeled a banana, and approached the door. Levon rose to his feet, following after me with a knowing smile. "So eager, hm?"

"I need a distraction," I confessed.

A smirk tugged at his lips as he raised his brows. I rolled my eyes even as a wildfire of sparks danced up my spine and ignited within my chest.

I quickened my pace down the hall and descended the grand staircase into the courtyard.

He started jogging toward the left side of the castle, and I followed suit. We ran along the castle's edge, circled the garden, and took a path leading to a hill scattered with trees and shrubs. My legs burned as we climbed the hill, but I welcomed the physical exertion, letting it distract me from my thoughts. I pushed myself harder, feeling my lungs squeeze with each exhale. The sun hovered just above the horizon, though its heat caused sweat to bead along my hairline.

Just as we neared the top, Levon suddenly swerved to the side, blocking my path, and unexpectedly tackled me to the ground, knocking the air from my lungs. I cursed as he let out a laugh. Our limbs tangled, and we rolled back down the hill. I shoved him to the side and dug my heels into the ground as my foot found purchase.

"Are you insane?" I yelled, anger coursing through me, making my already burning body feel even hotter. I rubbed my arm, already swelling with a bruise from the fall.

"Make it to the top, you win," he rasped, catching his breath. "Don't make it to the top, I win." He flashed me a devilish grin, squaring himself in front of me.

"What do I get *when* I win?" I breathed, hoping to distract him long enough to sneak around him.

His grin widened as he opened his mouth to respond, but I bolted to his side, shoving his muscled arm away.

A laugh bubbled from his lips as I dug my feet into the crisp ground, hauling myself up and forward. He lunged, grabbing hold of my right ankle and sending me sprawling to the ground. Quickly catching myself, I whipped my left leg toward him, and he barely dodged my boot aimed at his pretty face.

Trying to retreat, I stomped on his arm with my leg. Despite it all, he kept smiling. "How are you going to escape?" he taunted, still holding tight to my ankle.

"Not by having a conversation," I spat, throwing myself back down the hill, quickly twisting my body so that Levon lost his grip and tumbled after me. I found my footing swiftly and darted diagonally toward the right side of the hill. A laugh burst from my lungs as I glanced back at him chasing me, pumping his arms as quickly as mine. I abruptly changed direction and headed straight up, my legs screaming in agony with each push against the ground as I neared the top of the hill.

"Give up?" I hollered, looking back to see him only steps behind me right as I collided with a solid body and was knocked to the ground.

My vision blurred as I saw the familiar end of a leather cloak flicker into view. Two hands pinned me down, and I saw Kaizen's smirking face above me.

"Took you long enough," Levon panted, looking down at me with a smile. Beside him, Kaizen's amber eyes sparkled with pure enjoyment at seeing me pinned beneath him. I wiggled under his grasp, but Kaizen only held tighter.

"Seems like you've been caught, orphan," he mused.

I pursed my lips at him with a snarl, demanding he let go, but he only smiled.

"You're still a cheat," I barked at Levon, who walked up the last of the hill, effectively winning.

"Find your way out," Kaizen growled, still pinning me to the ground.

I grunted, feeling frustration bubbling within me, and strained against his weight, attempting to free my hands from beneath him.

"Free yourself," he barked, his eyes ablaze with a feverish passion.

With my legs partially free and my head clear, I quickly surveyed my surroundings, noting that I was still slanted on the hill, my head positioned lower than my legs.

Gritting my teeth, I dug my heels into the dirt, feeling the earth give slightly beneath me. I braced myself, preparing to use the force of my momentum to throw him off.

With a determined grunt, I continued to wiggle and squirm beneath him, putting on a convincing display of resistance despite the weight pressing down on me.

"Do it, Eliah!" he yelled just as I hoisted myself up and twisted, sinking my teeth into his forearm.

He cursed and hissed as his coppery blood filled my mouth. At that same moment, his weight shifted, and I clutched his arms, throwing all my weight into him and sending us both rolling down the hill. He finally let go as we tumbled forcefully down the hill.

A laugh escaped him as we tumbled to the bottom, lying on the ground and gazing at the bright blue sky scattered with fluffy clouds. Our breaths were staggered, but a sense of comradery settled between us.

Levon came running, his white tunic damp with sweat clinging to his chest. His bright smile emerged as he reached me.

"One day, I might let you win," he teased, chuckling as he hoisted me up. Kaizen was still lying on the ground, and the smile from moments ago vanished as he quickly rose. He started up the hill to retrieve his fallen cloak, clutching his blood-spattered arm.

His gaze met mine, a fire burning in his eyes—whether it was anger or acceptance, I couldn't tell.

"You'll pay for that," he asserted through gritted teeth.

I scoffed with a smirk and turned toward Levon, pushing his shoulder playfully. "You'll always be a cheat," I quipped, wiping Kaizen's blood from my mouth.

Levon grinned at me and headed back up the hill. "Let's do some real training now," he suggested. Energized by the sun's rays, I followed after him, ready to win.

My arms and shoulders ached from the continuous jabs and hook maneuvers, followed by a ruthless leg and arm workout that left me reeling on the ground, allowing the hot sun to soak up my sweat. Kaizen left quickly once practice started, only scanning the surrounding area as he stayed hidden within the tree's edge, then disappeared into the woods themselves.

We stopped our battle play once several carriages pulled to the front gates, deeming it time to hurry back inside to freshen me up for measurements.

———— • ✦ • ————

The tailor was almost a head shorter than me, with eyes that seemed too big for his narrow face. He was balding, with only a handful of black hair that wrapped around the back of his head, peppered with gray.

He helped me onto the small podium and promptly began taking my measurements, turning me around before he held up an outline of a dress with an air of disdain, poking me purposefully as I wiggled under his hold. He gave Levon a pointed look through his bushy eyebrows, hoping he might exert some influence over me, but only initiating an airy laugh from Levon.

I glanced at myself in the large mirror, remembering the last time I had a fitting. A few years ago, Calum had surprised me with new training attire, which inevitably earned him a few lashes from Jesri for using his money on me. As a result, Jesri threw out all my old training clothes, leaving me with no choice but to train in dresses until the new attire arrived.

"Hold still for just one moment," the tailor said, walking toward a table adorned with several pins, fabrics, frilly things, and lace. I kept my arms out wide, watching him gather items at the table reflected in the mirror.

"Sir Alder," he said, motioning for Levon to join him at the table. Levon gave me a quick wink before standing next to the tailor, towering over him much as Edmon towered over Levon. I stifled a laugh at the sight, eagerly awaiting to see what the tailor would bring over next.

"Eliah?" Levon said, returning to me. The tailor was holding a variety of colors, from dark blues to bright yellows, greens, and inky blacks.

"The tailor, Mr. Illeu, suggests a purple for royalty," Levon stated as the tailor held up a vibrant purple fabric that caught the light beautifully. Levon's eyes gleamed with a different idea. "But I suggest a crimson color for your passion, courage, and strength," he suggested.

The tailor displayed a luscious crimson fabric that almost shimmered in the light. "Perhaps we could also incorporate some complementary colors—gold, perhaps, with touches of white or black?" Mr. Illeu suggested, glancing at Levon, who then turned his questioning eyes to me.

"The crimson," I decided, slowly lowering my aching arms. Mr. Illeu eyed me, and I quickly propped them back up.

"Crimson it is," Mr. Illeu declared, walking back to the table of fabrics.

Levon walked back to my side, his presence comforting. "Red compliments you better," he whispered, sitting back on the sofa with a satisfied smile.

Mr. Illeu returned to my side and moved swiftly, measuring and noting, his hands working expertly with the chosen crimson silk fabric. He finished his last measurements before undoing all the pins and freeing me.

We exchanged thanks with the tailor before heading back to my rooms. The day had progressed well into the afternoon, and a nervous flutter danced in my stomach as I contemplated the challenges ahead. Facing the king, meeting the other contestants, dealing with Jesri and Calum. And then there was the looming prospect of being shown off like a prized horse, hoping desperately that no one in the Onyx Market caught any clues about who the Spellcasters were searching for.

Lost in my worries, I didn't realize I had stopped on the stairwell until Levon placed a comforting hand on my back, stirring me out of my trance. I looked up to see his saddened eyes, reflecting the weight of similar thoughts.

"You can do this, Eliah," he said, his voice carrying reassurance and concern.

I took a calming breath and accepted his outstretched arm, letting him guide me back to my rooms to wash and prepare for tonight. The gravity of the impending events pressed down on me, making each step feel heavier than the last.

We walked in silence until we reached the grand arched door, which seemed to be made for giants.

"I'm required to attend a sponsor meeting here soon, where we will find out more details about this Match. Once I get word Jesri's here, I'll send Aoife up to help you get ready," he said, his voice solemn with a regretful tone as if he wished he could stay by my side. He took my hands, holding them tenderly. "We should keep our distance for now," he apologized. His expression was heavy with sadness as he gently kissed my cheek, his touch lingering for a moment longer before pulling away.

I closed my eyes, trying to hold onto the fleeting moment of comfort, the sensation of his lips against my skin. When I opened them again, all that remained was the echo of his departing footsteps as he left me alone with my thoughts, the weight of his absence settling heavily upon me. With a heavy heart, I pushed open the doors to my chambers, steeling myself for the challenges ahead.

Lunch was laid out on the large table, and an array of small tea sandwiches were surrounded by sides of smothered vegetables, sugared fruits, and an assortment of confections. I sat in silence, mechanically taking bites of food, each morsel a futile attempt to quell the rising tide of anxiety within me. Doubt gnawed at the edges of my mind, leaving me uncertain if I could go through with the Match.

Throughout my life, others have always dictated what I should do and who I would become, but they have never acknowledged my soul.

The flame hidden within me rattled, stunning me to the core and zinging the air around me with electricity that seemed to dance on my fingertips. I sucked in a breath, quieting my anxieties but feeling every nerve ending in my body on edge, pulsating with an intensity that threatened to overwhelm me. I expanded my lungs, inhaling the sweet air, desperately trying to ground myself amidst the tumult of emotions and sensations that surged within me.

As I sat at the table, the amount of food before me only added to my frustration. Without thinking, I seized a bag and hastily filled it with the remaining food. Racing to my trunk, I grabbed another bag and stuffed it with clothes and a soft blanket from the large closet, hoping it wouldn't be missed.

Without a second thought, I slung the bags over my shoulder and stormed out the door, taking the same back stairwell that Levon and I had used the night before. Emerging onto the bustling city streets, I felt a surge of determination coursing through my veins, hoping to remember my steps to find that poor mother. The sun arched in the sky as I navigated through the tangled alleys. I stopped often and distributed food to anyone I encountered, offering warm words and as much comfort as possible.

Finally, I arrived at the small alcove where I had last seen the mother and her children. I found no trace of them besides the remnants of their things and took in my surroundings. A broken chair leaned against the corner, a makeshift shelter fashioned from thick clothing hung from a loose brick to the other side of the small corner, and a scatter of worn clothes, shoes, a rusty plate, and a wooden bucket. Without hesitation, I unloaded the bags, arranged the clothes and blanket within the cloth shelter, and placed the bag of food on the chair. I lingered for several moments longer, wishing she would return, but as I watched the sun dip lower in the sky, reality set back in, knowing what awaited me.

With a heavy heart, I turned away, retracing my steps and passing by those I had given food to, their expressions of gratitude still echoing in my mind. As I reached the final secluded alleyway leading to the castle's edge, I imagined the mother's face upon discovering the clothes, blanket, and food. A pang of longing tugged at my heart, and I wished I could see her again, learn her name, and offer support.

My thoughts drifted back to the present, to the daunting reality of what was transpiring with my fate in all this madness.

I sighed, listening to my boots scrape against the stone when my vision began to blur right as an oily darkness washed over me like a crashing wave, engulfing me in its suffocating embrace and pulling me deeper and deeper into a pressurized abyss.

I felt my muscles tensing and convulsing, unable to lift my hand as my legs gave out, and I fell to the ground with a sharp jolt that sent a wave of pain shooting through my left shoulder. Memories began to blur and rush past, fleeting and fragmented, each a painful reminder of my tortured past.

Agony erupted in my head, washing over me with so much pressure, worming its way through the ruts of my mind. Darkness scraped at my vision as I fought against it, feeling a sizzling fire within me recoil and squirm under its oily touch. I tried to scream but was consumed and plunged into a realm where I was no longer in control.

Their rotting touch was more evil than before, crawling up my body, ready to consume every inch of me as I thrashed against it.

Control it, Eliah, because that will be all you have left.

The memories stopped for a fraction of a second, sending ripples throughout my seizing body as fear crept and licked at every ounce of my soul. I gasped in terror, but no sound escaped my open mouth as I lay paralyzed in my own body.

You must let it happen.

The fear gripped me tighter like crashing waves threatening to consume me, driving me to flee blindly from its suffocating grasp and sensing its spidery tendrils chasing me into the deepest recesses of my mind.

Focus on what it feels like.

More memories surged, a relentless onslaught threatening to overwhelm me with its oily and wicked grasp. Amidst the tempest, a fleeting image emerged from my childhood of tranquil woods bathed in the gentle light of dawn. I seized the happy memory with desperate determination, refusing to surrender any further. I honed in on the sensory details—the fragrant aroma of flowering trees and the delicate caress of spring air against my skin.

Light surged, colliding with the oppressive darkness and forcing it to recede, pushing the haunting memories further away as it scraped my mind, sending pain crashing down my body.

Channel your anger.

I harnessed the roaring energy of my wrath, feeling it burn deep in my core, and allowed it to swell within me. Every ounce of anger fueled the blaze until it consumed me entirely, sucking all sensation with it. With a blinding flash of light, a cavity sliced through the veil of the dark abyss, revealing the cobbled alleyway and the distant glow of the castle before me. I screamed out against the encroaching darkness, feeling its oily tendrils rake across my body, but I pushed back harder against the pressure. My anger slashed through the darkness, deepening the cavity until it sizzled and shrank into its final icy breath, receding completely before finally ceasing.

I snapped back into control, tasting coppery blood swell in my mouth, and gasping for hot air for the first time in what felt like hours.

Weakness engulfed my trembling limbs as they slowly tingled back to life. Through a hollow tunnel, the city's sounds slowly filtered back into my consciousness. Despite the lingering throb in my head, I focused my mind to let the city chatter awaken me.

Tears blurred my vision, streaming down my cheeks unchecked, as I cried out into the empty air, uncertain if my words were mere whispers or anguished cries or if I said anything at all. With each passing moment, the sun sank lower, casting long shadows that seemed to mirror the depths of my despair, knowing I could be killed for not showing. The weight of my predicament pressed down on me, suffocating any semblance of hope.

Gasping for air, I struggled to steady my erratic breaths. The cool touch of the evening breeze offered a fleeting reprieve from the turmoil as I lay paralyzed against the cold stone. I gulped a few more deep breaths, forcing myself to settle and wait, scolding myself for venturing out here alone.

Click.

The sound shattered the silence, sending a bolt of fear coursing through my veins.

Click, click.

I held my breath, trying to hear where each click was coming from but each click echoed off the walls like a countdown to some unspeakable horror.

Cllliiick.

A cold chill gripped me as I felt a soft touch brush against my skin, icy fingers of terror tracing patterns of dread across my flesh. I dared not move, praying desperately that it was merely the chatter of insects crawling home for the night.

Click.

Tears filled my eyes as I slowly turned toward the source of the sound, my heart pounding so hard it echoed in my ears like a death knell. A slithering scrape grew louder, echoing off the alley walls with a sinister resonance as if it were announcing the arrival of something far more terrifying than any nightmare.

With trembling limbs, I blinked through my tears, my body aching as I struggled against the paralysis, desperate to move my arms. A dark creature swayed from side to side, creeping closer with each slow, high-pitched click. I blinked harder, and as the beast came into full view, a wave of terror crashed over me, sinking deep into my soul.

Its black, writhing form was like a grotesque and monstrous centipede that came from the depths of a nightmare. Each shaft of its body twisted and swayed unnaturally. Jagged, contorted legs—long and skeletal—ripped into the ground with razor-sharp claws, dragging its huge body forward with a slow, deliberate scrape. Every inch it moved sent a fresh wave of terror through me, as though its twisted form was a living embodiment of dread itself.

I whimpered as the creature crept closer. Its eyes were empty black voids, completely devoid of light, and its gaping mouth dominated its twisted face. The back of its body tapered into a thin, narrow end, where a bloody stinger jutted out. Waves of terror surged through my trembling body, my heart pounding furiously in my chest. Desperately, I cried out for help, my voice hoarse and frantic, as the horrifying realization hit me: this was a Breva.

"Help!" I screamed, the words torn from my throat in a desperate cry for salvation. But the alley remained eerily silent, save for the sinister clicking of the creature and its thick body slithering against the ground.

My senses flickered in and out as the world spun around me in a dizzying blur. I shouted as I fought to reclaim control, feeling the tendrils of darkness of Their presence taunt me.

A shout rang out behind me, bouncing off the alley walls, followed by the rapid sound of footsteps racing toward the Breva. I stared in horror as the creature hesitated, its movements faltering. Then, with a piercing, high-pitched squeal, it jerked violently as a flash of steel sliced through the air, severing its stinger with a sickening crunch. Black blood sprayed from the wound, splattering across the cobblestones in dark, oily streaks.

"Kaizen," I whimpered out, my voice barely a whisper as my arms slowly tingled back to life. I began dragging myself away from the gruesome scene, the eerie black blood splattering around me like a morbid painting. The clicking sound of the Breva filled the air, turning my bowels watery.

With a swift, deadly grace, Kaizen sprang into action like a silent guardian among the carnage of horror. He leaped off one wall, using its momentum to propel himself toward the Breva's grotesque form, his sword slicing through the air with lethal precision, finding its mark in the creature's flesh. It emitted a blood-curdling sound followed by fast, unrhythmic clicks.

As the sensation returned to my legs and upper body, I sat, urgently slapping my legs to recover faster. I glanced at Kaizen, now bathed in the creature's dark blood, his cloak now tattered as the monster squirmed chaotically under his hold and charged straight for me.

Kaizen's amber eyes burned with vibrancy through the dark blood smeared across his face as he drove the sword deeper, putting his full weight into the thrust. The Breva let out a guttural shriek, its mouth gaping wide, and it slammed its body into the unforgiving stone wall with bone-crushing force. The impact drove Kaizen into the wall, piercing the sword through the creature more. Kaizen swiftly leaped off its trunk, driving the sword up its writhing body and through its skull, raining us with its blood and building a cacophony of nightmarish sounds. Its body slumped in a pool of its own blood, cut in two from the waist up.

The stench of copper hung heavy in the air, mingling with a sickening rancid odor that threatened to overwhelm my senses. I retched violently, emptying the contents of my stomach until I was left dry heaving, my body wracked with involuntary convulsions. Gasping for air as Kaizen approached, his eyes ablaze with an enraged fury that pierced even through the darkness.

His teeth were bared in a feral snarl and his eyes blazed with such intense rage that it seemed he might strike me down. Yet, despite the murderous fury reflected in his gaze, he lifted me effortlessly and cradled me in his powerful arms. As he held me tightly against him, his bloodied body trembled with a sudden, profound sense of relief that seemed to flow through him, mingling with adrenaline and a worrying sense of dread of what could have been.

With each step, the world around me became a blur, the pounding of my heart drowning out all other sounds except Kaizen's beating heart. As he carried me away from the scene of horror, I counted each comforting beat, trying to center my thoughts away from such raw and tangible fear.

"Don't let it win," Kaizen whispered urgently into my ear, his voice trembling with desperation as the darkness closed in, threatening to consume me. "Stay with me. Fight it." The weight of the void pressed in, too overwhelming and heavy for me to resist. I surrendered to its cold embrace, slipping into unconsciousness as Kaizen's desperate pleas faded into distant echoes.

28

The shock of freezing water splashing against my face startled me awake. My head bobbed to the side before I jolted upright. My limbs tingled intensely as I regained consciousness. I coughed up the water, hissing in discomfort as I tried to steady myself, feeling solid hands gripping my arm to support me.

Brushing my wet hair out of my eyes, I saw Calum standing before me, his features etched with worry. Beside him was Aoife, her face mirroring Calum's concern. As the fog of confusion lifted, I realized I was back in my room, fully clothed in the clawfoot tub, soaked with freezing water and black blood that smeared the entire front of my body.

Cal's golden eyes frantically scanned mine before he pulled me into a tight embrace, soiling his cream tunic and blue vest.

"You idiot. Stay put, that's all you had to do," Calum cried into my hair before placing a gentle kiss on my hairline.

"I'm...fine," I lied, pulling away before Aoife tightly embraced me. The two of them were now dampened with the black blood.

"Sir Alder said you fell into mud as you passed out! Are you still having those episodes?" Aoife's voice trembled with fear, and my heart ached with love at the sight of her concern. Tears slid down my cheeks, cleaning my face as they fell. She cupped my cheek, and Calum's eyes bore into me, knowing it was all a lie.

"Calum, tell your uncle she is awake. We need to hurry," Aoife urged, shooing Cal out of the bathing room and closing the door behind him.

I couldn't stop the tears as they continued to fall harder and more profoundly, remembering all of it.

I embraced Aoife again with every fiber of my being, her gentle hand caressing my wet hair as she wept with me.

"I missed you, my dear," Aoife said, pulling me back and looking deep into my eyes. She cocked her head as a wave of confusion washed over her eyes. "Your...eyes," she muttered but quickly shook it off as she helped me out of the tub and turned on the water.

"We must hurry now; the feast is less than an hour. Take off your clothes and wash quickly," she pleaded, pausing to look at me with endearment in her brown eyes. "And wash twice, Eliah, you smell," she teased, opening the door. "I need to let the team know you're okay; I'll be back in a moment." She gave me a final smile before closing the door, her footsteps fading over the plush carpet.

I quickly peeled off my clothes and threw them into a pile in the porcelain sink. Sliding into the warm water, I let it melt away the cold and began scrubbing every inch of my body vigorously. I soaped my hair and body three times, still feeling the sticky blood coating me, still seeing the rank flesh of the Breva being slit in two.

Inhaling deeply, I begged the fear to drain from me but couldn't push away the oily feeling of the mindscraping, unsure how it paralyzed me.

I splashed my face, palming my eyes to calm my breathing.

I'm okay.

Because of Kaizen.

I exhaled as I stepped out of the tub and wrapped myself in a clean towel, beginning to dry my hair. Aoife's soft knock came at the door, and she opened it, exposing her smiling face. She took me over to the partition, allowing me to change into my underthings before pulling out the gorgeous gown Jesri had bought me for Spring Harvest.

"He demanded you wear it in front of the king," Aoife said with sad eyes.

"No," I snapped more harshly than I intended. "I'll wear my own gown."

Aoife's eyes gleamed with understanding as she helped me into a stunning, silky gold gown Levon had bought me. It hung low on my back, supported only by thin straps at my shoulders. The fabric cascaded down in a creamy, shimmering waterfall, making me feel beautiful despite the lingering phantom stickiness of the Breva's blood on my skin.

Aoife gave me a heartfelt smile. "You look different. Free," she remarked, squeezing my shoulders before leading me to the vanity.

"I'm so happy you're here. Life has been...different and dull without you," I lamented, genuinely grateful she was with me.

"I don't know if 'dull' is the right word," she teased, a mischievous glint in her eyes. "Seems like you've been on quite an adventure."

She brushed my wet hair, skillfully pulling it back into a loose plait. With practiced hands, she artfully tugged at sections to add volume, giving the braid a soft, romantic feel. Delicate flowers were woven into the braid, their petals peeking out as she pulled out several wisps of hair to frame my face, carefully finger-curling each strand to create soft, cascading waves.

"I don't know if *adventure* is the right word for it either," I replied, smiling as I watched her in the large crystal mirror as she worked.

Several other ladies' maids entered the room, chatting as they arranged a cosmetics tray on the vanity table. Aoife greeted them and graciously moved out of the way so they could begin working on my face.

They patted my skin with powder, added a rosey shade tint to my lips, darkened my lashes with charcoal, and replaced the flowers in my hair with sparkling gems.

"I liked the flowers," I stated.

"You're meeting the king, sweetheart, not a commoner," one of the ladies retorted, finishing gluing the gems in place before motioning the others out. Venom coiled in my veins as my anger pulsed, but Aoife's soft hand on my shoulder grounded me. Her familiar motherliness straining the anger out.

"Thank you," Aoife said to the departing ladies, her tone polite.

Aoife hurriedly helped me into my heels, and we rushed out into the hallway. Levon stood waiting, resplendent in a royal blue overcoat adorned with gold buttons that shimmered in the light. I wondered how regal he would have looked in the Royal Gaurd. His eyes sparkled as they met mine, causing my powdered cheeks to blush.

He extended his arm, bowing slightly to Aoife. I squeezed her hand in silent thanks before I let Levon escort me to my moment of dread.

"What were you thinking going out alone?" he whispered with worry.

"I wanted to help," I replied in defiance.

"Don't," he spat, his tone sharp and cutting. "At least not without me," he quickly added, his eyes flashing with a mixture of anger and concern. The memory of the energy I had unleashed to tear open the cavity for control surged through me as familiar as Aoife's comforting touch, yet it only fueled my anger.

"Do not patronize me. I didn't ask for this," I shot back, my frustration bubbling.

"Nor did I," he retorted, his expression tight with emotion as the air around us went taut.

We walked the rest of the grand hallway and silently descended the stairs, approaching the four guards clad in uniform by the large ornate doors. My anxiety flared like a roaring fire, but I forced my anger into silence. Levon squeezed my hand, giving me a subtle nod before leaning in to whisper into my ear.

"We are fourth in line for introductions. Jesri and Calum will already be there. I told Jesri to keep his mouth shut if he wants you to have a chance," he paused, looking deep into my eyes, and lifted my chin. "Hold your head up, Eliah. You're worthy of every eye."

My face heated under his solemn gaze, feeling he wanted to close the gap between us. Just then, the doors opened, flooding the room with light. We snapped back to attention before anyone could notice, and I held my head high, determined to face whatever lay ahead.

I am more than all this.

The grand dining room stretched out before us, glittering with opulence. Chandeliers hung from the high ceiling speckled with gold and hung like bouquets, casting a golden glow over the assembled guests. Navy and gold flowers were hung around the exterior, with similar banners of the royal crest billowing against a slight breeze. Various plants and expensive ornaments glittered on the dining table, making everything sparkle. The sound of murmured conversations and soft music filled the air but quickly subsided as they turned their attention to us.

King Thealor sat at the head of the large rectangle table in a deep blue overcoat also clad with golden buttons, ribbons, and star-shaped medals. His brown hair, woven with silver, was tied back with a black ribbon, while a peppered beard hung to the base of his neck. His queen sat beside him in a white flowing gown that was simple against her olive skin and long black hair that had no trace of silver for several years. She was an image of pure beauty.

Levon guided me forward, his grip firm yet comforting. Each step felt like a test, but I focused on Levon's words and the sense of purpose they gave me.

"Lady Eliah Archenon from Fernwen. Sponsored by Sir Levon Alder, previously of the King's Royal Guard," boomed a guard beside the door. The king's smile widened at Levon's name, and he bowed his head in welcome.

I gulped, determined not to let my gaze linger on anyone in particular as we crossed the ornate, polished floors. However, when Jesri's dark eyes came into view, a surge of fury ignited within me. I held his stare with an intensity fueled by malice, disregarding the attention it might attract, as Levon guided me to the spot across from him.

Jesri's eyes landed on my dress and his expression twisted into rage, teeth clenched, but he managed to compose himself. Beside him sat Calum, his usually tousled hair slicked back, exuding an air of regality, too similar to his *beloved* uncle. Despite his proximity, Calum refused to meet my eye.

Four other contestants were called, each emerging from a different door, escorted by their sponsors, who had ensured they were polished to perfection. Among them were three other females and five males, spanning a range of ages. I appeared the youngest among them, followed by a dark-haired boy named

Astor Flemming from Kleads. His dark almond eyes conveyed a palpable sense of anxiety. I felt a surge of empathy, a desire to reach out and reassure him that he was not alone in his apprehension as he sat beside me.

The king rose from his seat, his imposing figure commanding attention. "Welcome," he began, his voice surprisingly soft as it carried over the length of the table. "I appreciate not only those participating but also those mentoring and preparing our contestants for this adventure." His smile widened but did little to ease the knot of unease that had formed in my stomach and left my mouth dry.

"This year is very different from previous tournaments," the king began, his voice carrying a note of excitement. "It will be the first of many for the entire Kingdom to enjoy. In the past, we kept the contestants within my court's lands. But this year," he motioned to the lot of us, "we have selected an individual from each of the regions who has shown the most courage, the best abilities, the strongest will, and accompanied by the most well-loved sponsors with a dedication to succeed."

His excitement radiated like fireworks lit on Yulemas, causing a stir among us all. My stomach turned leaden as he continued. "Tomorrow night, each of you will be celebrated and presented to my court, marking the commencement of the tournament festivities. So, enjoy yourselves while you can tonight and tomorrow, and then the real entertainment begins. But now—let's eat! Fill yourselves fully, drink deep, and accept my deepest gratitude, my dear contestants."

Clapping followed as the king's words hung in the air, amplifying the anticipation and anxiety rippling through the room. All the doors opened, revealing a procession of servants carrying platters of food. They set them on the table before us, presenting a feast beyond my wildest dreams. Platters overflowed with crisp roasted meats, their savory aroma mingling with the scent of freshly baked bread. Bowls of spiced vegetables, buttered potatoes, and mouth-watering soups were placed before me. But the dizzying array of desserts was staggering—delicate pastries dusted with confectionary sugar, towering cakes embellished with fresh berries, and decadent, flavorful chocolates that glistened under the warm chandeliers.

The food was piled so high that it obscured Jesri's wicked face from view, a small mercy amid the overwhelming display. As I looked around at the other contestants, I saw similar reactions of awe and disbelief. The sheer abundance of the feast seemed surreal.

The tantalizing smells made my stomach growl, but despite the feast laid out, my appetite had vanished, replaced by a knot of tension, of anger, knowing that so much food would be going to waste when people outside these opulent castle walls were starving.

It made me want to scream, grab every pastry and stomp on them, overturn the table and walk out cursing them all, throw each buttered turkey leg at the king and dirty his perfect face, his perfect castle, and his perfect sadistic life.

Anger shot through me like a rocket, firing up every ounce of blood until it was boiling, making me shake. Levon grasped my knee under the table, squeezing hard, trying to anchor me as that metallic tang of rage pulsated in the air, energizing my fury even more. He clutched harder, glaring at me to stop, to calm down. Calum's usually calming, golden eyes darted up to mine, silently pleading while Jesri entertained himself, chatting about his pompous life.

"Eliah, stop this now," Levon whispered urgently into my ear, letting go of my knee and clutching my trembling hands. *"Stop or else you won't see any ounce of that freedom."*

Calum's eyes darted between Levon and me as he pretended to eat the delicate meat served.

"Eliah," Levon hissed through a forced smile, reaching for a pitcher of red liquid and pouring me a glass.

The others around us didn't notice us and were too busy stuffing themselves full. Their laughter and chatter filled the air with static, coiling my stomach into more knots. I gritted my teeth as I took the glass, raising it to my lips without letting the sweetness touch my tongue. I set the cup back down and sat straighter as Jesri's black eyes pierced mine.

Eat, his eyes commanded, glaring at me and then at my empty plate.

Instead, I held my head high, defiantly turning away and placing my hands in my lap, pretending to care about the conversation from one of the female contestants who talked about a festival she attended a year ago where she first picked up a sword.

Act the part.

Levon brushed his hand against mine as someone called over to him, drawing the king's eyes to us. His gaze weighed heavily on me and remained fixed as he finished his plate, then another. Even long after everyone's stomachs were full and the savory air had dissipated into thin wisps of memory, his eyes never left me, and all I could do was try to remind myself to breathe.

The king stood, silencing the spacious room. "With the festivities tomorrow, I hope that tonight you sleep well, for we shall enjoy ourselves more tomorrow." He took one last sip of his wine and held his goblet up in a cheer. "To my contestants," he said as his eyes locked onto mine once more. "May Tarragon bestow upon you the honor of passage!"

I glanced to Levon in question at the king's words as crystal glasses clinked, signaling the end of the meal. The king swiftly rose from his seat, his wife at his side, escorted by a dozen guards. We all waited for their departure to be excused and disperse to our respective rooms.

May Tarragon bestow upon you the honor of passage. Why did that name sound so familiar?

I shook the thought away as Levon helped me up, leaving my untouched plate, preparing to face Jesri's wrath. His dark eyes beckoned us to follow him out. With Calum in tow, we made our way towards our main quarters with only the click of our shoes and the tension between us all palpable.

We all reached inside the large foyer, but before the door shut, Jesri was shouting.

· ✦ ·

"Make me a fool one last time, Eliah, and I'll end you myself!" Jesri's hiss reverberated through the open room, his anger filling the air like a suffocating fog.

Levon stepped forward to intervene, but I pushed him aside, bracing for the full force of Jesri's wrath.

"I am no longer your puppet, and after this, I am not coming back," I fumed, trembling with suppressed rage.

"You will," he ordered, his eyes blazing with fury. Calum stepped before me, shielding me like he had done many times before.

"Uncle, please. You've always been hard on her. She has come of age, and *you have no right to her,*" Calum interjected.

"No right to her?" Jesri scoffed, running a hand through his slicked-back raven hair. "I'd say otherwise." An evil smirk twisted his lips, sending a chill down my spine and igniting a fierce bitterness that drowned out even the pangs of hunger.

"What did you do?" Levon growled, advancing toward Jesri like a predator closing in on its prey.

"You have no place here, Levon, besides making sure she wins this wretched thing—" Jesri began, but Calum interrupted, his anger radiating off him like sparks.

"What did you do?" Calum spat, his voice low and dangerous, every word dripping with fury.

"Tyran, *please*. What any guardian would," Jesri said dismissively, waving his hand as he strode toward the lavish spread of food on his table, flanked by an array of wines. "I've made an arrangement for her to wed a noble Lord with substantial wealth. And one who will introduce her into society."

Levon and Calum's expressions drained of color, mirroring the deep despair that flooded through me, crushing me like a boulder.

Marriage.

The word hung heavy in the air, suffocating me with its implications as I faltered to the ground. I would forever be tied to Jesri. All my dreams of freedom vanished in an instant, replaced by a seething rage that burned like wildfire in my chest, dragging my heart down into a pit of hopelessness.

"*You self-righteous wretch!*" Calum cursed, his voice thick with fury, his fists clenched at his sides.

"He'll be here to congratulate you on your winnings, my ward," Jesri spat, his tone dripping with malice. "*So win it.*"

"Who?" I breathed, my voice sharp with anger as Levon stooped to help me to my feet. My nails dug into my palms as I shook with rage.

A twisted smile curled Jesri's lips. "Lord Winslow of Bricol."

The slimy wastrel, known for his old, touchy, wrinkled hands, was old enough to be my grandfather.

Acid lined my throat as the air vanished from me, remembering the last time I encountered Lord Winslow at the Spring Harvest, conversing with Levon before I intervened.

"No," I spat, my voice dripping with defiance.

"No?" Jesri cooed, his tone sickeningly sweet. "It has already been arranged, dear; he will be the one to take you home."

"*Burn in hell!*" I yelled, the words bursting forth like flames from a raging inferno. I spat in his face, the disgust and anger bubbling up from the deepest parts of my core.

His fury burned to the surface like dead fish in a boiling sea, and his features contorted with rage.

I stormed out, with Levon at my heels, before Jesri could retort. Behind me, I heard Calum's shouts echoing through the long hallway as my head felt submerged, muffling all sounds except my pounding heart. I stumbled over my own feet in these cursed heels, the skirts of my dress clinging to my legs like shackles, dragging me down with each step. It felt as though every thread of fabric was woven with the desire to see me fail, to drag me down into the depths with that *monster.*

Everything had a price, and now I was forced to pay it.

My rage drowned out Levon's desperate pleadings until he grasped my hand, forcing me to stop. I tried to twist out of his hold, but tears fell, blurring my vision as he pulled me into his warm embrace, only causing the tears to fall harder.

All that hope, all those dreams—I realized would *never come true.* That wretched tree was nothing more than a cruel bad luck charm, always cursing me with never-ending punishment.

"We'll find a way," Levon whispered through his own despair. "We have to."

"How? There is nothing we can do. I will always be under his chains," I replied, my voice choked with despair.

He pushed me away only enough to hold my tear-stained face in his calloused hands. "*I won't let this happen.*"

"It already did," I voiced, sliding out of his embrace and heading to my door. My feet feeling so heavy.

"*I promise you,*" he cried out, his tone turning to anger. I could only shake my head as the tears fell to the carpet as I forced myself to keep moving. "I won't let it happen."

All I could hear was the rage pounding in my ears as I closed the door behind me and fell to the floor in a heap of tears, wallowing in a darkness that crept over me with a threatening vengeance.

29

I refused to get out of bed, eat, or drink, hoping the hunger pains would rile me up, but they only left me feeling more desolate. Aoife, Calum, Levon, and even a few scullery maids tried to tempt me with food, but they all failed. The darkness in my mind grew more concrete; Their dark touch wormed deeper in the mindscraping, clinging to each memory like a ravenous parasite. It ate away at me, begging for more and more.

My body felt heavy as memory after memory flashed by. I couldn't remember my name as the thick, suffocating fog wrapped around me. The world outside my bed felt distant and unreal; the voices of those who cared for me were just echoes in a void.

I let the darkness take over, giving in to its relentless pull. My dreams of freedom and a life beyond this torment felt like distant fantasies. The crushing weight of hopelessness pressed down on me, overwhelming my spirit. This time, I didn't resist. I allowed it to take everything.

A vivid memory flashed by, dragging me deeper into the dark pit.

"What's wrong with her?" asked a young girl with ringlets in her hair, pointing at me. Her mother glared at my old, worn shoes and spat on the ground.

"Everything. Don't dirty yourself with that," the mother replied harshly. They walked off, leaving me with the sting of their disdain. My scraped, bloody knees

burned as I ran, my dress snagging on branches as I darted into the woods, running as fast as my small feet could carry me, heading for the tree. I clung to its trunk, weeping hard until the force of it overwhelmed me, and I fell asleep.

When I awoke, the setting sun bathed me in warm light, coaxing the fog out of my brain. Darius sat next to the tree, either asleep or pretending to be, as I looked down at my bruised and scraped frame. Earlier, Calum and I were playing a game of tag, which ended with me falling into a rose bush and tumbling down a hill. Fearful of the punishment I might receive, I had run to the river to clean up while Calum tried to distract his uncle, yet on the way, I had accidentally run right into courtiers who mocked me with disgust. I could still see the repulsion rippling off that mother, dragging her daughter away like I was some infectious disease.

Tears continued down my dirty face as I prayed to the tree and the stars above, hoping they would grant me my parents' return, praying for a better life anywhere but here. I prayed so hard, feeling the weight of despair crushing me.

Finally, after I stopped my tears, I found the courage to tap Darius on the shoulder.

He slowly smiled and turned toward me. I helped hoist him up with my young frame as he gently wiped away the tearstains.

"Don't listen to the darkness," he said. His soft and reassuring voice was a balm to the harshness I had faced moments before.

A tear fell from my cheek as the memory passed vividly through my mind. I let them take it and play with my wilted heart as another memory flashed.

"Harder!" Darius yelled as I punched his padded hand, almost splitting my knuckle. I exhaled, striking deep with every stab of pain. "Harder, Eliah!"

I roared, thrusting my whole body into each throw, exhausting myself and increasing the grumbling in my stomach. Darius stepped aside, letting my momentum fling me to the ground. I grunted, hissing at the fall.

"If you can't do it right, don't waste your energy," he snapped.

"What energy?" I spat blood, biting my lip in the fall. "This is ridiculous. I am not a warrior, nor should I be! I don't understand what Jesri wants from me?!"

I laid down, letting the cool stone bite into my exposed shoulders and arms, gulping deep breaths to calm my racing heart.

"He wants you to succeed."

I laughed, hearing the echo of it throughout the stone training room.

"Succeed in what? His plans? Life? Getting out of here? I'd say I'm failing quite terribly at all three." I sat up, wiping the sweat dripping from my forehead. "I cannot be like this forever. I can't live like this, Darius."

At just fifteen, I was hitting ladyhood later than most, yet I was more toned than many of the gentlemen in town. Despite this, ladies still glared and spread rumors about me, assuming most came from the snake himself. Jesri continued to push me harder every day while the cold food became scarcer due to one failed evaluation after another. It left me stuck in my sad, wishful life.

"I want you to succeed. I want you to be who you were born to be—"

Darius's words were cut off by the oily worm as it seized, shaking me under its pressure before it vanished, leaving a residue of dark build-up around every crevice of my mind. I sat up abruptly, taking in the large room as my stomach rumbled with pain, feeling breathless and hollow with self-pity.

"Finally," Calum grunted, standing up from the plush chair in the corner. I grumbled, falling back into bed, not in the mood for his games. "No, no," he said, grabbing my arm and hoisting me back up. "You need to eat."

I shot him a glare but didn't retort as I spotted a cluster of food on the back table that made my stomach grumble deeper. Standing, I made my way over, my limbs numb and my nightgown sticking to my salty skin; Calum snickered.

"Stop," I seethed, shoving a muffin and several other savory pastries into my mouth before cutting up a dragon fruit with Kaizen's ruby dagger.

"Where'd you get that pretty thing?" Calum said, swiping it from me and rubbing a thumb over its pommel.

"What do you want?" I spat, taking the dagger back, and finished cutting the fruit.

"Am I not allowed to be here to help my best friend?" He rounded the corner of the table, picked up a few berries, and popped them into his mouth.

"And how do you suppose you'll help me?" I challenged.

"Like I always have—" Calum began.

"By cheating?" I interrupted, brushing past him and heading to the bathing room to wash off the brine of darkness still looming within me. *Pathetic.*

I was being pathetic, letting this arrangement control my life. Perhaps, if I won, I would gain enough money to break the bond, give it to Jesri, and be free of him forever.

"I never cheat," Calum purred with a devilish grin, trailing a step behind me. Ignoring him, I turned on the gold faucet, letting the cold water sting my skin awake. "Well, while you were busy wallowing in self-pity, Levon told us more about what he learned at the sponsor meeting. But I suppose if that's cheating..." he trailed off, waiting for me to beg.

I turned toward him, stoned-faced. "And?" I mocked, dabbing my face with a plush towel.

He grinned, popping more berries into his mouth. "It's a race. Whoever makes it out first—or alive," he added under his breath, "wins the Match and will be crowned the victor."

"A race? That seems too easy."

"Levon said there are no rules besides finishing, so each contestant can do as they please in whatever manner to finish first."

My mind raced over Edmon's warnings to Levon about the animals. A sickening feeling settled in my stomach, knowing I wasn't just competing against the other contestants but also against whatever beasts they would unleash into the arena.

I grabbed the dragon fruit and finished it off, walking to the vanity. I grabbed my brush and began detangling my hair as he appeared in the mirror, arms crossed, exposing a more toned body than when I had last seen him. I rolled my eyes and tried to put my hair into a braid, but my hands shook with anxiety that wouldn't leave me be.

"El," he breathed with sincerity, "I had no idea he was going to do that. We'll find a way out, even if it means running away together. I'll protect you from him, and we can live the life you've always dreamed of."

"Run away together?" I muttered. "Why would I ever go anywhere with you?" My anger sizzled within me as I finally finished a sloppy braid. I stood and headed toward my partition as Cal rushed in, grabbing my shoulder before I could disappear behind it.

"Stop this—this isn't you, El!" he complained, desperation evident in his voice, a tactic he'd used countless times to get his way.

My only answer was a glare as I shrugged his hand off and continued behind the partition, changing into the new training attire Levon had bought me.

I brought my hands to my eyes, trying to push away the dreaded reality of all of this, knowing deep down that there was only one way out of this—and Levon wasn't part of it or any of my dreams of freedom. I stifled a cry while extreme despair washed over me once more.

"El, please," Calum's voice broke through the heavy silence, but it only stoked the roaring flames of anger within me, banishing the suffocating darkness that had enveloped me.

Stepping out, I confronted him with a venomous glare. "I think I am being myself for the first time in my life, Calum. I told you I am done playing your games. I'm not some trophy you get to take wherever you want," I snapped, the air crackling with the intensity of my frustration. His golden eyes turned dark as he shook his head, his hair swaying with it.

He loomed over me. "So now that you're some *contestant* of the king, you think you're superior over us?" he scoffed, his words dripping with condescension and bitterness. "Remember that I've been the one on your side your entire life. I wasn't the one who left. I've been the one rooting for you since we first met, and I will always root for you, El. You're not a trophy to me."

"All you've done is keep me weak," I retorted, my voice trembling with suppressed rage. "Playing your sick game of *who-is-better*. You've never rooted for me but caged me in your life so no one else could have me. *So I couldn't succeed.* Never have you asked what I wanted. You're just as prideful as your uncle."

"Like you're any better?" he seethed with venom.

"No. I'll never be better—that's the point," I shot back, my anger boiling over. "I won't ever meet your kingly expectations, and I'm done playing. What we had was some made-up—"

The door swung open, revealing Aoife. Her expression shifted from bright anticipation to dark tension as she sensed the palpable anger between us.

"Then win this wretched thing so we can be done with you once and for all," Calum hissed, storming past and slamming the door shut behind him. My anger boiled within me, threatening to burst through my clenched teeth.

"You two—" Aoife started to protest.

"Please don't," I interrupted, grabbing my boots and hastily lacing them up.

"You understand that his parents left him too. I know he can be difficult, as can you, but you two are all you have left. Don't spoil something good," Aoife implored, her voice tinged with concern.

Was it ever good? We had fun as children, but things had changed. I had changed. I couldn't stand idly by, letting my life slip away under their control. The world was vast, daunting, and full of more pressing concerns than worrying about Calum's feelings.

Aoife let out a long breath, her frustration palpable. "I'm angry too, Eliah. Jesri had no right—"

"He does, that's the issue. He's a Lord *and* my guardian, remember?" I retorted sharply, seeing the hurt in her eyes. I couldn't handle any more emotions today. "I'm sorry. I need to get ready."

I needed to forget.

She squeezed my hand, her expression softening. "You're better than this."

"They've left me no choice."

I left the room, resisting the urge to return, seek solace in her arms, and unleash my frustrations upon the world.

Just a bit longer. I could keep up the façade for a little while longer. But one thing remained resolute: I would not allow myself to become the wife of Lord Winslow.

— • ✦ • —

I returned from my run, my body drenched in sweat and my muscles protesting with each step. There was barely enough time for a quick bath before my fitting. The tailor sighed impatiently as Aoife assisted me in slipping into the new gown. Bathed in crimson, the gown boasted a stunning array of gold and black gems, intertwining along my figure before seamlessly blending into the hem of shimmering silk that billowed like liquid gold while hints of black tulle adorned the sleeves.

Despite its beauty, the dress reminded me more of a queen preparing for her death than for a glamorous event. I pushed aside the unsettling image and focused on the details of the attire.

I was stunning with a newfound elegance and no longer a little girl wearing the childish attire Jesri had imposed on me. I was no longer bound by compliance and refused to adhere to a life devoid of joy. Through years of enduring pressure and hardship, I had transformed from mere coal into a resplendent diamond.

Aoife skillfully arranged my hair into an elaborate coronet, intertwining red, black, and gold ribbons. As the other maids applied cosmetics, they painted my face into someone unrecognizable as the head maid drew out a large box. Our collective breath caught as she unveiled the box containing a stunning black diamond necklace.

"King Thealor offers courage for the night," the maid announced.

I couldn't help but scoff, earning a disapproving glance from Aoife as she clasped the heavy necklace around my neck. It felt eerily reminiscent of those dark, phantom fingers, still lurking and ensuring I knew they were watching and waiting.

Suppressing my anxiety, I allowed my anger to propel me, fueling my determination as I stood and strode out the door. This time, I opted for black slippers, disregarding the maids' protests that heels were preferred. With Aoife trailing behind, I made my way to Jesri's door.

Act the part.

Maintain control.

Just a little while longer.

As I pushed open the door, Levon's anxious worry was palpable in his bright eyes, perhaps realizing the insanity of his idea. I forced my expression to remain neutral and held my head high while Jesri was brimming with pride. His only remark was a slick smile as he led our entourage to the steps of the king's balcony.

Arriving last, I found all the contestants looking equally stunning. Some wore bright feathers and extravagant hats, while others were adorned with gems from head to toe. Each outfit was uniquely different, ranging from fluffy ball gowns to tweed suits.

The boy from Kleads donned a dark green suit embellished with silver buttons and trimmings. His almond eyes, lined with dark charcoal, added a hint of intimidation to his otherwise gentle smile that welcomed me. The king's gaze lingered on me and the black necklace I wore, his lips lifting in a smirk.

Clad in pure gold, he shone like the sun itself, accompanied by his dazzling queen. With a raised hand, he silenced the growing murmurs among us.

"One by one, I'll introduce you to my court, so stand tall. Please wait for my dismissal before leaving," he commanded. His gaze lingered on me. "And don't forget to smile." A smile crept over his cleanly bearded face, tied with a simple blue ribbon.

I met his stare, feeling a tremor run through me, but I brushed it off as Levon's hand skimmed against mine. Stepping away from his touch, I refused to let myself feel anything until it was all over.

"Lady Beth, you are first," announced a guard beside the king, who swung open the balcony doors to a resounding wave of cheers echoing in the distance. My stomach churned, heavy with dread, threatening to bring bile up my throat.

Levon leaned in, "You're radiant in crimson." His breath tickled my neck, but I leaned away again, holding my breath.

Lady Beth wore a velvety emerald green that complemented her golden skin and blonde hair, holding herself with regal poise. The anticipation hung heavy in the air, each of us preparing ourselves for what was to come—whether relishing in the spotlight or dreading it.

The king nodded to us before he and his wife stepped onto the balcony. A kaleidoscope of colors danced on the ground below, casting shadows of their figures on the wide doors behind them. The cheers grew louder and more fervent as the king emerged.

He raised his hands, bowing in several directions before gesturing for the crowd to quiet.

"Welcome to my annual tournament!" His applause was met with thunderous cheers from the crowd. "This year marks a special occasion—a Match. We have gathered skilled contestants representing each region from across our glorious kingdom."

Shouts drowned out his last words as the anticipation grew deeper within me, grateful I hadn't eaten since after I willed myself out of bed.

The king signed for silence again, "I extend my deepest gratitude to all of these brave contestants for enlisting in this courageous quest with sheer determination."

Enlisting?

His words faded into the background as wrath pulsed in my ears, stealing my breath.

They...enlisted for this?

Lady Beth stepped forward with her sponsor, twirling in front of the crowd—*twirling*. They all wanted to be here. They all *asked* to participate.

I tried to breathe again but lost my footing, and Levon quickly caught me as I leaned into him, hoping to dispel the aloofness. He held sturdy, helping me stand.

I looked up at each contestant, their faces bright with excitement and a vicious pride to be introduced to the King's Court *by* King Thealor himself. My breath stuttered out in a fiery wave.

The second contestant, dressed in a dark indigo suit adorned with silver, stepped forward. His fiery red hair seemed to mirror the blazing fury within me, urging me to scream and flee.

I gritted my teeth, clenching my hands into fists as the fear that had once consumed me now ignited into a fiery rage. It was the same fear I had succumbed to since I first understood the meaning of being an orphan, realizing that my parents were never coming back to rescue me from Jesri's clutches.

And no one was here to save me now.

As the third and fourth contestants took their turn, followed by the fifth, each raising their hands in joyous pride, I felt a surge of disgust welling up inside me.

Jesri grabbed my arm, yanking me back to face him. "Whatever you're thinking about doing, stop it," he hissed, barely audible above the roaring crowd.

I tore my arm away, my heart pounding with anger, the air crackling with tension around me.

"Do it, Eliah," the dark voice whispered, sinister and seductive, forcing an image through my mind. I gazed up at the balcony's edge, calculating the distance, the impact below.

"Do it."

The king called forth the sixth contestant. Levon's grip tightened on my hand, pulling me back from the brink, from the darkness encroaching upon my heart.

I shut my eyes, trying to silence the insidious whispers.

"You are *strong enough. Do it. You can finally find your freedom."*

Images twisted in my mind's eye, a sinister tapestry of power and darkness. I saw myself seated upon a throne amidst a river of blood, a crimson crown atop my head, my hair swirling in the shadows. The voices that once condemned me now cheered; their long fingers applauded. Red lighting flashed against the black sky as thousands hailed my name.

"You are fear, *Eliah."*

This...this isn't right. This isn't me.

"It is Eliah. This is *who you are—who you are meant to be,"* the sinister voice mocked.

Levon's grip tightened on my hand, urging me forward as my feet skidded against the slick floor, his eyes wide with terror as if feeling my fear.

"Eliah, don't let them win."

But I couldn't shake the vision from my mind. My black gown soaked in the blood of a throne before a cheering crowd, their chants echoing in my ears. A dark aura pulsed against the flames within me, threatening to consume everything.

"Come back to me," Levon urged again and again.

Control it, Eliah, because that will be all you have left.

I felt the maggot and grasped it, forcing all my anger upon it, feeling it squirm under my command.

I am in control.

I opened my eyes, meeting the king's dark gaze. His brows furrowing as he motioned me forward. "It seems that the lady is afraid of a crowd," he boomed, laughter rippling through the court below, joining in the mockery. My breath caught in my throat.

"Eliah," Levon said, turning me towards him. His gaze penetrated mine as his eyes flashed with a vibrant electricity, showing more of the blue in his turquoise eyes. I gasped for breath as his touch anchored me, reeling me back from that bloodied throne and not caring about Jesri's seething eyes.

Levon's hands cradled my face as he gently kissed my forehead, seared with a quiet fury, driving back the darkness encroaching upon me with an actual force that was warm, welcoming, and felt as old as the stars themselves.

"*My Regina*," he whispered, his words carrying a fierceness that stirred something deep within me, banishing the shadows that threatened to consume me and energizing my entire being with a faint light. Then he proceeded to say something in a tongue I didn't understand, his voice barely muttering words.

His voice steadied my trembling heart, replacing the visions of a bleak future with the warmth of love. With a steadying breath, I willed my feet to move.

"*Come back to me,*" Levon said as he released my face and approached the king, his figure illuminated against the colorful spectacle below. With a graceful bow, he acknowledged the king, then waved to the crowd.

Inhale.

Levon's radiant face turned towards me, his arm outstretched.

That rippling power compelled my feet forward into his hand. His smile widened, silver glinting in his eyes like stars in the night sky.

"Welcome back," he whispered, his voice a soothing melody as I stepped onto the balcony, greeted by a sea of cheering faces. The crowd stretched out before me, a vibrant mosaic of colors and energy. My heart skipped a beat.

"Lady Eliah Archenon of Fernwen!" The king's voice boomed over the applause, and I glanced to his side, meeting the queen's gaze. Her smile was bright, tinged with a hint of sadness as she nodded respectfully before turning her attention back to the crowd. The king ushered me back in line with the other contestants.

"To my dearest contestants! May Tarragon guide your path to victory!" The king's words were met with an enthusiastic chorus from the crowd, their voices blending together like a roaring, erratic symphony. A surge of energy coursed through me as my heart pulsated in a new rhythm. Filling me with a newfound sense of vibrancy as if my very core was ablaze with lightness, and the blood in my veins flaring in response.

Levon's grip tightened on my hand, and tears streamed down his cheeks. His smile wavered, a mix of relief and joy evident.

I squeezed his hand in silent reassurance, but as I attempted to retreat, the king's gaze bore into me, challenging me to take another step. Levon pulled me back to his side in a protective gesture.

The king cleared his throat, commanding the attention of the crowd. "Betting will take place at the front gates as usual. Remember the rules—one bet per family. Now, let the festivities begin: Eat, drink, enjoy the night, for tomorrow, the real enjoyment begins."

With a final gesture, he raised his hands, and streaks of glittering fire danced through the air above us. Fireworks exploded, illuminating the night sky in a dazzling display of colors.

I closed my eyes, allowing the vibrant hues to permeate through my eyelids. Taking a deep breath, I steeled myself, acknowledging the presence of the dark force within me. I refused to succumb to its influence, to the possibility it presented. Whatever they sought from me, I would face it head-on, ready to fight until the very end and allowed this new warmth and peace within me to take precedence.

I recalled the memories vividly, Darius's voice echoing in my mind.

Don't listen to the darkness.

His words lingered, urging me to push through.

If you can't do it right, don't waste your energy.

I refused to waste my energy fighting against the past, against false truths I had formed about my life, dreams, and future. I couldn't...wouldn't let the darkness of the Spellcasters drag me down with them in their evil schemes.

I sucked in a breath and opened my eyes, moving my view to the sky. Watching the radiating colors explode against the deafening blackness. It took my breath away and pulled my veins with something unfamiliar, something I hadn't *truly* felt since I sat wishing under that wretched tree.

Hope.

30

L evon held onto me tightly as we navigated through the throng of people. The crowd was thick, and I felt hands brushing against my shoulders, arms, and side as they praised my name with the unmistakable stench of hard liquor on their breath, their thoughts consumed by the festive atmosphere.

Feeling overwhelmed, I begged Levon to take me somewhere, anywhere but here, away from the cacophony and the chaos.

Levon merely smiled in response and guided me away, paying no attention to Jesri's persistent questions, which he continued to shout even as we moved out of earshot. Calum was nowhere to be seen and probably enjoyed the women's attention and free-flowing drinks.

My dress kept catching on the bodies pressed tightly against one another, making our progress slow and cumbersome. The crowd radiated with excitement, their energy tangible as they pushed forward, eager to reach the front where the betting was about to commence. The air was thick with anticipation, the noise of chatter and laughter blending into a continuous roar.

My stomach churned with anxiety, knowing that *tomorrow*, I would embark on the lifelong mission Jesri had set for me.

I forced myself to silence these rising fears as more people applauded me. Some even bowed deeply, and by the time they straightened up, I was already gone, no longer there to acknowledge their gestures. I didn't feel guilty or care about any of them. They were dancing, flattering, drinking, and laughing, living as if they had no concerns or cared little about anything beyond their revelry. It disgusted me, especially knowing children were starving in the streets and mothers struggling alone to care for them.

Levon must have noticed the disgust on my face because he glanced back, tugged on my arm, and gave me a sympathetic smile.

"How can so many people fit in here?" I shouted to him as we continued to make our way through the crowd.

"By pushing and shoving," he replied with a chuckle, demonstrating as he cleared a path for us.

We finally emerged into the open air, free from the tightly packed bodies. As we rushed into the empty city streets, the lights around us seemed more alive than the sweaty, chaotic crowd we left behind.

"How is the king supposed to control any of that?" I asked, still catching my breath.

Levon slowed our pace and came up beside me, taking my arm and pulling me close.

"He doesn't," he said with a wry smile.

I furrowed my brow in confusion. "What do you mean?"

He continued, "King Thealor only allows the ruckus as long as the people obey the rules. If they don't, more severe measures are taken."

"How does one control a crowd of thousands?" I pressed, genuinely curious and slightly horrified.

"Extreme force," he replied. Seeing the shock on my face, he quickly added, "Everyone knows the consequences, so they clear the square by one in the morning and continue their festivities elsewhere. We...they haven't had to use those extreme measures yet."

I nodded, still processing his words as we continued through the vibrant, quiet city. The contrast between the silent streets and the unruly crowd we'd left behind relieved my quelling stomach.

We strolled through a secluded, illuminated cobblestone archway flanked by vibrant, colorful houses. "Did you ever enjoy yourself during these festivities?" I asked, trying to ease my anxiety.

"Only in the early days of my employment, but I grew weary of it," Levon replied, his tone somber. I nudged his shoulder playfully, taking in the crisp night air as his expression turned serious. "You had me really worried earlier. I didn't realize the depth of it all. I...I don't know how to break you out of this—"

"I don't expect you to break me out of anything," I interrupted, halting abruptly. Clinging to hope, I refused to let despair about the future take hold—a future without him.

He turned me to face him and gently lifted my chin with his fingers. "My Regina," he whispered into the warm night air. "You are still worth every agonizing year of waiting, and I can wait a little longer." Cupping my face in his hands, his eyes filled with concern for what tomorrow might bring, for the inevitability of Jesri's tight grasp. "I will not fail you, Eliah. I made that vow long, long ago, and I will uphold it *forever*."

My heart raced at his proximity, longing for his lips to draw nearer, wishing to escape into a dream world where we were just ordinary people again, untouched by the complexities of our current existence, where we could defy the odds and live a simple life together.

With a heavy heart, I closed my eyes, feeling a wave of despair wash over me, and gently pushed away from his embrace.

"No matter what path I choose, you're not a part of it," I said bitterly. The pain in my words cut deep. It surged through me, coursing through my veins and settling in my heart. "We were never meant to be. This," I gestured between us, "was never supposed to happen."

I took a deep breath, my voice trembling. "Jesri will find out. And I can't allow myself to let *you* throw your life away for *me*. Save your money, your estate, your people—" Faces flashed through my mind: Saasha, Elise, Aveal, Edmon. "They need you."

"*I need you,*" he retorted, his eyes darkening with an irritation I hadn't seen before. He stepped back, running his fingers through his hair in frustration. "I need you," he repeated, his voice strained.

His face contorted with the growing despair of a life neither of us wanted. A life thrust upon me, filled with dark Magics and relentless pursuers of the Onyx Market.

It was unfair, all of it.

My frustration grew, with tears threatening to spill. How utterly exhausted I was of this life.

"I need you, Eliah. We all do," he said, his voice barely audible over the clamor of the crowd behind us chanting a song. "You—" he paused, reconsidering his words. "I...I know your—"

I waited, staring into his eyes, full of confusion and remorse. His mouth opened and closed as he struggled to find the right words. My thoughts were a tangled mess, my heart raging in all directions, torn between hope and despair.

"Your life isn't ideal," he began, his voice trembling with emotion as if he was withholding something from me. "It keeps dealing you a bad hand, over and over again. But you keep going. You still believe in a better world, a better life." He stepped closer, taking my hands in his, his grip warm and reassuring. "You *will* achieve that life, Eliah. I know it. With all my heart, I do."

The tears flowed freely, my raw pain mingling with hope, reopening that crater within me that still longed for that world, whether in this life or the next.

He took my face in his hands and gently kissed away my tears. "Don't lose sight of that dream," he said softly. "One day, you'll understand everything—the pain, the anger, the training, all the depressing days, and the long hours. It will all make sense. Keep fighting, keep going, and remember who you are: my Regina."

"I'm falling for you because of your light, Eliah. Be the source of light in this darkening world, and know that you are a *beacon* for goodness. Don't succumb to the darkness. You fight—let your anger guide you rather than try to suppress it. Embrace this unrelenting side to you and let it ignite your spirit. When you do, it *will* free you."

He pressed his forehead against mine, and his own tears began to fall. "I promise you," he whispered, his lips brushing mine in the faintest touch. We shared a breath before he pulled away, wiping his tears.

We lingered in that shared moment, drawing strength from each other, ready to face whatever came next.

"We should head back. Casmir needs to talk with us, and Admearin demands to see you before...tomorrow."

I nodded, letting his words sink into my racing heart as he led me back into the crowd of sweaty bodies.

We found them by the long table of sweets amidst the chatter of other guests who were at Levon's party. As they spotted us, their faces lit up.

"Eliah!" Admearin exclaimed, hurrying over to pull me into an embrace. Her short hair was elegantly pinned up with gold beads, complementing her flowing purple gown that hugged her figure.

"You looked like a true queen up there," she remarked, admiring my stunning dress and the king's black gem necklace that still felt like hands around my throat. "It's not fair for someone to look that beautiful."

"I'll say," I replied, gesturing to her equally stunning gown. She blushed but said nothing as she led me over to Casmir and Levon, who were already engaged in deep conversation.

Admearin cleared her throat, catching Casmir's attention. He looked up and took me in with a warm smile.

"You were spectacular up there. A true star," he said, kissing my hand gently.

I blushed, feeling a wave of warmth at his compliment. Glancing at the massive but fading crowd, I took a deep breath. Admearin looped her arm through mine, leading me away from Levon's worried gaze. I could sense his silent message: *Later,* his eyes seemed to say as he returned to his conversation with Casmir. My stomach coiled.

"Please tell me you've tried the confections? The flavor is exquisite," Admearin exclaimed with a grin.

I shook my head, mustering a smile. "I can't imagine stomaching anything right now, if I'm honest."

She patted my arm reassuringly. "Well, you'll just have to win this wretched thing so the king can bathe you in all the sweets."

Forcing another smile, I recalled what the king had said, not just during our presentation but also at last night's dinner: *May Tarragon grant your path.*

What did that mean? Tarragon—why did that sound so familiar? Perhaps Tarragon was a king, or noble faded away with the history of all those Magics. A history that *should* be known.

No, that's not it.

Swallowing hard in the stifling air, I longed to escape this dress, this crowd.

"I've never seen you in action, but based on all Levon has said, I know you'll do marvelously, dear. Believe in yourself," Admearin said, her voice soft with encouragement.

"Do you know who Tarragon is?" I blurted out, desperate for something to ground me in reality, craving answers, even if they were wrong.

"Tarragon?" she echoed, eyebrows furrowing in thought.

"At the feast last night and up there," I gestured toward the high balcony jutting out of the castle. "The king said: 'May Tarragon grant your path to victory.' I don't remember much from my childhood history lessons, but I can't recall anything about Tarragon."

She furrowed her brows in thought, searching her memory for any clue. "I can't recall either. Perhaps Casmir or Levon might," she suggested, pulling me back towards them.

I appreciated her sincerity, her friendship feeling more genuine than Calum's. I dismissed the thought as we interrupted the men's conversation once more.

"Darling, do you know who Tarragon was?" Admearin shouted over the racket of the crowd. Casmir turned toward her, his green suit complementing his eyes and silver hair.

"I don't think it's a 'who' but rather a 'what,'" Casmir replied. "As far as I know, Tarragon is a spice most used in baking or cooking; said it adds a spicier bite to it."

My heart plummeted into my stomach as I recalled the little black drawing of a dragon on the spice Elise used to season the chicken. My head spun as their conversation continued.

"Well, that doesn't add up," Admearin remarked, casting a doubtful glance at me. "What does the king mean by '*may Tarragon grant your path to victory?*'"

"Little Dragon," I muttered, interrupting, feeling the weight of its significance pressing down on me. May the *dragon* grant your path to victory. I sucked in a deep breath as my head spun with anxiety.

Admearin and Levon looked at me inquisitively, but Casmir's eyes widened with sudden realization, a fear that sent shivers down my spine. "Tarragon is known for its strong flavor, earning it another name: The Little Dragon."

I stepped back, my gaze rising to meet Levon's as the color drained from his face, confirming my worst fears. Admearin gasped beside me, and suddenly, the world around me seemed to blur into chaotic motion.

This morning, the basket of fruit left by the king was filled with dragon fruit. *Dragon.*

I stumbled backward, feeling dizzy and overwhelmed. Levon quickly reached out, grabbing my arm with a fierce grip. His eyes were ablaze with a mix of anger and disbelief.

"It can't be. It—it can't," I whispered, my voice barely audible over the noise of the crowd.

Levon's eyes met mine, searching for his own explanation.

Edmon knew it was some kind of creature...but a *dragon*?

It couldn't be. It had to be a mistake. Dragons didn't exist—or at least, they weren't supposed to. Neither were the Breva, Miehja, or any other creatures summoned by Them.

"H-how does one fight a dragon?" I rasped, the words escaping me almost involuntarily. Acid burned my throat as a flicker of fear seized its way in, but my anger wrapped around it, choking it off before it could burrow deeper and steal my breath.

Levon turned to Casmir, whose own eyes reflected the same fear. Then he looked back at me, scanning the crowd frantically for a way out. His panic was palpable, etched across every line of his body. When he met my eyes again, they were filled with worry.

"I promise you, we'll find a way," Levon rasped, his voice trembling and trailing off in an empty promise that filled my soul with dread.

"I need a drink," I panted, pushing through the crowd.

My heart thundered in my ears as bodies jostled me, buckling my knees and leaving me gasping for air, for relief from this—this life. Tears welled up, blurring my vision as Levon crouched down beside me, placing a gentle hand on my back as shock seized my body, rattling my breath.

"Breathe," Levon whispered, helping me rise as a loud bell rang out in the distance. The crowd fell silent, parting like a curtain as the balcony doors swung open, revealing a brilliant light and the silhouette of the king.

"My dear people! What a pleasure it has been to host such a special year with such special contestants," the king's voice boomed. "The betting has ended. Give your last wishes to our vigilant contenders." Cheers erupted, drowning out the tempest within me. Levon held me tighter, holding me close.

"And to our dear contestants, please return immediately to the front gates. Thank you!" With a wave, King Thealor disappeared through the doors, leaving a surge of excitement as people clamored to glimpse the contestants one last time.

My feet turned to stone, resisting every effort to move with the crowd's relentless pull. Clutching onto Levon, I locked into my memory his scent, the sensation of his soft touch, the strength of his heart.

He turned me into his chest and wrapped me in his arms, shielding us from the tumultuous sea of people, the cacophony of voices, and the looming tide of fear that shook us both. They could never erode the hope we clung to, the dreams we both cherished yet knew were doomed to fail.

"Remember your light, Eliah," he implored, his voice quivering with emotion. "Harness your anger and channel it. *You control it*," he cried out, his words stifled by his tears. "I'm so sorry," he breathed against my neck, his embrace trembling with emotions as raw as my own. "I didn't know."

Enveloped in a frenzied hush, we were washed forward by the crowd. Dark tendrils clawed at my mind, threatening to consume me once more as I stumbled forward until I reached the front gates with the others. Following the guards inside, we were greeted by the king's smile, a portent of the trials that awaited us.

Levon stepped back, positioning himself behind me as the other contestants filtered in, their mentors trailing behind them. Despite the gravity of the situation, they all wore smiles and exuded excitement, as if they weren't about to willingly step into the jaws of death.

"My spectacles, you performed admirably," the king expressed, his smile taking on a darker edge. "What a display you shall all provide."

Two footmen emerged with a clap of his hands, bearing trays of small glasses filled with a swirling blue liquid.

"As our final toast," the king declared, gesturing toward the drinks. The contestants reached for a glass one by one, swirling the liquid within as it shimmered in the light as the sponsors stood by watching.

Timidly, I took a glass, gritting my teeth as I forced myself to calm my breathing.

Inhale.

Exhale.

"To our land of Creos," the king proclaimed, raising his glass. The other contestants followed suit, echoing his sentiment. "May we usher in a new era of civility and compassion for all within our beloved kingdom."

"To our beloved kingdom!" Several contestants cheered in unison.

"To civility!"

"To compassion!"

I lifted my drink a little higher, forcing down the trembling in my fingers.

To a better world.

Lowering my arm, I brought the glass to my lips and downed the blue liquid in one swift gulp. Not allowing myself to enjoy its sparkling flavor or to let my anger spark as all the contestants clapped, handing their empty glasses back to the footmen, who quickly rushed away as if they, too, could not stand to be under the stare of the king who now smiled sinisterly.

I swallowed, feeling an overwhelming tug tether me to some unknown oblivion as something within me stirred, sputtering and reaching for me as if begging for release.

Struggling against the hollowness that began to swell in my ears, I fought to draw in a breath, but each inhale felt like a strenuous effort. A heavy weight settled over me as I staggered backward, my weakening body no longer able to keep me standing. Darkness pulsated through me as I felt Levon's presence grasp me while I spiraled down into a heavy abyss.

With a rasping cough, I managed to utter a plea, but my words were lost in the thickening haze of my fading consciousness. My vision was beginning to blur as the shadows closed in, surrendering to the inevitable, and collapsing in a mindless heap.

Oblivion beckoned with a soothing embrace.

31

I stirred to the sensation of a chill wind caressing my neck while gravel dug into my cheek and ear. Gasping, I inhaled sharply, the frigid air biting at my throat, causing a sudden cough to erupt.

Blinking my eyes open, I found myself greeted by a watery, gray light, the sun's warmth drowned out by a cascade of dark clouds. A shiver rippled through my body, jolting my sluggish mind awake.

Drugged. He drugged us.

The realization hit me like a physical blow.

I spat a curse under my breath as I slowly rose to my feet, brushing gravel from my cheeks and gloved hands. Taking in the vast expanse of the desolate mountain range that stretched as far as the eye could see, feeling a sense of isolation wash over me. Glancing around, I noticed two other contestants asleep nearby, dressed in similar slick, black attire that shimmered like scales in the faint, watery light. Thick, black boots encased my feet, their laces reaching up to my shins—sturdy enough for traversing the terrain yet heavy enough to hinder swift movement.

I turned my gloved hands over, feeling the strange material flex and stretch against my fingers. Whatever this fabric consisted of, I hoped it would hold up to this desolate landscape of ice.

Pushing myself upright, I focused on shaking off the remnants of grogginess, allowing the biting cold to slice through me, waking me fully to the bleak reality of my situation.

To my left, a rugged expanse of towering mountains stretched out, their jagged peaks crowned with a thick layer of snow, while dark clouds swirled ominously overhead, casting a sense of impending doom. Ahead of me and to the right was a sheer fatal cliff that would send anyone who misstepped into the Afterworld. Behind us lay a thicket of dead bushes and a path leading downward, promising potential shelter. If the supposed dragon didn't claim us, surely the merciless elements would.

"Some match for compassion," I scoffed bitterly, remembering the toast everyone chanted before the king drugged us. I eyed one of the contestants who jerked nearby, her dark braid swept over her face.

I shook out my limbs, searching for anything that could serve as a weapon, but found only a barren landscape of frozen, brittle terrain.

I crouched beside the girl while the boy to my left suddenly awoke with a loud groan, his voice piercing the silent mountains.

I tried to shake her awake, but she remained unresponsive while the boy's groans grew louder, drawing attention to our presence.

Rushing towards him to muffle his sounds, he unexpectedly swung a punch at my side, knocking the wind out of me and sending me crashing to the ground. Pain shot through my knees as they hit the rocky terrain. A cough escaped my lips as I struggled to catch my breath.

He scrambled to his feet, his blue eyes wide with disbelief as he surveyed our surroundings.

"Where are we?" he demanded, his blonde hair stark against the somber clouds. "What happened? This wasn't part of the plan!" His curses echoed louder than I'd prefer.

"*Hush yourself unless you want to be eaten,*" I warned, eyeing him warily as he sized me up. Rising to my feet, I still felt the lingering effects of the drug clouding my thoughts.

"What do you know?" he spat, his tone laced with arrogance.

I shrugged indifferently. "Clearly, the king drugged us and wanted us to stumble unwittingly into the monster's lair."

He staggered back as the girl coughed herself awake. She shot up, stumbling back into a prickly, dead bush. Cursing, she shoved her braid over her shoulder and hastily regained her footing.

"What's going on?" she spat, her voice laced with as much venom as I felt.

"Fernwen here thinks monsters reside in these mountains," the boy said, moving closer to the girl, helping her settle.

I shot him a glare. Fernwen? They knew I was from Fernwen, yet I knew nothing about them, but perhaps that was my fault.

"Monsters, huh?" the girl coughed, brushing herself off. "As if she knows anything besides how to cower in fear."

The boy smirked, casting a knowing glance in my direction.

"What *was* the plan then?" I scowled at them, my voice edged with frustration.

"Like Tyran would I tell you. Remember, only one wins," the boy retorted defiantly.

Gritting my teeth, I surveyed them, realizing they were just like Jesri, like all those at the king's party—hungry for fame and money.

"Do you know anything about survival in these conditions—"

A deafening roar erupted from the cliff behind us, shaking the ground beneath our feet and assaulting our eardrums. The girl collapsed to her knees, hands clamped over her ears, and screamed in terror, her voice bellowing just as loud as the roar. Instinctively, I lunged toward her, covering her mouth as we all crouched in frozen fear.

She quickly shoved me off and bolted down the jagged mountainside path. The boy followed suit, struggling to maintain his balance against the pull of the steep slope. I cast one last desperate glance around, searching for any sign, any clue that could aid us, but found nothing.

I quickly staggered after them, leaping from one jagged rock to another. We ran perilously close to the cliff's edge, its sheer drop stealing my breath.

"Move it, Zeph!" the boy hissed urgently at the girl, his voice strained with fear as he slowed down to assist her.

I rolled my eyes in disgust—so much for the idea that only one of us would win.

We stumbled down the treacherous slope as another thunderous roar reverberated dangerously close behind us. Glancing back, my heart pounded as I saw nothing but the swirling darkness of the approaching storm clouds.

Finally, we reached an alcove nestled within the side of the mountain and rushed inside, gasping for breath in the suffocating darkness.

"What...was that?" Zeph panted, hunching over as she tried to catch her breath.

The boy exchanged a look with me, his expression etched with defeat and frustration. "Maybe Fernwen was right," he muttered between labored breaths.

I glared at him, inching my way out to see if anything followed...*or flew.*

"Where are we?" Zeph slurred the effects of the drug evident in her speech.

"Judging by the towering peaks and the blanket of snow, my guess is we're somewhere along the Aduantas Mountain Range. The Unmarked Territory. Known for its unforgiving, icy terrain," the boy remarked, stepping up beside me to survey our surroundings. "And for the chilling tales spun to scare the wits out of children."

I furrowed my brow, recalling the map of Creos in Jesri's study. How far were we from the King's Court? Days of travel? A week? How had they managed to transport us here so swiftly?

"The Aduantas Mountains?" Zeph hissed, her panic pulling me back to the present. "This *wasn't* part of the plan. I didn't sign up for this! We were supposed to be in the King's Arena...not here, in the middle of nowhere!" She stumbled toward us, tripping over loose rocks in her disorientation. The boy rolled his eyes, a smirk playing on his lips, before turning his gaze back to me.

"I'm Osric from Samar," he declared, extending a gloved hand to me. I glanced down at his hand, then back up to his piercing blue eyes, before diverting my attention back to the daunting mountain range. Engaging in small talk felt insignificant in our situation. "Now you're supposed to say *your* name," he prodded, grabbing my shoulder and turning me to face him.

I sidestepped out of his grasp, planting myself out of his reach. "So what was the plan then?" I reiterated.

He chuckled, the sound grating against my nerves, his too-perfect teeth glinting in the dim light. "Tell me your name first, and then maybe I'll consider sharing," he said, stalking closer to me and folding his arms across his chest.

I exhaled sharply, irritation prickling my skin. "Is *Fernwen* not good enough for you?" I retorted.

Zeph snorted, stepping up beside him. "She's the lord's pet," she sneered.

My anger ignited like wildfire, coursing through my veins with searing intensity.

Osric held up his hands, attempting to defuse the tension. "No need to be unpleasant, Zephyr," he said smoothly. "Yet, hearing it would make for quite the interesting story."

"How much do you know?" I spat, reigning in my fury.

"Enough to realize you didn't sign up for this willingly," he replied, closing the distance between us and shoving me against the jagged wall. Towering over me by at least two feet, he leaned in close. "Now, let's get one thing straight. The one who was too afraid to join doesn't get to win. Got it?" he ordered between his teeth. His tone dripped with arrogance and malice, fueling my anger until I surged forward, unable to contain myself any longer.

I stomped on his foot with ferocity, relishing the surprise in his eyes. In a fluid motion, I drove my knee up into his groin, satisfaction coursing through me as his agonized scream tore through the air, echoing off the walls of the alcove with startling intensity. Doubled over in excruciating pain, he clutched at himself, vulnerable, and I seized the moment, thrusting my elbow upward with all my might, the impact reverberating through my arm as it connected with his chin.

He staggered backward, dazed, and I released his foot, pivoting to unleash a swift, punishing kick to his chest. The force of it sent him crashing to the unforgiving stone floor. He landed with a curse, his words dripping with venom as he condemned me to a fate worse than death at the hands of the monsters.

Zephyr spat at me, rushing to his side to help him up as he clasped his torn, bloody elbow.

So much for the fancy suit.

Zephyr curled her lip, assisting Osric to his feet, who now clutched his manhood. He began to laugh, a cruel sound that echoed through the alcove. "Impressive moves for a petty ward," he sneered.

I flexed my fingers, feeling the anger coursing through me like a taut bow-string ready to snap. Pressure built deep in my core, shaking my body with each inhale and exhale. Gritting my teeth, I clenched my fists and flared my nostrils, letting the pressure burn more profoundly until it melted and curved against my body like a second skin.

With a shuddering breath, a surge of crackling energy burst forth, illuminating the air with blinding light and scorching embers that crackled and danced around us. The force slammed us against the unyielding stone walls, a sudden onslaught that left us gasping for air, disoriented and shaken; as quickly as it had materialized, the light vanished, leaving only the echo of its power reverberating in the air.

The two looked at me with even more disgust and confusion, coughing as they got to their feet. With disbelief, I glanced down at my hands, rotating them only to find my suit scorched and riddled with holes.

"What the—"

A large smashing sound reverberated through the alcove, snapping my attention back to the two of them. Fear was palpable on their faces as they silently retreated into the dim light beyond the alcove's entrance. Another startling rumble of rocks stirred behind me, raising the hairs on my neck and causing the fire of defiance within me to flicker as if seeking refuge. I quickly got to my feet as a loud clicking noise emerged, echoing hauntingly in the darkness from the depths of the alcove.

I stood paralyzed, the very air fleeing my lungs and leaving me breathless.

The clicking sound echoed louder off the walls and penetrated deep into the recesses of my soul. Osric and Zephyr's faces contorted in frozen fear, their eyes wide with terror. I whipped around to see a Breva slithering into view, its grotesque form twisted and mangled, festering with a putrid infection that assaulted my senses. The stench alone was enough to make me gag. Frantically, I scrambled back as the creature's wide mouth clicked threateningly, sending another wave of terror coursing through us.

Zephyr screamed and sprinted out with Osric trailing her wake. I shot after them, falling and hauling my thick boots over the tumbled rocks.

A deafening crash and screech of falling rock thundered through the air as I emerged back into the watery sunlight, leaping over boulders and dead brush.

The Breva loomed before me, its massive body dwarfing the one that Kaizen sliced in two. Its black form was peppered with a sickly grey, and several of its legs were limp with atrophy from chunks torn out of it. The rumble of its jerking movements shook the very floor of the mountain as its clicking grew louder, the sound echoing off the canyon walls.

I caught up to Zephyr, who stumbled over her boots while Osric's blonde hair disappeared farther down the hill. With a cry, I grabbed her, hauling her with me as we tumbled faster down the mountainside, our bodies sliding over the sharp rocks and brush that littered our path.

Osric reached a flat landing and darted for a narrow path wedged between the two mountains.

"RUN!" Osric's voice pierced the chaos, drowned out by the thunderous cascade of boulders and bits of rock raining down upon us. Its clicking increased, diluting my head with a sharp agony of noise.

Osric plunged into the narrow gap, his movements urgent as he pushed his body through. Without hesitation, Zephyr followed suit, throwing herself into the tight space, and I swiftly followed behind. The coldness of the mountain bit into my ripped suit as smoky tendrils of air escaped from our hot breaths.

"*GO!*" Zephyr shrieked, her voice echoing through the narrow passage.

"It's too tight!" Osric hissed, his struggle tangible as the Breva crashed into the mountain behind me, dislodging small rocks that rained down upon us.

Zephyr's scream pierced the air, her hands shielding her head as the Breva relentlessly battered against the narrow opening again and again. Black blood sprayed from its broken, grotesque body mere inches from where I stood. I pressed against Zephyr's trembling body as more rocks pelted down upon us.

The air around us became thick with dirt as the mountain shook, fear slamming into my heart and suffocating me as I gasped for air. Osric slipped deeper into the heart of the crack just as the Breva's attack abruptly ceased, leaving an eerie stillness in its wake. Dirt wafted up, clouding my vision.

We stood in tense silence, hearing only the sounds of our racing heartbeats and labored breathing. The dirt around us gradually settled into an ominous quiet.

"Is it gone?" Zephyr hissed, shoving me toward the opening of the crevice. I shot her a sharp glare before I forced my feet to move.

I am in control.

Sliding cautiously along the stone walls, I held my breath, straining to listen for any sign of the Breva. There were no telltale clicking's or even the faintest rustle of movement. I inched my head out of the crack and peered out, nothing caught my attention until my gaze was drawn to the giant claw marks carved into the mountainside, the black blood still warm in the dirt below. Leaping over the viscous liquid, I crouched low and scanned the surroundings.

Nothing. There was nothing.

I stepped out cautiously, my eyes darting around, analyzing potential hiding spots, escape routes, or makeshift weapons among the scattered rocks. Glancing back, I waved urgently for Zephyr and Osric to join me, but I caught movement twenty feet above before they emerged from the crack.

My heart stopped as I beheld the Breva's sleek form clinging to the mountainside. Its blackened body was stained with blood, and its tail curled up with its stinger ready.

"NO!" I screamed, leaping to them just as Zephyr stepped out with Osric. My voice echoed throughout the mountain range, and the clicking resumed, louder and more ferocious. The massive body of the Breva leaped, hitting the ground with a bone-rattling quake.

Zephyr and Osric hurled themselves over fallen rocks, but the Breva instantaneously struck its stinger, piercing Zephyr's shoulder. She screeched, collapsing to the ground and clutching her wound. Osric hesitated, terror etched across his face, before rushing to my side. He cursed my name as blood pooled around her, soaking into the cold, dry dirt.

The poison worked swiftly, her screams turning into gurgles as the Breva's clicking grew more frenzied.

"You killed her!" Osric cried, watching the Breva slither up to her. Her foot twitched once, then went still, her chest barely rising. "You killed her!" He shoved me aside, rage and grief contorting his features, before sprinting down the hill.

My feet were leaden as I watched the Breva click up to her, its mouth lengthening wider. Kaizen's voice echoed in my mind: *Whatever you do, do not let one take you.*

Swallowing my fear, I spotted a sharp, broken branch jutting from a dead trunk. I gripped the branch, yanked it free, and charged toward the Breva before the fear sank in.

Its gaping mouth stretched wide, ready to swallow Zephyr whole as I hurled the branch. It pierced the inside of its throat and sprayed black blood over Zephyr's limp body.

The Breva let out a high-pitched shriek that resonated painfully in my ears as it clawed at its mouth. I lunged toward Zephyr, hauling her up by her arms and dragging her away. She was heavier than I expected, and with my feet sinking into the cold ground, I heaved her toward where Osric had fled. The Breva thrashed, trying to dislodge the branch, its blood pooling beneath it.

"OSRIC!" I yelled, praying he was still nearby. "OSRIC!"

I couldn't drag her much longer before the Breva found us again, as it successfully dislodged part of the branch. Desperation clawed my insides as I scanned the area, spotting a large jumble of rocks clinging together with a small hole at its center. I tugged harder, praying it was big enough for us to hide in.

The Breva's high-pitched scream ceased, replaced by a thunderous crash. I glanced up to see its massive body poised at the top of the hill, oily blood oozing from its maw. Its depthless eyes gleamed with a vengeance as if it had feelings and would not leave empty-handed.

I pulled harder, every muscle straining.

"Tyran, *please*! COME ON!"

I clenched my teeth, muscles straining as I exerted every ounce of strength and speed, leaning back against the resistance. The jagged rocks loomed mere feet away, their rough surfaces beckoning as the Breva's clicking resumed, now accompanied by a gruesome choking sound, as if the creature was drowning in its own blood.

It lunged toward us, its clicking punctuated by guttural gurgles that made me want to vomit. Its massive body crashed into a boulder, hissing at the impact and leaving a trail of blood.

Finding my footing, I hauled Zephyr up against the rocks. The opening was too small for us both or for me to pull her in wholly. I quickly dragged her body over one of the rocks and jumped in. With trembling hands, I laid her down and pushed against her knees, her body reluctantly sliding into the narrow gap, the jagged edges of the rocks threatening to rend flesh as I fought.

The Breva's clicks intensified, a morbid cry summoning other predators to our location. Desperation surged through me as I shoved Zephyr harder, the jagged rock scraping my skin raw as I pushed her into the narrow crevice. The acrid stench of the Breva's blood permeated the air, a thick, choking stench. Bracing myself, I barely had time to react as the Breva smashed into the outer rocks, a scream ripping from my throat. I ducked, curling protectively over Zephyr's limp body. Dust and debris swirled around us as I gave one final, desperate push, ensuring she was completely hidden.

Swiftly, I vaulted over the rocks, scrambling to escape. The Breva charged, its massive form bashing against the jagged stones. Suddenly, its clawed arm snared my foot, yanking me violently to the ground. Pain exploded through my body as I hit the earth hard, my vision blurring with the impact. The gurgling clicks of the bleeding Breva reverberated in my ears, its proximity freezing my mind with terror. The overpowering stench of its blood churned my senses.

Do not let one take you.

I lay paralyzed beneath its grotesque body, suppressing a scream as its cavernous mouth stretched open. The jagged remnants of the large branch jutted from its throat, and it choked on its own thick, black blood. Its fully erect stinger glistened ominously at the tip of its tail, clicking menacingly. My body trembled uncontrollably, but Levon's voice echoed fiercely in my mind.

You fight—let your anger guide you rather than try to suppress it.

Rage surged through me like a wildfire. My lip curled in defiance as the Breva staggered back just enough to create an opening. Seizing the moment, I lunged forward with a primal scream, thrusting myself into its gaping maw. My hands grasped the blood-slicked branch, and I tore it viciously from its throat. The creature's agonized wail reverberated through my bones, hurling me back to the ground, the branch still clutched in my shaking hands.

In less than a heartbeat, its stinger shot down, striking the ground mere millimeters from my neck. I rolled frantically, barely evading another deadly strike, as its viscous black blood splattered from its mouth onto my legs, burning with a rancid heat. It continued its relentless attack, its stinger smashing down repeatedly in a savage frenzy before its massive form slithered over mine, and I felt the sting of its razor-sharp claws grazing my thigh. Above me, the segmented shafts of its body writhed and swayed, revealing a gruesome gash on its underbelly.

Instinctually, I seized the broken branch, driving it with all my strength into the exposed wound. I screamed, pouring every ounce of fear and fury into the thrust. The Breva shrieked in agony, its cries a chilling mixture of wails and hisses as more hot blood spilled over me. It convulsed violently, its serpentine body coiling and writhing, encircling itself in a desperate bid to escape the pain.

With fury coursing through my veins, I leaped to my feet and raced downhill, refusing to witness the Breva's demise and unsure where else to go, praying nothing got to Zephyr before she woke up.

The already dim, gray light of dusk faded into an unnerving, inky black sky, making the warmth of the Breva's black blood on my skin create ghostly wisps in the chilled air. Despite the cold slicing into my lungs with each breath, I pressed on, driven by adrenaline, overriding the protests of my empty stomach and exhausted body.

I ran until the landscape became a blur, unable to distinguish between rocks and shrubs and until fatigue threatened to overwhelm me. By some luck, I stumbled upon a shallow hole in the mountainside. Hastily, I gathered dry brush to cover myself, seeking refuge from the elements.

As I huddled in the makeshift shelter, my sole focus was on silencing the chattering of my teeth and suppressing the fear that threatened to paralyze me. The cold night air seeped through, chilling me to the bone. Desperate for distraction, I grabbed a thicker piece of wood I had found next to the brush. With a sharp rock in hand, I began to carefully sharpen the stick, each deliberate stroke a futile attempt to carve away my mounting dread.

32

A howl startled me awake, jolting me from my restless sleep. I slammed my head against the low roof of the small hole I had taken refuge in, causing the remaining dried brush to tumble to the ground.

I exhaled sharply, watching my breath mist in the moonlight. Shivering, I licked my chapped lips, trying to steady my racing heart.

Another howl echoed across the quiet night, sending a chill down my spine. I curled tighter into a ball, hoping the darkness of my suit would enable me to blend into the shadows.

"I am not afraid. I am brave. I-I am," I repeated barely above a whisper, trying to summon courage against the encroaching fear.

I rubbed my hands together, trying to stop them from shaking, as another howl echoed nearby, followed by a scattering of small yelps from the hill below. The sound sent the hair on my neck to rise, and I struggled to calm my shivering breath. Suddenly, a sharp and chilling scream pierced the eerie night air. I heightened my ears to listen, ensuring I was not caught unawares by whatever was in these mountains, and waited.

A deep pressure ignited within me, like a stoked fire rushing through my body. My heart swiftly slowed to its normal rhythm, and a soothing warmth began to thaw my freezing limbs. I took a deep breath of the cold, crisp air, feeling it electrify my entire being as if every cell had been awakened and I had taken my first breath from a moment of drowning.

I glanced down at my hands in curiosity. The warmth spread to my fingertips, starkly contrasting the biting cold around me. My previously muted and numb skin was now vibrant with life through the suit's burnt holes.

What is happening?

I marveled, awe-struck by the strange and powerful sensation coursing through me. It was as if some dormant energy had been unleashed, filling me with a newfound strength and resilience.

I rubbed my face, ridding myself of the confusion, and felt the sticky residue of the Breva's dried blood. A shudder of disgust ran through me just as another scream pierced the vast silence, compelling me to peer out from my hiding spot.

The sky glittered with countless stars, their light casting an ethereal glow over the cold landscape beneath the waning moon. Despite everything, I couldn't help but feel a sense of awe. Each star sparkled and radiated as if eager to meet me, beckoning to something deep within my soul.

The celestial display seemed almost otherworldly, the stars shimmering with brilliance contrasting sharply with the grim reality around me. I breathed in the cold night air, feeling it fill my lungs with a crisp, invigorating chill.

I sat there, mesmerized; the fear and exhaustion of the past days seemed to momentarily fade as I stared at the stars, so distant yet so vividly present, offering a silent promise of hope and endurance, begging me to keep going. I had an odd sense of feeling at home, much like I did in the colorful woods behind Jesri's estate.

Cautiously, I stepped out of the small hole, stretching my cramped legs and pressing against the mountain to peek around it. The moon cast a blue, silvery glow over the haunting, dead terrain, very different from the vibrant life of the sky. Long, narrow shadows cascaded from the jagged, towering peaks.

My heart stopped, and my breath caught in the frigid air.

I've seen this range before.

My breathing quickened as I scanned my surroundings, clutching the makeshift dagger I made from the thick stick, hoping it would be enough for a fight.

Fear gnawed at my insides, cold and relentless. I looked back up at the mountain peaks, memories flooding my mind: dark reds and blinding flashes of light, the overwhelming terror, the cold metal of the manacles, the screeching monster, and the shadowy figure's fingers wrapping around my throat.

"No," I breathed, my voice trembling. "No, no, no."

Panic gripped me as I backed against the rocky surface, my eyes darting around for any sign of movement. The terrain seemed to close in on me; my increasing awareness of this place and the horrors it invokes were suffocating. Each shadow felt like it was coming alive, and every rustle of the wind was a whisper of impending doom. The memory of the shadow man, with his cold, menacing presence, flashed through my mind.

I closed my eyes, shaking away the images and the fear that threatened to paralyze me.

Inhale.

I am in control. I am in con—

A blinding pain seared through my mind, dropping me to my knees.

No, no, no. No!

I am in control.

Another wave of agony crashed over me, and I crumpled to the ground, convulsing in torment.

"Welcome home, Eliah," the sinister voice hissed, slurring and elongating my name as it raked down my spine.

My throat tightened, my breath stolen by the invasion. I fought back with every ounce of strength I had left.

GET OUT!

"Accept your fate, Eliah. Don't fight it—"

"GET OUT. GET OUT!" My screams shattered the oppressive silence, echoing off the towering walls of the alcove.

Desperation fueled my actions as I slammed my hand against my head, channeling my rage at the insidious presence burrowing into my mind. I latched onto its oily black tendrils, crushing them with a fiery intensity until they sizzled and convulsed like the Breva and vaporized to a dulling headache.

With a hiss, air rushed back into my lungs, and I uncoiled my body, lying flat on the icy ground. Gasping for breath, I stared at the dark sky that twinkled in an embrace.

"No...more," I gasped, a desperate plea to the uncaring void.

They know I'm here. This is their territory.

Swallowing my anger, I forced myself to sit up.

Did Levon know the Match would be here?

Flexing my fingers, I stood, unwilling to waste another second wallowing in pity.

The sooner I finished this, the sooner I could escape their domain.

I stomped down the hill, letting the eerie moon guide my way. I clutched the sharp branch in my hand and let this *energy* of my anger build up and steam off me, melting the frozen ground under my weight.

"What's *happening to me*?" I whispered, the weight of the past few months pressing heavily on my shoulders.

Every lie. Every secret. Every fight and aching limb.

Every kiss.

Was it all just a pretense? A lie to manipulate me into this? To make me comply?

The anger surged again, burning hotter as I started running. I grumbled as the black sky slowly turned a dull gray, heralding the cold sun of dawn.

None of this makes sense. What memories do they want? Why do they want me to join them?

The horrifying image flashed in my mind: the bloodied throne I sat upon, their cheers echoing as spidery fingers crawled up to choke me into compliance, with a crown of death on my head.

I shivered at the image, pushing it far, far away, and letting the overload of questions distract me as I continued down the slope.

"*Fernwen!*"

A hiss came from the right, halting me and sending gravel and dirt scattering. I scanned the area, seeing only the chasm's edge and the murky fog swirling below. I stalked toward where the voice came as a howl echoed off the mountain paths below.

Creeping closer to the edge, I spotted Osric's light hair as I peered over. Disgust and rage twisted my face as I saw him clinging to a dried root off the cliff, standing on a narrow slice of rock barely big enough for him. The deadly plunge below made my stomach lurch.

"Get down here!" he hissed.

I knitted my brows together and stepped back while my anger surged, hotter and more intense than ever before. My teeth clenched, and my fists tightened as I glared back at him, unyielding and defiant.

"*No way in Tyran,*" I spat back with venom.

His eyes darted down the hill behind me before locking back onto mine with a deadly glare. "Fine," he mocked sarcastically. "Hopefully, you'll satisfy their hunger."

I quickly pivoted to look behind me, bracing myself, yet nothing but the eerie breeze brushed past my cheeks, twirling my blood-soaked hair with it. I turned back just as Osric grabbed my ankle and yanked, sending me crashing onto the rugged terrain. Sharp rocks tore into my suit, and sparks of pain exploded through my vision as he pulled harder, dragging me across the frozen ground as I clawed desperately, forsaking my makeshift dagger.

I cursed, kicking at his arm, but soon felt the sickening pull of gravity as I teetered on the cliff's edge. Screaming, my nails broke with my desperate attempts, the jagged earth slicing open my black suit as I clawed at rocks, weeds—*anything* to stop the fall. My fingers found a small root jutting from the ground, and I clung to it desperately. My torso curled over the edge, leaving me hanging over the sheer drop of the cliff, my heart pounding in terror.

The rage in me boiled over, fueling my desperation. I shouted through gritted teeth, my voice raw and primal as I kicked his arm off. The wind whipped around me, adding to the chaos as I dangled, each second feeling like an eternity.

My mind raced, the adrenaline and fury blending into a maelstrom of emotions as fear swelled up into every fiber of my being. Osric grasped my shoulder, yanking my body, forcing me to let go and accept my impending fate. I screamed at him, cursing his name, and kneed him in the side before quickly swinging my legs with enough momentum to kick him in the chest. He faltered, barely clutching to the root. I didn't look to see if he kept hanging on as I curled my arms, lifting myself back onto the ledge.

I scrambled to find purchase and hoist myself up, sliding on my stomach as he grunted close behind and grabbed at my legs. I kicked his hand off, sending loose gravel and dirt cascading down his face and over the cliff edge in a puff of smoke.

He cursed at me as I crawled to my feet, sprinting away from the edge as fast as possible. The sound of feet smacking against the rough gravel echoed behind me. Within an instant, he was on top of me, tackling us both to the ground with a hiss. The rocks scraped painfully against my exposed skin under his weight. He wrapped his arms around my waist and heaved me upright as I kicked off the ground with all my strength, sending us both tumbling backward with an air-escaping thud.

He swiftly let go, grabbed my head, and flexed, putting me into a headlock. I clawed at his already shredded suit, turning my head towards him and catching the sourness of his dry breath. Desperately, I kneed him in the groin, where he released me just long enough for me to break free and jump atop him. I straddled him, raining down one hard punch after another, the sting of each impact fueling my rage until my knuckles were slick with his warm blood.

With a powerful kick, he sent me screeching across the rocky ground. "You killed her!" he screamed, charging at me with his bloody face. I struggled to find my footing right as he crashed into me with a solid impact, forcing the air out of my lungs. We smacked the ground, slicing open parts of my suit, and felt the tug of my braid stuck beneath my back.

"*You left us both!*" I hissed through gritted teeth as he pressed his weight into me, viciously smiling down at me as his blonde hair sagged in front of his face.

I heaved my legs up, trying to get him off me, hearing Kaizen's words blare through my skull.

Get out. Get out.

I squirmed, freeing my hand, and threw a solid punch to his cheek, but he quickly retaliated, gripping my arm and throwing several blows to my jaw, each strike sending a jolt of pain, driving me into the ground. I blinked back at the stars, feeling a welt erupt on my face.

Abruptly, my anger surged, blinding and all-consuming. The air around us crackled with electric energy; a gravitational light held us suspended for a millisecond before a sudden zap burst forth, throwing Osric off me. He skidded to a stop against a large rock, his body convulsing uncontrollably before falling limp.

My heart pounded as I fought for each shallow breath, staring at his limp body and then at my hands in disbelief.

No.

My mind raced through a hundred scenarios, each more implausible than the last, yet they all led me back to the impossible.

No!

This wasn't why the Spellcasters were hunting me—they wanted memories, not...*me.*

I'm nothing. *I'm normal.*

The notion seemed absurd, a fantasy I refused to entertain. But every confusing moment replayed in my mind: the heightened awareness, the uncontrollable anger, the incident that left Levon's face a brutal mess, and the Miehja attacking only those who posed a *threat.*

Swallowing hard, I forced myself to stay grounded. I needed to focus on finding a way out of here, not on wild imaginations.

Pushing myself up from the ground, I sat feeling a strange energy pulsating between my fingers as I wiped my bloody knuckles on my leg and brushed the hair out of my eyes, trying to steady my breathing and regain control.

The sky dawned into a somber grey, broken clouds pressing low overhead. I slowed my breathing and gingerly picked myself up, every movement sending waves of pain through my aching body. My jaw throbbed, a painful bruise forming, which I hoped would be hideous enough for Lord Winslow to call off the arrangement if I made it out of here alive.

Shifting my gaze to Osric, lying motionless on the ground with his chest still rising and falling, disgust churned within me. For a moment, I entertained the idea of tossing him off the ledge but ultimately decided to leave him for whatever animal might find him instead.

I scooped up my makeshift dagger before trudging down the steep hill, stumbling several times but using the momentum to keep myself upright. Thirst, hunger, and sleeplessness gnawed at me, each step feeling heavier than the last.

The gravel crunching underfoot for the mountain slope was my only companion, the silence punctuated by my labored breaths.

I kept walking and walking, driven by sheer willpower, even as exhaustion and pain weighed me down.

+ ✦ +

After what felt like hours of trudging, fatigue settled over me. My steps grew sluggish as I veered off the path, descending into a valley of dead trees and frozen greenery. There had to be a stream nearby and perhaps nuts, berries, or even squirrels.

I pushed deeper into the twisted embrace of the dead branches, the ground beneath me becoming soft and springy, giving me hope that water was close. The clouds above were now a dark, oppressive grey, hanging low and shrouding the landscape in fog. The cold, moist air chilled me to the bone, and I shivered as I moved forward, hearing the weight of my breath in each step.

Unexpectedly, a rustling noise sounded up ahead, causing me to freeze in place and hold my breath. I listened intently as the noise grew louder, something approaching through the underbrush. Clutching my makeshift dagger tightly, I slid up against a tree for cover, listening to my heart pound as I waited.

Heavy footsteps broke through the dead branches, sending rocks scattering. Peeking around the tree, I saw the younger boy from Kleads emerge into view. His face was covered in scratches, his suit was torn, his head hanging down, looking as desperate and worn as I felt.

I watched him for a moment, assessing his condition. His movements were slow and cautious, his eyes darting around as if expecting danger at any moment. Without thinking, I stepped into view.

Fear flashed across his face as he jumped back, holding out a large rock and a sharpened branch. His expression softened with relief when he recognized me, but he kept his weapons up.

"Astor, is it?" I rasped, my voice rough and crackling. I coughed, feeling the cold air slice deeper into my throat. He nodded, his dark almond eyes curious, examining every detail of my blackened, splattered face, down to my tattered suit and bloodied hands. "I'm not going to hurt you," I said, raising my hands in a gesture of peace.

"What happened to you?" he whispered, his voice barely audible over the wind picking up around us.

"The King's Match did," I replied, licking my chapped lips, my throat aching for liquid.

He lowered his makeshift weapons slightly. "I didn't think this was what it would be like."

I shrugged in agreement.

"Food?" His eyes conveyed his hunger, his pale skin mirroring my own desperation. I shook my head. "I-I found water. Maybe another mile back. I can take you there?" His voice sounded light and airy, causing me to wonder how young he was.

"Please," I nodded, grateful for his offer.

He quickly pivoted back to where he came from, and I followed, our bodies shivering against the wind, which now howled past our ears like a mournful lament.

Due to the thick fog, I was unsure how long we had been walking or what time of day it was when we finally reached the river, but I immediately kneeled, gulping the icy water, and let its coolness clear my mind. I splashed some onto my face, hoping to wash away the blood, but the biting cold stiffened my fingers, making it impossible to scrub.

"I heard you didn't volunteer for this. Is that true?" Astor asked, finishing his gulps of water.

I looked up at him, breathing warmth into my palms. "Yes," I whispered. "Though I'm guessing you didn't know what you were getting into either."

He shook his head sadly. "No. I don't think any of us did."

We sat silently for a few minutes, the only sound was the gentle bubbling of the stream over the wet rocks.

"Thank you," I said finally, breaking the silence. "For the water." He gave me a small, appreciative smile, one that gave me a flicker of hope in this wicked world. "Were you with others?" I inquired.

He nodded. "Beth from Aravel. We got separated, though. Something was chasing us. Something...dark." His youthful face mirrored a yearning to flee this icy, desolate tournament. "I don't know what happened. We were both asleep when we felt it, the fear, and bolted. I tripped over something and tumbled down a hill when I heard her scream—" He shut his eyes, shaking his head. "I shouldn't have agreed to this."

I placed my hand on his shoulder. "We'll find a way out," I promised, hoping my assurance could offer some solace amidst the overwhelming despair in his eyes. "You should get some rest. I'll search around for some food."

He nodded, and we made our way to an alcove by the stream, shielded from the biting wind by the towering mountainside. He sank to the ground, his breathing gradually slowing into a steady rhythm.

I lingered momentarily, watching him drift into slumber, pondering the cruel irony of this supposed tournament meant to foster peace among the Regions. With a bitter scoff, I turned to scour the murky landscape for any semblance of sustenance, venturing cautiously while keeping a watchful eye on Astor. Despite my efforts, I found nothing. Not a single crumb of food in sight. Anger churned within me, a tempest raging amidst the hollow pit of hunger gnawing at my stomach.

Returning to Astor, I settled beside him, endeavoring to quell the rising heat coursing through my veins. A heavy weariness draped over me like a suffocating haze. Leaning my head against the mountain wall, I found little relief in the stagnant fog that barely stirred against the fierce wind whistling through the small alcove, sending a haunting echo wheezing past.

Struggling to keep my eyes open, I sat in silence, listening to the steady rhythm of Astor's breathing and the persistent grumbling of my empty stomach.

I was abruptly pulled from the hazy embrace of exhaustion by Astor's urgent shaking.

"Wake up!" he hissed, his eyes wide with fear, jolting my heart awake with a surge of adrenaline. I leaped to my feet in an instant, sensing a threat. He quickly covered my mouth with his hand and pointed toward the stream.

A large grey wolf stood at the water's edge, its massive form casting a menacing shadow, its fur thick and matted. My heart raced as I scanned the area frantically, searching for any sign of more wolves. Wolves, I knew, usually ran in packs, and the presence of one often meant the presence of others.

I strained my ears for any signifying rustle or snap of twigs, but any sounds were engulfed in the howling wind, which seemed to swallow all other sounds. The tension in the air was tangible, every instinct urging me to remain perfectly still and silent but flee and escape at the same time.

The fog slowly dissipated, making our situation more precarious.

Gulping down the fear and anger that threatened to overwhelm me, I clutched the wooden dagger tightly, my knuckles white with tension. Positioning myself protectively in front of Astor, I observed the wolf as it drank from the stream. Quickly analyzing our escape route, I leaned close to his ear and whispered a plan.

We maneuvered cautiously along the mountainside, hugging the terrain as much as possible until we reached a point where the slope jutted out at an odd angle, leaving us dangerously exposed to the wolf's back.

"When I tell you to run, you run as fast as you can," I commanded, gesturing toward his own makeshift weapons, which looked like they would shatter with a single swing. We need to get back on the path," I whispered, nodding in the direction we had come from. Astor nodded in agreement, his shallow breaths betraying his anxiety, and began to creep back step by careful step until the wolf was no longer within sight behind the jut of the mountain.

"Run," I urged, pushing him forward. With adrenaline coursing through our veins, we sprinted as fast as our legs could carry us, weaving through the dense forest and leaping over scattered boulders and rocks. Astor proved to be faster than I anticipated, leaping over each boulder as if they were mere pebbles. We continued to run, the watery light filtering through the clouds above, threatening to expose our position. A solitary howl pierced the air, followed by several others, seeming to encircle us from all directions.

I grabbed his arm, propelling him forward. "Keep going! We're almost back to the path," I panted, my eyes fixed on the incline ahead. The sight of the sloping road gave me a burst of hope. We ran in tandem, our breaths ragged and visible in the cold air. Each inhale sliced through my throat, sending goosebumps cascading down my neck as a pounding of feet and guttural snarls echoed through the air behind us.

We slowed as we reached the hill's slope, the incline making each step more arduous in the loose rocks. I glanced back again, noting that nothing seemed to be following us. I sent a silent prayer of gratitude to the heavens, hoping we would safely reach the bottom of the road.

"Stay down," I panted, licking my cracked lips. "Let me make sure we are clear."

Astor remained pressed against the rocky hillside, his black hair contrasting with the light gray stone. I shifted my weight, digging my fingers and boots into the rocks, sending some tumbling down the hill. Another howl pierced the air, and I pushed down the rising fear.

Peeking over the ridge, I listened intently for anything unusual amid the silent wind, praying that neither another Breva, a wolf, nor the Spellcasters were nearby since I was in their territory.

I scanned the area to the right and left, seeing and *sensing* nothing except the faint howl of several wolves scattered behind us. Sliding back down to Astor, I dug into the loose gravel, my movements careful but swift.

His dark eyes were filled with fear. "The sooner we get to the bottom of that path, the quicker we can get out of here," I said, hoping to give him the courage to keep fighting. I nodded upward. "Let's go. Hopefully, we can find some food at its end."

Astor followed me up and over the ridge, staying low as we scanned the vast landscape for any signs of danger. Our hearts pounded, and we tried to slow our breathing against the wind that wove around us, chilling us to the bone. The howls echoed closer, urging us to move quickly.

We descended the path in a rush, our steps uneven on the loose gravel. Each stumble and slip sent small rocks tumbling down the slope, the noise unnervingly loud in the otherwise quiet surroundings. Our stomachs grumbled loudly, a painful reminder of our hunger and a sound that could easily betray us to any predators nearby.

This part of the path was steep and treacherous; the jagged rocks and rough terrain demanded our full attention. The cold wind bit through our tattered suits, sapping our energy and adding to our discomfort.

As we moved, I glanced back at Astor. His young face was set with determination, though fear still lingered in his eyes. He mirrored my movements, his footsteps as cautious as mine, but his determination strengthened me.

The howls behind us grew fainter, but we didn't slow down. We couldn't afford to. The landscape stretched out before us, a mix of dead trees and rocky outcroppings, offering little shelter or promise of food. Yet, we had no choice but to keep moving forward, hoping each step brought us closer to getting out of here.

33

"Why did you enter?" I asked as we trudged down the rocky hill, navigating the switchbacks. The sun was setting, casting a blue tint across the murky sky. We might not have felt so frozen if it weren't for the relentless wind.

"For my family...we need the money," Astor replied somberly, his eyes fixed on the swirling grey clouds above. "My father is sick."

"Oh," I murmured, feeling a pang of sympathy.

"It's life, right?" he said, turning to look at me with sadness. "I'm the eldest of three sisters, so I had to do what any provider would. My mother was furious when she found out I was accepted," he stopped, slightly smiling. "I wish I could harbor her face on dreary days," he said with a small laugh. I glanced at him with a smile, feeling it so very odd to have a family that he loved and loved him in return. A family that was worried for him.

He cleared his dry throat, "So it's true your guardian made you do this?"

I gave him a weary smile. "How many know?"

"All of us."

I laughed despite the deep hunger gnawing at me. "So much for secrets."

"That's why you didn't touch your food at the dinner?" he observed.

The thought of that meal made my mouth water, wishing I now had it in front of me.

I shrugged. "Among other things," I expressed, more bitterly than intended. The image of Lord Winslow waiting for me crept into my mind, and I shivered. "Let's hop off the path here and see if we can find any nuts or wood for a trap. I'm not sure how much energy I will have without food."

We veered off the path, pushing through the underbrush until the foliage began to change, welcoming us with tall evergreens and pines shooting up like swords into the sky. The ground was uneven and covered in a layer of dead leaves and twigs as the cold air bit at our exposed skin.

As we searched, the forest seemed eerily silent, the usual sounds of wildlife absent, causing me to wonder if there was anything around to catch. The wind rustled the branches above, adding to the sense of desolation. We moved carefully, scanning the ground for signs of edible plants or potential trap materials.

Astor paused beside a cluster of pine trees, examining the pinecones. "These might have some nuts within," he said, reaching up to check the branches.

I knelt down, digging through the litter of leaves, hoping to find something useful, yet every rustle and crackle seemed amplified in the stillness. "Keep an eye out for any thick pieces of wood we could use for a trap," I advised, my voice low as he dug into the pinecones, splitting them open with a rock, and continued doing so, pinecone after pinecone.

Minutes felt like hours as we scoured the area.

Finally, Astor held up a small handful of nuts, his face lighting up with a hint of relief. "It's not much, but it's something."

I nodded, grateful for even the smallest find. "Let's gather what we can and set up a trap nearby."

The process was slow and painstaking as our fingers were numb from the cold, but together, we worked quickly, gathering materials and setting a rudimentary trap. We put the pine nuts underneath it, hoping it would catch anything.

We hid behind a large boulder nearby, waiting in tense silence. My energy was nearly depleted as night loomed closer, and the cold began to seep deeper into my bones. We made no sound except for the shivering patter of our breaths, keeping close to one another for warmth as we watched the sun's light disappear into an indigo blue.

"Maybe we should keep going," Astor rasped, barely above a whisper.

I nodded in agreement, feeling the weight of exhaustion mingling with a surge of frustration.

We stood up, took the pine nuts from under the trap, and set off. Our feet grew heavier with each step as we finished the juicy nuts and found the path again. The moon and stars illuminated our way, casting a pale light on the rocky trail. My feet throbbed with each step, and each breath became shallower as the cold pressed deeper into my bones. We walked in silence, the darkening sky our only cover.

The path ended at the base of a large mountain alcove, which cut smoothly into a dark, eerie, narrow canyon that looked barely big enough for one person to walk through at a time. The canyon walls rose steeply on either side, their surfaces rough and jagged, looking like the deepest, darkest trenches where nightmares dwell. The air within the alcove was colder, and the shadows were deeper, making it feel as if the canyon pass was the entrance into the mountain's belly.

We stepped to the canyon's eerie opening, and the sound of our footsteps echoed in the confined space. The oppressive darkness shook me to my core, begging me to run. It was too dark to see anything except a few feet before us. We were cornered against the mountainside with nowhere to go except back up the path or continue through the dark tunnel of the canyon.

"You're not actually thinking about going through there right now?" Astor whispered with terror in his voice.

I looked back at the deadly canyon, fear spiking through me, knowing what might be ahead.

"Maybe there's another way?" he said, already stepping back several feet. "We should wait until morning."

"And then what?" I snapped. "Wait until the other beasts eat us with nothing to protect ourselves?"

His only response was a single blink. "But we don't know what's through there," he said, pointing to the terrifying darkness. "I'm not going through there. We can wait until the first light."

I huffed, letting my anger sizzle through my shivering and hungry body. My stomach ached for more food, and my eyes were heavy with exhaustion.

"Fine, I'll take the first watch—"

"No, you need sleep. You're running yourself dead," he interjected with the same bitterness.

I clenched my jaw and fists, reluctantly letting him win this battle. But deep down, something didn't feel right. The need to run was more urgent than before, a burning desire to escape this icy, dead terrain.

"Anything. *Anything at all*, and you wake me," I demanded, pointing my finger at him.

He nodded as we both sat down by the wall, exposed and knowing—*feeling*—that this wasn't right. But I dozed off before thinking more, letting the weight and exhaustion pull me into a light sleep.

———— + ✦ + ————

The cold air cut into my raw wrists and ankles, and the screeches of deadly things curdled my insides. I shivered naked on the freezing, rocky ground as flashes of red lightning lit the inky, oppressive sky.

"Give me what I want, and I'll let you go." Pain erupted in my head, blinding my vision with shrouds of white. I turned toward the horrible, oily voice of the shadowy figure. *"Give it—"*

"*No.*" Realization sank in as I scrambled to cover myself. "No. *No, no, no.*"

"I will always have you locked up here, Eliah. So either give it up, or you can join me."

The figure laughed, echoing deep into my mind as his spidery tendrils caressed over my hips and up to my neck.

I screamed, diving deep to find that anger and letting it consume me until I ignited the entire area with electricity.

The figure shrieked, slashing me down the forearm with its dark tendrils and sending a radiating pulse of fiery pain surging through my body.

"I'll *kill you just like I killed them all!*"

I jolted awake to the black sky and the dark canyon pass looming before us. My heart pounded in my ears as the blinding headache remained, along with the phantom pain of the slash on my arm.

Astor jolted in response to my sudden awakening, fear flashing in his gleaming eyes.

"I'm sorry," I breathed, falling back against the stone mountainside, trying to calm my raging soul. "I'm sorry, it was just a dream."

He slumped down next to me, pulling his legs in close as he shivered through shuddering breaths. It was well into the night as the stars continued to shine. The wind had died out completely, leaving an eerie silence nestling into the icy alcove.

"Sleep," I demanded, trying to calm my chattering teeth as I shifted closer to his side. He said nothing, curling his head around his knees and leaning on me. We sat there, shivering in the deadly quiet as I watched the stars twinkle, wondering what Levon might be doing.

Was he worrying about me? Was Kaizen beating him senseless, knowing that the Match was in the Spellcaster's territory? Was I a fool for falling for his kindness despite all his secrets? Or for his radiant eyes that still somehow melted my heart?

I let out a long breath, hoping his face would follow it.

I looked to the dark canyon to my right, feeling a need to run. As if the Spellcasters knew precisely where I was and waited, prowling to capture me.

The shadowy figure's phantom nails still stung my arm as I focused on controlling my thoughts, not letting the fear creep back in for them to take hold.

I'll kill you just like I killed them all.

The voice rang through my skull, over and over, as if I were tumbling down a steep hill right into their grasp.

Killed them all. Who else did he kill?

I shook away the thought, zoning in on my breathing to calm my racing heart.

A skitter of rocks tumbled down upon us from above, echoing off the mountain walls and shattering the quiet night. I brushed the dry dirt off, looking up only to see the towering mountain wall and the twinkling stars above, right as a shriek echoed from the towering mountain above, followed by more pebbles raining down on us.

My body seized in a panic, constricting my heart and compelling my whole being to run.

Control it.

I breathed in, forcing my anxiety to calm as a gurgle of choking sounds came from the left of us. More pebbles tumbled down, hitting our heads. Astor groggily awoke, groaning as a larger rock hit his shoulder. I clapped a hand over his mouth as his dark eyes shot to mine.

Fear spiked deeper, a metallic taste shooting through my nose and radiating down my veins, turning my blood into fire as an unexpected force gently tugged at my mind.

"Run."

I leaped up, pulling Astor with me, as my heart pounded in my ears, feeling the oily darkness before I saw it.

"Run! Eliah, RUN."

The voice came a second before a dark figure emerged around the paths bend. It stood several feet taller, it's arms looked too long, too peculiar, to be human with something glinting in the moonlight at its side. An aura of spoiled acid radiated from it, and wisps of black smoke pulsated around its being. I shivered at the icy feeling that stabbed straight into my heart as a deadly, contorted smile formed on the figure's mouth.

Astor swore, and I swiftly grabbed his arm, pushing him forward into the black, narrow crack of the mountain without a second thought. The figure lunged toward us, compelling us to run as fast as we could in the darkness. We sprinted in silence, our panting and pounding boots hitting the rocky floor echoing in the confined space.

"Faster!" I hissed to Astor, my voice echoing as I pushed him forward. Behind us, rocks shifted, and the figure's feet thundered toward us, slamming into the canyon's opening with a shrilling crash. Its tall, lanky body seemed cumbersome, but its long legs kept pace, closing the gap with each step.

A deep, sickening laugh echoed through the dark canyon, paralyzing me to my core. Dried roots and branches jutted out from the narrow canyon walls, slicing into our cheeks, arms, and shoulders as we collided with them, along with freshly spun webs that caught in our throats. My legs screamed from the exertion as fear threatened to paralyze me. I grunted as the canyon seemed to stretch endlessly and offer no escape as we practically tumbled over each other.

The canyon narrowed further, forcing us to run single file, my feet barely avoiding Astor's heels in front of me. Our panting breaths echoed loudly against the moist walls, drawing a chorus of howls and yelps from a ledge above and behind us.

What do we do?! What do we do?!

I kept running, my throat raw and bleeding from the icy air. Glancing back, I saw the tall figure still pursuing us, now wielding a long black blade at its side.

What do we do?!

Up ahead, a gray, eerie light barely illuminated the dark path.

"*Go, go, go!*" Astor yelled, propelling himself faster.

A wet snarl echoed from a ledge above us, joined by two more as a dried root slashed deep into my jaw, tearing a screech from my lips along with warm blood.

Oh, Tryan. Help us!

I crashed into Astor, who broke my fall as the canyon abruptly gave way to a vast, bowl-like arena resembling a massive theater. A labyrinth of pathways spiraled down into its center, converging at a small black hole. Four large, loosely packed rocky slopes marked each entrance, ending in a perilous drop. Surrounding the rocky landslides were descending switchbacks that snaked their way down the steep slope of the bowl.

A shrill, oily scream cracked behind us, sending a jolt of terror through my body. We jumped without hesitation and tumbled into the sharp rocky slope that cut into our skin as we began sliding uncontrollably down to the lethal cliff at its end, pulling us down like quicksand.

Astor cried out as he collided with a large rock that held firm in the landslide and broke his fall with a painful thud. I managed to catch hold of a dead branch a few feet above him, gasping for air.

I whipped my head back, bracing for the figure to lunge out of the canyon, hearing its oily screech echoing perilously close. Just then, a glimmer of light caught my eye to the left of me. I looked over to see a pile of weapons clustered together at the start of each of the switchbacks, having a dreading feeling that this was the start of the finale.

My eyes locked onto the shaft of a bow and arrows amidst the pile, and with a surge of adrenaline, I swung myself over to the switchback landing, pain shooting through my knee as the jagged rocks tore into my flesh. The oily figure leaped onto the bone-crunching rocks. Its ebony skeletal form was draped in tattered black robes that billowed like wraiths against its frail, patchwork body of rotting flesh. All the air left my lungs as my mind raced back to that book of monsters in Levon's library. Believing them nothing more than fables. I watched as the bony black figure scrambled for purchase, and my heart sank.

Dark Magics known as *Skinners*.

No—it can't be.

Astor's scream echoed through the canyon as he jumped away from the figure onto the adjacent switchback path.

I scrambled towards the weapons, desperation lending speed to my movements as I swallowed my fear. Astor screamed again, forcing me to run harder. I heard a brawl of movement close behind me as I reached the bow with a skid, scraping open my suit and feeling a painful warmth trickle down my knees.

With trembling hands, I seized the bow, feeling its weight as I swiftly nocked an arrow into place and whirled back toward Astor. Before I could react, the monster slammed into me with bone-jarring force, sending us both crashing to the ground in a violent tangle of limbs. I cried out as the bow and arrows slipped from my grasp, the rough terrain digging into my skin while the bony figure pinned me to the ground.

The foul stench of decay enveloped me, making me gag as I struggled to breathe. With desperation clawing at me, I reached for the sword lying just inches away, my fingers barely brushing its hilt as I kicked and punched frantically, trying to fend off the relentless shadow. Its eyes were as black as the night, only visible by the mere gloss they reflected from the waking sky with a rotting patchwork of flesh overlapping its black frame, confirming my dread. Its spidery fingers cracked and popped, tightening around my throat.

I shifted my body, trying to throw the putrid figure off. A Skinner.

"Xaldruk will love the feel of you," it hissed out. The snake-like voice sent thousands of shivers down my neck and spine. *"Perhaps he'll share your creamy skin."*

I grunted, closing my eyes and squirming beneath its crushing hold, pushing with all my might. My fingertips went numb from clawing and stretching for the sword, barely grazing its pommel but unable to grasp it. I cried out as the Skinner's black tongue flicked out like a snake, licking the Breva's blood from my face. Fear and disgust rippled through me as my lungs threatened to collapse under its weight.

"You killed it!" The figure shrieked, its grip tightening like a vise, cutting off my air supply. *"YOU KILLED IT!"* Its scream reverberated off the rounded mountains, waking everything in its path, unsure what it meant.

I squeezed my eyes shut, tears mingling with the dirt and blood on my face as despair sank deep into my ravaged heart. I abandoned my efforts to reach the sword and clawed at its fingers, gasping for air.

Help!

Levon's face flashed into my mind, recalling the comfort of his embrace in the market square. His voice pulsed through my veins and soul, causing more tears as my vision blurred and receded on the edge of oblivion.

Don't succumb to its pressure. Fight. Let your anger guide you instead of suppressing it. Embrace it and let it ignite your spirit; when you do, it will free you.

A blood-curdling roar shattered my eardrums, causing the figure to loosen its grip and turn toward the noise. Alarm spilled off the sinister being as it frantically searched for the source. I seized the opportunity, grabbing one of its bony fingers and snapping it, then swiftly shoved my knees into its chest. It screeched, its rotted teeth snarling, clutching me tighter.

Anger boiled deep within my core, pulsating in solid, vibrant waves, pushing up against the fear and igniting it like fire to paper.

I kicked the decaying Skinner's chest with all my might, just enough to gain some distance and move closer to the weapons. I screamed, throwing my body toward the sword. The creature tightened its grip again as I reached the sword's hilt and swung it towards its head.

The sword plunged deep into the Skinner's thin neck, unleashing a torrent of bubbling, red, and black blood that splattered down upon me, its stench as foul as death itself. The monster released its grip and staggered back, clawing desperately at the sword while choking on its own vile blood.

I coughed and gasped for air, the fiery anger within me igniting with a sizzle, jolting me awake. I welcomed the surge, feeling tiny pricks of electricity zinging through my veins, saturating my heart like a long-lost friend that finally returned. A warmth coursed through my body, as familiar as Levon's words.

I inhaled the cool, sharp air and snarled at the dying abomination, writhing and wailing in agony. With a fierce grip, I seized the slick, blood-soaked pommel and yanked the sword free, eliciting a gurgling shriek from the Skinner. Without hesitation, I lifted the dripping blade and brought it crashing down, cleaving through bone. I watched with grim satisfaction as the putrid head flew from its shoulders, the body convulsing uncontrollably before tumbling off the ledge to the path below.

An electric jolt surged through me, sharp and intense, making me feel more alive than ever. I was soaring on a wave of exhilaration that could sustain me for a lifetime.

Another roar thundered across the sky, reverberating through my core. I turned my eyes upward, above the carved out bowl, just in time to see the shadow of a colossal wolf leap onto a man running across the lethal slopes. The beast tore him apart, his shrill screams echoing through the arena.

Quickly, I pivoted, desperately searching for Astor on the other side of the rocky slope. I spotted him running, jumping, and sliding down the hill toward its center in frantic haste. My heart stopped when I saw what chased him, two matted and ferocious wolves, and I screamed at him to keep running.

I frantically grabbed my bow and arrows, nocked one, and released it without calculating. It struck the rocks before the wolves, bouncing off into the dark, dawning sky.

I sprinted forward, leaping off the ledge to the path below where the Skinner's body lay. Rolling with the impact, I quickly bound toward the middle, rocky landslide. I skidded across the sharp rocks to the large boulder and nocked another arrow, not caring about the blood that trickled down my arms and legs. Its feathers tickled my lips as I calmed my breathing, letting the electric energy within me force the world into silence.

Inhale.

I refused to let terror erode my concentration and focused on the gray fur just a few feet ahead, practically aiming at Astor.

Exhale.

I released the arrow.

34

T he arrow plunged deep into the eye of one of the wolves, eliciting a bone-chilling yelp and stopping its pursuit. Another roar blasted through the crater, startling me and breaking my focus. I tumbled to the ground, sliding against the sharp, jagged rocks. My ripped gloves offered little protection as my bloody fingers scrabbled for purchase on a dead tree trunk, its bark slicing into my hand. Desperately, I dangled from the cliff's edge, screaming in pain as the agony radiated up my arm.

The energy within me sizzled away my panic, flooding me with adrenaline and giving me the strength to hoist myself onto a lower ledge, splitting my nails against the hard soil.

I found my footing, hastily pulling out another arrow, when I saw a red-haired boy plummet down the opposite rocky slope, followed by a shorter raven-haired girl. Their screams, piercing and desperate, mirrored the agony I had just endured. I tore my attention away from their cries and spotted Astor. He leaped across another slanted rockslide closer to the center, only to catch one of the rocks and tumble down it. He looked up in terror as the large gray wolf followed, yelping as it scraped against the sharp rocks.

I nocked the arrow, tracking the wolf's movements with trembling hands, and released it. The bowstring snapped, echoing off the crater's walls as the arrow soared through the air, embedding itself deep into the wolf's shoulder. The beast tumbled forward, crashing straight onto Astor.

"*Astor!*" I bellowed, panic flooding my voice. I sprinted towards him, leaping over the first dead wolf, and watched Astor scramble for footing while the beast snarled, slashing and biting. Astor's desperate cries propelled my feet faster, leaping off each switchback until I reached his level closer to the crater's center. The sight of the wolf's fangs, inches from Astor's face, sent a surge of terror through me.

I nocked another arrow and let it fly into the wolf's back leg as I sprinted faster toward him. The wolf howled in agony, falling farther down the slope until it plunged off a cliff, smacking the center in a sickening crunch. Astor swiftly grabbed a low-hanging tree branch. Blood streamed down his arm, staining the rocks below as the cold light swallowed the darkness of the crater.

"Hold on!" I screamed, sprinting faster towards him. My lungs felt like they were about to burst, and my legs begged to give out as exhaustion began to overtake me. I slung the bow over my back and leaped across the next slanted rockway, scraping my legs against its jagged surface. I reached the other side, frantically leaping down each switchback until I finally reached him, his eyes brimming with tears as he grasped my bloodied hand. His body slammed into the sharp rocks, spilling more blood before I managed to pull him over.

Astor shook uncontrollably, blood bubbling from deep teeth marks on his arm and a long gash that ran down his thigh and one on his stomach. Tears spilled from his eyes as I sat paralyzed, staring at the blood pooling on the dirt path beneath us. The sharp scent of copper filled the air, sending my heart into a deep despair.

Quickly, I grabbed a sharp rock, using it to cut jagged strips from my suit, wrapping them around his leg, arm, and stomach. The blood soaked through almost instantly, but it was all I could do to try and staunch the flow. My hands trembled as I pressed against his stomach.

He hissed in pain. "What was that thing?" he cried out, slumping into me, his voice filled with pain and terror.

None of this should be happening.

None of it.

I opened my mouth to answer, but no words came out. I didn't *know* if it was a Spellcaster, but it had to be that monster written in that book.

I sucked in a coppery breath, glancing out to see the two other contestants running down the switchbacks into the exit at its center, long blades and daggers in their hands.

"We're almost there," I rasped, my throat dry and scratchy. "We need to keep moving," I urged, looking back up to the dark slit of the canyon we had entered through, praying no more skeletons or wolves would appear, especially with the scent of blood in the air.

"I don't know if I can—"

"*You must, Astor!*"

I tried to lift him, but he grunted in pain as more blood spilled from his open wounds. Our breaths came out hot against the cold morning air as my mind raced through every possibility.

Leaving him would make him an easy target for predators and death itself. Taking him would slow us down and put us both at greater risk. Finding something to help move him would take time we didn't have, and there was no guarantee I'd return to the crater in time.

I glance at my trembling and blood-soaked hands, knowing he had minutes before—

NO!

I tore off more pieces of my suit, fashioning crude bandages to slow the bleeding. From the sight of the spewing blood, I feared the wolf's claws had hit an artery.

"Astor, please," I begged, praying this wasn't real. "We have to move," I pleaded, my voice cracking with fear and exhaustion.

He shook, his breath sputtering.

I stood up, holding Astor under his arm. "This is going to hurt," I warned.

I tugged him upright, causing him to cry out and leave a trail of blood in our wake. My heart sank as I looked down into the crater's center, seeing how far away we still were, but I kept pulling, each step more agonizing than the last.

Tears stung my eyes with each pull, sending an exasperated cry from Astor. My arms burned as I pulled harder. We managed to pass two switchbacks when a roar froze us in our tracks; screams followed after.

This was it.

This was the end.

More screams bellowed beyond the crater as a roar stifled the contestant's cry.

I stopped, panting, unable to move forward. Nothing good waited for me at the end, only the wrinkled, old arms of Lord Winslow. The thought of him made me sick, mingling with the coppery smell of Astor's blood and causing me to dry heave. My stomach churned up acid, burning my already raw throat. I slumped down, holding Astor in my arms, completely depleted of energy, thoughts, and hope.

"Go," Astor whispered, his voice hoarse and stale. "Eliah, go." His lips had turned purple, his skin pale and clammy. He was losing too much blood too quickly.

"*I can't leave you,*" I whispered back, tears streaming down my face. The thought of abandoning him was unbearable.

I looked down at Astor's swelling leg, swiftly ripping off more of my suit to wrap around his calf. He made no sound as I pulled it tight. His trembling hand grabbed mine, coated with dirt and grime.

"I'll be okay," he heaved barely above a whisper.

"Astor, you'll die."

"Then win it...for...my family."

Tears welled in my eyes, falling onto his dirty forehead. My heart ached at the sight of his frail, slumped figure. I held tightly to his hand.

"No," I grunted. "*No!*"

I stood back up, pulling him along, not accepting this fate as rocks tumbled down the rocky slope from the canyon we came out of. Stark blonde hair appeared, tumbling down with a cry.

My heart skipped. "Osric," I whispered.

He fell steeply, the cliff only inches from his feet, before he took hold of one of the path's roots and pulled himself up. I kept pulling Astor's limp body, watching Osric scour the weapons pile, grabbing a hatchet and a long sword, and stowing several things too far to see in his boot. He began running down the switchbacks with a pronounced limp, stopping a few times to grunt in pain before continuing.

"Osric!" I yelled, my voice raw and weak. "Osric!" He looked up at the echo of his name, his eyes meeting mine as I dragged Astor. "Please!"

He stopped in place, limping towards the edge of one of the paths. He looked back up to the slit he came through and then back at me, his features ablaze with fury.

"*Die with him, you wench*!" he screamed, his voice echoing throughout the crater. Each reverberation grew louder, burrowing deeper into my anguished heart and igniting my anger. He continued running until he made his way down to its center.

Desperation clawed at me as I watched Osric disappear. I turned back to Astor, his breath shallow, his skin pale.

"We have to keep moving," I whispered, my voice trembling as tears streamed down my face. I pulled him with every ounce of strength I had left, but his body had become heavier, and the cold air bit into my exposed arms and scraped-up legs. I stopped, inhaling a deep, freezing breath, seeing his blood smeared on the ground, a crimson trail marking our slow progress.

"Astor?" I breathed out, my mouth as dry as the desert. "*Astor!*"

I shook his limp body before laying him on the ground to examine his wounds. The second wrap was soaked through and caked with mud. My heart dropped as I felt for his unresponsive pulse.

"*Astor! Wake up!*" I shook his shoulders, unwilling to let this be his end. "*Fight it!*" Hot tears streamed down my cheeks, blurring my vision. "*NO,*" I sobbed into his chest.

"*Eliah, move.*"

I whipped my head around at the familiar harsh voice, hoping for a miracle, but I saw no one there and was utterly confused by his voice.

No, that's not possible.

My heart raced as more screams and shouts echoed from the crater's exit, followed by a thundering rumble that quaked my heart into motion.

I picked up Astor, tugging—

"Move!" Demanded the warm phantom voice against the slight breeze.

I swallowed, turning around again to find the voice. "No," I whispered back into the open air. "I can't leave him here. I can't leave him like this!"

I can't.

I slumped to the ground, my heart heavy with despair. Anger, sadness, confusion, and numbness swirled inside me.

"Astor, please," I wept in desperation. *"Please fight it."* I palmed my dirty face, scrubbing it over before crying out, my anger engulfing my being. My cry bounced off the crater walls, quaking the ground and surrounding area. Bits of rocks tumbled into the center as the rage blasted from my heart.

I gazed down at Astor's lifeless face, his chest no longer rising, and a crimson pool expanded beneath him.

"MOVE, ELIAH! NOW!"

The voice thundered in my head, causing me to falter and cover my ears before several bony Skinners emerged from two of the canyon openings as another jarring roar bellowed into the murky sky.

"I'm sorry," I murmured, pressing a tender kiss to Astor's brow before leaping down to the lower path, continuing faster down the labyrinth.

The Skinners quickly advanced, their tattered black cloaks billowing behind them as I leaped from the last narrow path towards the dark exit. It was a pitch-black hole, only large enough for one person to pass through, and it appeared to have been somehow drilled into the earth. Another roar echoed from within the cavity, sending chills down my spine. I looked up at the dark figures tumbling down the switchbacks and took a deep breath before plunging into the cold, dark hole.

35

The frigid embrace of the tunnel's icy walls sent a sharp sting across my exposed skin, threatening to wrench a scream from my throat. Deeper and faster, it spiraled, engulfing me in pitch-black darkness until finally ejecting me into the watery light. Fighting the urge to scream, I slammed onto the slick, unforgiving rocky ground. Pain exploded through my side at impact and forced the air from my lungs.

Gasping for air, I surveyed the terrifying, black, rocky expanse and slowly got to my feet. The terrain was filled with thousands upon thousands of small obsidian pebbles that gleamed against the faint light. Low clouds swirled around towering masses of black stone that loomed tall and as far as the eye could see. Their jagged forms reached skyward like ancient sentinels while shattered remnants jutted out like deadly spears.

Large, dark boulders formed a formidable barricade around the area before me, creating an impenetrable wall. I scanned the surroundings once more, desperately searching for a passage through the wall of boulders, but found none. The only option was a series of scattered stones that led up and over one of the massive boulders.

I looked up to where I had been thrown moments before and spotted the small black opening several feet above, carved into the towering mountain. The chill in the air deepened, and a layer of ice coated the ground beneath like a corpse, stealing my breath.

Quickly, I retrieved my fallen arrows, urging my trembling legs into motion, unwilling to linger for the Skinners. I forced myself to run against the exhaustion pouring into every crevice of my body. I scaled one of the large black boulders, scrambling up its rugged surface before swiftly descending the other side, determined to put distance between myself and the dark figures.

To my back and left, the towering Adauntus Mountains framed the sky with their dark, jagged edges. Skidding to a stop, the black, wet pebbles sprayed outward from the force. Turning in frantic circles, I began calculating advantageous points but only found ones that would expose me like a beacon.

I drew in a shaky breath when suddenly, I heard uneven, shuffling footsteps against the black pebbles and muffled cries up ahead. Panic surged through me, and before I could think, I lunged into action, scrambling up another larger boulder to get a better view. A blistering screech tore through the air, causing me to lose my grip and crash back to the ground. The closeness of the sound ignited every nerve, screaming at me to run, hide, and escape.

Without hesitation, I scrambled back up the boulder's rugged surface and bolted, leaping across the top of each boulder. From here, it looked like the boulders were a maze among the tall, jagged stones that shot up high into the sky. Beyond the boulder maze, a sea of the black pebbles spread wide. Dark black crevices of the terrain sloped down, touching the base of the towering mountains where a looming dark cave sat. My heart pounded wildly, and I cursed through gasping breaths as I kept leaping over boulder after boulder, letting the sheer panic of my situation drive me forward.

A sudden crash of black pebbles echoed behind me, followed by a sharp wisp cutting through the air. Before I could react, a searing pain ripped through my side, knocking the breath from my lungs and hurling me backward off the boulder. The scream tore from my throat, raw and uncontrollable, as the pain exploded through my body with brutal force. My head collided hard with the scattered pebbles, sending a shockwave of agony through my skull. Warm blood streamed down my forehead, dripping onto the cold ground below. I blinked rapidly fighting against the hazy blur clouding my vision.

Groaning, I turned over with a wheezing cough, expecting to see my demise, but only gray clouds drifted by as I felt my eye begin to swell. Fear spiked through my heart as I scrambled to my feet, struggling for balance and feeling absolute exhaustion fighting against my every movement. I touched my right side, where the sting had sent me flying through the air. My suit was sliced open, revealing a narrow red welt. Each breath sent sharp pains through my ribs, which felt as if they were collapsing with every inhale.

I hissed at the pain, desperately hoping I hadn't broken one, and wiped away the blood trickling into my eyes. Through the daze, I saw a flash of black to my left.

Instinctively, I notched an arrow, my trembling hands barely steadying the shaft, and started running in the opposite direction, away from the mountain range and toward the open sky.

The loud crunch of pebbles underfoot echoed with each step, contradicting every instinct I had to stop, blend in, and silence myself. But there was nowhere to hide and disappear, so I kept running as fast as my legs and the pebbles that sucked at my feet would allow me.

The pounding in my chest matched the throbbing in my side. Each step a battle against the searing pain, and every inhale sent a sharp sting through my ribs, threatening to steal my breath.

Wiping the blood from my eyes, I frantically scanned the area for any sign of a dragon or the Skinners. A sharp scream cut through the air, followed by a deep, terrifying rumble that shook my bones. I pushed myself to run faster, zig-zagging through the maze of jagged rocks, stumbling over loose stones. Suddenly, I burst into an open area, no longer surrounded by the towering black boulders. Instead, I stood before a vast sea of dark pebbles leading to the menacing cave in the distance.

Up close, the entrance revealed several winding black columns spiraling downward, resembling a slick slope that led deep into the enormous cave below where I stood.

I cautiously stepped out from behind the wall of black boulders, calming my ragged breathing and desperately searching for another escape route. I did not want *that* to be the exit, knowing it would take me right into the dragon's lair.

Suddenly, a massive black shape darted to the left, and my feet locked in place. Terror surged through me, my breath coming in ragged, uneven gasps as I struggled to think clearly, desperate to escape this nightmare. The looming threat of death pressed down on me, every instinct screamed for me to run, yet I stood frozen, paralyzed by fear, unable to tear my eyes away from its serpentine form.

I saw its massive, black, metallic body before I comprehended what it was. Its sinister scales gleamed with a dark, menacing sheen, interwoven with jagged patches of crimson that seemed to pulse with electric energy, like veins of molten lava. One eye burned an intense, fiery red, casting an eerie glow, while the other was a void of inky blackness, mirroring the darkness of its body.

One of its wings hung in tatters, shredded and clinging uselessly to its side, while the other remained poised for attack with long, sharp claws that protruded at each bend. Its long, snake-like tail coiled protectively around it, the tip twitching with a lethal readiness. The dragon exuded a humming aura of raw power and primal terror of red that radiated around its body; its very presence was a harbinger of fear. Every detail of its form spoke of pain and fury, a creature forged in raw darkness, hatred, fear, and saturated in violence.

It leaped into the air, snapping its tail, and vanished back beyond the boulders without a sound. My throat constricted as I realized it was the dragon's tail that had struck me off the boulder earlier, unable to comprehend how quietly it could creep, especially against the clattering of the obsidian pebbles.

Dread flooded my entire being as I edged slowly back toward the maze, my heart hammering with each labored breath. I crouched low on the slick, obsidian pebbles, desperate to blend in. My eyes darted around frantically, noting the eerie similarity between the pebbles and my shredded suit.

I gritted my teeth and channeled my anger and fear into a single, harrowing decision—I wasn't going through that cave; I'd find my own way out.

Backing away, my eye locked onto Osric's blonde hair, visible on the farthest edge of the area. He leaped onto one of the winding paths and slid down, oblivious to the looming danger. In an instant, the dragon was back and lunging toward him, its monstrous body rippling with predatory malice. Osric's scream pierced the silent air as the dragon's mouth opened, releasing a thick, suffocating black smoke that began to engulf him. His screams rose higher and full of agony.

I watched in horror as Osric hit a small landing, his form contorting in torture as he uselessly tried to lift his sword overhead. The dragon's smoke swallowed him whole, extinguishing his screams immediately as if it were poisonous. My heart pounded with fear as I waited for the smoke to dissipate, my mind racing as I weighed my options for escape.

I could *feel* the Skinners closing in, their evil presence scratching at the door of my mind, relentlessly hunting me, making me believe they were part of the Spellcasters. Panic surged through me, urging me to choose before it was too late.

The dragon's desperate attempt at flight was impaired by its injured state, causing it to lurch awkwardly before crashing into the black pebbles with a thunderous impact. A wave of obsidian stones cascaded away from its thrashing feet as it swiftly pivoted, its movements sinuous and predatory, reminiscent of a giant serpent as it leaped out of sight.

I tore my gaze away from where it bounded, only to be met with a horrifying sight—Osric's body, once vibrant and alive, now a grotesque mass of blistering red flesh. I choked back a gag of revulsion as the realization washed over me that his skin was no longer intact but had melted grotesquely around his dead body. Hot tears spilled from my eyes as I covered my mouth to silence my screaming and gnawing fear.

My hands trembled uncontrollably as movement caught my eye from the far left. The red-haired contestant slipped back into the maze of rocks, surely witnessing Osric's death as he scrambled away, desperate to escape the dragon's wrath.

Shaking frantically, I followed suit; my mind clouded with terror and re-pulsion. I raced through the labyrinthine passages, hitting one dead end after another but putting as much distance as possible between myself and the night-mare behind me. Though no matter how far I ran, I couldn't shake the image of Osric's dead, blistered form from my mind.

Once again, a piercing screech shattered the quiet of the morning, propelling me forward faster against the slick, icy pebbles that clattered loudly beneath my feet. I hugged the ground, darting in erratic zig-zags around the towering boulders of the maze, the pebbles clinging to my shoes, threatening to betray my position with their noisy protest.

Another deafening roar erupted, so close that it knocked me off my feet, sending me sprawling into the jagged pebbles. My breath came in short, pan-icked bursts as my heart hammered in my chest. The dragon's searing heat radiated from behind the massive boulders at my back, the force of its presence suffocating me with panic. Without thinking, I dropped my bow, my fingers trembling as I clawed desperately at the pebbles, knowing every sound I made only served to draw the beast closer.

I scrambled into the tiny crevice I made, forcing myself deeper into the earth, frantically piling the cold, black pebbles over my head and body. Their icy edges scraped my skin, but I didn't care—all that mattered was staying hidden. My heart pounded violently in my ears as the dragon's snout came into view, its hot breath washing over me in waves and sending out tendrils of smoke in the cold air. The creature's nostrils flared, searching the path I lay hidden in.

Half-buried and half-exposed, I froze, every muscle locked in terror. My breath caught in my throat as I trembled beneath the mound of pebbles. Every second stretched into eternity as I prayed it wouldn't find me, seeing Osric's raw, dead body in my mind.

The dragon's massive form twisted up and over the boulders, then slammed down with a bone-shaking crash that sent pebbles scattering in all directions, uncovering more of my trembling body. I clamped my teeth together, swal-lowing my scream as I watched in paralyzed horror. The monstrous creature hovered above me, its overwhelming presence pressing down like a suffocating weight. My heart pounded so fiercely it felt like it might burst, and I could only silently pray for a quick end as the fear clamped tightly around me.

Pebble after pebble cascaded off, revealing more of my quivering form as the dragon's colossal foot crashed down beside me, narrowly missing my head and discarded bow. It dug a massive claw into the ground as its snout hovered over me again, inhaling and taking my breath with it before emitting a repugnant snort that sent shivers down my spine. It shook its head and backed away, belching a deep grumble from its throat, almost as in repulsion.

A cacophony of howls and screeches ripped through my terror and wrenched the dragon's attention away. With lightning speed, it twisted its massive body towards the source of the noise and leaped, its sinuous tail barely missing my arm as it soared past. I remained frozen in place for what felt like an eternity, struggling to remember how to breathe, how to move.

The deafening chorus of viscous screeches, howls, screams, and roars reverberated through the air, melding into a deadly symphony. Amidst the chaos, Kaizen's voice fluttered into my mind, cutting through the fear and stirring me into action.

Control it, Eliah, because that will be all you have left.

All you have left.

All you have left.

I repeated the mantra to myself and letting it anchor me. With trembling limbs, I began to move and swallowed hard, centering myself back into reality as my body pumped with adrenaline. The black pebbles slid off me in a rocky cascade, clattering to the ground as I crawled toward my bow. I grasped its cold wood tightly, swallowing down the rising tide of panic that threatened to engulf me and wondering why it didn't attack.

It knew I was there.

I scanned the black pebbles around me, searching for clues as to what might have spooked the dragon and caused the repulsion. My gaze fell upon my own bloodied form, and realization dawned with a chilling clarity—I was covered in the grotesque blood of the Breva.

The sticky, dried, dark fluid clung to my skin and suit, its foul stench still filling my nostrils, overpowering my own coppery blood.

Slowly, I rose to my feet, finding my balance, and swiftly set off again, pushing back against the suffocating grip of fear.

Control it, Eliah.

Inhale, exhale.

I returned to the breathing techniques Levon had taught me, forcing the fear out of my heart.

Inhale, exhale.

I forced my ears to focus on the shifting and clattering of the pebbles underfoot, refusing to let my mind conjure the horrors that could accompany such chaos that screamed beyond the boulders. The air was electrified with more howls, gnashing of teeth, and screeches that erupted perilously close.

Nocking an arrow, I sprinted toward the expanse of open air, praying for some semblance of escape away from such sounds. I honed in on my breathing, channeling my anger to propel my legs forward despite the profound exhaustion and gnawing hunger threatening to drag me down with each step. A deafening snap reverberated to my right, coming from the other side of the boulder wall, followed by guttural screeches that sliced through the air.

Leaping over broken rocks, I hit an end wall that led right to the cacophony of horrid sounds. Confronted with a choice, I had to either scale the towering boulders and risk becoming a target for the dragon or possibly face the snarls head-on, praying they were in another part of the maze.

Digging my feet into the pebbles, I scanned the sky, thick with ominous clouds, searching desperately for a sign.

With a heavy heart, I took a step toward the screams, cursing myself for the decision.

Bow raised and arrow drawn taut, I advanced cautiously, my breath irregular against my ears. Each step felt like a burden as I navigated around scattered rocks amidst the sea of pebbles, muscles straining from the tension of holding the arrow at the ready.

I slowly walked forward, following the twists and turns of the maze, pressing myself against its side walls for cover. With each quick turn, the screams began to fade along with the obsidian pebbles, spurring me to quicken my pace against the hard black terrain.

The maze abruptly opened into a broad, open space strewn with dark, molten rocks that glistened with the same residual, eerie glow as the obsidian pebbles. The ground was a chaotic scatter of jagged, blackened stones, that promised to cut your skin if you faltered. I crouched behind the last massive boulder, my heart racing as I scanned the surrounding landscape with wary, watchful eyes. Each rock seemed to shift and shimmer with a menacing light, casting long, flickering shadows that danced across the uneven terrain. The air was thick with the acrid scent of scorched earth, heightening my sense of unease as I tried to make sense of the treacherous new environment, wondering if there was another dragon with fire-breathing abilities or if the black dragons' poisonous smoke could do this.

The eerie silence of the new area did nothing to ease the growing knot of dread in my stomach. Every sense was heightened, every instinct screaming at me to stay alert. I took a deep breath, trying to calm my heart, and took several cautious steps into the open expanse, scanning the long line of rocks.

Unexpectedly, a grotesque face lunged toward me, stealing my breath. Instinctively, I released my arrow, closing my eyes at the motion. I couldn't stop the scream that escaped my lips as a Skinner tackled me to the ground, cutting open my skin on the rugged obsidian rock beneath me. Black blood bubbled out of the Skinner's throat where the arrow had pierced straight through, the close range ensuring a fatal shot. Its long, bony fingers clawed desperately at my skin, leaving deep scratches as I struggled beneath its weight. I could feel the creature's jagged nails digging into my flesh, and the stench of its foul, viscous blood threatened to overwhelm me as it drenched my clothes and pooled around me.

Desperation surged through me. I grasped the bow and slammed it into the side of its head, making it topple off with a sag. I scrambled to my feet as crunching rocks heralded another attack before a second Skinner slammed into me, throwing me to the ground and causing me to lose my bow in the fall.

My head struck the molten rock hard, dizziness blurring my vision and blood trickling down the base of my skull.

I thrashed against the new attacker, much larger and more menacing than the last two I encountered. It straddled me, its bony fingers digging deep into my forearms. A cry left my lips as I glimpsed another figure through my distorted view. With a desperate effort, I threw my legs up into the creature's torso, but it barely shifted. Its rotten grin oozed a slimy green, the stench making me gag as my fading vision begged me to succumb to the darkness.

"*Keep fighting!*" roared the familiar voice in my head that stirred me to stay conscious.

Reaching for an arrow, my hand fumbled as the dragon's deafening roar assaulted our ears, momentarily stunning the Skinner. Seizing the opportunity, I drove the arrow into its side. It screeched out, tightening its hold on me as I tried to find this odd, angry energy within me, but it only flickered in response as if it, too, was depleted.

The dragon's black body slithered up, tackling another Skinner running towards us before leaping in our direction. Snarling, tendrils of smoke billowed from its mouth and nose.

I screamed as the Skinner on me shifted, angrily screeching at the dragon. Desperation fueled my actions, and I jabbed my thumbs into its cavernous eye socket, feeling pus swell around my fingers. It slashed out, opening a wound across my chest before collapsing backward.

Blood oozed from my chest as I scrambled for my bow; my breaths deteriorated, and I panicked, facing the giant, snake-like dragon hovering nearby.

The Skinners backed up, screaming at the dragon in fury is if they were trying to talk to it. The dragon snapped its jaws, the crack reverberating through the air and stealing my breath.

I nocked an arrow while still on the ground when a loud snarl from behind the dragon caused the Skinners to stop their screeching. The dragon turned its massive head towards the noise, and my eyes followed. A massive, golden-brown wolf with streaks of coppery oranges came into view. Saliva was dripping from its snarling maw and charged towards us.

Seizing the shift in attention, I stumbled to my feet and bolted, running back the way I had come, aiming for the entrance of the maze.

But the Skinner was relentless and leaped towards me, plunging its sharp, bony fingers into my leg. I cried out as pain erupted, shooting up into my back. I slammed into the ground just as the massive wolf tackled the creature, ripping it off me, and quickly snapping its neck. The other Skinner, still bleeding profusely from its neck wound, slashed out at me but had no chance as the wolf shredded it apart, then continued its attack by tearing apart the remaining morbid stolen-flesh creatures.

Terror surged through me as I forced myself up, grabbed my bow, and limped away, leaving a trail of blood in my wake. The dragon advanced, jaws open and snapping, tendrils of its poisonous smoke puffing out. It brushed against my right elbow, and a searing pain consumed me as a burning fire spread through my body in a blur of agony. I plunged forward, each step leaving a bloody footprint from the gash in my leg.

The massive wolf leaped from one of the large boulders onto the dragon's back, its claws sinking deep and sending the black, metallic scales clattering to the ground. The dragon thrashed and stopped spewing its poisonous smoke as it tried to dislodge the massive wolf. Its tail whipped against the black rocks and shook the ground beneath us. The wolf sprang from the dragon's back to its outstretched wing, snapping down on bone and shredding through the thick membrane of its wing like paper. The dragon's roar of pain echoed through the air, so intense that I had to cover my ears.

I stumbled, my vision blurring from the pain and blood loss. The dragon's tail lashed out, narrowly missing me and striking the ground with a force that sent shards of rock flying. The wolf continued its relentless assault, tearing into the dragon's flesh with savage ferocity. Blood, dark and metallic, sprayed across the ground, mingling with my own.

I crawled away, my body trembling, each movement a battle against the agony that gripped me and screamed at me to stop, to accept the dark oblivion. The dragon's screams grew more frantic, a mix of rage and desperation, as the wolf tore segments of its body apart, the ground littered with chunks of flesh and shattered scales.

I collapsed behind a boulder, trying to catch my breath, my entire body shaking in pain and the loss of blood. My right elbow burned as my leg pulsated with my warm blood that oozed out from the Skinners grip. I clutched my bow, knuckles white, and forced myself to remain conscious.

I watched in horror as the dragon snapped its wing, sending the wolf hurtling through the air. The wolf hit the ground with a sickening thud, landing just inches from me. A pained yelp escaped its throat, and our eyes met—its vibrant amber eyes locking with mine, filled with a familiar, desperate worry. The sight of its golden coat and fiery gaze triggered a flood of memories, taking me back to my last evaluation at Jesri's. The image flashed vividly in my mind—pulling four bloodied arrows from its soft fur after it attacked the terrorizing black beast.

My brows furrowed in confusion as I struggled to make sense of the familiarity, the glow of those amber eyes stirring something deep inside me that I couldn't quite understand in my murky mind, and the growing pressure in my head built, threatening to pull me under.

The wolf staggered to its feet, swiftly rushing towards me, its snout nudging under my arm. I hesitated, torn between fear and desperate need of help. Meanwhile, the dragon snapped and snarled, its tongue lashing out like a serpent. The wolf's amber eyes bore into mine, filled with an urgency that sent familiar shudders down my spine as it snarled at me in anger.

"Get on, now!" shouted the phantom voice barely recognizable within my disoriented mind.

With a final glance at the advancing dragon, I tightly grasped the wolf's coat, hauling myself over its massive body. The rough fur scraped against my blistered elbow that left my skin barely hanging on, but I held on tight, determined to survive.

The wolf took off, charging straight towards the dragon, forcing me to hold on. Smoke billowed from the dragon's mouth as it leaped after us with a deafening roar. The wolf dashed around the dragon, running faster and harder, its powerful muscles rippling beneath me.

I clenched my teeth, the strain to hold on almost unbearable as I clung to the wolf's golden coat, my blood staining its fur with dark streaks. We hurtled across the boulders, hitting them each with a jarring impact that felt like it might throw me off.

Behind us, the dragon's thunderous roar echoed through the blur in my mind, its monstrous presence charging after us with a fury that shook the very ground. My vision blurred with adrenaline and fear, but amidst the terror, a thin thread of hope flickered in my chest, urging me to believe that I might just make it out alive.

36

The wind screamed past my ears as we raced faster and faster, leaving the dragon behind with its broken and bloodied body, its screeches of anger and pain fading with the wind. A fleeting pang of pity stirred within me as I glimpsed back at the creature struggling with its broken wing, but I quickly banished the thought, recalling the malevolence I had sensed emanating from it.

I clung desperately to the wolf's mane, fighting to maintain my grip as it bounded, ducked, pivoted, and sprinted with relentless energy. Before I could fully comprehend our trajectory, we were in the air, leaping from the highest boulder and landing on the side of the mountain.

The wolf's breaths were deep and ragged as it began scaling the slanted mountainside, overlooking the vast expanse of the dragon's dark, pebbled domain below. A lump caught in my throat at the height of the mountain, and I pressed my legs more tightly against the beast's sides, holding on for life.

In the distance, I spotted another contestant making their way toward the spot where Osric's dead and blistered body lay. Yet, even as we continued our ascent, the dragon continued its pursuit, its massive and tattered body slowing it down. Its claws gouged deep into the mountain and spewed billows of poisonous smoke our way, but it was caught by the high wind and swirled away.

A deep grumble roared from the dragon's mouth as we rounded the steep range onto a landing. The wolf abruptly stopped, launching me off its back, and I landed with a thud, a loud groan escaped my lips. Ignoring me, it began madly digging and clawing at the mountain's edge, sending dirt and rocks flying off the side. The wolf dug faster and faster, jumping slightly as more debris scattered around the now-soft ground gouged out in the center and slumped. Suddenly, it stopped and leaped toward me, nudging me to climb back on.

The wolf sprawled on the ground to help me get on its back, and I did so with great effort. As soon as I was on, it stood up and sprinted away just as the dragon's claw slammed down right where the wolf had dug. The dragon struggled for purchase as another claw followed, scrambling for hold on the soft ground, but failed.

I looked away towards the slopes of the Adauntus Range, not wishing to see the dragon perish. The dragon's roar boomed, and I heard frantic claws losing grip. A wave of terror washed over me as a blaring roar split the air, its echo growing fainter and fainter as it fell into the depths below. Moments later, a bone-jarring smack reverberated through the surrounding mountains, resonating off the rugged terrain.

The wolf soared across the range's peaks, high above the rocky-cold expanse below. The frigid air bit my wet, bloodied skin as we passed through one dark cloud after another. The fog was thick with moisture as we leaped over a man in royal colors, his blood splattered on the ground, followed by two more bodies farther along the crater that still held Astor's dead body. We continued to run, reaching the alcove where Astor and I had waited for daylight to navigate the canyon before the Skinner attack. The realization hit me hard as I glanced down at the wolf. I was now convinced it had been responsible for sending those rocks tumbling down on us, rousing my senses and alerting me to the impending danger.

My thoughts ceased as darkness delved deeper into my mind, radiating a headache through my skull; my only tether to consciousness was a single thread of warmth that quivered with exhaustion. We descended along the back of the mountain range, emerging from the clouds and into the open sky, hitting the valley floor.

My hands ached from gripping so tightly that I let go for a moment to flex them but tumbled to the ground with a crash.

I coughed, clutching my aching stomach as my whole body shook in effort. Closing my eyes, the adrenaline completely subsided, and I felt the full extent of the pain and exhaustion strike deep.

The wolf's damp nose pressed against my neck, sending shivers across my skin, making it prickle with tiny bumps. I was overtaken by violent, uncontrollable shaking as I lost my grip on reality, my mind opening to the presence of the Spellcasters. I could feel their oily darkness seeping into my thoughts and soul with a menacing force intent on consuming every part of me.

A deep, vicious snarl broke through the darkening haze. Forcing my eyes open, I saw the wolf glaring at me with a rage so intense it seemed ready to tear me apart. I attempted to move, but my body remained frozen, paralyzed by the overwhelming exhaustion and pain. Everything felt distorted—overwhelmingly vast yet oppressively close, a maddening contradiction that left me trapped in a swirling vortex of fear and confusion as I struggled to keep breathing.

Another harsh nudge from the wolf rolled me to the side as it snapped its teeth. I looked up at its eyes, which were now gentle and pleading.

"Please. Hold on a little longer." A soft voice rippled through my mind.

I...can't.

I gazed into the wolf's desperate eyes as my vision began to darken, swallowed by the intense pain and gnawing hunger that engulfed me. Just as I felt myself slipping away, I was lifted off the ground by warm, strong arms. The comforting strength of the embrace was the last sensation I felt before oblivion completely took over, pulling me into unconsciousness.

• ✦ •

"*Eliah!*" A familiar voice quivered, jolting me into consciousness as I was moved into another pair of warm, strong arms. "*Eliah!*"

"She's going into shock; we have to give her this!" Another voice growled, urgent and frantic.

"No! She's too weak. It could kill her!"

"*She will die if we don't!*"

Fingers pried open my mouth, and a burning hot liquid consumed my throat and soul, engulfing me in a fiery abyss. I tried to scream against the flaming tendrils lashing through my every vein, seizing every cell and stitching it back together in a hot flare. I quivered, desperate to wake up and stop the liquid from consuming me whole. More poured down my throat, choking me as warm arms pulled me closer.

"I have her! *GO!*" A warm voice commanded.

An angered grunt faded away as I began to shake harder against the fierce fire that burned inside me. I gasped, struggling to breathe as the world around me lurched into motion. Dizziness and pain erupted in every ounce of my being.

"Please," the desperate, familiar voice cried close to my ear. "Come back to me." Lips pressed against my forehead, and a warm blanket covered me as the fiery liquid turned icy, coursing through my veins and into my extremities. I wheezed, feeling my fingers ice over.

The air left my lungs, and a deep pressure settled on my heart, which abruptly slowed, causing me to black out repeatedly until an electric shock zapped through me, thrusting screams from my throat until it was raw. I felt my swollen, torn leg, stitch back together, along with the cut at the base of my head and the poison on my blistered arm calm.

The familiar voice cried out, clinging to my limp body and praying to names unknown to me. Slowly, vibrant emerald-blue eyes came into view, and all I was left with was a blinding headache and gnawing hunger; all my pain had vanished.

I felt a soft kiss caress my forehead and caught sight of his teary smile as understanding hit.

"Levon?" I coughed out, my voice raw and depleted.

His lip quivered with a smile as he embraced me, rocking me back and forth. "I'm so sorry. I'm so sorry," he wept repeatedly, tears dampening my blood-soaked hair. He let go, holding my face and looking into my eyes, his own filled with guilt and determination. "I'll never let you go again. Ever."

"Water. Food," I whispered, my voice barely audible. He moved me to the side, and I looked up, seeing shadows of trees passing through the window, realizing we were in his carriage.

"Can you sit up?" he asked, holding a canteen before me. I nodded slightly, wincing as he shifted his arms to help me sit against him, pressing the cold metal to my lips. I drank slowly at first, savoring the cool relief, then deeply until I consumed the entire canteen.

He held out some nuts, an apple, and hard cheese. My stomach growled at the sight, and I devoured the cheese and nuts, reaching eagerly for the apple he gave over with a tease.

He laughed softly at my scowl, kissing my forehead again, his touch gentle and reassuring.

I felt a growing warmth awaken deep inside as a ripple of energy sizzled within my core as if it hummed with realization and familiarity of home. My mind flashed back to all the unexplained instances throughout the tournament—the unexpected surges of light that coursed through me, the soothing warmth, the voices in my head.

"Levon, what's happening to me?" I rasped, my voice cracking with a mix of fear and confusion having a foreboding feeling he knew what was really going on.

His eyes darkened as he sighed, looking away as if hesitating to answer. "You'll likely be hunted by King Thealor and his men for not finishing the Match *and* by Jesri...but you're not going back. You've come to a point where we had to intervene." He took my hands in his, his eyes lined with silver.

"Eliah, when I first saw you dancing at the seashore, it wasn't then that I decided to protect and care for you. I promised my mother I would," he said, his voice breaking slightly.

My heart pounded as I struggled to comprehend his words, my brows knitting in confusion.

"We had been searching for you for years, terrified you were lost in the Cataclysm," he continued, his words coming out in a rush. I tried to interject, but he continued. "I couldn't tell you with everyone watching...with Jesri watching and spewing so many lies. He would have taken you straight to the king or sold you to the Onyx Market, where the Spellcasters would torture and use you. So, we had to play along."

"After finding you, I closely watched Jesri and his idiotic schemes. He tried to sell you off to the highest bidder, but no one wanted to marry a girl so young. So, he created another revolting idea to make you a bounty hunter within the Onyx Market, but that would only put you in the line of fire. So, we spread lies and bribed the men to believe you weren't worth it, especially not against the king and his—" he stopped abruptly before his eyes darkened with sadness. "His personal executioner."

My heart sank as I saw tears streaming down his cheeks.

"I was the fear...to so many people," his voice trembled. "But I made sure to reach that rank to find you, to infiltrate every part of the politics within these cursed lands; it was the only way I could protect you. And when I finally left that life, I came searching for you, making plan after plan to get us all out and keep you safe. I made sure to steer Jesri to that tavern, without him knowing I was behind all his failed plans for the orphan he did not care for. This Match was the only way to make Jesri give you up willingly and without drawing too many suspicious eyes."

A lump formed in my throat, and I stopped breathing, pressing my hand against my chest to quell the pounding. "Why?" I breathed, my voice shaky. "Why me?"

He stared deeply into my eyes, his breath heavy with unspoken truth. "The convulsions, the change in your eyes, the incident to my face—they're all signs of something far beyond ordinary. Your ability to regenerate strength faster, heal within a matter of hours, and push through when others would have succumbed to the void. And your anger that burns so fiercely...*it's not human,*

Eliah. All of it points to the Ethereal—a power that's been dormant within you and has been waiting to be unleashed."

He paused, his expression a mix of sorrow and awe while my heart seemed to stand still. "You are a Magic, Eliah, one of the last of a rare and ancient kind in this world. But you're not just a Magic—you're something otherworldly, something celestial, and divine. That energy within you isn't just growing; it's unfolding in ways that transcend even the highest of Magics here in this world and in others. Your true nature is emerging, and it's something that can no longer be hidden or suppressed. Your abilities are awakening, and they will only grow stronger. We can't hide this anymore."

His words sent waves of hysteria through me. I quickly sat up, gasping for breath.

No, this couldn't be happening. I didn't want this. The idea of being a Magic *and* something celestial was too much to understand.

"That's why I couldn't tell you," he continued, his voice a mixture of sorrow and urgency. "Nor would you have believed me if I had. It was too dangerous, and you would have been killed if *anyone* found out. We simply couldn't take that risk."

My mind reeled. The world around me blurred as the truth sank in. All the strange occurrences, the inexplicable moments—they suddenly made sense, yet it was a reality I was desperate to reject. How could this be?

Tears stung my eyes as I struggled to find my breath, my chest tightening with the weight of my unwanted destiny.

There were still too many questions.

Too many fears.

Too many unknowns.

Too many suspicions that I didn't want to be true.

For me, an orphan, to be something more than what I was.

A Magic. An actual Magic. And something *celestial?*

No. It can't be true. *It's not true!*

"No, I'm—I'm no one! I'm normal—not a Magic and far from celestial!" I spat, desperately trying to reject the truth yet somehow knowing all along that some*thing* was always different within me.

He squeezed my hands, his gaze intense and unwavering. "You're not just anyone, Eliah. You are extraordinary."

I sat there, stunned, shaking my head in disbelief. "I-I don't understand! I'm a nobody. H-how?"

He cupped my blood-stained cheek in his gentle hand. "I'll tell you everything, I promise, but we must get you to safety first. Many people are likely already searching for you, especially after we took you out of the Match. I had no idea the Match would be here, in the Unmarked Territory—" His voice hitched, and his lip quivered. "I'm so sorry, Eliah."

I struggled to catch my breath, to understand, but even with whatever elixir I was given that dulled my pain, I felt utterly drained.

"That's why the Spellcasters want me. Why the Onyx Market placed a bounty on my head? Because I'm Magic?" I asked, trying to calm my rising panic.

"No," his expression shifted, becoming more apprehensive. My brows furrowed as my head swirled with questions. "The Onyx Market is searching for the lone Magic," he continued, "and we still assume they haven't figured out it's you. No leads are pointing to you; we've made sure of that. Kaizen has been silencing any bounty hunters who had leads."

He averted his gaze, looking out the carriage window, then hesitantly returned it to me. "But the Spellcasters, they want you for something entirely different."

"What?" I demanded, frustration and fear tightening in my chest.

Levon took a deep breath, his eyes brimming with concern. "The Spellcasters know you hold the key to this ancient power, something that will alter the course of time and reality itself. They don't just want to capture you—they want to control you, break you until you become a part of them."

I breathed out, the vision of the bloodied throne still haunting my thoughts, the echoes of chanting skeletons still ringing in my ears.

"They want you for control, domination," he stopped, looking deep into my eyes. "And to gift them with immortality in this world and the Cosmos beyond so they can reshape it all to their liking. You're a beacon of power and light, Eliah. A catalyst for something *much* larger than *this* reality."

My head swam with confusion, overwhelmed by too many surreal notions that refused to make sense.

"I don't understand," I muttered again, slumping against him. "I don't understand." Hot tears streamed down my face; none of this could be true.

I was not a Magic...I couldn't be. Nor a key to something.

He held me close, his touch soothing yet stirring up a storm of anxiety and bafflement. "We'll explain everything," he said softly, stroking back my hair and gently kissing my forehead.

A sudden loud crash hit the carriage from the outside, tearing a scream from my throat and whipping Levon's gaze towards the door.

Abruptly, the carriage lurched to a stop, throwing us both off the seat. We tumbled across the floor, hitting the opposite wall with a thud. Pain flared through my already battered body, and I groaned, clutching my side.

Levon scrambled to his feet, helping me up with careful hands.

"Are you okay?" he asked, his voice tight and concerned, as he quickly scanned the area outside the window.

I nodded, gritting my teeth against the pain.

He glanced towards the front of the carriage, his expression darkening.

"We need to be ready for anything," he demanded, handing me a dagger from one of his bags, his eyes meeting mine, displaying a fierce tension.

He helped me back onto the seat and pounded on the carriage's roof, signaling Kaizen. The carriage lurched forward with a violent jolt, sending us crashing into the opposite wall. It accelerated rapidly, rattling harder with each passing second. Levon cursed under his breath, his voice tense with urgency, as he leaned down to help me.

Kaizen started screaming something, his voice filled with panic but was instantly cut off by the sharp roar of flames erupting around us, consuming our entire beings and engulfing the carriage in a fiery inferno.

37

I barely had time to scream before the shockwave hit, a massive force that seemed to rip the very fabric of reality apart. A deafening roar shattered the air around us, sucking the breath from my lungs as an intense heat erupted, engulfing the carriage and obliterating it into splinters that flew in every direction. Shards of wood and glass cut into my skin as the blast hurled me through the air, slowing time to a crawl.

I slammed into the rocky road with a bone-jarring impact, knocking the wind out of me and barely hanging onto the edges of consciousness. The world around me blurred in fire, and all I could feel was the crushing pressure and searing heat of flames that licked my flesh with agonizing intensity. My ears rang with a high-pitched, continuous scream, and my head swam, disoriented and heavy with the shock.

Debris began raining down around me, crashing onto the road with startling force. Muffled shouts, distant and distorted, intruded into my mind, but they were dulled out by the persistent ringing in my ears and the pop of fire, sizzling beside me. I struggled to process what was happening, but everything blurred together in a cacophony of confusion and pain—so much pain.

Smoke plagued the air, thick and pungent, making breathing almost impossible. It choked me, sending me into violent coughing fits that wracked my battered body.

I blinked slowly, trying to clear my vision and regain some sense of my surroundings. My limbs felt numb, tingling with the desperate need to move and grasp something solid.

The area around me lay in ruins, shattered and consumed by flames that licked hungrily at the air. Thick smoke enveloped me as a suffocating blanket pressing down like a tangible weight. Each breath was a battle, my lungs burning with the effort to draw in air tainted with ash and soot.

Rolling onto my back, I choked for air, seeing flames paint the smoky sky with an ominous glow. Towering pines stood behind like daggers, their shapes morphing and twisting in the swirling haze.

A figure emerged from the blur, reaching out to grasp my arms and pull me from the scorched earth. I cried out in agony as his touch seared my blistering skin. Coughing, I blinked repeatedly until Calum's golden eyes slowly came into focus. A black cloth partially concealed his face, and his dirty blonde hair spilled out from beneath his hood.

It felt like a dream, a surreal and hazy nightmare of fire, smoke, and ash.

"Cal?" I choked out, my voice weak and trembling, not believing he was there.

Tears welled up in my eyes as I reached for him, hoping he was real. His hands closed around mine, sending a painful jolt up my burning arm.

He was real.

I shook my head, trying to clear the ringing pressure in my ears.

"El," he breathed, his voice thick with emotion as he took me into his arms. "I-I didn't want this. I...had to," he stammered, his voice breaking.

I clung to him, fighting to stay conscious. "What...what are you...talking about?" I slurred with a cough.

Calum said nothing and only held me tighter in his arms. I slumped against him, too tired to speak as an uncomfortable feeling raged within me. My gaze caught sight of fire devouring the remnants of Levon's destroyed carriage. The surrounding area was covered in scattered flames that threatened to lick our flesh right off as it began scaling the tall pines within the dense forest. Dark, thick smoke swirled low as crackling embers sparked, snapping more pieces of debris into the air. The sound of burning flames overtook the painful ringing in my ears.

Levon.

My head lolled to the side, panic rising in my chest. "Levon," I rasped, coughing on the thick smoke. "Cal, where's...Levon?"

He kept moving forward, trudging through the debris, flames, and thick clumps of ash that fell like soft rain.

"Cal, stop," I pleaded, my voice barely above a whisper. "We have to find Lev—"

"*It doesn't matter anymore! None of it does,*" he snapped, his tone sharp and final, muffled through the cloth he wore. I wheezed, the pain biting into my skull like a hammer.

"What...are you talking about?" I demanded, anger sweltering within my disoriented mind.

Calum's grip tightened, sending pain rippling through my burnt flesh as he shook his head with hatred carved into his eyes. He picked up his pace, and I coughed into his chest, blinking away the fog right as he tripped forward, throwing me from his arms.

We both crashed to the ground in a tangled heap, and I cried out as sharp rocks bit into my burned arms and legs. Thick smoke stirred, and I shrieked out in pain, coughing for Calum. I tried to lift myself, sinking into my seared forearms when I saw Kaizen's silhouette, his tattered leather cloak billowing behind him.

The smoke swirled around Kaizen's movements as he swiftly dragged Calum away from me and pinned him to the fiery dirt road.

Calum yelled in defiance, throwing a punch at Kaizen's face that snapped his head to the side, his untied hair following with the impact. Calum reached for a dagger in his boot, but Kaizen was quicker and began raining punch after punch on Calum with vicious ferocity. Each blow landed with a sickening thud, splattering blood onto the dirt.

Calum yelled, squirming under his hold, his arms flailing in a desperate attempt to defend himself and attack simultaneously. But Kaizen was a relentless force, a different breed that kept attacking, his eyes burning with a savage intensity.

I struggled to find my voice amidst the ringing in my ears, the acrid smell of smoke stinging my nostrils.

"Stop!" I rasped out, scarcely above a whisper, and crawled towards them. Each movement sent jolts of pain through my body, but I pushed on, the sight of Calum's battered face spurring me forward. "*Stop!*"

Calum managed to knee Kaizen in the groin, eliciting a small groan from him, but barely shifting enough for Calum to crawl out from his hold. Calum's face was a mess of blood and bruises, his eyes swollen and barely open. He scrambled towards me, his hand outstretched in a plea. Just as I touched the tip of his fingers, Kaizen's boot connected with his face, the impact sending a spray of blood splattering into the air and my face. Calum crumpled to the ground, unconscious, his body limp and lifeless on the burning dirt, his face now unrecognizable.

Kaizen sucked in a rasping breath, coughing deeply before he turned his attention to me; his amber eyes were burning, and his face was grimy with sweat, blood, and ash. Blood oozed from a more extensive cut at his hairline. His hair stuck against his face, while his cloak barely hung on, flowing in tatters against the roaring flames that threatened to overtake us.

Anger ignited within me, and a fierce snarl escaped my lips. *"WHAT DID YOU DO?"* I screamed, hearing my voice echo throughout the dense forest.

He moved swiftly, grabbing my face and wrapped a cloth around my mouth as I jerked back, trying to free myself. I threw a punch to his side and kicked against him frantically, desperate to escape.

"Eliah, stop!" he growled, his grip tightening around my jaw.

"*What did you do?!*" I screamed again, my voice muffled by the cloth, as he hoisted me over his shoulder. I pounded and clawed at his back, my legs kicking weakly. The pain from my burnt skin was overwhelming but not compared to the anger surging through me that was on the brink of eruption.

He cursed under his breath, coughing as the smoke thickened around us. He ran through the choking air, stopping several times to spin in frantic circles before pressing on.

Each movement was agonizing, every jolt sending fresh waves of pain through my body. He pivoted and lunged forward, coming to an abrupt halt before swiftly crouching down to grab a brown satchel that he put over his shoulder before continuing.

He coughed again, and I felt it rumble through his strong body as he skidded to a sudden stop. Crouching down, he let out a gasp of dismay, his grip on me loosening, and I slipped from his grasp, hitting the ground before coughs overtook my frame.

I twisted toward where Kaizen was looking to see Levon sprawled out beside a more significant part of the carriage that hadn't been obliterated in the explosion.

"*Levon!*" I screamed, the smoke choking down my cry. Kaizen gripped my hand, holding me back. I clawed at his hold, my nails digging into his flesh as I saw the haunting sorrow fill his eyes. I turned back, taking in Levon's bloodied body, charred and broken.

Horror flooded my soul as I sunk to my burnt knees and clasped my hand over my clothed mouth. A sharp, jagged fragment of the carriage impaled Levon's chest, and his blood pooled around him, glistening dark and ominous in the firelight.

"*LEVON!*" I wailed, my voice cracking as hot tears spilled freely down my bloodied face. I pushed free of Kaizen's hold, trying to reach him.

Kaizen quickly pulled me back and hoisted me over his shoulder again, his grip unyielding. He was up and running before I could save Levon, before I could even touch him one last time. The sight of Levon's lifeless eyes haunted me, frozen in my mind and sending hot tears rolling down my cheeks.

I kicked and punched and clawed at Kaizen, my heart shattering with every step he took away from Levon and Calum.

"*I'll kill you!*" I rasped, coughing out tendrils of smoke that burned my lungs. "*I'll kill you! I'll kill you!*"

I pounded on his back, my fists weak but relentless, driven by a fury and sorrow I had never known. My screams turned to sobs, and exhaustion overtook me, leaving me hanging limply over his shoulder. "I'll kill you," I rasped out with a cough.

Shouts and voices echoed through the dense forest that now wrapped us in its deadly grasp, while the world around me turned into a blur of tears, smoke, and despair.

"Geisha, bless us," Kaizen heaved, gently setting me down beside Levon's horse with bits of its flesh burnt and bubbling. Kaizen stooped down to grab his bow and arrows before slinging them over his back.

My heart, body, and mind were numb as he grabbed the reins of Levon's bay mare, extending his hand to me, but I couldn't lift my arm to his.

I didn't want to. I didn't want to do anything anymore.

"Eliah, please!" he choked, coughing.

"You left him," I breathed, feeling the tears stream down my face, barely able to hold myself up. More voices and shouts echoed through the deep, smokey darkness that cloaked us. My lips curled back as I looked at his burning gaze glowing against the darkness. "YOU LEFT—" I screamed, only to have Kaizen cup his hand over my mouth, cutting off my words.

"I took an oath to protect you, not him!" he hissed into my ear. "He knew what he was getting into. Now get your rutting behind on the horse before I have to force you."

"Over here!" A voice boomed nearby. Kaizen's bright amber eyes locked onto mine, filled with unease as he held his finger over his bruised lip, still holding my mouth closed.

"You're a coward," I seethed through clenched teeth, shoving his hand away. "You let him die."

"You think I wanted this? You think I had a choice?" Kaizen snapped, grabbing underneath my arm and yanking me into him.

"You always had a choice!" I spat back with tears, my voice shaking with rage, not backing away from his infuriating face, mere inches from mine. "And you chose to run."

Kaizen's grip tightened as he looked down at me with ferocity. "I'm choosing to save *your* life. So move, or so help me, I'll drag you through this forest unconscious."

The fear and anger in his eyes mirrored my own as we stood there, locked in a battle of wills.

"Someone call for help!" The shout came closer, and Kaizen's eyes flicked towards the sound, his fear palpable. His hands clasped around my waist, and before I could retort, he growled, lifting me onto the mare that pranced nervously.

I clung to the horse's reins with little strength as he swung up behind me, his ragged cloak hanging to the side. He wrapped his arms around me, taking hold of the reins as I slumped into his warmth reluctantly, unable to stop the weight of sorrow stabbing deep into my mind.

He clicked his tongue, urging the mare into a gallop. The tall pines blurred past us, the crackling flames and the shouting faded into the sound of the mare's hooves slamming onto the ground.

Kaizen wheezed out another cough as we journeyed deeper into the dense forest. My mind swelled with exhaustion, grief, despair, and sorrow that turned my thoughts depressive and overwhelming.

I began to cry, not believing this was happening to me.

I am just a pathetic orphan of no importance, not a Magic or whatever extraordinary person Levon thought I was. I'm nothing and should return to nothing.

More tears streaked my soot-lined face.

"Don't say that," Kaizen snarled behind me, his voice a low, dangerous growl.

I snapped my head back, glaring at him in confused anger. I opened my mouth to protest, but he cut me off, his eyes flashing with fury.

"We're going to a safe haven, but we won't get there until late," he replied, his grip on the reins so tight his knuckles turned white. "So rest. You need it."

The tension between us hung in the air as we rode in stifling silence. Minutes dragged by until I couldn't hold my tongue any longer.

"Why did you do it?" I seethed through gritted teeth, forcing my tears back, seeing Calum's swollen and bloodied face haunt my mind. "Why did you hurt him?"

"Calum isn't who you think he is," Kaizen warned, his voice raw from the smoke.

"*You know nothing about him!*" I snapped, my voice hoarse. I leaned away from his warmth, my skin on fire from the burns.

"He was the one who blew up the carriage, Eliah," he growled into my ear. "*Levon is dead* because *of him.*" I shook my head in doubt, anger billowing in my core like the swelling smoke. "He found out about you—your Magic. I didn't think he would truly want to be a part of the Onyx Market, let alone try to bring you in—"

"No! *You're wrong!* He'd never hurt me!" I interjected, my voice trembling with anger and despair.

His body tensed with frustration. "He wanted to hurt you, was sick of living in your shadow."

"My shadow?" I scoffed with irritation, not believing him for a second.

"I watched and followed him but never saw signs that he knew until that night he kissed you under your wishing tree," he grumbled.

I struggled to remember that night, which seemed like a lifetime ago. He pleaded with me to stay so he would take my place or find another way to keep me, but I refused, and after, he had become so odd...so cold. His abrupt kiss that ignited an actual spark of pain that stung my lips before I saw startling amber eyes glowing in the dark.

I choked back the image, unwilling to believe it was true. I tried to steady myself, struggling with my ragged, hoarse breaths. My hands shook uncontrollably as my mind spiraled.

My mind flashed back to Calum towering over me outside Jesri's library, where I felt, for the first time, he wanted to hurt me after I found the book of the Leonardian Trials and *dismissed* the footman as if they were working together.

I closed my eyes, still hearing Calum screaming at Jesri in his study, begging me to stay, to his deep hug pleading my forgiveness as I left for Levon's estate. To his odd smile after I woke up from my coma.

It was a coincidence. He wanted to keep me safe, to help me *stay* safe.

I shook my head, disbelieving it all.

"You're lying," I seethed, wanting to get off this wretched horse and run far, far away from him.

He huffed out in annoyance. "Believe what you want. But you can't deny that you're part of something bigger than all this. Levon wasn't lying—"

"Stop with the cryptic nonsense!" I snapped, my voice echoing through the swaying pines. I turned away, shaking my head. "For all I know, *you* could be taking me straight toward the Spellcasters! *You could be the one behind all of this!*" Fear spiked through my tired soul, and I hoped it wasn't true. I hoped none of this was true, and I'd wake up from this nightmare. "*Why should I trust* anything *you say?*" I fumed.

"*Because* your mother *entrusted me to protect you!*" he yelled, his voice cracking with the weight of the confession.

My heart stopped as more confusion overtook me. I struggled to breathe and think above the roaring disbelief.

"My...my mother?" I whispered, the statement hitting me like a tidal wave.

Kaizen took a deep breath that rumbled in my ear. His posture straightened, but his voice softened. "We knew you wouldn't believe us," he scolded. "*This is exactly why we didn't tell you anything.*"

"You knew my mother?" I asked again, feeling absolutely absurd I was having this conversation *with him!*

He abruptly stopped the horse, pulling on its reins and tightening his legs around its body and my hips. I arched my head to look at him, his jaw flexed as if hesitating to continue. "Your mother," he paused through gritted teeth, "was the last reigning Queen of the Seraphs before the Cosmos plunged into the Cataclysm. Levon, me...your mother, and several more Seraphs were thrust here in the collapse. And *I* am bound to the oath to protect *my queen* at all costs in this light-forsaken world we were never meant to be brought to," he muttered.

"So don't trust me, hate me—I don't care. But you have a destiny to fulfill, and I'm going to make sure you achieve it and restore order," Kaizen declared, his eyes blazing with resolution.

I could only stare at him, dumbfounded, my mouth wide open. Confusion swirled in my mind, clashing with a torrent of conflicting thoughts. My brain struggled to process what I was hearing, leaving me at a complete loss for words.

How could this be happening? Nothing made sense, and the more I tried to grasp the situation, the more bewildered I became.

"When we reach the haven, I'll explain everything," he added, his voice rough with exhaustion and punctuated by a rasping cough that shook his body. He clicked his tongue, urging the mare forward at a faster pace.

I turned my gaze away, struggling against the smoke that still clung stubbornly to my lungs as a paralyzing shock coursed through me.

How could this be real? These were the things of fables and stories, *not my life.*

Amidst the tumult of my swirling thoughts, something deep within me stirred—a warm, almost nostalgic feeling that seemed to flare in response, calling me home like the twinkling stars that had always brought me comfort.

As we rode deeper into the forest, shadows lengthened, and a coldness gnawed at my skin as the sun bled across the sky. The air grew crisp, filled with a quiet power that hummed with my every heartbeat as if the world itself held its own breath at the truth.

I felt the weight of their lies and schemes slipping away, unraveling like the strings they'd once used to control me. And as the truth settled within me—brighter than any sunset and more alive with colors I'd never dared to claim—something new and unstoppable awoke, filling the hollow spaces carved in my heart.

I was no longer the obedient pet of a haughty lord. I no longer had to play the submissive puppet to obtain freedom, or to be trapped in a future not of my choosing. I was no longer an unwanted orphan to parents I'd only known through Jesri's lies, and had always believed were as arrogant and selfish as him.

But instead, if what they said were true, I was the daughter of a Seraph *queen*, with a *power* that could reshape everything. And for the first time, I felt whole, unbound, and endless—ready to claim the life that was always meant to be mine and I would stop at nothing until I had the freedom I deserved, and the life I was ready to seize.

As the night grew thick, that nostalgic warm feeling settled in me again, deeper this time, helping me to realize that this was only the beginning.

Acknowledgements

Where do I even begin?

I am filled with more excitement and gratitude than I had as a little girl on Christmas day. And that's saying a lot.

When I was younger I absolutely loathed reading and writing because I couldn't do either. I was put into one literary intervention club after another because of my horribly low reading and spelling levels. You couldn't pay me to go to Disneyland to touch a book—let alone write one.

Yet here I am, almost 20 years later, with a love for story making so profound that it keeps me up all night long and I'm not even upset about it.

Books and the stories held within have absolutely reshaped my life. From the battles of good and evil, to heroes and heroines facing their fears, to magic and joy, to sadness and trauma. Each story holds *life* and is so important.

And *every* story is worth telling. *Even yours.*

So, first and foremost, I want to give all glory to my Heavenly Father and my Savior, Jesus Christ. Their guidance and unwavering love have been a constant source of strength and inspiration throughout my life journey. This year, I have seen a lot of dark days—days that I wanted to give up and wasn't sure how to keep moving forward. Yet, light has a way of slowly seeping in, even in the darkest of times. And that light is Jesus Christ. He is, and always will be *the* source of light and joy for anyone seeking it. And all you have to do is turn towards the Light and become apart of it. No matter the hard days ahead, God prevails—so let Him prevail in your life. I promise, if you do, your life will change for the better.

Now, to my beloved husband and best friend, thank you for your endless support, patience, love, and encouragement. You have been my rock, my cheerleader, and my confidant—always believing in me, even when I have doubted myself. Thank you for listening to my countless ideas and for helping me come up with new and better ones. For reading page after page, being my anchor when things got rough, and watching our cutie boy to let me write (or sleep). Your love and unwavering kindness mean the world to me. I love you, forever.

To my incredible editor, Tabitha Chandler, thank you for your keen eye, your honesty, your dedication, and your support. Your expertise and insight have helped shape this work into something I am truly proud of. I am SO grateful for your partnership and for the countless hours you've poured into bringing this story to life. You're amazing.

To my beta readers, thank you for being my first audience, for calling me out when I needed it, and for cheering me on through each chapter. Your feedback and friendship are priceless, and I couldn't have done it without your insights and encouragement. THANK YOU!

To my family, who's always been my biggest cheerleaders from day one. Thank you for always being there with open arms, with excitement, and with love. It's because of you this dream of mine has never dwindled. I couldn't ask for a better crew to have in my corner, and I am endlessly grateful for each of you.

To my incredible street team—you all are the absolute best! Your enthusiasm and help have blown me away. Thank you for spreading the word, sharing the love, and helping this book find it's way into the world. I couldn't have asked for a more passionate group of readers and friends. You make this journey so much more fun and worthwhile. Thank you from the bottom of my heart.

And last but certainly not least, to *you* dear reader—thank you from the bottom of my heart. You're the reason these pages exists, and knowing that you've chosen to dive into this story mean the *world* to me. Your time, your curiosity, and your willingness to journey with me through these words are gifts I don't take lightly. I hope this continued story of light and darkness stirs something in you, makes you feel, and leaves a lasting impression. Thank you for being a part of this adventure and for allowing these characters to live in your mind and heart. I cannot accurately express my gratitude.

About the Author

Dreamer, full-time baking enthusiast, cultural lover, and theatrical soul, Emmory has always been captivated by the power of storytelling. Her one true dream has been to become a published author, weaving tales that transport readers to new worlds and experiences.

Hailing from a quaint town in Utah, best known for its pristine snow-capped mountains and vibrant, colorful springs. She lives with her supportive husband, playful son, and their beloved fur baby.

She enjoys indulging in hot baths, filling her space with fresh, fragrant flowers, savoring the delight of homemade chocolate chip cookies, and is constantly day dreaming.

Whether she's lost in the pages of a book, experimenting with new baking recipes, or exploring the rich tapestry of cultures and theater, Emmory's life is a testament to her creative and passionate nature. She hopes to share her vibrant imagination and heartfelt stories with the world, inviting others to dream, and to remember that 'happiness can be found, even in the darkest of times, if one only remembers to turn on the light.'

Follow Emmory on Instagram @authoremmoryjarman for future updates in The Lightbringer Series.

READ ON
FOR BONUS CHAPTERS

6

Kaizen

My anger roared with absolute hatred as I followed Calum through the bustling market, cursing Levon and promising to skin him alive if he let anything happen to her while I was away.

The town was alive with people dressed in pastels, their clothes fluttering as they carried bags of goods, while the poor withered in the corners, their eyes hollow and pleading. Streamers of spring flags fluttered lightly in the breeze, casting intermittent shadows across the cobbled road. The air was thick with the rich aromas of spices, mingling with the earthy scent of fresh produce and the sweet fragrance of blooming flowers.

With my hood pulled low over my face, I stayed within the shadows of the alleys, sharpening my focus on Calum. Watching him turn down a secluded alleyway and vanish from sight. I quickly moved into the daylight, my steps silent and calculated as I blended seamlessly into the clamor of passing carriages and the din of the market, along with the chatter and laughter of pompous aristocrats.

I stalked into the alleyway, pulsating with a rage that threatened to consume me. Calum wanted to start work within the Onyx Market, but I knew I had to keep him alive. We were so close to getting her back that we couldn't risk anything now. I wouldn't allow it, even if that meant keeping a possible threat.

The alleyway opened into a dim, rank part of town, a stark contrast to the lively, bright market. My eyes scanned the open area, taking in every detail, every shadow. The atmosphere was heavy, the air thick with the stench of decay and neglect.

The buildings here were dilapidated, their walls covered in grime and graffiti. The ground was littered with debris, and the few people who moved about did so with furtive glances and hurried steps. The alley led deeper into this forsaken part of town, where light barely penetrated, and the air felt stagnant.

I moved cautiously, my senses on high alert as I watched the dim light cast eerie shadows, and every sound seemed amplified in the oppressive silence. There was no trace of the fresh fragrance of spring here, only a murky odor reminiscent of the tavern Calum had taken Eliah to the other day.

I could still feel her smooth yet calloused hand in mine, unable to resist the urge to touch her...just for a moment. Anger still radiated through me that Calum had taken her there and allowed her to have one of the strongest drinks, knowing full well how important her meeting with Levon was. His sabotage was transparent, and I wouldn't let all our efforts be ruined by a mere drink. Eliah's slender frame couldn't afford to be inebriated, and I was keenly aware that Levon had a façade to uphold with Jesri, even if things went awry.

I clenched my teeth in frustration as Calum's voice echoed through the foul-smelling area. He was laughing with someone who remained stone-faced, unimpressed by Calum's charm. I crept forward, watching as the tall man usher Calum into a crumbling brick storefront that looked like it had never been repaired after the Creos Civil War. Bricks still crumbled around its exterior, and the clay roof barely held together. The only thing that appeared intact was the door, which slammed shut behind them.

The sight of the decaying building filled me with unease. Its façade bore the scars of past conflicts, a stark reminder of the turmoil that had once engulfed this place and the thousands who had withered away because of Xaldruk and his legion.

I forced the memories out of my head as I approached cautiously. My senses heightened, but I did not allow myself to open the power gate. I scaled one of the crumbling buildings as the sun descended, casting glowing oranges and pinks across the sky. It was one thing that was beautiful here, but it also indicated the start of the party that Calum should be at.

I perched at the top of another crumbling building, nestled in a spot that gave me a clear view through their watery, firelit window, offering the best vantage point. I inhaled deeply and carefully opened my power gate enough to enhance my hearing.

"Now, what do you mean he *knows* something?" Growled a voice thick with menace as if it belonged to someone who perpetually held a cigar in his mouth.

"He is right here and can speak for himself," Calum retorted sharply. "And yes, I've got a lead on a potential Magic."

The gruff man let out a guttural laugh, audible even from my perch without enhanced senses. "So, you, Lord Jesri's kin, are willing to give information?"

"Oh no. I'm not giving anything away unless there's something in it for me," Calum shot back, his tone dripping with disdain.

A tense silence hung before the gruff man spoke again, his voice low and dangerous. "Fine, spill it. What do you know, and then I'll decide."

Calum's laughter turned bitter. "I'm not one to be naïve," he taunted.

"What do you want?" The man snapped, his impatience evident.

"I want in," Calum declared with cold determination.

My jaw clenched fiercely, grinding my teeth together as fury surged within me, restraining the urge to strike him down then and there. I couldn't inform Levon until this entire ordeal was over and Eliah was safely away from the Archenons, knowing that even though Levon could put on a face, he wasn't good enough to hold back his temper which would ruin everything.

"Geisha," I swore under my breath.

"And what exactly do you have?" The man demanded, his voice now a menacing growl.

"I said I have a lead, didn't I?" Calum spat.

"I need more than just a lead, boy!" The man bellowed, the sound of his hand slamming down on a table echoing through the conversation. "I need proof. We can't afford mistakes anymore, *especially* not when it involves someone like Lord Jesri, boy. Too many eyes," he added darkly.

"Fine, I'll get you your proof," Calum replied sharply, his tone now edged with a hint of sinister determination, yet I heard his pulse heighten and wondered if he had the guts to do it.

I shut my power gate, observing from above as Calum scurried away. The light was fading into an inky indigo as I leaped from roof to roof, barely making a sound while keeping pace with him. We reached the market, now lit by fire-light and sparsely populated. A few scattered people milled about, some ladies snickering at Calum, who eyed them with pleasure before jogging down to a store with a bell that dinged as he entered.

I quickly slid down a pipe, jumping from one rafter to the next before rolling to the ground without a sound. Calum emerged with a brown bag and began walking swiftly back toward Jesri's estate, nodding to several ladies and men as he passed as if nothing from his previous encounter had happened.

It was dark by the time we arrived at the estate, the crowd from the party still bustling with activity. I reached into my mind, feeling my tether to her pulse with life, and relief washed over me. Scanning the crowd, I spotted Levon chatting with other lords and ladies that Jesri had introduced him to. Calum slipped into the back of the estate, his form visible through the illuminating crystal windows. I waited, watching and scanning for any larger threat than the boy Eliah called a friend.

As the night went on, people began to depart, the stars twinkling to life above. Eliah walked inside after speaking to several maids who were cleaning up.

I had always been so close to her, felt her cry and mourn, felt her joy and infatuation. Yet, I had never been able to touch her, to mourn with her, to tell her she wasn't alone. To tell her that her mother had loved her so much and had never wanted to let her go.

I squeezed my eyes shut, unwilling to let the memories sweep back in—the pain, the anger, the relentless guilt of knowing I had failed my queen. The weight of it all threatened to crush me, but I couldn't afford that guilt now.

I sucked in a breath, forcing myself to stay present as I watched Eliah slip out with a dark shawl wrapped around her shoulders, now dressed in her training attire. She moved with a grace that spoke of how well she pieced herself back together every time Jesri laid a hand on her, taking me to my breaking point to not throttle him. Wishing I didn't have to go along with Levon's plan and that I could just take her, train her, and keep her safe. But there were only a few of us left, and we were nowhere near strong enough against Xaldruk without her.

As she disappeared into the woods, I quickened my pace to keep up with her, adjusting my eyes to the darkness. My heart pounded with a mix of urgency and anger. I vowed to protect her and intervene if it became necessary, not daring to let her out of my sight. Not now. Not ever. The thought of losing her—of failing again, was unbearable.

I pushed forward, determined to protect her, to make up for the past with her mother, and to finally prove that I could be the high guardian she needed.

"What took you so long?" Calum's voice pierced the darkness, instantly flooding my being with fire. How did he get out here without me noticing?

"It's not midnight yet, and I'm not going to wish anyway," Eliah lamented. I could feel her pain—dreams and wishes that never came true because they already had; she just didn't know it.

Calum laughed as he walked closer to her. "Glad you're enjoying the shawl."

"Please tell me you didn't skip the entire party just for this?" Eliah remarked, her voice laced with annoyance.

"Oh, I had other important matters to attend to."

So help me, if he laid a hand on her, I won't be able to hold back from killing him right here.

"Important?" Eliah laughed. "What could possibly be more important than a party with plenty of ladies who—"

Her words were cut off as his lips pressed against hers. A snarl escaped my lips as I watched her melt into him, her breath hitching before he kissed her again.

My heart pounded in my chest, and I couldn't stand the sight of him touching her or her responding to him. Rage surged through me, and without thinking I snapped my power gate open, sending a controlled wave of energy toward them. It was soft enough to avoid hurting her but strong enough to force them apart. I flexed my jaw and clenched my fists, struggling to reel my anger back in as I saw Eliah and Calum stand back in confusion and anger.

"*What was that?*" she hissed, her eyes wide with irritation.

I saw the malice in his eyes, the malicious smirk forming on his lips, realizing I had just given him the proof he needed. I swore under my breath, watching him smirk only boiled my blood even more. In my fury, I stepped forward onto a stick that snapped loudly in the eerie quiet of the forest.

I cursed as they snapped their heads toward me, but I was already out of their line of sight, stalking to their left. Calum raised his finger to his lips as they both listened intently. Eliah shifted her gaze toward me, and the determination in her gray eyes flooded me with pride. Even though she looked small, she wouldn't back down from a fight. My mind flashed back to her solid punch to that disgusting man's nose in the tavern, and I couldn't help but grin.

Opening my power just a fraction, I allowed my eyes to adjust to let her see me...just for a moment. I blinked as her eyes locked with me. I swallowed hard before I shut my power gate and moved back into the shadows.

As if summoned by the universe, a fawn stepped into the clearing, its presence almost symbolic, reminding me of our duty to protect and restore balance. The delicate creature stood still, its eyes wide and curious, seemingly aware of the tension in the air. It felt like a sign from the Cosmos, a reminder of the stakes and the urgency to return home. The universe knew how difficult this was and how much it needed us to succeed and protect what remained.

Eliah, still focused on where I had been, eased her posture as she turned her attention to the fawn. I took a deep breath, calming my racing heart.

"Scared of a fawn?" Calum teased her before she shoved him away and walked toward her wishing tree as he followed suit.

I sat and listened, seething with anger at each of Calum's ridiculous notions. My patience wore thin until I could no longer contain my fury. In an attempt to distract myself, I opened my mind to scan for Levon, hoping that his plans for tomorrow's evaluation were in place. The thought of having to be locked up before sunrise only added to my frustration.

My breaths came in heavy, angry huffs as I struggled to maintain my composure. Each word out of Calum's mouth felt like a provocation, pushing me closer to the edge as he begged her to stay, knowing full well she had an important evaluation tomorrow. I clenched my fists, the urge to lash out and throttle him was nearly overwhelming.

Desperation clawed at me. I couldn't let my temper jeopardize everything we had worked for. Levon's plan had to be flawless, and I needed to keep my focus. Yet, the thought of being locked up and caged like an animal gnawed at my sanity, knowing very well that Calum would do anything to find proof while I was helplessly trapped and could do nothing to protect her.

I bit down on my frustration, forcing myself to remain silent, hoping that morning would come quickly and bring some semblance of order to this chaos and bring us one step closer to finally getting her back.

19

Kaizen

The mental line tugged with a sizzling spark, igniting through the open doorway to her.

I lost my breath and stopped dead in my tracks, the mud and dirt scattering as I pivoted and sprinted back to her with all my might. Her awakening power radiated like a guiding light, pulsating faster and faster within me.

"Eliah!" Levon's voice, filled with fear and desperation, reverberated through the forest, my power amplifying his voice. My heart pounded, and I quickened my pace, feeling the overwhelming raw power threatening to consume her.

I ran faster, tapping into just enough of my power to propel me forward but to keep the Miehja at bay. Fear gnawed at me as I gritted my teeth, seeing a flash of ethereal light pulse ahead of me. Her scream of agony pierced the air as I felt the Ethereal Power engulf her.

I reigned in my panic, and my heart stumbled, feeling her searing pain as her raw power sputtered to life in a world she could destroy if fully unleashed. I abruptly stopped, raising my hands and commanding the light to me. My fingers burned with the force, and I missed the sensation of my full power in our celestial world.

The eruption of blinding light reversed, quickly sucking back down as if swallowed, then billowed toward me like lightning. It hit me like a fresh breath of air, but my body shook as I struggled to contain the power of a queen, a protector of the Cosmos. My skin flared to life with its original vibrant, ethereal golden glow but quickly faded as I shut my power entirely off.

I sprinted back to the estate, feeling my skin tickle to life. My power begging to stay awake, to breathe and protect. But the king's annoying Miehja were still in the area, and I had no time to fight them off.

Her pulse tugged along the tether of our minds before drifting farther away, spurring my feet to move faster.

Curse this rutting Match—the wretched façade we must maintain to avoid the relentless scrutiny of Jesri, the king, and their prying eyes among the Onyx Market. It infuriated me that I couldn't start her Ethereal training now. Yet, I knew it would be unwise to fully open her powers before the Match, knowing that every eye would be watching her and there wouldn't be a way for us to help without repercussions. The frustration of the entire situation gnawed at me as I cursed Xaldruk, cursed his legion of darkness that took everything from me, disrupting the balance of all existence within the Cosmos. Spreading his darkness in every realm, leaving life vulnerable with no Seraphs to defend with the Veilgate closed.

I pushed the bubbling anger down, wishing time would move faster, knowing the danger Eliah remained in without proper guidance with her Ethereal power.

I reached the clearing with clenched teeth, seeing Eliah and Levon's limp bodies sprawled on the ground. Panic surged through me as I charged toward them, scanning the area to see if anyone had noticed or if any Miehja had breached the area. I reached Levon first, who lay face down in the grass several feet from Eliah.

I tugged his limp body onto his back. His face was a mess of blood and bruises, evidence that Eliah had repeatedly slammed her power into him, and he had taken it without fighting back. My heart clenched at the sight, fear and concern battling for dominance.

"Emil!" I shouted desperately, searching for Levon's guard. "EMIL!" He was supposed to be stationed outside today, but there was no sign of him.

I knelt beside Levon, my mind racing with worry. I cursed silently for not having my pack of elixirs to help him, but I reassured myself that he had endured worse. Leaving my bow and arrows behind, I sprang to my feet and sprinted toward the stables, fueled by a mix of fear and anger. Emil appeared in my path, jogging toward me.

"Emil," I called out urgently, pointing back toward Levon. "Get Levon to Saasha!" My voice shook with a combination of rage and desperation. Emil's eyes widened in alarm as he took in the gravity of the situation, but without hesitation, he turned and rushed to Levon.

I reached the stables and grabbed a bucket of icy water, seething with frustration that I couldn't use my power to cool her down. The rutting king's dogs were still too close for comfort. My worry for her eclipsed everything else, and I cursed the constraints that had thrust me into this dire situation.

Swiftly, I ran back to Eliah, my heart racing with concern as I saw Emil dragging Levon inside. I knelt down next to her, feeling the intense heat radiating from her body. Panic seized me, realizing she wasn't breathing, and my heart cracked at the sight of her limp form.

I delved into the tether of her mind, desperately trying to reel her back to the surface. I grappled with each tremor of her awakening Ethereal, knowing that every second was critical.

"Eliah!" I barked, my voice trembling with fear and urgency, daring to open the power gate to touch her as I frantically examined her body. My heart pounded in my chest as I looked down at her lavender dress and realized the problem.

Damn, these bloody corsets!

Without hesitation, I unsheathed Sabene's ruby dagger and tore open the front of her dress. Her chest rose with a shallow breath, flickering hope amidst the panic that gripped me. I quickly poured the icy cold water onto her, watching as steam rose from her and exposed her tan skin beneath her wet petticoat.

I held her close, ignoring the burning sensation in my palms and arms from her overheated skin. She gasped for air, and I frantically searched her eyes, seeing the usual dull gray-blue begin to shift, revealing a cosmos of color—like every Seraph Queen, each uniquely different.

She jerked upright, trembling, but relief flooded me, knowing only two outcomes awaited Seraphs in such moments and praying it was the better of the two.

"Geisha, bless me," I rasped, gently cupping her face and slowly opening my Ethereal to soothe her.

She pushed me away with a wince, then slumped back into my arms, gasping for air. Panic widened her features as she glanced down at her wet form and the torn clothes beneath her, shivering uncontrollably.

Rutting idiot. I cursed at myself, hastily holding her with one arm while I unclasped my cloak and draped it over her chattering body.

"Breathe," I whispered into the shell of her ear, my hair coming undone and falling across her face. I held her close, feeling the softness of her skin against mine, before cradling her in my arms and rising to my feet. I hurried toward the estate door, my heart racing as I scanned anxiously for any sign of the Miehja that were bound to appear.

"Levon," she rasped, her voice hoarse. I gritted my teeth, suppressing my sudden frustration. "Levon?" she repeated.

I hushed her gently as I unlatched the door, hearing murmured voices echoing through the opulent estate.

"Ka—"

"Save it, Eliah," I sharply interjected, not wanting her to exert any more energy than necessary. I held her closer, feeling her trembling fingers against my chest and her soft cheek against my neck.

Bounding up the stairs and across the hall to her room, I opened her door and gently laid her down on her plush bed.

I rushed to her bathing chambers, frantically turning the faucet on to hot and plugged the bottom, only to realize my shirt was stained with blood from taking out a Bounty Hunter from earlier. In a panicked flurry, I tore off my bloodied tunic and tossed it aside, my mind racing with fear as I heard her whimper something, the tether of her mind convulsing.

I hurried back to her side, watching her entire body convulse with tremors.

No, no! I cursed within my mind, terrified of the other, darker ways her pulses of Awakening could seize control, especially here in this foreign world where no first Awakening should ever be experienced.

"Geisha," I swore, praying to the first queen not to strike me down as I leaned over Eliah. *"Eliah, stay with me!"*

I rushed to the door, knowing Elise or Saasha would be nearby. "Elise! Saasha!" I shouted desperately, needing to reach my elixirs of raw power that wouldn't attract the Miehja, but was unwilling to leave her alone. Hurrying back to the bath, I turned off the water and returned to her now freezing body. I quickly removed the cloak, forcing myself and my eyes to remember that she was *my queen*—not the formidable, daunting lady I had grown up watching and protecting.

Crouching beside the bed, I gently slid off her wet stockings and shoes before standing up and pulling her limp body into my chest, swallowing the forbidden closeness that threatened to overwhelm me.

"Kaizen," she trembled into my neck, sending hot flashes coursing through my body in a rage.

"Hold onto me," I begged, wrapping her arms around my neck and then carefully pulling her forward to unlace her skirts, resisting further reckless imaginations.

Gritting my teeth, I hated myself for savoring the touch of her skin against mine as I gently lifted her and removed her skirts, before carrying her in my arms to the hot bath. I lowered her into the water, hearing her sigh in relief as the pulse of her mind slowed ever so slightly.

I quickly stepped back, clenching my fists in frustration, desperate to escape the turmoil inside me. Rushing down the hall, I shouted for Saasha and Elise again before bounding down the stairs and crossed the foyer to the room Levon had created to store Seraph relics fallen during the Cataclysm. I thrust open the picture of Hyenah, Levon's mother, who had always been the best of us, revealing the door behind it. Swiftly descending the stairs, I grabbed a calming elixir, hoping it would dull Eliah's powers enough to buy us more time and take away her pain.

Running back up the stairs, I closed the frame and hurled myself up the steps two at a time. Elise's blonde curls disappeared into Eliah's room, and I sucked in a breath before stepping in after her.

"She's ice cold. We need to reheat the water," Saasha declared, holding onto Eliah's arm as she kneeled beside the tub. Eliah's bare back was now exposed and pebbled with tiny bumps prickling her skin.

I cursed under my breath, looking away and clenching my jaw, knowing how the cold could threaten to consume her, turning her into a pitiless shell.

"Saasha, go help Levon; I brought up your kit," I lied firmly, my voice tinged with urgency, desperate to create a moment of privacy. "Elise, go make some hot tea and prepare her bed."

"No," Eliah breathed weakly. "My head..." she trailed off, and Elise and Saasha exchanged a glance before hurrying out, their footsteps adding to the commotion of the estate.

I hesitated, torn by the conflicting desire to hold her close and to comfort her. I approached cautiously, pushing away such lustful thoughts that lingered in the back of my mind as I dipped my finger into the water, focusing on easing the tiny shivering bumps on her bare skin. Opening the power gate just enough, I sizzled the cold water into steam.

I held my breath, watching her sink into the warmth, quickly averting my eyes and stepping away, wrestling with forbidden emotions that threatened to overwhelm me.

"Here's the tea and a robe," Elise said softly, walking into the room with a tray bearing a ceramic teapot and a cup, which she set down beside the bed along with the warm robe.

"Help me lift her out," I rasped, my heart pounding with concern for Eliah's condition, needing to get this elixir to her before another possible power surge.

Elise nodded curtly, moving to unplug the tub before turning Eliah around. I averted my gaze, locking onto a blood stain on my boot, as I took Eliah under her arms while Elise supported her feet, and we lifted her out. Elise quickly helped her into the robe before I swiftly cradled her in my arms, laying her back onto the bed while Elise pulled the covers over her.

I hurriedly retrieved the elixir from my pocket and flipped open the cap, pouring it into the teapot. After mixing it thoroughly with a small spoon, I turned back to Elise, my mind focusing on Eliah's flickering light within her mind.

"I'm going to Levon. Make sure she drinks all of it," I instructed, not trusting myself around her any longer.

I snatched up my bloody tunic and cloak, every fiber of my being longing to stay, but anger filled my senses as I stormed out of the room, closing the door behind me. Instantly, the sharp, acrid rank of oily darkness collided with me, signaling the breach of the invisible perimeter I meticulously set up around the estate.

"*Cursed dogs!*" I spat out, my voice tight with frustration and rage, sensing the predatory presence of the Miehja closing in. With a quick intake of breath, I hastily pulled my shirt over my head and flung my cloak back on, the fabric swirling around me as I quickly descended the stairs.

My adrenaline surged as I raced across the foyer and onto the estate grounds, headed to the field where I had stashed my cache of poison arrows and other bow. I hoped my reckless chase would distract them away from the estate long enough for her powers to subside.

A screech shattered the forest's silence, sharpening my focus. I grabbed my bow and arrows with swift, practiced movements and expertly nocked one into place. A Miehja emerged onto the open grass; I snarled in defiance and quickly released the arrow with deadly precision, watching the arrow sink deep into the creature's eye as it let out a sickening shriek.

I turned and bolted towards it, running into the forest and seeing several others yipping and clicking with a deadly pleasure.

I took in a breath and flung open my power gate, my skin blazing gold, as they halted in their tracks before rushing to me with predatory force.

I sprinted away, the Ethereal propelling my limbs to move faster than I could in my weak human frame, and lured them after me.

30

Levon

"**S**he's *gone! She's gone!*" I screamed, pounding on Tazina's door, my voice cracking in the stillness of the night. It was well past two in the morning, and my legs were on fire from the desperate run. The night sky seemed to sparkle with an overwhelming dread, every star pressing down on me, making it harder to breathe, and voicing their dismay.

I yanked at the handle again, ready to break down the door, when it finally flew open. Kaizen's eyes blazed with fury that would sear me into ash.

I failed again. I failed her.

"She's gone," I heaved. "They took her straight to them. I-I didn't know! It was supposed to be like the other Matches within the Arena," I rasped out, feeling my lungs collapse against the dread, the mistake.

Kaizen's anger flared, his amber eyes burning with a terrifying intensity, as he swiftly disappeared into the darkened room. Tazina emerged, a green shawl hastily thrown over her shoulders, worry etched into her face as she touched her mouth in shock.

Kaizen reappeared, thrusting the Seraph pack into my shaking hands as he flung his cloak on.

"I did it," I muttered. "I initiated the full Awakening." His jaw flickered with enough power that I took a step back.

Tazina stepped in. "What happened." Not a question, a demand.

I told all of it. The suspicions of a dragon, the drinks, how they forced me away as they stripped her down and chained her to the inside of a wagon like a prisoner, pilled with all the other drugged contenders.

They were headed straight for the Aduantas Mountains, where sentinels perched on every peak, watching, reporting, and waiting at the end for the champion.

Tazina steadied herself against the door frame as Kaizen brushed past me, slinging his bow and arrows over his chest.

"The tunnels," I muttered. "They took them through the tunnels."

He flashed me a sharp snarl, looking down to the Seraph bag in my trembling hands. "*Do not fail again,*" he scolded, his voice dripping with wrath. "You know the escape route, be there or I'll hunt you down and tear you apart if you're not." He quickly turned before running into the night.

Anger and fear coursed through me, intertwined with a seething hatred for failing to uphold my vow...again.